S0-AZR-463

Avignon

Marianne Calmann's previous
books include the history *The
Carrière of Carpentras* (OUP).
She is the only British
member of Avignon's prestig-
ious Académie de Vaucluse.

asb

Marianne Calmann

Avignon

First published in 1999 by
Allison & Busby Limited
114 New Cavendish Street
London W1M 7FD
http://www.allisonandbusby.ltd.uk

Copyright © 1999 by Marianne Calmann
The right of Marianne Calmann to be identified as author of
this work has been asserted by her in accordance with the Copyright,
Designs and Patents Act, 1988

This book is sold subject to the condition that it shall not, by way of trade or
otherwise, be lent, resold, hired out or otherwise circulated without the
publisher's prior written consent in any form of binding or cover other than
that in which it is published and without a similar condition including this
condition being imposed upon the subsequent purchaser.

A catalogue record for this book is available
from the British Library

ISBN 0 7490 0446 0

Printed and bound by Biddles Limited,
Guildford, Surrey.

With warmest thanks to
Jennifer Luithlen and Peter Day

Chapter 1

The year was 1346, and Pope Clement VI – brilliant, grand and generous – had ruled Christendom from his palace in Avignon for the past four years.

That June was sultry and hot, even hotter than usual, and the mistral had been blowing through the stinking streets for three days. When it blew, crimes multiplied in the overcrowded city, especially crimes of passion. Tonight, under a full moon, Avignon lay in the crook of the river's arm in exhausted, murmuring sleep.

Across the Rhône, at Villeneuve, along the steep and winding street just back from the river, stood a great house belonging to a member of the papal court, cardinal Le Gor; near enough to obey a sudden summons from the Pope, far enough away for privacy, which Le Gor needed and prized.

The bells rang out four o'clock. In his ornate bedchamber, rivalling the Pope's opulence across the river, Cardinal Le Gor, his silk robe slipping off his shoulders, stood breathing in the cool breeze at the window. He stared across the river at the golden square of light formed by a window high up one of the towers which stretched heavenwards from the bulk of the papal palace.

'Either the Pope has insomnia or a recurrence of last year's dropsy,' murmured the cardinal. His companion tossed the damp, crumpled sheets aside and, snatching up two purple figs from the platter by the bedside, cooled his feet on the marble floor as he joined Le Gor at the window.

'Last year's infected tooth, my lord. Not dropsy. You said such an infection might well spread. But it didn't. The doctors did well, you said.'

'Thanks be to the Lord.'

The night breeze cooled their naked bodies and stirred the grey curls on Le Gor's head and the snaking golden locks which fell onto the broad shoulders of his companion.

'Come away from the window!' Le Gor said sharply, suddenly.

'But he can't possibly see us.'

'Just as well. I'm in trouble enough.'

Soon after four o'clock, Guillaume de Saint-Amant, knight and comptroller of the Pope's household, had finally fallen asleep on his cot in the papal palace, despite a suffocating headache due to the mistral. Had he dreamed or was that a hand on his shoulder? He started up and shrank from the dark form of a monk, bulky in a beam of moonlight from the tiny window. The monk whispered in his ear, urgently, ending with the words:

'—now, *chevalier.*'

'Can't you find someone else to go?' asked Saint-Amant. A pulse hammered in his head and his eyes stung after two days of the cursed wind. The monk shook his head, and moved out of the shadowy cell. Anxious, concerned about the news, Saint-Amant dressed, threw a dark cloak over his official clothes – important to show that he was indeed on official business – and felt his way down the familiar maze of corridors and stairs. He had to wake the guard who was sleeping against the door in the outer wall, who shook with fear when he saw who had caught him napping, then let him out. Another guard, on the perimeter wall, didn't even see him. The town was swarming with able-bodied men looking for work at the palace, and he'd replace these two tomorrow, thought Saint-Amant sourly. Today.

Holding his lantern tightly, Saint-Amant made his way towards the parish of Saint-Pierre, which lay closest to the huge mass of the palace. As he passed huddled figures in doorways – the town was filled to bursting with clergy, merchants and lawyers, snug in their beds at this hour, but also with artisans, peasants and beggars, many homeless and bedless – he felt ashamed. Can't you find someone else? he had asked the monk, when there was such urgency. Surely there were doctors in the palace?

The Chevalier de Saint-Amant was used to the streets of Avignon, but he knew them in daylight, and from the saddle of his horse, with two outriders making a path through the crowds for him, a high papal official. He was on the present errand because of the necessary secrecy, and therefore alone . . .

Now the narrow street led him past a churchyard and he heard and smelled, although he could not see, a herd of swine snuffling among the graves. Where else could the swineherd . . . Holy Saints! His delicate red leather shoes slithered into a slimy mess from which arose a stench which was seeping into the leather, he could feel it. It might well prejudice his standing as an official where he was going. But no, of course not, the place smelled to high heaven from streets away. And he had arrived.

A locked door set in an archway blocked the street.

He was breathing hard. He had never been inside this loathsome place.

He knocked – a sound so loud that Saint-Amant himself was startled. Above him a window opened, and a lantern swung, lighting the porter's face from below, and catching Saint-Amant's ruddy Norman complexion and red gold hair, just visible to the porter in spite of the black cloak which billowed in the night breeze.

'Ah! No, sir. No Christians in the Street from nightfall until sunrise. Pope's orders.'

Saint-Amant tried not to breathe. Putrid smells seeped under the ghetto gateway. He gagged. A shooting pain travelled from temple to temple.

'I'm on duty,' he snarled. 'Open up, porter.'

'They all say that,' said the porter, smirking. 'Many gentlemen like yourself knock on this door every night. In consequence I don't get much sleep. That has to be paid for, sir.'

'I'm in a hurry, porter. Open the door.'

The porter unlocked the door, mumbling under his breath, and both men went inside, the porter locking the door from inside the Street, as the ghetto was known in Avignon. The porter stood, waiting. The two previous transactions that night between himself and men with well-filled purses – one at eleven, one at midnight – had been normal. The porter held out his hand:

'Enjoy yourself, sir.'

The porter watched with surprise and dismay as Saint-Amant began to unwind his cloak, revealing long hair, parted in the middle, curled under and just touching an azure silk tunic. A gold decoration briefly winked in the light of the lantern. The porter cursed silently, then whispered, 'I was joking, sir! I only ever allow doctors in at night, sir, and pregnant women out. In what way may I be of assistance, sir?'

Saint-Amant stood, staring at the Street before him, as he sank further into the detritus which by now covered his ankles – sodden rags, mule and horse droppings, rotten vegetables, scraps of meat. Rats rustled. There were plenty of lanes in Avignon as disgusting as this but he felt that the Street harboured another kind of rottenness he was still waiting to experience.

The porter stood by his side, waiting for instructions. Let him tremble, let him worry about his livelihood. Saint-Amant thought about the other visitors who would have known where to go. He himself had not been into the Street during the day to make an assignation. No girl was waiting to lead him through the system of stairs and corridors.

The porter could have told him that the five-storey houses had corridors on each floor, so that the inhabitants could escape from the law along all the floors from end to end on both sides of the Street, as well as up and down the stairs. Christian visitors would be smuggled by the girls from house to house, till the gates opened in the morning when they would be lost in the throng pouring into the ghetto to buy and barter in the little shops on the ground floor.

Saint-Amant remembered his purpose. 'Get the doctor – er – Bonivassin. He's needed at the Palace. Now!'

Saint-Amant covered his face with his cloak. If they didn't hurry, he would surely faint.

'There are five hundred people here and there are two doctors and I'm not sure, sir, if one of them isn't—' the porter whined.

Saint-Amant drew his sword, and the porter disappeared, returning within two minutes with a pale Jew with frightened eyes, who beckoned Saint-Amant into a doorway. 'I know where he lives, sir, the best doctor, sir. Follow me, sir. Don't touch the walls, sir.'

I won't touch the walls, thought Saint-Amant, pulling his cloak tight. The walls look as though they had leprosy; what were those stains? The smell of urine was overpowering, ordure clung to all surfaces. The house wrapped him close like a fetid sheet. He heard stirring, groans, shifting, as he followed his guide up the stairs, then a woman's cry. He too could just have been a visitor here. A door would open for him and a woman would draw him into a room, and that would be terrible, disgusting, forbidden. Exciting. He wasn't well, the mistral . . . the house was a huge animal, it was alive, pulsating . . . he gasped with effort. They had reached the top of the stairs, this must be the fifth floor, the top floor, why did the Jews build so high? Now they stood before a door and when the guide held up the lantern, Saint-Amant read the name: THOROS BONIVASSIN and, underneath, *magister in medicina de Montepessulano.* Doctor Bonivassin, trained in Montpelier. Good enough.

Behind their door on the same landing, Astruc and Blanchette heard the steps on the stairs, voices, Thoros replying, receding footsteps down the stairs. Nothing unusual: Thoros, the doctor, was called to a patient in the night.

Blanchette, in her thin flaxen shift, felt the heat from her husband's body so close to hers on the narrow pallet, doubly unwelcome in this fetid heat. Or in the cold, come to that. But the heat was intolerable on their side of the Street, not least because the window had been boarded up after Sarah, the fool, had emptied a bucket of night-soil over the street just as a procession of penitents passed, carrying the cross and chanting. After that the community had paid a large fine and all those windows overlooking the Christian side had been boarded up. Her husband Astruc had knocked nails into the boards to make holes so that tiny breaths of air were able to enter the narrow room. Not that it made a difference. Now if, instead, they had a room on the other side, looking into the Street, like Thoros, they'd be able to have the window open.

Blanchette returned to sleep, to dream of Thoros, her husband's brother.

Astruc's eyes remained open. He put out his hand to touch her. He was going away for a whole week. Wasn't he her husband? He had his rights.

Astruc and Blanchette had married four years ago when she was thirteen, fat, with a dull face and an obedient manner. She was very good with her needle, unpicking seams, turning and sewing so that he could sell these clothes as new in the villages around Avignon. And gradually his cabbage had become a rose. She lost weight, her face tautened, the fat rolled away from her body. Gone also was her respect for him, her obedience. As for him, he was now nineteen and had grown neither stronger nor taller since he married her. Although she greeted him after his week away among strangers with the Sabbath customs and the welcome due to him, he felt an absence.

The first cock crowed. Astruc rose and said the first prayer of the day. Blanchette slept on.

'Blanchette, I have to go soon. Blanchette . . . shall we . . . ?' He touched her cheek.

Her eyes opened and she looked at him with such cold aversion that his throat tightened. But the look was already gone as she spoke:

'I am going to the baths.'

Once a month the women went to the ritual baths to be cleansed. The baths were forbidden to men, and it was forbidden for husbands to touch their wives until they had been cleansed.

'But,' he said, confused,' last week you told me that . . . weren't you . . . ?'

She turned her face to the wall and he left without another word. The mistral made his scalp prickle, and his anger choked him. What did the Talmud say about the obedience of wives, what did it say about beating a wife, what about murder? Whoever had written the Talmud did not know what a man felt like when the mistral blew.

He did not unclench his fists till the porter unlocked the gates, to let the throng of men out of the Street, some on foot, some with mules. He washed and drank at the fountain with the other Jews; there was no water in the Street. An armless beggar jostled him as he made his way to the gates of Avignon, but Astruc would not vent his rage on a cripple. Outside the gate, pushing against the crowd of country people on their way into Avignon, Astruc set down his pack. Already sweat had soaked his shirt. With anger churning the bile in his empty stomach he pulled his hat out of the pack. The brim offered some protection, but he hated the colour – deep yellow, the colour of a buttercup.

He strode along. Under his yellow hat his face was burnt the colour of terracotta, and with his reddish brown eyes and strong nose he looked like any other traveller along the road to Carpentras – if it weren't for his hat, which told everyone who he was. If he took it off, he'd be fined. If he kept it on, sooner or later he'd find himself in a fight. As he was slight of build, he usually preferred to run away. If he could. He stopped to tie a rag over his mouth and nose to protect him from the whirling dust raised by horses' hooves and the wheels of the carts bumping over the ruts. Along the dusty road shade was rare. Some pilgrims were gathered under a group of plane trees whose rustling leaves responded to the mistral. Astruc trudged on, looking for shade without the complement of travellers who would not welcome him. There were carts and peasants under the grove of cypress trees offering an oasis of shade further on, but the hostility in the eyes staring at his yellow hat forced Astruc onwards. Hardened by years of exposure to the cruel sun, he kept going for a further two hours, when his body demanded rest, and he found a remembered place where the verge dropped steeply down to a brook. Astruc climbed down and washed his face and feet, then dipped his hat in the water and rolled it in the grass, till it looked stippled like a Cavaillon melon. Let them make something of that colour!

He was alone on the bank, among the sweetly scented lavender and rosemary, far from the fetid smells of the Street where the Jews were penned up like cattle, where they built upwards as the Street could not hold them all. To be alone among the herbs and the trees and the rushing clear water in the stream below, that was the best thing, the reward for all the hardships a pedlar must expect. He washed his face among the boulders of the fast running stream, then crept between the waist-high bushes of gorse, myrtle and rosemary and thought of Blanchette, no longer with rage but with longing; and then he slept.

When he awoke, his pack had gone. He was also aware of movement in the gorse bushes behind him. Whoever had taken his pack was still near. There were sounds of stifled laughter.

Two men who had been watching him from behind the gorse enjoyed the sight of Astruc's rising panic, the way he searched for his pack. They knew what he was – a Jew. The popes, in their wisdom, had decreed that Jews must wear either a badge or a yellow hat. The men were stonemasons from Arles, come to join the hordes to whom the Pope gave employment, for the Pope was still building. The streets of Avignon were paved with gold, there was work for all.

'Are you looking for something?' called the bigger of the men, rising to his feet; huge, slow and cumbersome like an ox righting himself between the shafts of a cart. The smaller man grinned and gestured in the manner used to a cuckold. His misshapen small body, warped from childhood by heavy loads, looked insignificant by the side of the huge man.

Astruc saw the couple. Their grins were malicious, they stood above him on the slope, menacing. He sought a means of escape, maybe across the stream? But he needed his pack if he and Blanchette were to eat.

'My pack. It's my livelihood,' said Astruc. And three weeks' needlework by Blanchette, he thought. Two against one, and they had the advantage of the slope. In any case, Jews did not fight.

'Is this your rubbish? Come here and fetch it,' said the large mason, swinging the pack above his head.

'Yes,' said Astruc, but he did not move.

The ox-like mason opened the pack and took out a jerkin of chestnut velvet, on which Blanchette had spent many hours, the best garment in the pack.

'Stinking rag,' said the big man lazily. Then, looking round at the remains of a meal the two had eaten, he picked up a fowl carcass that was humming with flies and disturbed them briefly as he stuffed the bones and rags of meat into the pack. He then looked around for the jar of wine and poured the dregs into the pack, adding two oiled crusts of bread. Wiping his mouth on the jerkin, he said, 'And where's your hat, Jew?'

The hat, as Astruc saw, was in the big man's fist. Astruc said to himself, we are God's people. I will not fight him. One day this will end, the Messiah will come and our persecutors will fall silent.

'Come closer,' said the big mason and, turning to the small man, he asked in a reasonable voice:

'How do we know he is a Jew, though? He hasn't got a yellow hat on his head. He's not wearing a badge. Shall we make sure that he's a Jew? They did kill a lot of them in the kingdom of France, but in Avignon they're safe, I don't know why. I will examine him.'

Astruc waited for the questions: Why did you kill our Lord? Why will you not see the error of your ways? Why do you poison wells to kill Christians? Of course Astruc would promise to convert, or whatever they asked.

He was astounded by the speed of what happened next. No questions. The big man leaped on him like a wolf on a sheep and knocked him to the ground. With one hand he gripped Astruc by the throat, the other tore at his short cloak and his robe, ripping it with a tearing sound; then he stripped Astruc of his nether garments while Astruc retched and tried to twist his neck away from the iron grip on his throat. When he was finally naked from the waist down, the big man suddenly released the hold on his throat with a triumphant shout:

'Yes! He's a Jew! A circumcised . . . swine!'

Astruc lay on the ground, with the big man straddling him as though he were a deer he had slain. Nineteen years of submission and fear were extinguished in Astruc at that moment and thirteen hundred years of learnt and accepted behaviour vanished in a roaring of blood in his head, with the pain throbbing in his throat and the breeze blowing shamefully around his naked body.

Though thin, he was wiry and his legs were the strongest part of him. From where he lay, he aimed between the big man's legs. The man screamed and fell on top of Astruc.

'Kill him, Bernard!' cried the little mason, as the two men, now entwined, with their hands around each other's throats, rolled further down the steep bank and into the stream whose water, running fast between boulders, cooled their bodies. But the boulders and pebbles were slippery and when Bernard managed to rear up his wet shoes slipped on a slimy patch of moss and the big mason lost his balance and fell backwards, heavily. The sound of his head striking a rock remained in Astruc's memory for the rest of his life. The water changed colour around the head of the fallen man as Astruc, lying next to him in the shallow water watched him in fear, uttering a few words of prayer, begging God for deliverance; and God heard him, for there was no movement. Astruc raised himself slowly to peer at the gross face. Blank eyes stared back. The brook continued to run red around the head.

He fell onto a rock, thought Astruc, watching for the other man, the little man, but there was no sign of him, he must have gone for help.

Astruc dragged himself up, gasping with pain and effort. He must get away before the smaller man arrived with others. They would surely kill him when they saw the body in the stream. He picked up what was left of his clothes with trembling hands, then stumbled through the stream to the other bank and ran across the stony, harsh ground towards a screen of trees, young chestnuts and pines. They swallowed him up in their green, whispering embrace and there was silence.

Chapter 2

At Villeneuve, Cardinal Le Gor had broken his fast with curds, melons and nuts, and was studying his notes. Pope Clement made plans; and it was Le Gor who was responsible for making sure they went smoothly. The Pope had decided to visit Cardinal de Périgord in four days' time. This caused Le Gor a great deal of work, though of course he had done it all before, working with the Chevalier de Saint-Amant, the comptroller, whom Le Gor found fussy and conceited. A major task was finding lodgings for accompanying cardinals, courtiers, and hangers-on, servants, messengers. And, discreetly, for the ladies; officially for the Pope's sister and diplomatically for the unofficial ladies. Without scandal, and efficiently, Pope Clement was going on to Gentilly, to stay with Cardinal Annibale de Ceccano – a hugely expensive venture, as usual. Any house in which Clement stayed would have to be decorated, and the host would be expected to put on an entertainment. Clement paid for that, too.

Benedict, the last pope before Clement, was surely turning in his grave at Clement's spendthrift ways. Le Gor had served under Benedict, that parsimonious, austere Cistercian, but he much preferred Clement; after all, he, Le Gor, shared the current pope's tastes.

'Food, flowers. Hangings, tapestries. Decorations. Horses, mules, standard-bearers, guards, provisions, musicians, cooks, servers. Check uniforms, washer-women, messengers with Saint-Amant—'

Le Gor stopped writing and thought back over the night. He was about to lose his heart, he knew, and the thought gave him no pleasure. He was too old, he would be cuckolded. Could he still withdraw? No. He stared at the list he was making and deliberately broke the point of his goose quill.

He was on the verge of disgrace, anyway, but the blow hadn't quite reached him, though the signs of his coming fall had multiplied recently. An hour ago, a messenger had come from the palace with a letter, perhaps the very letter – and he had left it unopened, the splendid papal seal intact. Why should he open it as he was almost sure of the contents? Of course he had made plans. Calm now, he rose and returned to his bedchamber. His companion had gone long ago, leaving memories, rumpled sheets and the indentation of a head on the pillow.

What, said Le Gor aloud in the empty room, if I had been found out? A nine days' wonder, probably, no more. And who at the papal court would be prepared to cast the first stone? For what is the relative veniality of the sins I commit here, and those committed over the river in the palace?

Well, there was the matter of the papal coinage. Five kinds of papal coins were struck at the château of Sorgue, among them golden florins and *gros* and *demi-gros* of silver. Rather too many of all these were in Le Gor's possession. But as to villainy of this sort, there was an embarrassment of choice at the court. And Le Gor was quite simply essential to the smooth running of Clement's life.

He sniffed the letter. Surely he imagined the scent of over-ripe melons, of rottenness emanating from it. With his short dagger which he wore under his cloak, he broke the seal.

My Lord Cardinal, he read, *His Holiness begs you not –* NOT *– to attend him today.*

'My goose is cooked!' he said to the empty room and thought, Now is the time to call in old debts.

Blanchette did not rise until an hour after Astruc had left her. She dipped some bread in oil, chose a ripe peach, and crossed the landing to knock on Thoros's door. He didn't reply and she opened the door a crack. He still had not returned from the confinement, or whatever had taken him away in the middle of the night.

She ate the bread and the peach, in Thoros's room, thinking of the two brothers. They were unalike except in their strong affection for each other. For Astruc, prayers and work, making love, making a little money, eating well on the Sabbath and enough on other days, now and then a little gambling, some gossip, some grumbling was the sum total of his daily life. But Thoros had attended university, he was a healer, loved and respected by everyone in the Street. He held magic in his hands and his eyes could detect the seat of sickness in a body. Not for him the selling of clothes . . .

Old clothes. She went down to the shop and began to unpick a deep blue velvet jerkin, a lovely thing to hold and work on, to stroke. It must have been worn by an important person.

A man darkened the doorway of her shop: old Jacob, bent like a bow, dragging his right leg. He wore not only a battered yellow hat, but the parti-coloured badge. He was liked in the courtyards of Avignon where people readily gave him cast-off clothes. He placed a bundle at Blanchette's feet and said in his hoarse voice, 'I saw a Jew in a red hat today, Blanchette! The Pope doesn't allow that colour. I'd like a red hat, though.'

Blanchette sorted through the bundle and smiled at the old man. 'What would you sooner have – a red hat and a beating, or your old yellow hat and peace to go about your business? Here's your money and a peach, some bread and a goat's cheese to go with it.'

God required them all to give to the poor, and she was richer than old Jacob, a poor widower. She saw Jacob leave, eating the peach, and took up the jerkin again, while briefly her thoughts turned to Astruc, and a whole week's freedom till he returned to her and the Street. Then she called into her mind and heart, as always, Thoros.

Thoros was wrestling with a bear and awoke with his face pressed into the fur of the animal. By the light of a candle near his head he saw that he was indeed lying on the fur of a bear, one long since dead. Around him on three walls were brilliant-feathered fowls and fowlers, leafy woods with game running, small birds on the tendrils of vines and honeysuckle, hunters with dogs and blue sky with skipping clouds, miracles of a painter's art. He jumped up, his heart beating – he'd fallen asleep. How did he come to abandon his patient?

In the light of the sun, just rising, he peered through the open door into the next room, where he saw the sick man on his bed, his folded hands resting on the coverlet and a whippet at the foot of the couch, like an effigy on a tomb. In a few strides Thoros stood next to his patient, whose eyes were closed. A deep furrow divided the fore-head. Thoros noted the waxy pallor, but the sick man's chest rose and fell.

I didn't lose him, thought Thoros. If I had, they'd burn me at the stake.

He noted a monk on his knees, praying, and a woman in a white robe, staring at him. No one spoke. Thoros walked to the window to breathe, and collect his wits, the very window which all Avignon knew to be the Pope's, which Cardinal Le Gor had seen illuminated from the other side of the river. He looked down onto the Street, far beneath him, where he worked, a Jew among Jews, then he turned back to his patient, his since four o'clock this morning. Pope Clement VI.

Avignon was the centre of Christendom, but it was also a small city, and Thoros had heard all the gossip. Clement was generous, the greatest monarch in the world. He had said that he wished no one ever to leave his presence dissatisfied, and that a pope should make his subjects happy. In the Street of the Jews they said of him: Clement in name, Clement in deed.

The woman in the white cloak spoke. 'You worked a miracle, Master, and I let you sleep for a little while. When my brother was taken ill, we asked the comptroller of the household to get the best doctor in Avignon. He came back with you.'

'My lady—'

'I am Guillemette de la Jugie, Master.'

' Where was the Pope's own doctor? Surely—'

She shrugged. Thoros saw a face in middle age but unlined, grey eyes, calm and competent. He had never been so close to a Christian woman. She was waiting for him to speak, he saw.

'This is not finished, my lady. I fear it will return, and we must prepare.'

The sick man had begun a movement of the head. Thoros took his pulse. 'He is weak after the intense pain of the attack, my lady.'

Clement suddenly opened his eyes and whispered, 'God took my pain from me. Guillemette, please see that ... the *medicus* ... receives ... three ... gold florins ...'

Thoros called to the monks of the bedchamber for towels, hot water and wine, clean robes and linen, so that they could be ready for the next attack which he saw advancing from the look in Clement's eyes and, as the monks of the bedchamber hurried in and placed everything within reach of Thoros, they heard a stifled groan from the couch.

'Doctor! Help me!'

Spasms of pain made Clement's body arc and his legs kicked away the silken coverlet and the dog. As Guillemette and Thoros attempted to support the sick man, Thoros thought, I knew it would return, and the worst is yet to come; and though he is the Pope he must suffer like any man until the stone has left his kidney. And Thoros wrestled with Clement like Jacob with the angel for hour upon hour until midday, when the stone was washed out of Clement's body, the pain ebbed and Clement, without the strength to speak, slept.

Thoros and Guillemette, in their sweat-stained clothes, moved to the window. Even the mistral was welcome.

'Thank you, *maître*,' Guillemette whispered.

She turned her head and looked at him, the doctor from the Street. It was the closest she had ever been to a Jew. He had a handsome face, she thought, black curly hair above a wide forehead and eyes which looked right inside her mind. She blushed. If he could read her mind, widowed as she had been for twelve years, he might well see feelings which surprised her, which she had forgotten; she, Guillemette de la Jugie, with two grown sons far away from here in the Holy Land, doing God's work to free Jerusalem from the infidel. It must be twelve years since she had lain with a man . . .

'My lady. The . . . Holy Father, my patient, has four doctors accredited to the Household – two *medici* and two *surgici*. As you know, I have both competences. But the edict forbids a Jewish doctor attending to Christians. Why, then – do you feel faint, my lady?' His voice was soft, soothing.

He guided her to a fragile chair, supporting her with practised arms and as she looked into his eyes she felt the security and the warmth which had been missing from her life since her husband was slain by a Turk outside the fortress of Acre. And she saw that he felt something for her – pity, compassion; he gave her his strength. A man the age of her eldest son. A Jew.

'My brother asked for you by name,' she whispered, 'as soon as the attack began. You, Dr Bonivassin. You cured him. He thought you would.'

He took her hand – and she wished that he would never relinquish it. He had the power to cure all ills by his presence. That was why the pope had called for him . . .

'I did not cure him, my lady. You must know that God disposes of our lives.'

She looked surprised.

'We worship the same God. Doctors have few means of curing illnesses at our disposal; a few books the ancients wrote and a few palliative medicines. Otherwise our – my – most efficacious medicine is my wish to help. And my belief that the patient, if God wills, will live. We have studied tricks to help us effect cures, but we know little. What I find myself doing is to put my over-whelming desire for an end to a patient's suffering at his disposal. Sometimes, this time, it works.'

He touched her pale face, streaked with tears and sweat. 'Rest, my lady. You have done what you could.'

Guillemette de la Jugie nodded and walked to the door, reluctant to leave. 'I want to go to Mass; can I really leave him now?'

Thoros smiled and pointed to the door. Guillemette resisted the impulse to embrace him and was gone. Thoros watched the *chambrier* monks remove the soiled sheets and, when Clement stirred, bathe him and help him into a clean gown. The whippet returned to its place at the foot of the Pope's couch, and stared at his master with unblinking eyes.

When Thoros was a student at Montpellier university, the moral teaching there deplored the use of Jewish doctors by Christians, be they surgeons or physicians. For their pains, students were taught, these Christians would learn that such treatment would aggravate their disease. But if no Christian could be found, a Jewish doctor might be sought – and this had happened to Thoros. And his patient was no ordinary . . . no ordinary . . .

He sat down. He felt his head, lighter than a feather, detached from his body.

He clasped it with both hands. I diagnose great tiredness and the greatest responsibility I have ever had, he thought. A short rest.

He slept again for ten minutes and dreamed of peace, so deeply that he must surely be safe in Abraham's bosom. Then he woke, stood up and felt his head clearing and resuming its weight on his shoulders. Galien and Avicenna had written about the onset of a disease with these symptoms. Was it Galien? He would consult his books, Galien first.

His books were in the bag, at his feet, but too heavy to lift just now. Later.

He must get home. Having arrived in the dark, so many hours ago, he remembered only vaguely the long journey through silent halls and passages, aware sometimes of fluted ceilings just above his head, at others conscious of great height above him when the echo of their footfalls took many seconds to reach the roof of a great chamber. He and his guide had knocked into abandoned carts and sleeping forms blocking the way in the corridors . . .

Who was going to lead him out of the palace now? There was a great deal of coming and going in the bedchamber but nobody noticed him. All these Christians look the same in the papal livery or in their monk's robes, he thought sourly. I have done the task for which they fetched me and now I need to go home. I'm ill.

'I am his Holiness's *chambrier* prelate, my name is Eble Dupuis,' said a voice. 'Will you follow me?'

'I need to return to the Street, Maître Dupuis.'

'This way, down these stairs. People do not know what a *chambrier* prelate's responsibilities are and you, from the Street, are not likely to be aware that I hold a position of great trust. I attend the Pope when he rises and when he retires and am present at all masses he attends. Most important, *maître*, we select from the crowd—'

'I am not well. Please lead me to the entrance, now.'

'Directly. We select from the crowd who importune the Holy Father – they ask for money, or position, or for help with litigation—'

'For pity's sake!'

'Not far now. Down this corridor. But just let us stop here . . . I will just use these keys . . . you see? His Holiness has two rooms one above the other, which contain nothing but his clothes and here . . . here are his furs, one thousand and eighty ermine furs! Here . . . oh, very well, I thought I was rewarding you for succouring the Holy Father, I wanted to show our gratitude. I will just lock up. This way, *maître.*'

Thoros sighed with relief and, walking slowly behind the *chambrier* prelate through endless halls, thought of his patient; his broad, fleshy face with a beaky nose and sagging folds under the chin. The eyelids hiding prominently set eyes. A frown marked a vertical and two horizontal folds on the forehead. Thoros had never seen the Pope in health, but here was a man who had experienced suffering, not for the first time.

Let him be well, thought Thoros, dragging his feet over the endless stone floors, walking strangely behind the little official, but was that because the floor was undulating? The massive stone walls bent out of his way like willows in the breeze – and the crowds of petitioners and workmen and a man driving geese through the corridors to the kitchens; the monks and priests – crowds of people frustrating his passage out of the palace.

At last he found himself standing alone by the palace wall in the huge square with the sun striking fiery sparks from the cobbles. The heat was terrible. How could he cross the square without any shade?

I have saved the Pope and am I now to lose my own life? he whispered as he slumped against the wall of the palace, fixing his mind's eye on the prayer for the dead. Heat. Soon he would lose consciousness. Water . . . if he could just drink . . .

Someone bent over him. He saw that it was a woman, his mind was still capable of that, and that she was young. She carried a basket of cherries on which his eyes fastened. Without a word exchanged between them, she gave him a handful which he ate avidly, reviving.

'You do not look well. You should see a doctor.'

'I am a doctor,' he said to her with what he thought was a laugh, but turned into a groan.

'If you are, I'm the Pope's mistress. You're a pedlar the cooks didn't like the look of. You're filthy. Clean yourself up and try your luck in there again. They'll buy anything, food, clothes, anything. Where's your pack?'

Thoros pointed at the bag, with his instruments, at his feet.

'I'll take you back in with me. The cherries get me through the gates. I'm selling something else.' She winked. 'Don't shut your eyes just as I'm showing you!'

He wrenched his eyes upward, and saw her pulling back her cloak. Her upper body was dressed in a transparent veil which showed her to be naked to the waist.

'You look half dead, pedlar. Doesn't this rouse you?'
But he had not heard her.

For many minutes, in the searing heat, she watched for a sign of life by his side, muttering a prayer and keeping a look-out for help. But who was going to stir during the midday heat?

While she waited, Jeanne Poisson cast a professional eye over Thoros. Men – there was little to chose among them except that some paid more than others. With the town crowded with men helping the Pope to spend his money, Jeanne, born in a hovel at the foot of Mont Ventoux, was much in demand – for the present. But too many girls came from the villages now seeking a living, and in a few years others would take Jeanne's place.

She observed Thoros; face like ivory, black curly hair matted. Jeanne crossed herself. Life was short.

'Jeanne!'

A neighbour, with a small handcart. Both of them bent over Thoros.

'Take him in the cart!' said Jeanne, 'and do a good deed.'

'Me? No. He's dead.'

'We can't leave him here. The dogs will get him.'

'The guards will see him from the Saint-Laurent Tower, and fetch him in.'

Two papal officials passed, in black robes, deep in talk.

'Sirs! Reverend sirs! We have a corpse here. We would accept your advice, please help us, reverend sirs.'

The men stared at Jeanne. One said, after a pause: 'The Holy Father, in his generosity, has founded ten hospices. Take him there.'

'It is true,' said Jeanne, watching them walk away, 'that the Pope gives away money to anyone who asks him. Well, the cockroach is right for once.' She spat. 'They'll give him a proper burial at the hospice.'

Between them, they lifted Thoros's body into the cart. Jeanne placed his bag at his feet, then looked inside.

'Poor soul,' she said, 'he was selling copper pots and scissors to the kitchens. I may use these myself. He no longer needs them where he has gone.'

The carter drew Thoros's three books from the bag. They looked at the books longingly; neither could read.

'These are books on magic,' said Jeanne, 'see the signs? I'll sell them, and share with you.'

They pushed the body and the empty bag at its feet across the burning square into the deep shadow of the maze of little streets leading down to the river, where there was a hospice. The bells were ringing but Thoros no longer heard them.

Chapter 3

Alone in her shop, Blanchette was finishing the hem on a woman's cloak. Among the remnants which Jacob had brought, some reminded her of summer fruits in colour and she stitched these together to fashion bright lozenges of colour. Now she had a fiery sunset of a cloak, and she draped it around her. In the cracked mirror she looked at herself.

'Fit for a cardinal! ' she said aloud.

Not for a cardinal, nor for Astruc's next pack, but to be worn by Blanchette herself. The mirror told her every day that she was beautiful. She deserved beautiful clothes.

I did not look like this when I got married, she thought, as she examined herself and the cloak in the mirror. Her mother, the fattest woman in the Street, made her help in the kitchen. She taught Blanchette to make honey and almond cakes, pine kernel biscuits, candied chestnuts, sugared peaches, cherries and plums; and Blanchette, in the kitchen all day, tasted everything. The Jews in the Street and people in Avignon outside paid well for these foods, and with the money Blanchette's mother had put away for her dowry there was enough to buy Astruc as a husband for her fat daughter.

Astruc; shy, thin, in need of a wife, brought his brother Thoros to meet his bride.

'He is all the family I have,' said Astruc.

Blanchette cried when the brothers had gone.

'I want Thoros, mother.'

'You're not a beauty, my love. But you're a good girl and you'll make a good wife for Astruc. As for Thoros, I reckon he'll marry Bonaventure Carcassonne – her father's got two houses. She's the only one rich enough for Master Thoros.'

So Blanchette and Astruc were married, and lived in Thoros's back room. Then Blanchette discovered linens and velvets and silks, while helping her aunt Miriam, who washed and turned old clothes. When Miriam died, Blanchette carried on alone; in love with the textures and colours of the clothes that old Jacob begged from cardinals, courtiers and ladies.

But the children Astruc hoped for did not come. He brought her roots and plants to make her conceive, but she could not.

Thoros advised her only to eat at night and on the sabbath, when Astruc was home. Soon the fat melted off her body and her face emerged, oval and small with regular features, from its disguise of double chins and ballooning cheeks. Her large dreaming eyes looked out from beneath a frame of dark curls, short on her forehead, cascading in ringlets down the nape of her neck.

Now men looked at her. But not Thoros. She accepted his even-tempered kindness with pain, and suffered an aching longing, sleeping across the passage in her lonely bed all week, while Astruc roamed the countryside with his pack.

In the third year of her marriage, only a few months ago, something happened which was to change her life.

Her friend Esther called in to the shop to show Blanchette her new coral necklace.

'Did Hananel give you that, Esther? It's beautiful.'

'Hananel! Of course not, Blanchette.'

'You've always got money, Esther.'

'And you've never asked me how I come by it. Wouldn't you like to know?'

Blanchette remembered something her mother had told her. 'You've got night visitors. Is that true?'

'Yes.'

'Is it because of the money?'

'No, it is not. Like you, we have no children yet. I'm bored, locked up in this stinking cage of a street. We're as pretty as the Christians. We can hold our own with the prettiest ladies in Avignon.'

'Who says that, Esther?'

'My lover, and he should know; he's a Christian.'

She was still wearing her fiery cloak when the figure of a customer, a man, darkened the doorway. In the dim light she saw that he was from outside, and by his clothes, that he was important.

Guillaume de Saint-Amant carried a purse with the three gold florins which the Holy Father had promised Thoros. He looked at Blanchette with amazement – a beautiful flower growing on a dungheap, he thought. The cloak caught a beam of sunlight from the doorway and flashed its burning colours at Saint-Amant. When Blanchette looked up at him, every sense in his body urged him irresistibly towards her, so that he had to catch hold of a wooden stanchion to arrest his movement.

'Are you the wife of Thoros Bonivassin?'

His voice sounded hoarse. He had to remember where he was. She flushed, he saw. Why?

'The wife of his brother, sir.'

'His Holiness has sent Maître Bonivassin a purse for his good offices this past night. Is he here?'

'No, sir. He has not returned. I will keep the purse for him.'

Their eyes met.

Saint-Amant broke into a sweat. His heart was racing. He *must* find a way to . . . but no – in his position, what he contemplated was suicidal.

Blanchette thought of Esther's lover.

At first Astruc, running, panting, hardly noticed where he was but now there was no spiky gorse to tear his bare legs and he let himself drop to the ground in the deep shade of the oak and chestnut forest. Men shunned the forest, and for good reason, but for the moment he felt safe.

I didn't kill him. He fell, thought Astruc for the twentieth time.

Then, suddenly, he heard the faint sound of pursuit. The sound grew stronger. He had no strength left, they were going to catch him for he had killed. And as his body tensed for flight, he abandoned thinking as a man: he was a beast, hunted by bestial men. His eyes fell upon the branches, like rungs, of an ancient oak and he climbed it till he was twenty feet above the ground.

Broad of back, brownish black, majestic and evil smelling, the wild boar made his way through the undergrowth. Under Astruc's tree, the animal lifted its long head with the gleaming tusks. Its brilliant black eyes set

in the blackish stubbly mask looked directly up at Astruc.
Behind the boar, the herd of wild pigs, powerful long
shapes, wound their way round the trees and were gone.

So they had not found him. He thanked God, and
spoke to Him, asking what He considered Astruc should
do: I have no pack, no hat and what was left of my
clothes is torn. Almighty God, have you decreed that I
should become an outlaw?

Within him, he knew he had been heard, and an
answer would be provided.

Before setting off in the direction the pigs had taken,
he wrapped the chemise around the waist and thighs,
but that left his chest and back bare. He could stay in the
forest, but without forest skills he would soon die. If he
made for the road, back to the Street, he would be
caught. He might beg, till the news of the mason's death
had become stale. Other beggars banded together; in his
mind's eye he could see them begging at wayside crosses.
They would chase him away, or kick him to death like
black crows kill a white crow.

Astruc lived by God's rules, as they were taught in the
Street. He obeyed the positive laws as explained by the
rabbi, of which there were 248, and the negative laws of
which there were 365; the exact number of veins in a
man's body and the number of days in the year.

Lord, said Astruc, breathing in the clean fresh smell
of the canopy of chestnut leaves, I cannot remember all
the laws, there are too many. I am sure I have broken one
or two, but not deliberately. I say my prayers, I try to be
an obedient Jew.

He touched his face, and felt caked blood around his
nose and mouth, and as he did, he heard a faint sound

which delighted him; surely that was an ass braying? He set off. The Lord would lead him to help. But the sound was a will o' the wisp, he heard it to the left and right of him, forward and back.

Suddenly he stood on high ground, overlooking a narrow valley. There was no sign of a village, but below him stretched a field of lavender and, half hidden by cherry trees, huddled a house and a barn. Astruc began the descent to the house. There were low bushes and, crouching, he made his way from one to the next till he was within sight of the single window of the house.

He waited for shouts, dogs, men – but there was no sign that the place was inhabited. Now he was close enough to see the skull of a boar which was nailed above the door. He waited for movement, slept a little and woke to the sound of movement.

The door was open and a woman let a huge dog out, then followed it, standing for minutes with the dog, watching its pricked ears and roving eyes; then she called it back into the house and closed the door.

I will throw myself on her mercy, thought Astruc, in spite of the dog. He rose very stiffly, his body marking injuries he had not noticed during the fight and slowly dragged himself downhill towards the house. Turning as always to prayer, he had reached the door by the time he had uttered the last word. Then he knocked and called out. 'Please help a poor traveller who cannot hurt you, and needs rest and food!'

There was no answer.

'For God's sake, lady, do not set the dog on me, I am injured!'

'Go into the barn, traveller,' said a woman's voice.

He hobbled across the farmyard where work had been abandoned and where a ladder and baskets lay about. The barn was open and he found a mound of hay on one side and fowls pecking at the beaten earth. It was dark. Astruc crawled into the hay and fell asleep at once.

Marie had heard the man's steps across the farmyard. Her dog – his rough coat bristling, his eyes seeking hers – sat by her, waiting for the command to chase the intruder away.

Whether he was a beggar or a vagabond, she would give him food and shelter, for a little while at least, in the hope that good people would do the same for her Roger. He too might be walking into a farmyard somewhere, afraid of the dogs, hungry and thirsty; so for Roger's sake, she would help this man. And maybe . . . her eyes turned to the abandoned ladder. Twice the child in her womb had been stillborn and, since then, although her arms were still strong, a weakness in her belly and a trembling in her legs became a constant companion.

Perhaps the traveller could help her.

Astruc, in the barn for hours – or was it days? – had slept, woken and slept again. He remembered eating bread and drinking goat's milk. Now there was less exhaustion but more fear again. All his limbs were working, he found, as he stretched arms and legs. He calculated how he could escape when the man who lived in the house returned from the fields and found him in the barn. Who had brought the bread and milk? The woman, and she had been alone. She had put the food down on the ground, not close to him, he remembered. The dog was by the door, growling, ready to spring. He tried out his legs now by walking to the door, and found it closed and locked.

He was trapped in the barn and the key was on the outside.

Astruc threw himself down on the hay. All his life he had listened to the rabbi reading in the synagogue – about Moses, David, Joseph, Joshua, all heroes, all brave men. Not like him, Astruc, a weak man, a coward even. But he had fought the big mason, so once in his life he had been brave, forced to be brave, and what had that brought him? What kind of a man was he? He could not even father a child. Blanchette had turned away from him.

He could not bear his thoughts and began looking for a way out of the barn.

A sliver of light showed him that there was a hole next to the door. He peered through it and was in time to see the woman cross the yard with the cur close by her side. She moved out of view, gone, he thought to fetch her man from the fields.

A memory bored into his head.

One Sabbath morning the women's rabbi, from Poland, had told the women about a group of Jews the Polish peasants had killed because a well had been poisoned. The peasants locked them in a barn, yes, the women and children as well. Blanchette had cried when she told Astruc what happened: the peasants set fire to the barn. A locked barn. Astruc's bowels cramped, he crept into a corner, his bowels emptied, his legs trembled. A rat watched him.

Astruc lived by the rules: and his mind was unused to independent thought, nothing he had been taught seemed to fit. Well, any action at present was better than his thoughts and there was one thing he must do: clean himself. He found a rag and did his best. When he had finished, his faith returned and he called to mind texts which he had been learning since he had been very young.

He draped a piece of sacking, dirty as it was, over his head, like a prayer shawl, and chose the words of the song which David sang when the Lord delivered him from his enemies:

Thou deliverest humble folk
Thou lookest with contempt upon the proud.
Thou, Lord, are my lamp,
And the Lord will lighten my darkness.
With thy help I leap over a bank,
By God's aid I spring over a wall.

As he searched his mind for the next verse, the key turned in the lock and the door was opened.

It was the same woman as before and, as before, the dog was with her. But she was smiling. A good-looking woman, thought Astruc. And still alone. Astruc's fear left him, for wasn't she smiling?

'Here,' said Marie, 'eat this. And do not touch me, or Loupiot will tear your throat out.'

The dog's tongue emerged at the sound of his name and hung to one side of his huge teeth.

'You have slept two days. What happened to you? There are armed men about.'

'Looking for me.'

He eyed the food she had brought – bread, olives, honey – but could not eat.

'They knocked but I did not open the door. And I had locked you in. At present . . . my husband is not here. What have you done?'

'I fought a man. Much bigger than me. Then . . . I ran away.'

She laughed and he noticed how kind her face looked.

'You were afraid of him?'

'I was very much afraid. I am a pedlar, a peaceful man. I have a wife in Avignon whom I want to see again.'

Marie hesitated. She was not tall, Astruc saw. She had wound a cloth tightly over her head and tied its ends twice round her neck, so he could not see the colour of her hair. She wore a grey chemise over a brown *cotte*, and a belt drawn tightly round her waist which had a medal pinned on it. Thick linen hose and shoes tied around with twine. As he looked at her, she watched him, then made up her mind and spoke, hesitantly. 'They may be looking for you. Did you kill the man?'

'He's dead, I think, lady. But he fell. It was not my fault.'

'Then . . . I think, if you like . . . till they stop looking, you might stay here. You could sleep in the barn. I could give you food, and maybe other clothes.'

Astruc looked at her eagerly. But why would she do this?

'For . . . it is harvest time, and I – we – could use another pair of hands.'

Later, he propped the ladder against the large cherry tree. He wore strong leggings and on his feet were his host's strong shoes. An overshirt covered him from neck to knees and a cowl protected his head from the sun. He sang as he picked great handfuls of the gleaming fruit, a song which Marie did not recognise.

He had not told her that he was from the Street in Avignon. She had not told him that her husband was not coming back that night or, she feared, any other night.

Chapter 4

Mid-afternoon and the heat penetrated even into this lofty chamber, facing east, where Cardinal Le Gor sat immobile before a huge looking-glass. Rivulets started between his shoulder-blades and his hair lay in damp curls on his head. He often passed the scorching afternoon hours in this high vaulted room, dressed in a loose white robe which gave no indication of his rank. The room smelt cooler and fresher since a servant had sprinkled rosewater on the marble floor.

Le Gor stared into the mirror and bit his lip. Dark eyes stared back, and the mouth whispered: 'Chastity . . . I failed on that. Yes. Poverty . . .'

Le Gor took his eyes away from the looking-glass and surveyed the room. Against the south wall huge woven hangings from Florence covered the bare stone, and below this wall stood two chairs with silk and gold embroidered seats. A sky-blue silk canopy encrusted with silver and rose-coloured stars hung in swags from the ceiling; Le Gor had it brought from Arabia. The red and white marble slabs under Le Gor's gold embroidered slippers had been imported from Italy, as had thirty other pairs of slippers.

'Yes. Yes. But my burdens are heavy, as you know perfectly well. And God has given us our senses to enjoy His world—'

The black eyes in the looking glass smouldered above prominent cheekbones set in a face still young. Below, the dull black folds of a monk's robe half concealed a young man's body, and the smooth skin of a young man gleamed cloister pale, much paler than Le Gor's florid complexion. As the cardinal watched, the face in the looking glass darkened and the lips formed words:

'Fornicator! Excess is what you crave; excess and power. When did you last fast? Wastrel, voluptuary, is this how you carry out Christ's commandments? The broken, spoilt food from your kitchens is sent to the hospice, but do you go there, do you succour the sick? You attempt to live like a prince, like your master. The poor and sick of Avignon starve and die, while you revel in debauchery—'

Le Gor's clasped hands felt the marks of his nails, digging deep into his palms, when he heard a knock.

Gui, his page, entered, and looked anxiously at his master, sitting without movement in front of the looking glass. Le Gor turned to him and cleared his throat several times before he spoke:

'News from the palace, Gui?'

'Yes, my lord. I thought I heard voices—'

'I was talking to myself, Gui. Well?'

'I mingled with the crowd, my lord, in the square before the palace. They say that the Holy Father was taken ill in the night and a wise woman, some say a witch, was called and she pronounced a spell – and he is well again sir, my lord, and resting. I would like to meet a witch, my lord—'

Le Gor looked at Gui with irritation. But I hate myself, not you, he thought.

'No, no, Gui. Witches do not heal, only God heals sickness. Prayer helps to heal, doctors try their art. You are at the papal court, not in your wilderness. You are displaying ignorant superstitions which are not accept-able in a cardinal's household.'

Gui closed his eyes briefly, hearing the contempt in his master's voice. He was young, and new at the court and Le Gor often went out of his way to make him feel the country boy he was. Except last night, when he had been happy and even, he thought, loved.

'Before your time and mine,' said Le Gor, 'forty years ago, the popes came to Avignon. Nobody thought they would stay, and everyone rented out their hovels, or their town-houses, to the popes and their retinue. And people have flooded into the town ever since, for the papal court has remained here against all expectation. Everyone came to seek their fortunes – just like you. Your father sent you to see what you could earn—'

'To see what I could learn, my lord.'

'We always thought the popes would return to Rome, but they are still here, and the town is like a madhouse. Like fleas, like lice, they batten on the body, let us say the bounty of the Church . . .'

Gui's eyes would not meet his, and Le Gor bit his lip. How could he tell Gui what he felt?

'Did you see Giacomo? Go and see if he has returned.'

Gui met Giacomo on the stairs. Giacomo, larger than Gui and dressed in the scarlet cloak which was his badge of office as the cardinal's messenger, slapped Gui on the back with such force that Gui stumbled down the rest of the flight to the wide entrance hall below, while Giacomo knocked and entered the cardinal's retiring room, where he handed over a note.

'From the Chevalier de Saint-Amant: He told me the contents, my lord; the Holy Father suffered from a kidney stone, and has recovered.'

'Thank you, Giacomo, you may go. Ask Gui to wait on me with wine.'

Giacomo did not scowl till the door of the cardinal's room had closed. Then he ran down the stairs two at a time and stopped at the marble bench where Gui sat, awaiting any summons.

'Come here, you swollen-headed rustic. You—' and he cuffed Gui's right ear '—are wanted upstairs. And when he's finished with you—' he cuffed Gui's head once more, 'you . . . painted whore, I want to talk to you, in private. Oh, and my lord wishes you to bring some wine.'

Gui gave no sign of having felt the blows. He was the son of a landowner, and Giacomo the son of a peasant. But all of Le Gor's household feared Giacomo's temper, and Gui had learned to keep silent at his taunts. Gui called on the cellarer and took the wine and glasses carefully up the stairs again, knocked and was called into the private apartments.

He poured wine for Le Gor, who looked at him critically; he had invested in Gui, as in any other work of art.

Gui was sixteen. Today he wore a cherry red shirt which reached to his knees and a blue woven cloak, full as far as his elbows, from where it dwindled into two thin strips, ending in points. These hung down from his elbows and often caught in the furniture. A long belt was wound twice round Gui's waist and held his sword in an embroidered sheath, more for show than use. A cap of gilt mesh kept his long fair hair from falling into his eyes, which were green. His nose was straight and his lips full. No one could fail to be moved by his beauty.

Le Gor looked at him coldly. He really must not speak gently to this beautiful boy, or in any way reveal his true feelings; for he was not prepared to give such a hostage to fortune.

Why did he need to flaunt the most beautiful page in Avignon at court? There were reasons – all of them bad. Well, tonight he would sleep alone and for once need not justify himself to the young monk in the mirror, particularly because he would also visit the hospice by the river, and see what help he could offer. Today, or tomorrow at the latest.

He dismissed Gui with a wave of the hand and without one kind glance – for which he would blame himself over and over for many months.

In the vestibule Gui found the major-domo waiting, with instructions to show three visitors the cardinals's residence. One was a painter, the two others architects. They were to report to the cardinal after the tour of the building, to discuss further embellishments which Le Gor envisaged.

I might become an architect, thought Gui. No, he would enter the Church and become a cardinal. Le Gor had told him that he was not just a beautiful face – he had talent, and for the past six months the cardinal had taught him manners and the ways of a great household. Meanwhile, he showed the visitors the majestic great rooms, and the chapel with the statue of the Virgin from Perugia, over which they exclaimed.

After they had left, with their notebooks filled, Gui returned to the entrance hall and his bench, where

Giacomo joined him, gently tapping him on the shoulder. I should have asked the Virgin for protection, thought Gui, but no, bah! For all his size and bulk Giacomo was one of the cardinal's servants, like himself. He would not risk an attack during daylight hours.

'Follow me,' said Giacomo softly. 'My lord's orders.'

Giacomo left the residence through the main door and crossed the central courtyard, turning round from time to time to check that Gui was following. Giacomo's face was calm and watchful. The two young men passed under an archway, used at the moment by three horsemen, and having waited for the frisky, prancing animals to clear the narrow passage, Giacomo made for the stables on the right, lying at this time of the afternoon in deep shadow.

Giacomo stopped and leaned against one of the two stone lions which Le Gor had brought from Rome, while grooms led more horses from the nearest stable out towards the archway.

'We need to talk,' said Giacomo quietly. 'Let us go into this stable, it's cooler in there.'

And then the nightmare began.

The crowd of pilgrims and travellers crossing the bridge late that afternoon made way hurriedly at the sight of a young man on a grey horse, riding like the devil over the cobbles of the bridge without regard to men or even animals. When he was forced to rein in his horse to pass a slow herd of oxen, the drovers remarked that the rider's face was streaked with sweat, or it could have been tears; and they certainly heard him utter a stream of obscenities. The rider reined in his horse again near the chapel half way across the bridge, and a priest, observing his grimy, distorted features, thought he heard him pray, briefly; then the young man was gone on his magnificent steed. His gilt mesh cap fell off as he spurred the horse, and the priest picked it up and, entering the chapel, placed it before a picture of the Virgin.

When he reached the gate by the river, the rider turned right and followed the road around the perimeter walls, till he came to a narrower road which he took without hesitation, murmuring now instead of cursing and crying.

The grey horse was going well in the cooler air, and Gui left the reins slack on the horse's neck, while he breathed deeply to quieten his heart, and the rage and despair which filled it.

He was going to Montolieu, where he had been born. Beyond the village, the surprised traveller would come to a tall tower, rising four storeys out of the thickets and trees, which had grown so high that Gui and his father could not see out of the first- and second-floor windows. On the third floor the huge, dank rooms were cool in summer, cold and clammy in winter. From the tapestry icy drops fell on the stone floors in winter, despite huge fires. Gui and his widowed father lived like birds in the treetops in these little rooms on the top floor.

Gui saw the tower in his mind's eye. In an hour he must face his father. Meanwhile, he wound the extravagant sleeves around his arms, and brushed some straw out of his hair. I'll kill him, a voice murmured inside him. How would his master, the cardinal, take his disappearance, what would . . . but now there was a blank wall between him and what had so recently . . . he shook his head. His mind had turned away and would not come to his rescue.

He rode towards Montolieu along the dusty highway, breathing in the lavender fields, greeting the olive groves and the almond trees along the way.

Gui was almost sixteen when a restlessness seized him. Hunting, riding, swimming, reading the books which his father had brought back from his travels as a young man, were no longer enough. His father, a lonely man who, in default of friends, barely left his son's side, loved his son enough to recognise his needs.

'You had better go to Avignon,' said the Chevalier de Montolieu. 'The city, they say, is now the centre of the Christian world. Pope Clement has come from the luxurious court of France. I could have told you a few tales about that court myself, but that was long ago and not suitable for your ears. The Pope has created a multitude of court offices. There must be a place for you somewhere. You could begin your career as a page . . . all that activity and brilliance! You'll find a great change from our peaceful life.'

'You don't want me to go,' said Gui, suddenly hoping that his father would make objections.

'At your age I travelled and saw the world. And sinned.'

'You've never said that before, Father.'

'I envy you. Think of serving at the court of the Pope! Generous, magnificent, the greatest monarch of our day.'

Maybe he missed me, maybe he will be pleased I've come back, thought Gui, riding along. He'll be startled to see me back so soon, although if it hadn't been for

. . . if . . . and again his memory encountered a blank wall, behind which crouched monsters. Well, he himself had also sinned, but his father loved him, and once he had told his father . . . like a horse refusing a jump, his mind stopped there with a jolt.

The horse. Once home, his father would ask a groom to take it back to Le Gor. The cardinal would be puzzled, or perhaps angry, and he would look for a new page, one who was less ignorant than Gui.

As he approached the little wood beyond which his home and his father awaited him, Gui's spirits began to lift. Twilight had come and the grey was forced to pick his way carefully along the narrow path through the darkening wood.

The tower stood silently, no light showed. In the small courtyard the low building where his father's two servants lived was also silent and dark. Gui thought that everyone was in the cherry orchard picking fruit before the light failed altogether. He dismounted and tied his horse to the stone ring near the majestic door. It was open, so his father could not be far.

The tower had been built, by Gui's grandfather, in such a way that each floor contained one large and one small room. The stairs from one floor to the next were lit by window slits – the tower served as a fortress against the lawless bands which plagued those who lived in the country, away from other habitations – and Gui had to climb the stairs now in almost complete darkness. He felt the silence which told him, somehow, that he was in an empty building. On the second floor he turned the handle of the great door into the large room. The door opened into impenetrable darkness.

Gui climbed to the third floor which also lay empty in silence and darkness, then to the fourth floor where the bedrooms were. After the . . . the . . . what had happened in the stables, he was suddenly overcome by apprehension and terror. Before opening his father's room, he knelt to pray to the Virgin, his one source of comfort amid the injury and senseless harm which had been done to him. Protect me, he prayed, and my father.

When he opened the door to his father's room, the scudding clouds released the light of the moon for a brief moment, and he saw disorder, a broken chair, scattered clothes, a broken ewer and the mattress which had shed its entrails onto the floor; and when a cloud extinguished the light of the moon and the room had returned to darkness, he began to search with his hands, searching for his father, perhaps his father's body. It was not there.

Gui hoped that his father must be alive, somewhere, and that he had better rest until dawn and then begin searching again. His own room had also been ransacked and his bed destroyed. Gui spent the night on the floor, sleeping briefly, and rose at dawn. Where were the servants? There had been no sign of them last night. He ran down the stairs to question them. When he reached the yard, he saw the old couple standing by the well; they had drawn water for the cardinal's grey. They ran towards him, falling to their knees, and Gui knelt down as well and embraced the old woman, then her husband.

'What happened? Where is my father?'

But they both began to sob and could not answer immediately. Then the old woman spoke: 'We slept in the cave, Master Gui, we thought they would come back for us.'

'Who came? When? Come over here, sit down on the step, and tell me.'

Toinette's fingers held a tiny bunch of herbs, which she tore into little pieces, while Yves's round, flat face turned away from Gui.

'Yves! Is . . . is my father . . . dead?'

'No, no, master,' said Yves at once. 'He went away with them, the men. They looked for his money. He gave them some, but they looked for more. It happened like this: the master came back from Vaison and there were naked men with him, with the blood streaked on their bodies. And the master said', Yves choked on the words, 'He said, "Tell my son – if he ever returns from Avignon – that I have gone to live a great adventure, for Christ. Besides, this is . . ." Forgive me, Master Gui, but I cannot remember the rest.'

They sat in silence by the well, in the morning sun.

Gui questioned Toinette and Yves, but they knew nothing more. Gui made up his mind to find his father. A great adventure? He thought of the slashed mattresses, the bodies streaked with blood, the open door of the tower, the scared servants, and he remembered the evil he had experienced in Avignon.

Chapter 5

Pope Clement, on his knees in his chapel of St Michael, where he could pray alone, rose unsteadily; he was barely able to control his trembling calf muscles. High time to plan his tomb. A good sculptor would need about two years to work on his effigy; he would insist that the artist did not flatter, obtain a reasonable likeness. He suddenly cried out with pain; once again the old injury to his left leg plagued him.

How much longer would God grant him? He sank back on the embroidered bench next to the prie-dieu. Benedict, his immediate predecessor, was crowned in January 1335 and died seven years later. Nicholas, before Benedict, resigned after two; before Nicholas, Pope John had served eight years. As for me, thought Clement, I am now fifty-seven and I've been Pope for five years. I haven't finished my task, oh Lord, I need more time.

He managed to descend the stairs where Saint-Amant and his sister Guillemette waited, watching him test his legs on every step.

He dismissed Saint-Amant with the charming smile which he offered everyone, nobles and servants alike and asked Guillemette if she would keep him company in his private apartments, as she had done so often since they were both children at the modest Château de Maument, in that wild and arid part of the Limousin landscape where they had been born, when they were called Pierre and Guillemette Roger.

'I don't know how long I will be permitted to live, Guillemette. Time to take stock.'

Guillemette, seated in her usual chair opposite her brother's, stitched away at a hare on her tapestry. She knew what her brother wanted to hear; every evening since his recent illness he had begun their conversation with these or similar words. She marshalled her list. 'Pierre, I shall tell you again. First, you completed the palace and it will stand for centuries to come. You brought painters and sculptors from Italy and Germany and France to Avignon – poets, scholars. They praise you for your generosity—'

'Yes. They also call it luxury unfitted for a religious court.'

'Luxury? You improved on that fortress Benedict had built, more suitable for keeping out attackers than housing a prince of the Church. When you came, there were no proper kitchens, no rooms to receive petitioners, just a warren of bare cells. You found engineers to bring water from the meadow to the tank, with pipes—'

Clement laughed. 'Am I to be remembered for the lavatory tower?'

'Why not? And the new system of sealing off the corridors and stairs against attacks. The vegetable and flower gardens—'

'Stop, stop. My love of the arts, and the money I have spent on them, is what excites the critics, but I tell them that it is a means of celebrating the beauty of the world, which God has enjoined us to enjoy. Though how long I

myself will do so . . . Guillemette, I want my tomb to be
at the Chaise Dieu, and I count on you to see to it. When
I was ten years old, the abbot there believed that I was
called to serve God a special way. There I became a
Benedictine, and there I will be buried.'

He put his head in his hands.

'And . . . ? Tell me, Pierre,' said Guillemette.

'The war between the English and the French; both
sides expect me to mediate, as head of the Church. The
results are inconclusive, negligible. And, as you know, I
appealed to all the princes of the West, regarding the
fight of Christendom against the infidel – a cause to
touch men's hearts and minds, you would think. There,
too, confusion and jealousy. What have I achieved? How
can I rest? I must work, I cannot be ill. I cannot die yet.'

Guillemette rose and kissed him.

'You will live, you are much stronger than you think.
And I know what you want to know, and I'll tell you
before you ask. But remember that sometimes, what I
hear is based on ignorance and gossip. I carried food
and wine from the kitchens to the hospice today, and sat
talking with the abbot and his helpers in the refectory.'

'Do they know who you are?'

'Oh yes, though I keep the veil over my face. They
know you will hear what they say about you and I think
they want you to hear. I have told them of my vow to visit
the hospice until my husband returns from the Holy
Land safe and sound. Oh, Pierre, it is so long since he
left . . . Of course you want to know the gossip in the
refectory. They say that since you bought Avignon, you
were the prince as well as Pope. One, a priest, quoted
you: "Clemency and I have grown together since—"'

'"—since I was a child,' continued her brother. 'I drank it with my mother's milk, it is my promised bride; but clemency has no existence without justice, mercy, and respect for truth.'

He smiled, and his eyes blinked, then closed. Guillemette sat for a while, then put away her needle and, rolling up her tapestry, rose softly from her chair, ready to leave Clement, when he opened his eyes.

'I beg you, sister, don't leave me before we have finished. I am aware that you want to shield me from adverse criticism, but let me know what else was said.'

'If you insist. They say that you have risen in the Church by service to the King of France, rather than to the Church. That you were a Frenchman.'

'So I am.'

'That the papacy in Avignon is nothing but an instrument of France.'

'Ah!'

'That the court is luxurious and sumptuous – and wasteful and profligate.'

'Luxurious – do I not share with many? Does not the show enhance the lives of many wretched people? Are we not all stalked by illness, misery and death? Is there enough joy in this city? Must Christians deny themselves joy? Must I not provide as much as I can, to relieve the black despair which is every man's condition, only too often?'

'Yes. Yes. And are you content now, Pierre, now that you have heard adverse criticism?'

'I should hear it, I must hear it, it is my antidote to pride. Good-night, Guillemette, you have helped me as you always do.'

At the hospice by the river, the abbot sat with two of his helpers, adding and subtracting and pushing piles of money across the table.

'Without the food Madame de la Jugie brings from the kitchens, we would not have enough for tomorrow. She is a good woman – another would send the cart with a kitchen servant, but she comes as well and enquires after – What has happened? Speak!'

A helper novice stood trembling before him.

'A man has risen from the dead, Father. I saw it, I was there. Brother Artaud and I were in the mortuary to remove the bodies to their coffins. On the tables, the trestle tables, there were only three bodies, Father, the fourth was on the floor. When we bent down to lift the corpse onto the table . . . we did not understand how he came to be on the floor, he was in his shroud, Father— he moaned. The Lord has worked a miracle!'

The abbot hurried to the mortuary where a group of hospice monks had just unwrapped the man from his shroud. He was incoherent, and too ill to be asked questions, but touched his head and back. He spat out green and yellow matter and they heard him cry out several times. The abbot and the monks knelt down where they stood in the mortuary, praising God and giving thanks, then carried the sick man to a bed.

The evening light fell slanting at the feet of the two women, in their little waiting room, in a world where pope, cardinal or abbot, powerful in Avignon and far beyond, played no role.

'Eat a *coudolle*, do,' said Lea to her daughter Blanchette, offering her a honey-cake.

'Oh no, Mother, I can't. There goes the bell again, from the convent. We've waited half an hour.'

'And they'll keep us waiting another half. You know what men are. And remember the *baylons* are paid to talk. Eat.'

'It's an honour, Mother, they're not paid.'

'You believe that? Jessue doesn't sneeze without getting paid!'

Blanchette took a *coudolle* and ate it, waiting for the *shamas*, the beadle, to fetch them from the little waiting room in the *escole*.

The huge building which the Jews called the *escole*, the school, thrust its bulk above the tall, narrow houses of the Street towards the light. The building housed the vital organs of the community; here they prayed, met in committee, butchered their meat and baked their bread. An underground stream fed the women's bath. Three times a day Jews entered the *escole* to pray and to gather strength for their struggles.

As a child, Blanchette had crept away from the others, whispering that she had to use the women's closet, creeping down to the semi-basement, to the black pool where the women took their ritual baths. She knew all the meeting rooms, the special kitchens and the great oven.

The *baylons* were meeting in the Mahama, as a Grand Council, to discuss the disappearance of Thoros. That's why they want us, thought Blanchette, but what could they do? Fear for him sat like a stone in her breast.

'Who says they're grand? Just Jews, like the rest of us,' Lea was saying, through a mouthful of *coudolle*.

'Much richer than us, mother.'

'That's as maybe. They eat and drink and fall ill like the rest of us. Mind you, they can buy themselves out of trouble. Did I ever tell you when your father—'

Thoros, thought Blanchette. He may be dead. She wondered whether her anguish showed; her mother noticed nothing.

'So the rabbi from the Holy Land stayed five nights, and ate everything! It was our turn to look after visitors, but I tell you, we couldn't wait to get rid of him—'

Blanchette sat listening, twisting her hair which stood up in two peaks like horns on either side of her forehead, exactly as the law required.

Suddenly Muscat the *shamas* stood before them and asked them to enter the meeting room.

Blanchette and Lea knew all the *baylons*, the elected officials of the Street, in whom the community had vested great power. They made all the laws, and enforced them. Even Lea fell silent as the two women sat down, facing the men: Daniel Naquet, Cabri Montel, Michel Aron, Abraham de Monteux, David Rougier, Vidal Farrusol and Rabbi Liptois de Mehier. At the head of the table sat Jessue de Carcassonne, well dressed, fat and overbearing, father of Bonaventure, who planned to marry Thoros, Lea knew, and bring him a considerable dowry. Jessue was the richest man in the Street.

'Rabbi, will you put the questions we have prepared?'

Rabbi Liptois shook his head and blushed. He was from Poland, had been appointed women's rabbi and had just started his three year contract with the Avignon community. The mixture of Polish, Provençal and Hebrew which he spoke was hard to understand. Cabri Montel whispered in Jessue's ear.

'Well, yes,' said Jessue. 'Maybe I'll put the questions myself. Now tell us. Is it correct that Thoros and Astruc have no other family apart from you and your mother?'

Blanchette nodded. As if they didn't know!

'And you have today visited several sick people in the Street to discover whether he had called on them today – and he had not?'

Blanchette nodded. They already knew the answer, everyone in the Street knew. Jessue droned on. 'About five o'clock you received the visit of one of his Holiness's officials, and he paid you for Thoros's attendance on His Holiness last night?'

'Yes, sir. I have already said so once to the rabbi, sir.'

'You and your mother may now withdraw.'

Blanchette knew Jessue to be a bully, whose wealth had made him arrogant. Today, she feared no one. She needed to know how they would set about finding Thoros.

'I will not. Mother, sit down. We're not going. I want to find Thoros. My husband is away. I and my mother are all the family Thoros has. Please help us find him.'

A ripple of displeasure ran around the table. Blanchette was to obey, not question. Jessue held up his hand. Outside the Street, he was just another Jew, but in the Street he was powerful. The *baylons* watched to see whether he would have the two women removed by the *shamas*, by force if need be.

Among the *baylons*, two represented the richest group, two those of middle income, and the remaining two spoke for those of little income. The poor were not represented.

Jessue now turned to Daniel Naquet and to Cabri Montel who, after him, were the wealthiest men in the Street. They nodded, and Jessue addressed Blanchette – a woman who had just spoken like a man. This can be turned to our advantage, said Jessue's smile, and besides, she is really beautiful. Something might well be done with her. He cleared his throat. 'We have considered and reached the conclusion that this is the usual trick. We will soon hear more and then be asked to pay, as usual. This year alone, there has been the land tax and the tax on possessions and of course the poll tax, and we have been asked to contribute to the papal coffers four other times. Tomorrow, friends, we'll very likely receive the visit of an official and we will be told the amount to pay, and they will then give us back our best *medicus.*'

Into the silence Abraham de Monteux ventured: 'I do not contradict what Jessue has put so well. But Thoros is our best doctor. And now that the Holy Father has seen what he can do, what if . . . what if the Pope has detained him, with promises of gold?'

'Then why,' cried Blanchette into the silence, 'did the official come from the palace to search for him at home? He could have paid Thoros at the palace!'

David Rougier lifted his hand. He represented those of little income. Blanchette knew that he lingered by the shop as often as he could, when Astruc was away.

'I think – if you will permit me – the doctor saved my life, you know. God guide his steps and his hands! I know I am the poorest here and I represent the poorest, but when it comes to the society for the care of the sick and the burial of the dead – *Bicur Hollim* – have I ever missed a duty?'

'David,' said Jessue. 'Come to the point, friend.'

'I think,' said David Rougier, 'that Maître Thoros has had an accident. Not, I think, an attack on his person. Because he would not have been recognised as one of us, would he?'

A hubbub arose.

'For he wears neither the hat nor the badge – as a doctor, he need not.'

'He would have sent a message,' said Blanchette.

She is clever, thought Jessue. We should make use of her.

Rabbi Liptois raised his hand, and spoke in Hebrew. 'My advice is this. No one except Blanchette has seen the Pope's messenger. Only Blanchette will recognise him. She must look for him, in Avignon, perhaps in the palace itself, and question him. Not alone, of course.'

David Rougier translated for the benefit of Lea and Blanchette who had no Hebrew. Then he offered to accompany Blanchette.

'I will give you a purse,' said Jessue with a sigh.

'It goes without saying that I will accompany my daughter,' said Lea, but her face was pale.

Blanchette smiled at all of them: 'None of you, nor my mother, nor myself,' she said,' knows Avignon like Old Jacob does. I will go with him.'

Chapter 6

Guillaume de Saint-Amant returned to his room reluctantly, although the hour was late and he needed sleep. All day long his duties had kept him from thinking but, once alone, the demons seized him, night after night. He looked out over the roofs of the town below his window and then closed it so that the canary could be released from its cage. He watched the bird flutter towards the watery moonlight, then circle the room.

Guillaume threw himself on the pallet, as he had done every night for a week now, hoping for sleep, but this night, too, his mind and his body tormented him.

His position at court gave him much pleasure and a great deal of power. His work required decisions regarding the spending of great sums and the channelling of money into his particular areas of responsibility for the palace – from buying horses and mules to food, wine, stuffs, furs; and the disbursements to innumerable tradesmen. But power seemed to preclude friendship, and he became more and more conscious of his isolation.

Yet there was one who was not envious of him. Raimond Durand was a cleric who taught theology at the university. They both came from the extreme north-west of France, from Quimper, and had formed a friendship at the papal court. The bells tolled midnight when Guillaume could bear no more and decided to seek help from his countryman. If I don't solve this, he thought, the obsession will take over my life and ruin me.

The residence of the preaching friars, where the teachers of theology lodged, was closed at this hour, but the night porter recognised Guillaume and let him in. Guillaume found his friend writing in his cell, wrapped in his robe, with a glass of Beaumes de Venise on the table and a cat on his lap to keep him company. The candle flickered in the draught from the door.

'What disaster brings you here?' said the friar. 'It must be important to keep you out of bed, and I had hoped to have a couple of hours' sleep before Lauds. I presume this is an important moral problem?'

'There are areas of knowledge with which you're familiar and I am not.'

'For example?'

'Erm . . . well . . . the attitude of the Church to the Jews and other infidels.'

'Guillaume, you're teasing me! You can't sleep without knowing the Church's position? You're here . . . no, I see this is serious. Well, shall I begin with the Jews or with the infidels?'

'The Jews. I'm sorry, Raimond, to keep you from your bed.'

'I may take it then that you're in trouble – or you want to forestall it?'

'To forestall it. There are things I need to know, Raimond.'

The friar rubbed his tonsure, which was beginning to sprout hairs.

'Of course I'll do my best for a countryman. So, firstly, what do we learn from the papal bulls on the subject? It is, of course, the Holy Father of the day who gives us guidance on this, as on all matters concerning the faithful, but I had better go back a little and begin with Pope Honorius's bull of 1215 . . . what is the matter?'

Saint-Amant was staring at him with bloodshot eyes. 'I'm not one of your students. Is this relevant?'

'Oh, go to bed,' said the friar crossly. 'Leave me to write tomorrow's lecture. I'm behind as it is.'

'I've offended you, and I do need to know. I am sorry. Please tell me what is essential, it is important, I do assure you—'

'Or you would not be here now. I must guess your needs . . . let me see . . . you want to know, probably, what is and what is not permitted to Jews?'

Saint-Amant nodded, and the friar pushed the bottle and a glass towards his friend, as the bells chimed one o'clock all around them, from every church in Avignon.

'Jews,' began Raimond Durand in the voice he used to teach, 'must wear distinctive clothing, in case they are mistaken for Christians, for they often look indistinguishable. Under our Pope Clement, they must wear a badge and a hat. The Talmud, their book of commentaries on the Holy Bible, is forbidden. It is impious and contains recipes for sorcery. Jews must not carry out public functions. Very important: Jews and Christians must not live together—'

'Under one roof? Or does that mean as man and wife?'

'Neither, of course. You know that really, don't you? They must attend the sermons which we preach, so that they may be converted to the true faith. They must not enter brothels or public baths, except on designate days – is that the sort of thing you want?'

'Yes. I suppose so. Is there much more?'

'Yes. Many of these laws are broken constantly, by the Jews and by Christians too, and recently by the Holy Father himself – but there were extenuating circumstances, no doubt—'

'I know about that one: Jewish doctors may not attend Christians. Please go on, Raimond.'

The friar scratched the emerging blond stubble on his chin. 'You could help me by specifying . . . no? Where was I . . . they may not sell flour, bread, wine, oil, shoes or new clothes. They may not build new synagogues. The guilds bar them from weaving, metalworking, mining, tailoring – that is, new clothes – goldsmith work, carpentry – have you heard enough?'

'More than enough, thank you. But why can't we treat them as neighbours? They seem to me – they seem to be very like us.'

The friar looked at him without a smile.

'You have forgotten what they did. They crucified our Lord. We need the Jews as testimony, to remind us of the reality of the New Testament, for they bear witness to the reality of what took place which no Christian – which you, Guillaume – should not forget.'

Guillaume de Saint-Amant stared at the candle and the flickering light showed him not the friar, but the beautiful face of the woman who haunted him.

'If a Jew converts, we will protect him against those other Jews who have not yet seen the light—'

'And do they? Convert, I mean?'

'They do not. A stiff-backed generation . . . And did you know, Guillaume, that there is a decree nailed on the door of the synagogue in the Street, and the same one on the doors of all the churches in Avignon, forbidding intimate relations between Jews and Christians? No one can pretend ignorance, can they?'

'Perhaps I should explain . . .' said Guillaume, after a pause.

'No. Remember I'm a man as well as a friar. Go and see your confessor. I hope that you will now be able to sleep after this short, tedious and probably unwelcome lesson.'

Saint-Amant nodded, and the two friends embraced. The friar closed the door after his departing visitor, and offered up a short prayer for his countryman, asking God to be lenient to Guillaume who was on his way to sin, without a doubt.

Saint-Amant negotiated the short distance back to the palace without seeing the dung, the puddles of urine and vomit, the humped figures in doorways, the mule asleep on his feet, the sentry at the gate who saluted him. He moved in a waking nightmare. As he climbed the last stair and reached his own corridor, a hand plucked at his sleeve. Saint-Amant raised his lantern. 'Bitch!' he shouted.

The girl shrank away. The sentries were supposed to keep them out of the palace, but it was like putting a drunkard in charge of the cellars. There were scores like her, running hither and thither through the passages like rats, and the devil had sent her, too. He groaned. He now found himself in a worse position than before his visit to the friar; before he could have pleaded ignorance. The visit had been an error. Satan had shown him the most beautiful woman he had ever seen and had cunningly offered him a snare exactly matching his weakness.

Gui left the grey in his father's stables and saddled the old mare, who remembered him with a whinny and a soft, trusting glance. She picked her way down the hill behind the tower along the path they both knew well, across the meadows, which were bright with a myriad of poppies into the one street of Montolieu village. At once the sun was blotted out, for the houses stood close together, leaving no room for the scorching sun to enter.

Gui was on his way to the priest for help; not only for news, he hoped, of his father, but for some release for his feelings of shame, his desire for revenge and his impotence to prevent the scandal which would involve his master, the cardinal. Last night he had felt little except fear for his father but this morning his memory of the anguish in the stable filled his heart.

The priest's house at the other end of the village was small and decrepit. The door was open. Gui tied the horse to an iron ring in the wall and called out: 'Father! It is Gui de Montolieu.'

The priest came to the door. His sullen face expressed no interest in Gui. He led him into the single room on the ground floor, indicating a chair. From the corner of the room a dark-haired small boy with the same narrow, delicate face as the priest looked silently, as did his father, at the visitor

'A beautiful boy,' said Gui.

The priest looked at Gui morosely.

'When your father last came here – and that was more than a year ago – he said to me: "You and your son look as alike each other as two eggs." That's what the master of Montolieu said to me.'

'And so he does. I am here today to go to confession, Father. And to ask whether you have seen or heard—'

'And your father asked me, Master Gui, why I sold indulgences for sins committed, why I did that, with my own sin staring me in the face.'

'Do you know where my father—'

'I told him that there were plenty of priests in Avignon who had fathered bastards. But there the priests' bastards and their mothers go begging, compounding the sin. But I care for my boy and his mother, Master Gui. Your father, about whom you are anxious should have bought an indulgence. You may guess that he has sinned, your father; I am in a position to know. Worse, he used his influence as master of Montolieu so that none of the villagers has bought indulgences either, so they will fry in the flames of hell. Then when the bishop sends for the *sous* I am supposed to have taken for the sale of indulgences, I can't give him any. In turn he may decide that he cannot give me my stipend.'

'My father—' Gui began again.

'I do not expect you to atone for the sins of your father.' He paused. 'So you have returned from the city of sin, the Babylon of the West, as Petrarch says. I have obtained a page copied from the book. It may interest you.'

He unrolled a parcel tied in cloth and took a frail piece of vellum from it. 'This has been passed from hand to hand, among those who feel like I do. I will read you . . . Petrarch says . . . yes, here.'

The popes, successors of the poor fishermen of Galilee, are now loaded with gold and clad in purple. I am living in the

*Babylon of the West, where prelates feast at licentious banquets
and ride on snow-white horses decked in gold, fed on gold,
soon to be shod in gold if the Lord does not check this slavish
luxury.*

'Oh no!' cried Gui. 'My master, Cardinal Le Gor,
explained to me that Petrarch is a lapsed cleric and
that he denounces what he does not approve of. He
seems to have some quarrel with the Holy Father, who
values him highly, my master told me – and he exag-
gerates. For instance, the horses are only decked in
gold for processions . . . Father, please. I need your
help.'

But the priest had not finished. His small son flinched
as the priest's voice rose in denunciation:

'The clergy sin in Avignon, even more than the
common people! What should humble clergy like me
think of the behaviour of great dignitaries of the
Church? It is said that some cardinals make love to a
different high-born lady every day – and even to pretty
boys,' he ended maliciously, staring at Gui.

'Yes. Will you hear my confession, Father? And I must
know what happened to my father. Do you know?'

'Yes,' said the priest grimly. He looked sharply at Gui's
pale face and his voice became gentler. 'I will say Mass
now. Come with me.'

Gui followed him to the church.

When Mass had been said, and Gui's confession
heard, the two men returned to the priest's house. The
priest sent his boy out to play.

'So now you know about me,' said Gui. Confession
had cleansed him for the time being. He waited minutes

for the priest to speak, and with every passing minute he lost all hope of hearing good news.

'You will put your life in Avignon behind you,' said the priest at last. 'As for your father – prepare yourself, Master Gui.'

Chapter 7

Giacomo helped Cardinal Le Gor into the saddle with a great show of solicitude, hoping for a smile or a few words, but Le Gor mounted the piebald with his face turned away, silent and deep in thought, and rode towards the bridge, leaving Giacomo in his usual state of sullen resentment. Giacomo had hoped that with Gui gone, he would be appreciated and maybe even promoted, but for many weeks now the cardinal had become very withdrawn.

Le Gor let the piebald amble towards the bridge and allowed the horse to pick his way through the crowd, dense as always on the bridge. When he reached the chapel, Le Gor decided to dismount. His head was full of questions, but lately his anxiety had carved out a new channel. Only prayer could bring him peace.

Once inside the familiar small chapel, cool air stroked his brow. He nodded to the priest who came towards him, but retreated again as Le Gor shook his head and knelt awkwardly in the shadows of the narrow back pew. He closed his eyes.

Prayer had become very difficult in the past few weeks, ever since Gui's inexplicable departure; so sudden and so unexpected. Now, whenever he began to pray, repetitive and unrewarding thoughts and questions insinuated themselves between the familiar comforting words, and today, too, the prayer turned into painful, useless ruminations. Release me Lord, he prayed, from these thoughts: but they pushed away prayer remorselessly and filled his mind.

Gui, for whom I care and who cared for me, Lord, yes, I am sure he cared for me – yet he left me without a word to me, Lord, or to anyone else and I have wearied myself and my household with questions. Who is lying to me and why, who knows but will not speak? Has he been seduced away by my enemies, will they use him against me? I have transgressed in abusing my position, Lord, and I do expect to pay one day – is it to be now, Lord? Strangely, I believe that I would feel relief if that should happen – my mind will be eased. But my heart, my heart . . . Lord, help me . . . Lord, you know that I used the money I took wisely and that the poor benefited . . . if only I knew where Gui is now . . .

As he lifted his eyes to the altar, his gaze was caught by a glimmer of gold. A circlet of gold mesh had been attached to the wall of the chapel, beneath a picture of the Virgin, to which it seemed to call attention . . .

Le Gor rose at last, carrying the same burden in his heart as when he entered and wishing, as he did constantly, that he knew where to seek relief, and left the chapel, to find a crowd admiring the piebald. As soon as the beggars saw his scarlet cloak, they displayed the stumps of arms and legs, sightless eyes and suppurating wounds. As always, he gave away all he carried in his purse; every coin given to a beggar eased his mind.

Le Gor had one call to make before riding through the town to the palace on the Rocher des Doms. The hospice lay outside the town gate, close to the bridge, and the cardinal spurred the piebald to trot smartly into the hospice courtyard. A friar led his horse to the stables, while the abbot hurried forward anxiously as though propelled by a torrent of complaints.

'The hospice is full, Cardinal, every bed is taken! I am at my wit's end, how will we fare? Certainly the money will not stretch to accommodate all these folk. I need money for gruel, we have had to burn sheets, I need linen, the provisions sent from the palace kitchens have not arrived and meanwhile—'

'Yes, yes,' said Le Gor, noting the abbot's words without surprise. 'I shall be riding on to the palace and will remind – Saint-Amant, is it? Meanwhile let us do the rounds of the sick, Abbot.'

Le Gor and the abbot entered the cavernous room where helpers were swabbing the floor. The two men went from bed to bed.

'And this,' said the abbot in a low voice, 'is the man who returned from the dead.'

'I saw him last week. Have you noticed any change?'

'No.'

They stood by the bed, one on each side. The man's beard, curly and black, was in curious contrast to the hair on his head and his eyebrows, which was white.

'All his hair was black when they brought him to us,' the abbot whispered.

'Do you know who he is, yet?'

'No. He has not spoken. He does not reply to questions.'

Le Gor bent over the sick man and looked carefully at the sunken face. 'He is still in a fever. I fear—' the sick man's eyes were open, staring at the ceiling, '—that he is on his way to God.'

The man who had returned from the dead heard their voices but the words meant nothing to him. Pictures rose in his mind like bubbles. A hand held him under the small of his back, another supported his head. His whole body, a foot long, submerged again under water. Bubbles rose and burst. Later, warm liquid flowed into his mouth and calm enveloped his rocking, swaying body till he fell asleep.

Cardinal Le Gor and Guillaume de Saint-Amant had been sitting in the Pope's *studium* for the past hour. It was agreeably cool and Clement was in good humour.

'The repast should mark the occasion without osten-tation,' said Clement. 'And now let me hear what else you have planned, Cardinal.'

'Matteo Giovanni tells me that he has prepared some painted screens which will be lit from behind with candles and are said to be extraordinary. I have also obtained the services of Raoul de Ferrières. He will be singing ballads, love songs, lays. That is, of course, if you approve, Holy Father.'

'Good. And you, Knight?'

'The cooks will be preparing the meals in the Secret Kitchen, Holy Father, and serving in the little *Tinel*—'

Clement winced and clutched the small of his back. After a long moment he smiled. 'Just a momentary indisposition – but it reminds me. You took a purse to the Jewish *medicus*, Saint-Amant – I may need him again. Tell him so. Tell him I want to retain his services.'

'Holy Father,' said Saint-Amant. 'The Jew left the palace and has not been seen since. I took the purse to his house where his sister-in-law awaited his home-coming in vain—'

'Find him, Saint-Amant.'

After every last detail for the forthcoming celebration had been settled, Le Gor returned to his house across the Rhône, while Saint-Amant moved like a sleepwalker, unseeing but safely, along the endless passages and wearisome stairs to his own room in the palace.

He fell onto his bed and with open eyes resumed a now familiar daydream. It began with an actual event, which at the time had seemed like a dream. Blanchette Bonivassin, the most beautiful woman he had ever seen had sought him out, here at the palace. She had begged him, with great dignity, to trace the doctor Thoros Boni-vassin, her husband's brother. Blanchette then offered him a purse, donated by the Jews of the Street. She had begun her visit calmly, but suddenly burst into a torrent of tears which hardly disfigured her beautiful face but moved Saint-Amant so that he had to repress his own tears.

But he did not touch her.

Ever since his second visit to the Street, Saint-Amant had found the time to slip away there to exchange a few words with Blanchette, although her eager, welcoming expression whenever she saw him changed quickly to indifference when she realised that he had no news of Thoros.

And now his daydream took control and spun him a beguiling tale: standing close to Blanchette in her dark shop, he moved still closer, took her hand, pulled her against his body in spite of her struggles and kissed her while his hand slipped around her breast – could he make it happen? If she were to cry out, if he were seen, if someone should enter the shop, his career at the court would end. He thought briefly of seeking out one of the shadowy women who haunted the corridors. But no, he wanted her, the forbidden woman of the Street, the devil's offering; the witch, the bitch whom he needed and would have just once, to be free of the incessant unbearable longing.

He leapt off his pallet, flung a dull brown cloak over his vivid, tell tale clothes and hurried down the stairs and out of the palace. His work? He would see the cooks later, everything was in order, ready. Saint-Amant hurried through the afternoon streets and was jostled by the crowd in his brown cloak. Once in the Street he joined the curious who were peering into the dark little shops, buying or haggling with the Jewish women while their husbands, almost all pedlars, were roaming the villages.

He strode towards Blanchette's shop, where as always she was stitching together a garment. As soon as she saw him she looked at him eagerly.

'No news yet,' said Guillaume de Saint-Amant, avoiding Blanchette's eye.

She sighed and a small sound of grief and frustration escaped her.

'I will not keep you from a customer,' said a woman who rose from the shadows and left the shop with a nod to Blanchette.

'Yes,' said Saint-Amant, seizing on the idea. 'Make me a – a tunic. Yes. Take my measurements.'

Blanchette appeared not to have heard him.

'Where can he be?' she murmured. 'Where should we look? If he is still alive . . .'

Guillaume watched her, like a cat about to spring, every nerve quivering, muscles tense. Would she cry out? His right hand was ready to close her mouth, his left prepared to seize her by the hair, pushing or perhaps pulling her into the back of the shop where it was dark, almost totally dark. Blanchette was not looking at him. Was she crying? By God, he did not want her grief. Ten minutes – less – and it would be accomplished and he would be a free man again, master of his life.

'Will you measure me for a tunic? Have you not heard me?'

Blanchette sighed and rose. She began by measuring his chest. As soon as her hands touched him, he pulled her roughly towards him, ready for resistance and ready to clamp his hand over her mouth.

But she offered no resistance. Why not? Was this an ambush? She remained inert and turned her face away from him. He put his arm around her shoulders, astonished by her compliance, and made for a half-open door which he saw gave onto the stairs, and to his astonishment she preceded him upwards till they reached what he realised must be her room, as dark as the stairs.

The window was shuttered.

She allowed him to take off her clothes and he fell on her. At his climax he called her name – Blanchette! But she uttered not a word and lay, a silent ghost, on the narrow pallet.

I have lain with a she-devil, a Jewess, a witch, thought Guillaume, suddenly afraid. He crossed himself. He must find his confessor and rid himself of this sin. Perhaps he would be punished, perhaps his sex would rot or wither, perhaps he would become impotent? Or any woman with whom he lay would conceive and bear rabbits. He shivered although he was fully dressed.

And . . . and he had not enjoyed lying with Blanchette. Another thought struck him. Perhaps she had concealed her husband somewhere and suddenly some Jews would fall upon him with cudgels – on the stairs? – and split his head open.

'Your husband—'

'He has left me. He and my husband's brother, both.'

Guillaume saw that she was crying. She, who had enticed him to commit a sin from which he had not even derived pleasure. He could go now, it was over. He looked about him at the bare room and, after a moment's hesitation, laid two gold ducats on the table; a fortune.

Blanchette looked at the coins, then rose and wrapped herself in her cloak.

'I shall not make you a tunic, *chevalier*,' she said in a voice without any colour at all. 'Take these coins and do not return.'

Guillaume de Saint-Amant left without a word, and walked to the palace. Already he missed his obsession with Blanchette. As for the sin: would it have been greater if he had enjoyed it?

Chapter 8

After the very hot summer the people of Avignon looked forward to cooler weather but when winter came, it was a hard one and in February of that year of 1347, sickness struck Avignon.

The town was overfull when the sickness started and each warm hearth sheltered many more than the summer before. There was no shortage of work or food, but the people were herded like cattle: and fear ran with the contagion through the populace, for the sickness could be caught by touch.

In Avignon they called it *ladrerie* or *mesellerie*, as well as leprosy. It declared itself firstly on the skin, then in the mucous membranes, then it appeared in the internal organs and finally it attacked the whole nervous system.

When a man or woman caught the disease, the rules were strict. Lepers were forced to wear grey cloaks and hats and to ring a bell, so that people could avoid closeness and pass on the other side of the street to place coins in a bowl. No leper was allowed to handle any object without wearing gloves, drink from a public fountain or lower a bucket into any well except their own. They were forbidden to walk barefoot, or in narrow streets, or to touch walls, doorways, trees; they might not even sleep by the roadside.

A leper could only marry another leper. They were forbidden to make love; and, when they died, they were buried by other lepers in their own graveyards. So they had always lived, suffering and apart, treated by all with disgust.

That February, their numbers grew. Although groups of them lived in small houses outside the town, they suddenly seemed to be everywhere in the streets of Avignon. Where there had been eleven needing care in the hospice by the river last summer, there were sixty this February, and more begging admittance every day, for people had begun to throw stones at them in the streets. Only the hospices sheltered the lepers; but the hospices were overflowing.

At the hospice of the Friars Penitent by the river, the abbot awaited the weekly visit of Cardinal Le Gor in his courtyard and took the horse's bridle himself, for every friar and helper was occupied with the sick.

'Thank God you're here, Cardinal! I am at my wit's end as usual. I've had to put them on the floor!'

As soon as they were installed in the abbot's study, Le Gor asked for the abbot's list.

'Calm yourself, Abbot, do. You have placed how many and where?'

'All but two in the convents and monasteries: twelve with the Dominicans, three with the Benedictine nuns, four each with the Austins, Carmelites, Cistercians, ten with the Knights of St John's. But there are more sick, Cardinal, and now they are arriving with wounds – people are stoning them – and some have been savaged by dogs. The Reverend Mother Superior of the Benedictines could take more, I know she could.'

'Yes, yes, Abbot. Here, take this purse, I am sure it will help to place more of them. How many helpers are still with you?'

'All my friars, Cardinal, I am proud of them. And Laurent has turned out very well.'

'Laurent? Which is Laurent?'

'The one who returned from the dead. We call him Laurent, Heaven knows what his name is. Ever since he recovered last Christmas, he has served the lepers; washing, feeding—'

'He has remembered who he is, has he?'

'No, he has not.'

'Let me see him, Abbot. I have been very preoccupied lately.'

Laurent stood before the cardinal and the abbot, a gaunt figure whose black robe seemed to weigh him down, whose sunken features formed a map of hollows spread around a bony nose.

'Are you well again, Laurent?' asked Le Gor.

The man kept his eyes on the floor but nodded.

'I hear you are tending the lepers. God will reward you, whatever your sins were. Have you parents, or a wife, whom we could tell that you are better?'

Laurent looked up and shook his head, then stretched his hands out before him.

'My hands – I look at them ten times a day. Why can't they tell me who I am? I have been ill so long that they no longer bear the marks of my trade,' Laurent said in a low voice.

Le Gor had become markedly more understanding of human ills since Gui had left him.

'Kneel, Laurent. We are going to pray for your recovery together.'

All three men knelt in prayer. The Latin words echoed in the vaulted chamber.

'In the name of the Father, Son and Holy Ghost, Amen,' said Le Gor at last and, turning to Laurent:

'Try to remember where you were when last you heard these words.'

'I have never heard them before,' said Laurent.

'Of course you have,' said the abbot impatiently. 'You have heard them every day in our chapel. You may not understand them, as they are in Latin, but you have always heard them since you were a little child.'

Laurent stood still before the two priests. His brow furrowed and other muscles in his face contracted so that he seemed to be frowning and smiling alternately.

'I have heard them, yes, ' he said suddenly. 'But for the first time today I understand.'

'What do you understand?' said Le Gor, rousing himself from his thoughts.

'I understand Latin, my lord.'

After Laurent had left the abbot's chamber, Le Gor turned to the abbot. 'This man's plight interests me and, frankly, it would be a pity if – serving the lepers here as he does – the sickness were now to claim Laurent, considering he has returned from the dead, against all expectation.'

The following day, Giacomo dismounted outside the gate of the hospice and pulled over and over at the bell-rope until the jangling bell finally brought an elderly friar.

'Get the old man, the one with white hair and a black beard. My master wants him now, over at the residence. And hurry, this wind is cold,' Giacomo said gruffly.

'Come back another time,' replied the friar. 'We've our hands full with sick people.'

Before the porter could shut the gate, Giacomo had seized him by the throat.

'You'll be very sick yourself, porter, in no time at all! My master, Cardinal Le Gor, has arranged this with the abbot. Get him, now.'

A little later Laurent, bewildered and fearful, stood by the horse. As it pawed the cobbles, Laurent took a step back.

'Well, peasant, have you not seen a horse before?' jeered Giacomo. 'Get up behind me!'

The porter helped Laurent on to the rump of the horse.

'Remember,' said Giacomo, huge in his winter cloak, 'to hold on. I don't slow down over the bridge and I don't want you falling off. We'd become the laughing stock of every beggar.'

The nightmare ride left Laurent shaken and trembling. He slid from the horse onto the cobbles of the residence courtyard and Giacomo, cursing, was forced to help him up the marble stairs into the cardinal's study.

Giacomo propped Laurent against the doorway, and left, bowing deeply. For once Le Gor remembered to thank him. To Laurent, the big room seemed on fire; with candles in sconces everywhere, winking at their reflections in many gold-framed wall mirrors. At the hospice a single candle illuminated the room he shared with nine others. In a huge chair by the side of a marble fireplace where an olive wood fire smoked and hissed, Laurent's eyes discovered the cardinal, enveloped in his red fur-lined winter robe, and next to him Laurent saw a young man, dressed in honey and lemon velvets, holding a lute. The firelight caught the metal and gold of his dagger and the hasp on his belt.

'He is shivering. Geraud, get the robe,' said Le Gor, and Geraud put down his lute and reappeared shortly to drape the fur robe gently around Laurent's shoulders. As Laurent moved forward, he swayed under the unaccustomed weight, and the page caught him just in time to help him to a chair.

'Light as a feather,' said Geraud.

'You are lucky never to have been very ill, Geraud. Play, my boy, and sing for us, but softly.'

'*The malady of love is so pleasing*—' Geraud began the *ballade*, touching the lute only occasionally, singing softly and well.

Laurent's eyes closed, but Le Gor watched Geraud, metamorphosed into Gui, missing and missed since last summer. Tears rose to Le Gor's eyes as he listened to Machaut's ballad about true love. Until now, Le Gor had not given his feelings a name. The words of the lament reached his heart and the song spoke of what he could not name. Pages came and went; they turned from awkward boys into young men, like caterpillars turning into butterflies – and like a butterfly, Gui had gone at the end of summer.

The ballad was over.

'No more singing, Geraud. This ballad is too sad for me, and Laurent needs refreshment, if we can wake him.'

After wine had been brought, the cardinal turned to Laurent. 'I have asked you here for a purpose.'

He paused. Le Gor, in his usual spirit of enquiry – for informed was forearmed – had transferred his curiosity to an acceptable field for a man in Holy Orders. Since

God had made a miracle happen, Le Gor could perhaps, by probing, discover how death looked from the other side, reported by Laurent who had been with death and returned.

A few sips of wine had restored Laurent, but when the cardinal explained his purpose, Laurent excused himself. 'I am very grateful, my lord, and anxious to help, but weakened by the ride. What you ask, though, would depend on my recollections of my death, but my state is such, my lord, that I cannot even remember my life.'

'Come here, Geraud, and bring your lute.'

The tall young page with his good-natured air stepped forward.

'Laurent, whom you see before you, has alas lost his memory. He was brought to the hospice, lifeless. But he, with his face the ashen colour of a corpse, roused himself from the embrace of death. Now, he wants to know who he is. Let us test him, let us discover who Laurent is. He wants to use his hands, he thinks they will help him discover what he did. Give him your lute.'

Laurent took the lute. It lay awkwardly on his lap.

'Can you not play? I'll soon show you how!' cried Geraud.

'No, no, Geraud. He is not to be taught. We must find something which his hands recognise, and it may well take a long time.'

Geraud looked about him. Boredom was his enemy, this game would keep it at bay.

'Parchment and ink—' he began. But Le Gor shook his head.

'Later. Look, the wine has sent him to sleep.'

Across the Rhône, greyish-green under the cool February sky, the porter had just finished locking the gates of the Street, because the sun was setting, and with all visitors gone the Jews pursued their own lives, free from curious eyes.

Blanchette sat on the one chair in her workroom and, without rising, tried to cut the stuff lying on the table in front of her, ready tacked. But, because of her great belly she could not reach it. Her mother snatched the scissors from her to do the task.

'My poor Lolo,' said the old woman. 'At least you've still got me to help you. There. And the fish will be baked soon.'

'The smell of it is making me sick, Mother.'

'Fresh fish, cost me two *sous patas*. My only daughter, with child, and without her husband! It is a mercy you have me to look after you.'

'Mother, I really don't want to eat.'

'Good for the baby, the boy. I told you the *baylons* are coming, tidy your hair.'

'But I'm at home, Mother, where I can wear my hair as I like! I am not putting it up in horns, Mother, not for the *baylons* – not for the Messiah if he chose to come tonight.'

'I shouldn't tell you—' began the old woman.

'Then do not tell me.'

'I might as well tell you. You'll hear it soon enough.'

Blanchette waited.

'It's important. They have collected—'

'For me?'

'For whom, if not you? Who is great with child and has neither a husband nor a husband's brother? The

Society for the Care of Virgins in need of a Dowry, they have collected.'

'Then they have the wrong woman,' said Blanchette, laughing.

'Oh Lolo, you know who I mean. With all these societies you don't know where you are. The Society for Succouring the Sick—'

'And the Burial of the Dead. Good, Mother. I have something to ask them.'

'They are coming here to save your legs, any minute now. Be polite, be respectful. Ah . . . I can hear them – Where will they sit?'

The three officials were picking their way among the bales of old clothes and finished garments hanging from nails. First came the women's rabbi, Rabbi Liptois de Mehier, then Daniel Naquet and lastly David Rougier. They stood about awkwardly.

The Polish rabbi began in his halting Provençal mixed with Hebrew. 'We, as members of the Society, for which we receive no payment but the honour of belonging, are here to carry out our duty to succour you, under the twelfth *escamot*, the law – er – I cannot find the word—'

David Rougier interrupted. 'Blanchette, we wish to pay you a sum to relieve you and your mother of money worries during the absence of Astruc and Thoros. It is our duty.'

'I have no money worries,' said Blanchette.

Daniel Naquet blushed. 'We know that you are working very hard. Without your husband, how will you sell your clothes? Our duty is prescribed by law, and we will be rewarded for this *mitzvah*. You will be doing us a favour by accepting this purse.'

Blanchette had kept her head down since the *baylons* had entered her shop. She looked up at the men now for the first time, and it was they, all three of them, who looked away as she spoke with bitterness. 'I am the woman whose husband has run away from her. I know that everyone in the Street is pointing the finger at me, but at least I can be glad that I am the occasion for you to perform a charitable action.'

Rabbi Liptois placed the purse on the table, among tarnished buttons, torn uniforms and cassocks. Embarrassment and pity for the abandoned, angry, pregnant woman hung in the air.

A sizzling, acrid odour from somewhere above introduced a different note.

'My fish!' shrieked Blanchette's mother and hurried away.

The rabbi silently considered how best to help this headstrong woman. David Rougier tried not to stare at Blanchette and hoped that Astruc would never return, so that he could woo and marry this beautiful woman. Daniel Naquet, tired after a long day standing in his stuffy shop, wished he could sit down.

Blanchette forced her face into a smile.

'Let me tell you, sirs, that although my husband has not returned, he has sent me money. Twice. And now I would like to make a request of you. It concerns my brother-in-law. Do you believe he could still be alive?'

One after the other, the *baylons* shook their heads.

'Then . . . I want a funeral for him.'

Rabbi Liptois shook his head.

'The nature of a burial service is such that we must have a body. We cannot say yes.'

After the *baylons* had left, Blanchette and her mother sat in silence. The fish was too burnt to eat, but the *baylons'* purse was in the old woman's apron pocket.

'Why can't we have a funeral, Mother?'

'When your father died,' said Lea with a sigh, ' It was this time of the year. It was dark when we set off from the Street, because the Christians only allow us to bury our dead after dark. You were not two years old and we left you behind, of course. They had put your father on the bier, covered with a black cloth and the *baylons* – they're long gone – set off with the bier, out of the Street, and the porter locked up behind us as we walked to the cemetery outside Avignon, I forget outside which gate. And all of us that could walk went with him, Lolo, in our black hats and black cloaks to cover ourselves, even our hats. We chanted the psalms. But the wind and the rain blew out our candles as we walked and we only lit them again by the side of the grave. When you dig a grave, you know, there must be no bones in the earth when you dig it up. It is to be yours alone.'

She paused and wiped her eyes, and Blanchette put her arms around her mother.

'Then the *baylons* take the body from the bier. It is wrapped in the prayer shawl your father used all his life which becomes a shroud – there is no coffin. So when the *baylons* tell you that they cannot bury Thoros without a body, they speak truly and reasonably, my poor Lolo.'

Two figures moved stiffly, ungainly as wooden dolls, across the frozen puddles in the yard in front of Marie's house. Their arms and legs were swaddled in strips of cloth, cowls covered their heads and shoulders and two tunics, short over long, kept out the unusual cold.

In Avignon, leprosy raged. Here, wild animals approached the lonely house from the surrounding forest in search of food; and that was how Astruc had caught the wild pig that had fallen into the pit, covered with branches, which Astruc had dug as instructed by Marie.

Astruc threw a stone into the well to break the ice, lowered the leather bucket and drew up clear water. Marie skidded across the ice to the fowl-house, to lock it against predators – or men.

Months had passed since Astruc had come to Marie for shelter. He had not dared to return to the Street – had he really killed the big stonemason? If he had, they would come looking for him in the Street. But nowadays he often forgot his fear entirely. Marie lived alone, and there were a dozen ways he could help her in the fields.

Marie now called to Astruc and he carried the bucket into the house. Once they were both in the house, they were safe from the terrors of darkness in this lonely place. Sturdy planks held the door and covered the single window. The only light in the one room with the window closed was provided by the burning olive branches and the dry rosemary bush, flaming up on the hearth, crackled and sparkled.

Into the black pot hanging from a hook over the hearth, Marie put water, a handful of barley, a couple of onions, and then reached to the carcass of the pig to carve a piece from the flank, smoking as it turned in the heat of the flames below the hook on which it hung.

Astruc began the laborious task of unwrapping strips of cloth from arms and legs. As Marie unpeeled her garments one by one, lifting the skirts of her wide tunic to warm her body, Astruc scratched the chilblains on his feet.

'I spoke to a friar from Avignon today, Marie. A couple of them rode past the field and stopped to ask the way. The sickness, the leprosy, at Avignon is worse.'

Marie stirred the pot and the scent of cooking filled the room. 'Will you go home? If there is so much sickness . . . your wife will surely worry.'

'Not yet.'

They sat together, Astruc thought, like any married couple. They dozed in the warm, the dark. The dog sniffed the odours from the soup. They ate till they were full and the dog licked her bowl clean, amazed by the unusual taste.

'That smell is part of my strange life with you, here, Marie,' said Astruc, replete and drowsy.

'We never had pork either, in Caromb, what do you think! Oh, yes, once, a snout and trotters. Our share. It had to be divided between ten families.'

'In the Street, we do not eat pig. It is unclean.'

'Why?'

'It is a rule, Marie. It is forbidden.'

Marie put her hand on his arm. 'Something else is forbidden – for a married woman to sleep with a man not her husband.'

'It is the same for a married man,' said Astruc.

'So . . . will we stop?'

'No,' said Astruc, laughing.

'And will you go on eating pork?'

'Of course I will.'

Marie turned sombre, staring into the fire. 'I'm so afraid of Roger coming back. And of men searching for you.'

'I'm not afraid,' said Astruc. Astonished, he repeated it two or three times to himself. It was true.

Marie looked at him as he washed the earthenware bowls, later. He knew what she wanted to hear. 'You want to know whether I will stay. I can tell you that Blanchette will not pine for me, I'm sure of that. But my brother Thoros will miss me. I asked that Jewish pedlar to take a message to the Street: I saw him in Caromb, when I sold the eggs, remember? I will be missed by the *baylons*, though.'

'You are different, Astruc, and I like that, so different from my husband.'

'They'll miss me because of the dues. We pay them to keep the Christians off our backs. And for different charities. Or to send a boy away to study, like my brother Thoros. He attended medical school at Montpellier and came back a doctor, Marie.'

'In our village, in Caromb, no peasant studied.'

'I haven't studied, either. I am the stupid brother, but I earn, and pay my dues, and they'll miss those. You know, there are Jews from the Street who set up a little business in Orange or Cavaillon and leave the community. Their dues are missed, and when the *baylons* catch up with them, they're fined.'

'Will you go back, one day?'

'Maybe one day. I feel a different man, now. My brother earns well, he'll look after Blanchette and pay my fines. God send him a loving woman, such as I have found, in recompense.'

And they went to bed.

Lea was the first to wake. She lit a fire, filled the pot with water and when the bubbles rose put a handful of dry rosemary in the pot and carried the infusion to her daughter.

'Did you dream of your child to be born?'

Blanchette did not reply. She had dreamed of Thoros: these nightly dreams were all that was left of him. Mother and daughter sipped their infusion, thinking their own thoughts.

'Lolo, about the money,' said Lea at last.

'Yes, Mother, I should have told you. It seems that a man comes to the gates at dusk and hands a porter a purse, to be given to me in secrecy. I've never seen him. If the porter talks, or if I do, there is supposed to be trouble.'

'And you didn't tell your own mother. How long—?'

'Since last August, once a month. I think—'

'Yes, yes, I can imagine. Astruc is in hiding for some reason, he sends you money. Does he know you are expecting his child? Is there no message?'

'No, Mother.'

'Well, it is a sign of life. Your child still has a father.'

I don't want him back, thought Blanchette, I want my bed for myself and the child. She didn't need Astruc's presence, on the contrary. And the money was more than sufficient for her needs. What good were men to her? She had tried taking a lover, to banish her longing for Thoros. Of course it hadn't worked, he wasn't Thoros. Pain clutched at her heart – it wasn't the child, though it kicked her these days – but the incessant longing for Thoros, whom she would never see again.

A knock. Lea bustled to the door and brought a visitor for Blanchette. David Rougier entered, hesitantly.

'I thought you might like to talk to me, Blanchette. Without the others here, I mean. I know it is rather early.'

'Well?' said Blanchette listlessly.

David, his short hair bristling, looked at her with such admiration that she felt a little pleasure, in spite of everything.

'There's this society,' he began, ignoring her yawn, which she did not bother to hide. 'There are ten members, we serve for ten years, we have cast lots to choose officials. I have been chosen, to my amazement. We watch over dead bodies, the required time, we accompany the procession to the burial ground—'

'I know all about that, David.'

'The point is that everyone wants to give and we actually have more money coming in than good causes. You know I'm not rich, but, as an official, I consult with all, even the richest in the Street! We are united in bonds of great friendship, such as I couldn't hope to achieve with the leaders of the community otherwise, as I am poor. It is very important to me.'

'If you are offering money, I do not want it, David, once and for all. If you want to do something, find Thoros.'

David, attuned to every inflection of her voice, and every expression in her eyes, saw and heard the downfall of his own hopes.

'I thought,' said David, fighting to speak calmly, 'that, if your husband, that is if Astruc were . . . forgive me for my words . . . were dead, then—'

'Then?'

'As you must know, if a husband dies, the law says that the widow must marry the husband's brother. And if, as in your case, the husband's brother was also . . . no longer alive . . . then you and your child would be in need of protection.'

'You're very kind, David, but I am not in need of protection. I do need your friendship, though.'

David contemplated her.

'This money you say you receive – from Astruc. I have to say that we, the *baylons*, cannot accept that Astruc would not return to you and the unborn child, if he were alive. We believe that His Holiness, in gratitude for Thoros's efforts, is sending you money. His clemency is well known.'

'Maybe, David,' said Blanchette.

'We will say a special prayer for the Pope tonight, at the service,' said David, rising to go. He had got nowhere with Blanchette, but he had known that in advance. He would try again after the child had been born.

Near Caromb, Pierre and Jeannette Tavernier, old now, often cold, and with few *sous* between them, were out in

the woods gathering sticks. Jeannette had just hoisted a
bundle onto the back of her husband, when the fading
winter light fell onto a yellow mushroom. Jeannette's
eyesight was failing, but she told her husband that she
had spotted a mushroom.

'In midwinter? You're a silly old woman. Where? Yes,
you're right. No, it's a hat.'

The old couple looked about them, and found first,
an empty bag, such as pedlars use, then the pedlar
himself; dead, they guessed, since the summer.

'He's been dead for months,' said old Pierre,
unmoved by the sight of death, 'but let us see if we can
find his purse.'

In the end, they found no purse and decided to heap
sticks over the body, giving him the best burial they
could. Jeannette wanted to wear the hat, thinking that
there was still a good deal of wear in it.

Returning to Caromb, they had the misfortune to
encounter the priest, who stared at the hat. They
protested that they did not know that Jews wore yellow
hats, saying that they had neither of them ever been to
Avignon and knew nothing of the Street. The priest
made them take him to the body in the forest and,
because he was a good man, he gave the Jewish pedlar a
Christian burial. The priest saw no reason to let anyone
in the Street know of the death in the forest of one of
theirs.

Astruc's message to his wife and brother, which he had
entrusted to this pedlar – *Thoros, Blanchette, I am alive* –
was thus buried in the churchyard in Caromb.

Chapter 10

The spring rain was falling on Avignon as two lepers in their grey cloaks and hats, ringing their bells listlessly, made their way through the town and down to the river. They stopped in front of the hospice and rang for the porter.

'Is this where they care for us?' one asked him in a hoarse voice. The leper's cloak fell away from his livid face, which was covered in pustules. His eyelids were swollen and he had neither eyelashes nor brows. Through thick, cracked lips he whined again. 'The hospice?'

The porter nodded and told the lepers to enter.

Across the river, Le Gor sat opposite Laurent, one on each side of the fire. Rain and hail rattled on the windows while a couple of greyhounds lay close to the smoking fire.

'I have told you twice that you should not go back to the hospice. You are better, I concede that, but still too weak. Come, look at yourself in the mirror.' Le Gor said impatiently.

Laurent rose and moved to one of the twelve mirrors, the cardinal behind him. The two men contemplated themselves: Laurent's face had gained some flesh; the cardinal's full, square face, large mouth, wide forehead and hooded eyes seemed to belong to a different kind of species.

'I am better, my lord, and now I should return to the hospice where my life was saved.'

'Come and sit down with me, Laurent. We all know that leprosy is contagious. Every convent, every religious house in this town now cares for the overflow from the hospices. And I,' he continued with a searching glance at Laurent's narrow face, 'lack the company of men such as you.'

'Who am I then, my lord, that you lack the company of such as I?'

'You are a man who can phrase a question such as you have just put to me. Will you indulge my curiosity, and my loneliness? All but you, in this residence, are bought servants. All I give you is board and lodging, which I would freely offer man, woman or dog. I want you to discover yourself and I want to help in this task.'

Laurent rose, and bowed deeply to the cardinal.

'Geraud!' cried Le Gor to the page who had just entered. 'Bring parchment, a quill, and ink!'

Geraud hurried away with a grin. His greatest enemy was boredom, and he seized on any distraction, though he would have preferred something more energetic.

Laurent picked up the new white goose quill. Le Gor smiled as he watched Laurent dip it in the ink: so he knew what the quill and ink were for. The shadows of the three men, greatly magnified by the candle, hovered on the wall behind them, as Laurent began to write. He made the point squeak as he moved from right to left on the parchment and the ink splotched away from the quill, as long hooks, dots and rounded signs appeared. When he reached the left-hand margin, Laurent returned to the right and traced another row. He wrote three and stopped.

'I can write,' he said quietly.

Le Gor stared at the parchment. 'These are, I believe Kabbalistic signs. You may be an alchemist, Laurent. Whether you have been sent by Heaven or Hell is immaterial to me. It is possible that I could learn from you. Read to me what you have written.'

Geraud looked at Laurent with shining eyes. Sorcery! Le Gor, too, was breathing fast, but Laurent frowned as he looked at the parchment. 'I cannot do that, my lord.'

'I order you to read!'

'I do not know what I have written, my lord Cardinal.'

In the countryside, a five-hour journey from Avignon and its sick, the rough roads were washed by rain and by the overflow from swollen streams. Marie's house, set among the rocks and dripping forest of the Comtat Venaissin, was being prepared for the night. Marie had become very anxious, talking ceaselessly about marauders, robbers, lepers and even ghosts.

'It's different for us, now,' she said to Astruc, as he put all the defences in place.

The one large room was warm and bright. Marie this evening was sitting by the fire, and her lap was occupied by the head of her dog, looking up into her face. The scents of lavender and of ham drifted about in the room. The firelight glinted on the polished blade of an axe. A wicker basket held eggs.

Marie got up, rubbing the small of her back and groaning, to break pieces of bread into two bowls, ladle soup over the bread and add wine from the pitcher. They had sold their produce well last autumn and had not starved this winter.

Since Astruc had heard Marie's news, he had realised that he would not be going back to the Street and that it was up to him to let the laws of the Street guide him here, too. Marie began to eat, but before Astruc began, he washed his hands in one of the buckets, then glanced at the bread, the salt in its crock and the pitcher of wine, while he said a prayer. Then he looked in a corner and returned with a hat of no particular shape or colour.

'A man with a hat on in the house looks strange,' Marie said.

'Only because you have not lived in the Street, Marie.'

'Talk to me of your travels. Or sing me a song.'

When he had finished eating, Astruc began to hum a song, but stopped when he saw Marie's eyes had closed. Here he sat, an adulterer certainly, and maybe a murderer too. Not just an adulterer, but fathering the child of a Christian woman. Once the child was born, he must look after it too, without the help of the Street . . . He saw Marie's eyes open again after her brief sleep, and read in them love and contentment.

'I want to know, Astruc, about the two kinds of knife. You started telling me last night.'

'One for meat and one for milk, that is to say, cheese. Meat and milk may not be eaten together. They must be apart in preparation and on the table.'

'Because of leprosy?'

'No. These are our laws since we lived in the Holy Land.'

'Tell me again about Sunday – which isn't on Sunday.'

'It has started, for tonight is Friday and the sun has gone down. The sabbath begins as night falls. The women will have lit the candles, they burn in memory of Eve. The women will prepare three good meals; one for tonight and two for the sabbath tomorrow. Everyone washes very carefully, and we cut our fingernails, throwing the cuttings on the fire so that they cannot be used for sorcery against us.'

Marie crossed herself. 'And on the sabbath?'

'We read the law, we pray and sing. All work is forbidden – you may not kill a flea! Yes, that is considered work. Some of it is strange: you must not give too much grain to fowl, for what they leave might grow, and someone might say you had sown grain on purpose . . . And we eat garlic for it heats the blood and provokes thoughts of merrymaking. And of love . . .'

They smiled at each other.

'Another thing – on the sabbath we receive another soul, to gladden the heart. We have three souls. When we sleep, one goes to heaven, the other to the nether regions. The third soul is the one God gives us when we are born, and it will not leave our heart. That is the soul which dreams our dreams at night.'

'I know something about Jews,' said Marie, sighing. 'And it is very different from what you have been saying.' She hesitated. 'Roger hates Jews. If he returns, he'll hunt you like a wolf and when he finds me he'll kill me too. He has the right, Astruc.'

Astruc's heart beat painfully.

'Astruc,' said Marie timidly. 'You must try to understand how it was for us. We all owed the Jews. If we had a bad harvest the Jews of Carpentras lent us money. Roger needed a plough and borrowed from Juset, a Jew in Caromb. But we couldn't pay him back, not even after the next harvest. We were hungry all the time. My baby that I had then, died. I had no milk.'

Astruc turned his head away from Marie. The stories were not new to him, but hearing such words from Marie was heartbreaking.

'We lived in Caromb, Roger and I. The Lord of the Manor there was hard. Roger had to plough, turn hay, grind at the mill, and always the master's work came first. There was never time for us, so we never had enough time to work on our bits of field. We were always hungry – and in the end Roger joined the shepherds, with the other peasants, and all of them refused the lord their dues. That was the start of it all. Roger got put in the stocks. Well, the shepherds broke the stocks, and then they threw the bailiff in the river with stones tied to him. The rich live on the blood and sweat of the poor, so the shepherds told us, and they were right. Even the priest took our side and said the rich would howl in hell. We heard a prophecy then: that the poor would rise against the rich and the Church would be overthrown. And a band of shepherds came to Caromb. They were going south to the Holy Land, they had been burning castles and abbeys as they went, and when they came to Caromb, they started looking for rich Jews, to kill them. Jews and lepers were against us, they said. So Roger went with them. We had not long settled out here, to get away from the Lord of the Manor. One day Roger said to me, stay here, do what you can, we will march on Avignon and there we will make the Pope see the evil we perceive, he will understand. And he left me to my loneliness.'

'When did Roger leave you?'

'Two years ago, this month.'

She looked at Astruc calmly. 'It is a sin to say so, but I wish him dead. He beat me every night, when we lived in Caromb. But you are different . . .'

'What happened to Juset?'

'The shepherds killed him.'

'Of course,' murmured Astruc. 'Come, you have tired yourself talking, Marie, and upset yourself. Go to bed.'

The bed, made of planks laid across a large box, was built into a corner of the room. The mattress was stuffed with wool from Marie's sheep and the featherbed with feathers from Marie's fowls. While Astruc put a last piece of wood on the fire, Marie undressed and dressed again for the night in a long hooded gown. Astruc helped her onto the high bed, and in turn undressed and dressed again in a long hooded gown. After saying a prayer he returned to the table to see if he had remembered to leave a piece of bread, so that the bene-diction he had spoken over it would remain with them till the morning.

'Bring the axe,' called Marie from the bed.

They clasped each other, aware of the child in the womb, safe in each other's arms.

'Two of your souls will be away soon, Astruc!'

'Your guardian angel is watching them,' he said. 'If, by God's will, this should be our last night together, I have been happy with you, Marie.'

'And I with you.'

And with her arms around Astruc's thin body, she murmured as the priest had taught her. 'Lord Jesus, whose heart is full of pity, I appear humbly before you, repenting of my sins. May you watch over my last hours and what may befall me afterwards. O God our Father, who has taken care to hide from us the day and hour of our death, so that we shall always be ready . . .'

She slept. Astruc listened for the return of her husband, thinking of the axe near the bed, to hand. The wet February wind howled around the house of the adulterers all night, but neither wind nor rain entered.

Chapter 11

The storm raged around the tall tower of Montolieu, five hour's ride from Marie's house, all night, but for Gui and his father there was no sleep to be had. The sick man had asked for blankets, but they chafed his body, criss-crossed with scars as well as wounds which would not heal, bearing the marks of the leather whip tipped with iron spikes.

At first light, Gui heard the old serf coughing and cursing as he reached the top of the stairs. Yves had brought water, to wash his master. At the sight of the chevalier's body, the old servant crossed himself. 'Whatever demon did this to you, may he roast in hell!'

François de Montolieu, wincing with pain, was supported by Gui. 'My poor Yves, I've told you before. No demon did this. I did.'

Yves turned to Gui. 'Your turn to sleep now, Master Gui. I'll nurse him.'

Gui went to lie on his bed in the room next to his father's and listened to the rain drumming on the little window. In Avignon he would have sought out Guy de Chauliac, the renowned doctor, and begged for help. There was nothing for it but to return to Avignon, to plead with the doctor, though would the great man make the journey out to Montolieu in February? Not very likely, he thought, without the intervention of someone like Cardinal Le Gor.

Le Gor. Gui saw before his inward eye the imposing figure of his master, dressed for one of the many ceremonies which he organised for the Pope; on his head the wide red hat with the fifteen tassels, a tall and stately figure enveloped in his red cloak, the sapphire flashing on his finger.

At confession last summer Gui had promised to give up the life he led with the cardinal. Setting aside the sin he had committed, he knew that he could not return, knowing that his reappearance could expose his master to scandal and disgrace. Yet, without a doctor, his father's life might end soon: clearly, duty to his father ordered him to go.

His decision made, he slept after the exhaustion of the night; at first soundly, then fitfully and finally he lay awake on his pallet, watching the clouds scurrying past the tower, still threatening. The wind howled as Gui recalled what had happened to him.

He had begun the search for his father in the heat of the summer. From Montolieu he went east, for the priest had told him that they had gone that way, but before he left, Gui sent for the bailiff. The bailiff stared at the seventeen-year-old, whom he remembered as a boy and thought, without any liking for the conceited young chevalier, that adversity had at least made him a man.

'Until I return with my father,' Gui told him, 'the villeins owe us no labour. But give me what is due from the sale of wheat, pigs and fowl.'

Toinette sewed the money into Gui's money belt. The peasants of Montolieu, the bailiff, Yves and Toinette, gathered to watch Gui set off to find his father. No one spoke, no one wished him God speed but, as

Gui mounted his horse, the priest said loudly for all to hear: 'Remember: the flagellants are enemies of the Church.'

Gui sat uneasily on the horse, knowing he should speak to the villeins. His hose, shirt and hat were deep green, his crimson tunic was belted, his scabbard and shoes fashioned from tooled leather. He had found these clothes in a chest at Montolieu, witness to his father's life before he was born.

'I shall come back with my father,' he said into the silence.

'One more word,' said the priest. 'I trust that you will not be the victim of blasphemous counsel, as was your father.'

Gui laughed, shook his mane of curls and rode away.

'God bless him,' said old Yves to the peasant who stood beside him.

The peasant spat. 'Last year the brigands robbed me of grain. Jean lost his cart. Pigs have been stolen. And the Master of Montolieu wants his fees and our work. In return, he is supposed to protect us – only he doesn't. We give our service and pay in sweat and blood. If they never come back, father and son, what do we care? And you, Yves, like an old dog, waiting for them to toss you scraps.'

Yves had told Gui how the peasants felt about him when Gui returned with his injured father, and Gui did not forget those words.

But that day, and many to follow, Gui rode till he was saddle-sore. He rode along the mountain roads for over a week, sleeping where he could in barns or in the forest. By now he no longer resembled the beautiful youth who had ridden out from Montolieu. The bright tunic had faded, dust covered his clothes. An old woman told him that the flagellants had been seen two days ago in Rousillon, where a priest let him sleep in the stable with his horse and gave him bread and wine, while Gui, for the twentieth time, explained his quest.

'Oh, the flagellants,' said the priest. 'They were here. We will never forget them, the fear, the terror . . . they went on towards Apt, I believe. Do you know what they do?' And he told Gui.

At the papal palace, the Pope was closeted with his confessor. 'I am always beset by temptations. In spite of what is said and written about me, the sins of the flesh are not of importance to me, though once . . . but to return to my plan. I interpret and mediate, I do not share. I give to the poor, but I do not share; perhaps, with this plan of mine there is a way . . .'

After the confession, he questioned his confessor. 'Do you see any reason why I should not go ahead with my plan?'

'Holy Father,' began the priest. 'There is a certain amount of danger inherent in this enterprise. And it is an unusual step for a Pope . . .'

'Do we know that, Father? Such actions would not have been recorded, surely. I want to demonstrate to my critics that I care not only for princes and for pomp.'

'But no one except a few members of your household will know, Holy Father.'

'Yes. But I will know. You are right, my critics will not know; of course I am doing this for my own spiritual welfare. Yes, thank you, Father.'

'How often, how much time will you devote to your plan?'

'Perhaps an hour a day, perhaps more. It is in the nature of an experiment.'

The father confessor waited in vain for the Pope to continue, then inclined his head and withdrew from the chapel, thinking that Clement was truly an aristocrat of the spirit, and marvelling that such a man, the greatest lord of the Church, should be so sensitive to adverse comment. The King of France confides in him, thought the priest, yet he needs to prove himself an ordinary Christian . . . and he hurried down the draughty steps to the mulled wine in the confessors' room.

Clement sent for his *chambrier* prelate, Eble Dupuis. Dupuis found the Pope in his study, contemplating one of the pictures on the wall.

'Ah!' said Clement. 'I dream of these forests with the smell of the earth, a couple of dogs by my side and the scent of wild herbs under my feet.'

'It is February, Holy Father, and the trees are bare, the puddles are frozen – certainly the smells are better in the forest than here in Avignon—'

'I know,' said Clement gently. 'But it is permitted to dream, *chambrier*. It will not always be winter.'

Dupuis, small, corpulent and eager, nodded vigorously. 'Is His Holiness preparing to go into the country? Would His Holiness like the big fur robe?'

'Yes, I am going out, but not in the fur robe. Were you not born in the Limousin?' Clement continued, speaking the Limoges dialect. 'Yes, you were! Well, countryman, I need a plain robe.'

Eble flushed with pleasure and replied in the same

dialect. 'You have over one hundred. Specify the colour, please.'

'I want you to find me a friar's robe and cloak. Yes, Eble. I may count on your discretion, surely.'

Dupuis bowed. 'Holy Father! Of course. Let me see, a friar's robe . . . Carmelite? Franciscan? Dominican? Benedictine?'

'Benedictine. They wear black—'

'A black cloak over white robes, Holy Father.'

Clement smiled at Dupuis, and explained in a few words what he intended to do, leaving Dupuis bursting with importance but chagrined by the need to be totally discreet. He returned from the Great Closet within half an hour, holding up robes for Clement to see. 'This is for the use of the household, Holy Father, and a little threadbare though clean, of course. That is what you were thinking of, wasn't it? And . . . er . . . the household knows—?'

'No. Just yourself, *chambrier*, and my confessor. Not the Chevalier de Saint-Amant, not a single cardinal. And if word comes for me, even from an important visitor, I am not to be disturbed.'

'Do you wish me to accompany you, Holy Father?'

'No, why? I am going to start by attending sext, *chambrier*, dressed as a friar, to begin with. And then . . . then I'll see. Thank you, Eble.'

Eble Dupuis watched the Pope descend the private staircase on the way to the Clementine chapel, on the first floor.

Eble Dupuis stood for a long moment, fingering his keys. Like the confessors, the bedroom servants, doctors, treasurer and Eble himself were known as the Pope's family. No rivalries were tolerated in this small group, and they shared all information including the minutest change of plan.

However, the Pope had been adamant. Not a word to anyone.

Eble unlocked the door of the Great Closet again and wandered up and down between the rows of fur garments, rubbing the pelts the wrong way and smoothing them down again, till he was calmer.

Clement went to sit among the congregation of priests, monks, nuns and townspeople, attentive as the service flowed around the Clementine chapel. He prayed and sang; unrecognised, feeling free, all responsibility shed. He thought about St Benedict, whose robe he was wearing, who had attacked worldly pride and vanity. For an hour every day, said Clement, I, accused of worldliness, will be a humble friar.

Every day for seven days, he became this friar and, as he grew used to the robes, he felt bolder.

'St Benedict's Rule,' said Clement one day to Eble as the *chambrier* folded the papal cloak and handed over the friar's robe, 'laid down good behaviour in the monasteries. I fear we've adapted his *regula* to our purposes . . . he would not be pleased, I'm afraid. *Chambrier*, find me a Franciscan's robe.'

'Oh no, Holy Father, you wish to dress as a Franciscan? They wear nothing on their feet. In this weather? In February? Truly, Holy Father, the world is not yet ready for a new Pope!'

'Well said. I shall wear sandals.'

A little later Clement stood at the top of his private stairs. The robe felt very rough. He crossed his hands, hidden in their long sleeves, in front of his body, against the rope knotted around his waist. Surely he should have a begging bowl?

The door above him opened and a monk came out, who took a hard look at the Franciscan friar, so that Clement feared discovery.

'Be gone, friar, these are the private apartments of His Holiness!' he exclaimed severely.

Clement nodded, his face well hidden by the cowl and made his way down the stairs, confident that he would be able to deal with whatever came his way.

The first floor was thronged with people, who had no intention of making way for a friar. This was the floor where the great dignitaries had their rooms, and people were pushing each other in front of their doors, anxious to plead their case, hoping for injustices to be righted. Messengers and guards tried to keep order, and Clement, used to clear spaces wherever he went, felt a mounting panic.

Only yesterday his treasurer had read him – at Clement's request – the fifty-nine occasions on which the papal almonery gave food to certain poor, and dinners to the affluent. He thought he would see for himself how the poor were fed, and made what he hoped was his way towards the kitchens, following a throng of beggars. But all were stopped at the kitchen door by a scullion, who told them to go to a kitchen below, still in the same kitchen tower. Clement began to feel oppressed by the crowd, but turned to follow them, when he saw a kitchen maid beckon him, and thus he found himself in his own private kitchen.

There was a lot of hustle and bustle, and ribald comment on his appearance. 'If you've come to preach abstinence to us, go elsewhere!' called a scullion. 'This is the Pope's private kitchen. Even our rats dine on roast pheasant!'

I must speak to Saint-Amant, thought Clement, amused. But as he turned away, the maid who had beckoned him in tugged at his sleeve.

'Give me your bowl,' she whispered.

If he whispered back, surely his voice would not be recognised, thought Clement. 'Thank you, and God bless you but – but I've lost my bowl. . .' he murmured.

The steaming bowl which the girl thrust at him now sent up an evil smell as Clement backed away from the bawdy voices whose owners toiled over the great cauldrons; stirring pottages and turning spits holding the corpses of tiny birds. Acrid smoke and scalding, hissing steam searched for escape in the high ceiling. Does purgatory look and sound like this? thought Clement.

'Eat,' said the kitchen maid's voice in his ear.

'What is it?'

'Gizzards, fowls' gizzards. You must be hungry.'

'Out of the kitchen, friar,' growled a voice in his ear, and a hefty shove sent him though the door, which slammed behind him. He could not contemplate eating the cooling mess in the bowl and, seeing a one-legged man propped against a wall begging for alms, Clement offered him the bowl. At once, the beggar moved at great speed, on hands and one foot like an insect, scuttling into the crowd, and was gone leaving Clement, startled, staring after him. He stood where he was, when he heard the voice of the kitchen maid.

'Have you finished? I must have my bowl.'

'Tomorrow,' he whispered.

'Now,' she said. 'Please. Or they'll throw me out. They'll say I've stolen it.'

'Tomorrow,' whispered Clement. 'I promise you, tomorrow.'

The following day Clement, dressed in his Franciscan robes, returned to the kitchen. Eble had found him a bowl. Clement asked a passing scullion whether he might return a bowl to a kitchen maid who had given him food yesterday.

'Gone, with a beating,' said the boy. 'They thought she was a thief.'

'Please help me find her. It is my fault,' Clement hissed.

The scullion thought she lodged in one of the maids' dormitories and, after a long search, Clement found her in a room where there were rushes on the floor, neither beds nor tables nor chairs, and no window to the outside world. Her face was swollen with crying, her clothes were torn and there were red weals on her arms and legs.

When she saw Clement, she spat at him and cursed him.

He listened in silence. Today he felt as much humiliated as the bitterest enemy of the papal court could wish.

Back in the great closet, where Eble was waiting to robe him for Mass, he accepted the mitre on his head and the stole around his shoulders, before turning to Eble. 'There is a young kitchen maid who has just been beaten and dismissed from our private kitchen. They tell me her name is Elinor and she is fifteen years old.

Make arrangements to find her another employment, please, Eble.'

In the papal bedchamber, fresh linen was being unfolded and laid on the pope's bed.

'This is the second time I've sent away a friar from the private stairs,' said Matteo, shaking the covering of squirrel skins.

'The same man?' asked Bernard.

'Could be. But four days ago he wore a black robe over a white one, and today there was a Franciscan. I couldn't get a look at his face . . .'

The *chambrier* entered at this point and conversation stopped.

Eble watched the monks of the bedchamber finish their work and went to ruminate in the Great Closet, turning to the area where the robes for liturgical occasions were kept, looking at the double crown, the silver-white robe, the cloth shoes of white linen embroidered with a cross which the faithful were permitted to kiss when the chamberlain withdrew the hem of the Holy Father's robe. Another thirty pairs were ready on their shelves.

Physical illness, thought Eble, we are familiar with that; but what had disturbed the mind of the Holy Father to this bizarre extent? He scratched his head.

The monks of the bedchamber had noticed something, he was sure.

Chapter 12

The tall Franciscan with the broad fleshy face, large beaky nose and sagging folds under the chin climbed slowly with many stops to catch his breath up the steep path to the Rocher des Doms, close to the papal palace. Once he almost lost his foothold on the dry pine needles and loose stones underfoot. Arrived on the peak, he was rewarded by the view over Avignon below: the bridge, boats, the island, the distant mountains. He gazed across the agitated waters of the Rhône at the houses on the far bank, at Villeneuve, so near yet the territory of the King of France, trying to make out among the distant houses that belonging to Cardinal Le Gor. Le Gor, driven by his demons, had taken to strange behaviour . . . just then the April wind lifted his cowl, and hastily he pulled it well down over his face, for he heard the murmur of voices.

Just in time, he bent over his rosary.

But he did not pray – he listened, adding to the pleasure he derived from each foray into Avignon. Of course he had avoided his own officials, but innumerable others – beggars, market women, peasants and artisans – had spoken to him and given him a coin or food.

As Pope, his days were filled with the writing of letters in Latin, French, Italian: he was just now in the midst of delicate negotiations with Charles of Bavaria; working for many hours each week on reforming the Julian calendar; he had begun reading a new translation of

Cicero; and he was awaiting a *pietà* which he had ordered for Villeneuve. But his time as a Franciscan was dedicated to rejoicing in the simplicity and generosity of the men and women who gave him charity and, for moments, a share in their lives.

A cooler wind and the smell of a bonfire below briefly brought back his enthronement five years ago, watching the clergy place a pile of hemp before him, setting it alight, chanting SIC TRANSIT GLORIA MUNDI three times, as prescribed, and watching and smelling the hemp burn to powder. In the moment of his greatest glory and power, he was to be reminded of his earthly lot.

A coin dropped into the bowl at his feet. He murmured a blessing, without looking up, for he was now, as often, contemplating the glory of the world ending for him. As he drew in the sharp smell of burning, he saw himself lying in the papal bedchamber where his body awaited the ancient ritual questioning. Two cardinals would approach his bed, and deliver two taps on his forehead with a golden hammer, calling to him: 'Pierre Roger, are you alive or dead?'

Alive, he was His Holiness. Dead, he was Pierre Roger, for reverence was due to the office, not the person . . .

'Father—' said a voice, softly.

He looked up. A young girl, hardly out of breath after her climb.

He smiled and bent his head. She looked like . . . perhaps a little like Cicely, the comtesse de Comminges, supposed to be his favourite. Let them talk, he thought, and coughed his dry cough, like suppressed laughter. Favouritism – neither here nor there. Now his mind turned to a hasty decision which weighed on him. It had been a mistake . . .

'Father, please?'

Did someone speak? He had invited back clerics whom his predecessor had banished and who wished for a benefice. He had not properly calculated the consequences; because the petitioners only had two months to present their claims there had been such a rush to the court, hundreds and hundreds of petitioners . . . how to channel the flood? His officials were overwhelmed and in the end he had said that it would be his decision to adjudicate between claims. At once there were accusations of favouritism . . .

'Father! I've looked for you everywhere. I know it's you.'

Clement looked up and saw that the young girl was Elinor, the kitchen maid. She looked happy and clean and well dressed.

'I wanted to thank you. I don't know how you did it, but now I am apprenticed in the sewing room. The *chambrier*, he said it was to do with a stolen bowl . . . it was your doing, I know it was.'

Their eye met. He thought how pretty she was.

'Come and see where I work,' said Elinor. 'See what you did for me, Father.'

'Sometime; leave me now,' he said, smiling at her. She recognised him, but only as the Franciscan friar.

He watched her walk down the path, slender and graceful as a young cypress tree, and his mind returned to his problems.

Did all the beauty, luxury and display at his court interfere with the real function of the palace, as they said? No. All art, spectacle, finery, all beauty served but one purpose: it served, finally, the ends of God and His Church, for its greater glory.

He rose. This day marked his last appearance as a friar. He had reaped great rewards from this robe, but the experiment was over. He strode down the path towards his palace, refreshed, ready to resume all his burdens.

At a group of three slender umbrella pines Elinor was waiting for him. And, at her repeated urging, he followed her to the sewing room, whose occupants at that hour were at the domestic refectory, two storeys below. So they found themselves alone and remained undisturbed for nearly half an hour.

Eble Dupuis, searching for the Holy Father later that afternoon, found him, in his white robes, stretched full length and face down on the marble floor, before the altar, whispering.

Eble withdrew, deeply disturbed.

Gui's piebald horse picked its way carefully along a steep path winding down towards the little town of Apt, but shied away from a talking and gesticulating group of people sitting in the dust of the roadside.

'If you're going to the reliquary, you can't get anywhere near the cathedral,' a woman called to Gui. 'We need Ste. Anne to intercede with us, my mother is sick, and my husband too. We've come all the way from Cavaillon to be halted here.'

'But why—' Gui began, looking for obstacles along the path.

'It's not safe to go. Once you get across the bridge – can't you hear the noise? The crowd is too great, they'll crush my poor mother. And – Antichrist is in their midst.'

'They are Christians like us,' said her husband.

'They are not!'

'Are you speaking of the flagellants?' Gui asked eagerly.

'Yes. They say they are inspired by God,' said the man, whose face was covered in boils. Gui noticed with a shudder that one of his eye sockets was empty and that even in the open air a sickly smell emanated from him, and that one sleeve ended in emptiness; and he recognised the *mal boubil* which began in the private parts, then travelled.

'I need to touch the reliquary,' the woman wailed. 'But the flagellants are in the way. We cannot get through.'

'Well, young man, they'll dance again. After noon, in the square. A pilgrim told us.'

Gui saluted and wished them health, leapt on his horse and rode the steep path down into Apt. Crossing the bridge over the Coulon river, he saw that the square was indeed filled to bursting with people but, used to Avignon streets, he manoeuvred his horse on through the dense chanting mass, making for some raised steps in front of a house. Here stood a small family group: a knight, his wife and children. At the steps he swept his hat with the magpie feather from his head, explained his quest, and said his name.

Gui had chosen well. He was led into a large room, in which a thickset man with rolls of fat concealing his neck and a paunch straining his black robe sat eating and drinking. Broken bread and half a roast pheasant lay on a platter and candied plums and figs, vivid gold in a blue dish, caught Gui's eye. The man was just lifting a decanter to his lips. The head of the family, Henri d'Ansouis, and his wife Mathilde, stood respectfully watching while their guest ate greedily and fast, stared at by the d'Ansouis' three children, and by Gui.

'This is the lay master of the flagellants,' said d'Ansouis. Gui nodded and the master turned towards Gui and belched. There were grease stains on his robe. 'And this young man seeks his father, who is one of your band, Master, so he believes.'

Gui remembered some of Le Gor's advice: begin softly. 'I would like to know much about the flagellants, sir—'

'Master. I'm the Master, young fellow . . . whatever you call yourself.'

'As my ignorance is complete, Master. You are a priest?'

'No. I am elected Master for thirty-three and a half days. That represents our Lord's time on earth, in years. You, young man, do you want to join your father? Become one of us?'

'What are the rules, Master?'

'You must pledge us four *sous* a day for food and lodging. You must swear obedience to me and my successor. And obey the rules. Where there are two or three hundred flagellants, you must have rules.' He took a gulp from the flagon. 'Note this: you are forbidden to shave your beard, bathe, change your clothes, sleep in beds, talk with or have intercourse with women without permission. You must swear obedience to me.'

Gui remained silent, swallowing his dismay and looking at the d'Ansouis family for guidance; they, in turn, were looking at the Master with wholehearted admiration.

'Master,' Gui began. 'Your enterprise—'

'Enterprise?' bellowed the Master. 'What sort of language is this? I've travelled through the low countries: Flanders, Picardie, south, always south. We're bound for Avignon, for the fleshpots of the Pope! Not that we need him. We ourselves will intercede with God for all humanity! That's our enterprise. If it weren't for us, all Christendom would meet perdition. No priest can do as much! That's our enterprise, young man, and I hope it's enough for you.'

He crammed the rest of the sugared figs in his mouth and left the room.

The Chevalier d'Ansouis asked Gui to sit down and called a servant to bring a repast and, while he ate, Gui stole glances at his hosts. Henri d'Ansouis's long face betrayed no emotions. His features, regular and pale, seemed carved in stone; Gui noticed that the corners of his mouth remained turned down. As for his wife Mathilde, she had perceived one of his glances, and blushed.

'While you search for your father, we would be honoured if you would be our guest,' Mathilde said to him. Gui asked himself what her blush could mean.

'Perhaps one night,' Gui replied, rising and bowing. Do not stare, Cardinal Le Gor had said, but read their movements which may give you a truer picture than their words can – practise, Gui!

Henri d'Ansouis cleared his throat. 'So you come from Avignon, the cesspool of sin. You heard the Master just now; the Pope is corrupt, he maintains.'

'Oh no, sir. I served Cardinal Le Gor as page, and was present many times at discussions regarding the Pope. He is held in great esteem, sir, he is wonderfully erudite and generous – the Holy Father is much loved.'

Henri d'Ansouis turned his stony face towards Gui without speaking, and then away. He left the room with an angry gesture to his wife, which left Gui confused. This was his host; in the circumstances, shouldn't he leave? But Mathilde smiled. With her husband gone, Gui dared look directly into her face now and saw a beautiful woman, whose calm face was framed by the white silk cloth wound around her head and neck. Her cherry robe parted as she bent to pour more wine for him, and he saw the close-fitting damask dress with tight sleeves, sheathing her slender body down to her ankles. Her feet in gold slippers moved swiftly around him. The children had gone. They were alone. Without a mother, without sisters, as page in a totally masculine household such as Le Gor's, Gui had very little idea about women.

'My husband feels strongly, perhaps too strongly – these are olives from Nyons, taste them – he believes there will be a bloodbath in Avignon . . . This bread was freshly baked in our kitchen this morning. Do you like honey?'

Gui was surprised by a feeling of happiness; how could he be happy? With his father hurt? He mustn't waste time here.

D'Ansouis suddenly appeared behind his wife and Gui noticed the anger in his face, and stood up ready for whatever would now follow. D'Ansouis was barely able to restrain his anger. 'Let me tell you a little more! The lay masters hate the Church. They don't need her. A Master can hear confession and grant absolution – and your precious Holy Father is terrified of their power! When the wild shepherds reach the town and when the flagellants join them, you will see such a conflagration! They must be trembling, the cardinals and courtiers, they'll be hacked to pieces . . . you must have heard?'

'But, *chevalier*, the Holy Father is loved and revered!' Gui whispered, moaning and whimpering in his dreams on his pallet in the tower of Montolieu. Yves, in the next room, was roused from his contemplation of the sick master by these sounds and entered Gui's bedroom, while the wind whistled around the tower. The old peasant put his hand on Gui's shoulder.

'Mathilde,' whispered Gui. 'Stay, stay with me . . .'

Chapter 13

Gui stood ready, in a clean dark-hued tunic which Mathilde had given him.

'You will be spent, you will have suffered; whether you've found your father or not. Return to us; no hostelry will accept you, people are sleeping in the streets and under the bridges. Wait for the bells.' Mathilde instructed him.

When the bells rang out, followed by a high carillon, d'Ansouis and Gui left the house and made their way through the throng to the other side of the square where Henri said they would be dancing; until they were stopped by a solid wall of people, five or six deep. Their fine clothes, which would normally have ensured them a respectful passage, counted for nothing here. The noise of prayers, but also of groans and curses, did not rise above a ground bass, till the look-outs in the branches of the plane trees shouted, and Gui, who was tall, saw movement at the far end. The murmur of the crowd swelled with each passing minute but, above this sound, Gui heard wailing: shrill, piercing. And he could smell the approaching flagellants. He heard d'Ansouis say urgently that they must go no further forward, it wasn't safe . . .

I must see, thought Gui, however awful, I must see it. Without regard to those in his way he forced a passage till he stood in the path of the oncoming procession.

The crowd jeered at him, but Gui heard nothing; he saw and he smelt.

The flagellants had reached the square. In the heat the men's upper bodies seemed marbled with purple weals and crusted blood. Matted hair hiding their eyes, a phalanx of huge men strode in front, holding leather whips with iron spikes above their heads, like so many banners. Behind them thronged the other flagellants, many stumbling along, exhausted.

'Spare us!' the crowd moaned in sympathy.

More flagellants crowded into the square, and the sun beat down on their raw wounds, their bare heads and the tatters of their clothes, until the swaying bodies had filled the space, and crowd and flagellants formed one mass. The crowd knew what was coming. 'Christ have pity on us! Blessed Virgin, have pity on us!' they chanted.

'God spare us! Fall back!' a voice called, high above the others.

Gui was not prepared, so that when the whips began to whirl, and the crowd fell back, he and many others were suddenly lifted off their feet, unable to help themselves as fear swept the crowd back from the whirling whips. Those who were smaller and weaker fell and others stepped on them, some saving themselves, others never rising again from beneath the trampling feet, and the screaming began in earnest. As the flailing whips bit into the crowd, the devoted were still calling on God and the Virgin to save them while the flagellants, in their trance-like state, seemed unconscious of where their blows fell. They moved to and fro with their eyes closed, accepting lashes and scourging from the giants and from each other, chanting over and over: Christ have pity on us!

Gui, breathless and hardly in control of his feet, succeeded in escaping the whips and was borne over struggling or prone bodies like a boat over choppy waves until his momentum was stopped by a wall, where he was able to extricate himself, draw breath and with a huge effort pull himself up onto its stone slabs.

Now he could see that those of the flagellants who were upright had formed a circle, in whose centre appeared a priest who held up his hand for silence. And as he began to speak – Gui could not distinguish a single word – the Master appeared beside him. In a bellow the Master addressed the priest. 'By your presence among us, you who call yourself priest have caused this act of penance to be considered void! It will have to be done once more!'

A flagellant struck the priest with his whip and the man sank to his knees, while the crowd shouted: 'Scorpion! Anti-Christ!' At this, a group of women, dragging small children, terrified and crying, surged forward and approached the exhausted flagellants, dipping cloths in their wounds and dabbing their children's faces till they were bloodied.

'Heal my child!' cried one woman.

Another held out a stiff little corpse. 'Bring back my child! Intercede with the Virgin for my child!'

Gui, still winded and aching, followed the progress of the woman with the dead child and suddenly saw his father, trying to rise from where he had fallen, but unable to stand, disappearing again from Gui's sight.

Gui could not remember how he reached his father, but hands pulled at him and he was kicked and dragged along the ground. At seventeen he had the strength to persevere and, when he reached his father, he was able to gather him up in his arms. As he stood up, hands closed around his throat and other hands pinioned his arms and as he opened his mouth to shout a bloody rag was stuffed in it. He lost consciousness.

He returned to consciousness and was aware of silence. He attempted to sit up but his stomach muscles protested; they must have kicked him there. His mouth tasted of rag. He was lying on a pallet in a dark room, but his swollen eyelids made it hard to see where he was. Had he been crying? No, he had been punched in the face, his nose was swollen.

But someone was wiping his eyes. Mathilde and Henri d'Ansouis were kneeling by his side. 'Your father is safe, he is here,' murmured Mathilde.

Gui and François de Montolieu were visited by the doctor after a night during which Gui was cared for by d'Ansouis himself, his stony features making strange shadows in the light of the candle in his hand.

'You saved my life,' whispered Gui.

'After the flagellants left, I went out with my servants. Your father resembled you, he lay near where you fell and we carried both of you back here.'

'They're beasts,' said Gui. 'Monsters.'

'God is using them against the corrupt papacy,' replied d'Ansouis. 'The suffering they cause, and experience, is for the greater glory of God.'

He saved my life, thought Gui, and fell asleep.

The doctor examining the wounds told Mathilde to bathe them with water and wine. For François, whose wounds caused much pain, he prescribed poppy seeds crushed in olive oil; and against the heat of his fever, large draughts of grenadine juice boiled with honey and arabic gum; as well as fennel, to purge him. Gui shook off his aches quickly, and was able to help Mathilde with nursing his father. As they worked together, he observed her and marvelled at her: at her perfect oval face, the smoothness of her skin and the gaiety of her manner; and also what robes, silks, colours, what studded belts and elaborate head-dresses she wore, how cunningly cut her dresses and robes were. At times he was overcome, but stopped himself angrily. She took the place of a sister, or perhaps a mother, neither of which he had ever had.

Above all, what softness and gentleness she showed Gui's father and what laughter she shared with him, Gui, such as he had known neither in the grim tower of Montolieu nor in the cardinal's residence.

But, obstinately, his dreams mocked his waking self, they were beginning to be filled with the fluid movement of the silken garments and the scent of her hair as she bent over him to rub ointment on his bruises.

Every night, Mathilde brought the cup of poppy seed to François's bed and not until it had done its work, and the spasms which the pain and the fever caused relaxed, could she and Gui inspect François's wounds. Two – one on his forehead and a deep gash in his side were infected. Others were healing, but those on his back troubled him constantly. Only when François's body was shielded from pain could he bear their touch, and they stood waiting for deep sleep to overtake him before they were able to turn him on his cot. Gui was sometimes overcome by the sight of his father's back – the sight and the smell – but Mathilde in her silk dresses with the huge sleeves shrank from nothing and carried out every task.

Nothing disgusted her. And always an essence of summer flowers, myrtle, roses, lavender, hung about Mathilde, bewitching Gui in spite of his good resolutions.

It was midnight, two weeks after Gui and François had found shelter in the d'Ansouis house. In their chamber at the back of the house, father and son lay on their pallets; François in his drugged sleep, Gui assessing when his father would be ready to brave the long journey home on horseback. I long for Montolieu, François had said, and never spoke again of the flagellants. Once he enquired whether the cardinal had given Gui leave of absence, but Gui shook his head, and his father, weakened by his fever, said no more.

At the other end of the house, in the great bedchamber, Henri and Mathilde lay in the great marital bed, separated by a huge bolster. Henri lay rigidly on his back like a crusader on his tomb. To Mathilde, restlessly seeking sleep, he might as well be in his tomb. Her husband was dead, from the waist down. While in captivity – a pilgrim, he had been taken prisoner during his journey back from Santiago de Compostela – he had vowed chastity in his marriage should God permit him to escape, and God had permitted his escape. He had vowed to give up what he would not miss, thought Mathilde, there was no need for a bolster to restrain ardour he had never felt towards her. Duty had caused him to father their children.

The moonbeams shone on Mathilde's face, and she crossed herself at her thoughts, then moved to the window. Among the shadows on the rooftops, cats were stalking each other, fighting and mating on the steep slopes of tile and stone below the window. She envied them. Why should she not roam, too, in her own house?

Henri's sleep would last till cockcrow, come thunder witchcraft or fire. From a phial she shook some lavender oil onto her skin, and rubbed it into her throat, neck, breasts and thighs. By day she was a good wife but at night she found no answer from Henri for her needs. She unhooked her silk robe and tied it loosely.

She had seen Gui look at her. It was time she went to him. Such a chance would never arise again: she was thirty-one years old and life was short. She left the bedchamber on bare feet, on her way to the sickroom.

Gui had checked that his father was sleeping soundly, thanks to the opium, and quickly drifted into sleep himself. A dream visited him at once in which another body insinuated itself into his bed, gliding between the sheets and moulding itself against him and arousing him; and it was not until the violent pulse of lovemaking left him lying spent that his mind, shut off from his body during the invasion of his bed, told him the meaning of what had taken place.

It was not a dream. Gui was overcome with horror and revulsion. What had he done? He had made love to another man's wife, to the embodiment of motherly and sisterly virtues. He looked at Mathilde's pale face and closed eyes on the pillow beside him while his feelings of guilt and sin extinguished the passion and pleasure he had felt minutes before. Their limbs were still enlaced and he began, stealthily, to move away from her. She clung to him at once, murmuring words of love and holding him prisoner. Confused thoughts rose like bubbles in his mind about his life with Le Gor and the habits of loving into which he had drifted in Avignon – and that he had never made love to a woman before. But these thoughts were overtaken again by the larger sin: he had lain with a married woman, broken the laws of hospitality, injured a man to whom he owed his life . . . Henri d'Ansouis could kill him.

'Let me go, we have committed a sin,' he groaned.

'So, this is sin,' she whispered back. 'How sweet it is!'

For the next seven nights Mathilde came to Gui's bed. Although Gui was uneasy and unwilling, he could not resist her. He was learning the art of love from a woman; he was now a man like any other, but it was not long before he wearied of this, and Mathilde found to her great sadness that all her loving was to no avail. He finally told her that he could not love her, and held her close while she wept.

'Don't you love me a little? Love me, Gui!' she would implore, but he turned away, lying unmoving and incapable. One night she sat up in bed, contemplating Gui who looked back with pity for her, and, finally, understanding of himself.

'It is not only the sin we are committing, Mathilde, but—'

She thought she understood. 'You love another?' she asked. 'In Avignon?'

'Yes. Forgive me, Mathilde.'

Mathilde cried bitterly when Gui and François set off, two weeks later, for the slow journey to Montolieu; François still in pain from his wounds. Gui looked back and waved many times, his heart constricted by sadness. He did love Mathilde, but he knew whom he loved more.

Chapter 14

Pope Clement lay on his bed – Holy Father, you must rest, de Chauliac had insisted – digesting a repast shared with his sister, a nephew and two cardinals, of which his share had been only the coriander soup, a little pheasant pâté and a spoonful of blancmange. His mouth was very sore where de Chauliac had extracted a wisdom tooth, and his tongue ran over the remaining teeth in his mouth while his mind probed the sensitive corners of his conscience, and prepared for Cardinal Le Gor's visit. When the door to his private apartment opened, his dog Cola ran ahead, followed by a monk of the bedchamber with a glass of warmed wine and a silver spittoon, and behind him Eble Dupuis, fussing. 'Will you want to see Cardinal Le Gor? He maintains that you want to see him, but I told him about the tooth extraction—'

'Yes, Eble, as soon as I have rinsed my mouth.'

Le Gor entered in due course, looking travel-stained and weary.

'I came straight to the palace from Fontaine de Vaucluse, Holy Father.'

'Did it go well?'

'Yes, Holy Father; and no.'

The two men sat silently for a long moment, listening to the distant noise of building, the building of Clement's glorious palace, the raising of ramifications, courts and towers which continued year after year and testified to his optimism and energy. But my strength is intermittent, thought Clement, I am troubled by a multiplicity of aches and pains – each one of which could be the harbinger of an illness which my doctors, not even de Chauliac, could cure. I must hurry the building of my tomb.

At last Clement spoke: 'The gathering chorus of accusations is not new, Cardinal. There are the bands of shepherds, and the flagellants whose hatred for me and the Church rouse the rabble and the peasants in the countryside. But he whom I loved and admired, whom I gave a position here at Avignon! Why? Why has he turned against me? He is probably the greatest poet of our time, maybe beyond . . .'

Le Gor nodded.

'Speak, Cardinal.'

'Holy Father, I set off a week ago with my page and two grooms with the spare horses . . .'

'I remember your page,' said Clement, smiling. 'A beautiful boy, Gui de Montolieu—'

'Gerard, Holy Father. My present page's name is Gerard.'

The mention of Gui, for which he was quite unprepared, stabbed Le Gor in the heart. He turned pale and clutched the arm of his chair. Clement observed him in silence.

Le Gor took a deep breath and continued. 'You will remember Fontaine de Vaucluse as a wild and beautiful spot, a place where a man might think about religion and poetry and read and write. I left my attendants in the village and rode out alone to a narrow spit of land by the rushing mountain stream which flows very fast there between steep banks, such a deep green with leaping trout and the overhanging branches dipping their leaves into the sparkling foam-flecked waters – the beauty of it filled my heart, Holy Father – and saw two cottages. In front of the lower one stood a peasant woman, who pointed to the higher one, which was surrounded by the strip of garden, bright with flowers, about which he has written so much. His cottage is small, but there is room for his visitors: bishops, soldiers, friends from afar—'

'My dear Cardinal, I can hear how it affected you. So: you spoke of my dismay . . . would you hand me his book, which I have been reading, alas – I should know better . . . over there.'

Le Gor took the book; the *Eclogue* by Petrarch. A ghost of a harebell, pressed flat, marked the page.

'Read to me, Cardinal.'

Avignon . . . the miserable home of all the vices, all calamities and every kind of miser. Since my childhood, when ill fortune led me to this place, I have spent the greater part of my life here, chained to the town by various quirks of fortune. It is a town without pity, charity, faith, respect, fear of God. Here you search in vain for saints, for justice, reason, holiness, in short for humanity.

'Thank you, Le Gor. You asked him what is at the bottom of these extravagant accusations, and he said—?'

'The main thrust of his argument is that he wants the papacy back in Rome. St Peter and his successors were bishops of Rome, he says, the Court is after all called Curia Romana. The Popes do not like their bishops to reside elsewhere but in their diocese; so why do they not

follow their own precepts? Petrarch says that Rome is a
city widowed by her spiritual husband and true
protector . . .'

'I like that phrase. And Petrarch has a point there.
Others have said the same thing of course. You gave him
my prepared answer?'

'I quoted your words verbatim, Holy Father: "The
state of Italy is chronically disordered and violent and
makes it impossible for me to return to Rome."'

'I said so plainly when they came from Rome to
congratulate me on my election in May 1342, and now I
have settled in Avignon and have no intention of leaving
it, Cardinal. There is the new palace . . . no, Rome is far
too disturbed. And now that I have bought the town
from Queen Joanna, and the *comtat* Venaissin also, it
would be madness to return to Rome. Petrarch may be
furiously annoyed, but he cannot change the situation.
What else did he complain of?'

'The role of money in this town. He said that people's
only hope of salvation is placed in gold; gold opens the
heaven and, finally, Christ is sold for gold.'

'Nothing new there, Cardinal. What else?'

'Well, Holy Father, I challenged him on a passage in
his *Book Without a Name.* Mainly because he goes close to
the bone, as he is writing about cardinals. If you have the
book . . .'

The book was searched for and brought by a monk
from the Holy Father's study. Le Gor found the place
and read aloud:

*Among the cardinals around Clement, there is a little old man.
Like a goat, he is so lascivious that he is ready at all times to*

mount another . . . every night he needs to celebrate a coupling . . . his procurer scours the streets of Avignon for young girls . . . once he impressed a young whore whom he had enticed into his bedchamber but who would not let him touch her until he returned wearing his cardinal's hat, saying, I am a cardinal, girl, fear nothing . . .

'Really, Le Gor, such stories are commonplace, we should not pay attention to them. A man of your gifts and eminence, my dear Le Gor, cannot take these whores' fables seriously. Are there other, serious accusations?'

'Well, yes, Holy Father. I pressed him to say what really oppressed him and why you are the target of his venom. And he pointed to another passage in the *Book Without a Name* – I'll find it for you – here it is. Would you care to read it, Holy Father?'

Eble Dupuis entered and whispered in Clement's ear, who nodded and picked up Petrarch's book and read the passage which Le Gor pointed out:

. . . an enormous crowd of claimants were sitting, waiting, on the hard ground. As the papal officials entered they cried out and asked anxiously how the Holy Father had dealt with each one's request. At this, one of the clergy, unmoved by the clamour, began to speak, as one who had many times heard these desperate pleas, without feeling shame or commiseration for these unfortunates who, in their vain pleadings wasted their soul, their lives, their goods and their time. To them, the cleric, fabricator of lies, gave a wealth of spurious information, such as that the Pope had graciously listened . . . all believed him and departed . . . Another father, of a nobler nature, asked whether

he felt no shame in inventing the Holy Father's replies? At which, all around burst into mocking laughter. . .

Clement closed the book.

'Cardinal: Petrarch writes brilliantly, but here he is really wasting his talents. This is a matter of administration. The twelve new cardinals whom I have recently appointed will be asked to devise, as a first task, ways of allocating claimants better access to me. Eble Dupuis tells me that there is a messenger – an ambassador from Queen Brigitte of Sweden recently arrived, bearing an urgent message – I had better see him now – and you and I will continue another day. And thank you, Cardinal.'

Chapter 15

It was April. Avignon basked in the first real warmth of the year. Beggars, travellers and lepers, clerics and anxious claimants at the Court; all moved through the city more slowly, savouring the sun through the dust blowing from the many building sites. Merchants were besieged by people buying, stonemasons sang as they built for the Pope, and for those who made money out of the competition for house room, even the scrofulous mules moved faster through the streets already stinking of sun on ordure. There were fresh herbs for sale in the churchyard of St Marguerite. The women selling trapped songbirds in front of the great palace did a good trade. There was a steady flow of people through the gates in the wall around the town, and a hundred small boats bobbed about on the Rhône.

The Pope had just performed the ceremony most appreciated by the crowd: leaning out of the great gothic window next to the chapel, he had blessed the patient crowd with upturned faces waiting below in the square.

Daily, now, he walked through the new and spacious rooms which the April sun warmed up, admiring the dazzling richly coloured tapestries. The streets below had begun to stink, but fresh breezes blew through his rooms up here. He set off to watch the sculptors in his chapel working on the sculptures in orgon stone, almost finished now. The same stone had been used for the perimeter of the watchmen's walk and also for the new fountain in the garden.

In his study workmen were finishing the floor with its pattern of both square and hexagonal tiles, and this morning the steward came to tell him that the new hangings from Samarkand, three months on the road, were ready for inspection. Clement wanted murals between the hangings; abstract patterns of octagonal shapes, diamonds and six-pointed stars. Jean de Louves, his master builder, was waiting for Clement in his office, and with an anxious face confessed that he had – and by a large amount – exceeded his budget.

'I am entirely satisfied with the work,' Clement told him. 'You may keep spending. I am authorising a further 1000 *écus*; see me again next week.'

Then he continued his rounds, to see his organisation functioning as he had decreed. What does Petrarch know of my work, he thought, as he spoke to the scribes in his chancellery where documents and registers were drawn up and copied, then to his treasurers to check how the money was spent on a hundred projects; from feeding the palace to the financing of wars for the protection and defence of papal possessions in Italy. He next dictated letters, saw his couriers, spoke to visitors and to three of the fifteen confessors attached to the palace.

And as he walked through the corridors, climbed and descended the stairs, uniformed guards saluted and swept people out of the way. He was on his way to visit his special choir of twelve in their dormitory when he noticed a scuffle in the corridor. A man resisting the efforts of the guards to remove him; a man who appeared to have struck a woman, who stood crying but disappeared at speed at the sight of the Pope.

'Can it be—' said Clement. 'Surely not – Guillaume de Saint-Amant? You are ill, Knight. Return with me to my study—'

Saint-Amant's eyes were bloodshot. The guards must have been rough with him, thought Clement, who suggested a doctor. But Saint-Amant pulled at his clothes, which were dusty and torn – had he been thrown on the ground during the scuffle? – apologised to Clement, and, hugely embarrassed, left without an explanation.

Clement shook his head and let him go. He himself made one more visit: to the kitchens where to his glee he had timed it right, for the scent of newly baked bread – baked fresh seven times a day – permeated the great rooms. Here he tried to speak to the little kitchen boys who, overcome by his presence, could not be coaxed from under the great trestle tables in spite of the hissing geese, who had also taken refuge there. The Pope's immense charm, available to all, filled all his servants with love and admiration, and his visits of inspection were also triumphal progresses.

They love me, thought Clement. I can give them some happiness, but in Petrarch's view that is irrelevant. People are devoted to me, he thought; not as the Holy Father, available to the Christian world; not as the statesman, the arbiter between kings; but simply their own protector. They are drawn into my service for the glory and pleasure – and is this wrong?

The warm weather brought little joy into the Street of the Jews. The inhabitants and visitors picked their way through the dirty straw, sodden all winter with solid and liquid ordure, now steaming in the sunshine, while a fetid wind blew languidly between the tall houses. In the winter the street was swept weekly, in summer daily but the community was saving on daily sweeping now that the warmer weather was here. People slapped at the iridescent horseflies which had begun to torment the gossipers, mostly women, and the visitors, mostly Christian men. Among them walked Saint-Amant. He wore a large black cloak and a huge hat with a black feather. His eyes were brilliant. He stared at every woman he passed, and each one averted her eyes.

He walked to Blanchette's shop and saw it was closed. As he stood looking at it an old woman came out. Should he ask her? I'll not ask the porter, he thought, although the porter had handled the monthly transactions well. Much better ask a woman, who could tell him if it had happened, if the child had been born, his son – son or daughter, a soul to be won for Christ, away from the witches and sorcerers of the Street. What he needed was a wet-nurse, and he had one, a kitchen maid who had given birth. She was well and could suckle two children, a strong girl.

My money, he thought, has so far protected the mother of this little half-Jew whom he would offer up to Christ to atone for the sin of fornication with a Jewess, and thus make amends, to the greater glory of God, Amen. I must take the child . . . yet not appear too soon . . . maybe the child was not yet born? But it was weeks since I saw Blanchette so great with child that surely, by now . . . Anyway, all is planned. He nodded to an unknown passer-by.

David Rougier woke at dawn, rising when the sound of cocks crowing announced that the demons of the night had withdrawn, and began his morning prayer: 'Glory be to the Eternal, who has instructed the cocks to crow—'

Next, he washed with his left hand while his right hand followed the verses of Holy Scripture. A Jew could not pronounce the name of the Lord until he had washed out his mouth. When David had done so, he took the water in which he had washed and that in which he had rinsed his mouth and carried it down the three flights of stairs into the street, where he met others on the same errand, pouring water into corners and against walls so that no one could use it for casting evil spells.

All the time he carried out these tasks, David thought about Blanchette, about her and the child.

Back on the third floor in his room, he prepared for the *escole*, covering his shoulders with the prayer shawl and binding his forehead and left arm with the leather phylacteries. He continued to think about Blanchette as he set off for the *escole*, for morning prayers.

After the service, the congregation of men left the building walking backwards, so as not to show an indecent part of the body to the Ark where the scrolls were kept; and they walked as slowly as possible. God counts every step, David thought, and will reward me accordingly. If I were to meet a woman coming out of the service, I would have to close my eyes so that the sight would not give rise to impure thoughts. But he could not stop himself thinking, not impure thoughts exactly, more incessant speculations about what was happening to Blanchette. Where could the father be?

David had never liked Astruc very much. He thought him weak and a coward, by some mischance married to the beautiful Blanchette; although when they married, Blanchette was still hidden in her envelope of fat. And where was Thoros, Astruc's brother? An unlucky family. Once the child was born, surely Astruc would return from wherever he was. He was needed for the circumcision – surely he would come then, if he could? Blanchette had let it be known that he sent her money regularly; if so . . . he shook his head.

Astruc must have had good reason to stay away. He could be one of those who deserted their community, told a rabbi somewhere far off a pack of lies about persecution in Avignon, and was now living somewhere happily, maybe even with a new wife. David calculated his chances. Blanchette's situation had become irregular, she was bound to need him – David.

A week later Blanchette was lying quietly on her bed, while the baby Joseph, exhausted by his tears, lay asleep in her arms.

It had been an easy and quick birth, and she had quickly forgotten the pain. She had been well and happy and without fear, and no thought beyond the moment when she would hold her child in her arms.

She was woken at noon by her mother who had brought her a bowl of broth. The baby woke and the old woman took him in her arms, but her face was grim.

'Where's that husband of yours? Not here to see his own son, his first-born.'

If they do what they threaten, he'll be safe with mother, thought Blanchette. She said: 'I don't know where Astruc is, but he does send money, Mother,' she replied wearily.

'A fine husband! And Friday is the Zachar!'

On Friday, for the Zachar, all men in the street were invited to the house to say prayers and wish the parents of the newborn joy and happiness. After eight days, the circumcision would take place. Lea talked incessantly about who would come and what food she was preparing. Blanchette was aware that her mother had closed her mind against the evidence of the approaching storm. It was quite likely that no visitors would come, that all the food would remain uneaten. Blanchette was still very tired and, as she could not influence the outcome, fell asleep until her mother announced a visitor for her – at last.

Esther came into the room and sat on the only chair, smiling at her friend and the child.

'Mother—'

'I'll leave you to gossip,' said Lea and left the room.

Esther cooed over the little boy then turned her attention to Blanchette. 'I found out what I could, and I'll tell you, but I'm sure they will not carry out all of it. After all, think of me.'

'You?'

'I had a Christian lover too. No child was conceived, that's the difference.'

'You asked the *baylons*—?'

'Do you think I asked the *baylons* outright? You must be mad. No, I asked David Rougier; he knows all the laws and he is your friend and wants to help. It's a cruel law, Blanchette, and it would apply to me too, if they could prove anything against me, which they can't. David said that he cannot recall when this law was last applied.'

'And why wasn't it?' asked Blanchette.

'Because there would be so many of us, twenty at least.'

'You'd better tell me what the law says.'

'I have learnt it by heart, Blanchette, but remember, they probably won't apply all of it. It says: Those committing adultery are condemned, if it is wintertime, to plunge into a cold bath up to their mouths and to remain there for such time as shall be determined by the *baylons*. If the season is summer, they shall sit naked on an ant's nest, with their nose and ears plugged up. But if the case is a serious one, they should be driven through a swarm of bees.'

'So it is a swarm of bees for me,' said Blanchette calmly.

'No, it is not, Blanchette. This is your husband's son, conceived on his last night with you. Who can say otherwise?'

The two women looked at Joseph. The fluff on his head was golden and his eyes were dark blue. Lea bustled into the room.

'Finished your secrets?'

'Mother, doesn't a baby's hair and eyes change colour as the child grows?'

'Of course they do, certainly they do. And Joseph has his father's nose.'

'He has not, Mother,' said Blanchette sharply.

'Then more's the pity,' said the old woman. 'I'm not a fool. There's a lot, Esther, that I know and will not say about your ways, and I do not think my daughter learned good ways from you, but I will not ask. If you two take me for a fool, you're mistaken, both of you. But least said; and may God protect a fatherless child.'

Lea began to cry. 'Can you not comfort me?' she asked Blanchette.

'No, Mother,' whispered Blanchette.

Esther stood up and tossed her black hair, loose as was permitted in the house and hanging down to her waist.

'Joseph is Astruc's son,' she said loudly. 'Do you hear, Lea? Blanchette? I will say so to all I meet. The boy's hair is a sport, a freak of nature. And think about this: David Rougier would do anything at all for you, Blanchette.'

Saint-Amant woke and knew at once that he had a fever. If he was ill, what was the illness? It was strange that he had felt nothing before, but by now the danger was over. He had been deceiving himself; it was not over. He rose and looked at himself in the glass, particularly at his eyes. Were his eyelids swollen? He examined the state of his eyelashes: they were long and blond, and there seemed to be many of them left. Ulcers in his nostrils, another early symptom; but no. Nothing. He looked out of the window, at the roofs shiny from a recent shower, at the people far below from whom he could expect no mercy.

So far, the punishment for fornication had not been meted out to him, but it would be. All would happen in the way God had chosen, and his sin would become visible and separate him for ever from the people down below.

But why was he looking for signs of the disease on his face? God would punish him in the part of his body with which he had sinned. That was where the ulcers would start. He took off his shift and examined himself with care; nothing, yet. But just as the fruit of his sin took nine months to grow in the womb of the Jewess, his sin could well manifest itself now, nine months after the sin.

I will be walking the roads of Provence with my bell and begging bowl, he thought, and at the end they will care for me in one of the hospices, among the other lepers. He surveyed his unblemished body. He was still young, his skin was silky, the golden mat on his chest covered a powerful body, and the muscles were strong in his arms and thighs. He could ride, fence, play the lute, compose songs and sing them in his high tenor voice. He could speak Latin, French, Provençal and Italian and, by skill and intelligence, he had obtained his position, had carried out the many important and challenging functions of his office at Court; was he really to lose all this?

But what if he confounded the witchcraft by bringing a soul to God? Then God might prove merciful to him.

After Mass, Saint-Amant was called to the compound where 200 sheep had been penned up since they entered the city at dawn. The scribe who should have entered their arrival in his book had disappeared, lying drunk in some gutter, the Head Butcher supposed, but meanwhile he could not take delivery.

'Why do you need the book?' said Saint-Amant impatiently. 'Why do you not slaughter what you need for today?'

'The book shows what beasts have been bought and how many have been slaughtered this week. I don't want to get into trouble, and risk an accusation.'

Returning to his office, Saint-Amant found a man patiently waiting to report to the Pope that the Rhône had risen in the night and that the waters were menacing the shores, both banks.

'The Holy Father cannot see you today,' Saint-Amant told him, 'but I will ride out immediately, see what can be done and report to the Holy Father.'

This was work he enjoyed and called on many of his skills. He ordered a horse to be saddled, rode down to the bridge where the high spring floods were running fast through the stone pillars and then upstream as far as the flour mill, where he saw shacks and shelters, and a crowd on the bank near the mill. A cry went up at the sight of him. 'The Holy Father has heard us!'

These low-lying meadows had been chosen by those washing stuffs, linens, serges, hempen cords, using dyes, as well as by other artisans making parchment, for which there was a huge demand by the scribes at court. These trades polluted the waters of the Rhône, and the artisans had been allotted the meadows well away from the city.

There were people, Saint-Amant saw, who were in tears, for some of the shacks were already a foot or two under water and stores of dyes and parchment were getting wet. He quickly organised a chain of hands to pass stuffs, dyed garments and parchment to higher ground where they were spread on bushes to dry. A woman embraced him, many asked him to thank the Holy Father. Who does not even know about this, thought Saint-Amant; I'll tell him later. He will want food sent; I will ask the kitchen on my return.

While the work of rescue was proceeding – all they had needed was the assurance that the Holy Father knew and had sent an official to start the work – Saint-Amant felt a tap on his shoulder; surprised, he spun round.

'I have a message for you,' murmured the man. His face was hidden under the hood of his cloak. Saint-Amant felt a vague threat.

'Well . . . speak.'

'Come closer,' whispered the man. 'The message is for your ears and no other.'

Maybe a message from the porter in the Street, with news of the birth? He obeyed. Their faces were close together when the man pulled the hood from his face and Saint-Amant saw the weeping, bursting boils, the features eaten away and blurred by leprosy. The sick man's poisoned breath, as he exhaled into Saint-Amant's face, brought the putrefaction of the grave.

'You too will die! Justice! Chastisement, malediction!' he growled.

The combination of the sight of what might be lying in wait for him, and the words which might have come from his own conscience made Saint-Amant thrust out his hands to ward off the evil; the leper screamed abuse, but it was Saint-Amant who collapsed on the ground. To the man who brought him water, Saint-Amant said he was reviving; and who was the leper?

There was no leper, he was assured. They would not allow a leper near them and nobody had heard a leper's bell.

God preserve me from madness, Saint-Amant prayed as he slowly rode back to town. At dusk, he stumbled into the chapel but was unable to pray. Now Satan had sent a leper to blow disease into his nostrils, invisible to anyone but him.

He must have certainty.

A doctor could tell him whether he had the disease or not. Or whether he was going mad or not. Who knew how disease leapt from one body to another? Pustules from the leper's breath might be joining others, caught in the Street, in his blood, bubbling away as he breathed.

Who was the best *medicus* at the papal court? Guy de Chauliac had taught at Montpellier, the Pope and the cardinals spoke highly of him.

He dried his sweating body and put on a clean shift, blue hose and cloak, and called for the Chief Porter who told him where Guy de Chauliac's lodgings were.

An hour later, Guy de Chauliac told him to dress himself and told him the diagnosis.

'You do not have leprosy, *chevalier*, neither the major nor the minor form. Why do you believe you have it? Have you gone with a prostitute?'

'No.'

'From your fears I have drawn certain conclusions, so let me relate what the celebrated Roger Bacon has said on the subject. He noted that intercourse between one of his patients and a woman with leprosy had serious results. Two of his colleagues, John of Gaddesden, doctor at the university of Oxford, and Bernard Gordon, well known at Montpellier, have made the same observation, and I will tell you the theory behind it—'

Saint-Amant laid a gold florin on the table between them and rose.

'Thank you, *magister*, I am much relieved by your diagnosis—'

De Chauliac ignored the florin and waved to Saint-Amant.

'Sit down, *chevalier*. Now, you will wonder, and be edified, by this tale. Doctor Gordon tells of a countess who came to Montpellier to be cured of her affliction. A bachelor of medicine, whose task was to change her dressings, became her lover. He in turn developed this serious and dangerous affliction—'

Saint-Amant rose and held out his hand: 'My duties in the Household call me, I'm afraid—'

'Hear me out, *chevalier*. Jean Manardi, an Italian, writes that in his opinion the illness was spread from the town of Valencia in Spain, where a famous courtesan – for a price of fifty *écus* – accorded her favours to a knight who was suffering from leprosy, and she in turn infected 400 young men, some of whom accompanied King Charles into Italy and thus carried the disease into—'

'I did not sleep with a prostitute, *magister*. You are a learned doctor, sir. Do you believe that disease is sent as a punishment for sin?'

De Chauliac remained silent. A bell tolled in the town, then another and another.

De Chauliac looked at the wall of his room, where a small crucifix hung. When he spoke, he had abandoned his lecturing style, and Saint-Amant heard him speak as a humble man, intent on piercing the miasma of super-stition and ignorance with which he grappled daily.

'As a Christian, a believer, a son of the Church, I have heard many a sermon on the subject; that disease is sent as a punishment for sin. As a doctor, I have studied zoology, botany and mineralogy. I have attended dissections in Paris and in Montpellier. We, the doctors, are subject to ecclesi-astic authority, like all other Christians. But as to the causes of disease – here you touch on a difficult subject. We advance theories, of course. I myself am searching . . .'

He fell silent.

'Your answer?'

'No, I will not give you an answer to that question. You can will yourself into a sickness, though, you can will your-self to die of . . . let us say . . . fear. Yes. As an instance—'

'I've understood you, *magister.*'

'Suspend your beliefs, Knight. I surmise that your thoughts are making you ill.'

Chapter 17

When Astruc woke, Marie was still sleeping. The child had kept them awake but he was quiet now, suspended above the bed in a willow basket securely tied to a hook. Deep peace and joy filled Astruc's heart. He kissed Marie who did not stir and began the morning prayer. 'Glory to the Eternal, who has instructed the cocks to crow—'

It was confusing to be so far from the community, but he did his best.

In the yard he caught six hens, tied their legs together and placed them in the pannier, in another he put three dozen eggs separated by layers of fresh moss. The mule, fed and watered, allowed himself to be loaded, and was persuaded to trot to the market at Carpentras. As the sky grew lighter, man and mule rode through bright yellow thickets of gorse, past whole fields of flowers, red and violet poppies and blue cornflowers, and Astruc sang psalms and snatches of the songs they sang at Shavuot, when the mule suddenly stopped. Astruc listened and grasped his stick. He was still on the alert, he always would be, but these days the muscles in his arms had swelled with the hard labour of the farm; he was a burly figure nowadays and he felt confident that any attacker would get something he would remember.

But all the mule wanted was to browse for a while. He bent his head and pulled at the herbs, and the scent of bruised mint and thyme rose into Astruc's nostrils.

In all these months, nobody had come after him to be punished for murder: he supposed he could now risk returning to the Street. But why should he return, to his old life, to Blanchette? She had never wanted him. But Marie did and they were happy together, and they had made a son. He smiled as he remembered how he had explained to her that the child would have to be circumcised. Marie had shaken her head.

'He is half-Jew, Marie.'

'He is half-Christian, Astruc, and I shall take him to be baptised.'

'His name will be Bonjoue,' said Astruc. 'He will receive it when he is circumcised.'

'I shall call him Michel,' said Marie. 'But let there be peace between us.'

Astruc kissed her.

'Think; can you really take him to Avignon? What will your wife say? Baptism would be easier . . .'

She was right. To be happy, he had to shut his eyes to the Street. Adulterers both, Marie had told him, they must live as many happy days as God would grant them, and suffer in hellfire later.

'Hellfire?' Astruc had said to her. 'Don't you think we will be punished well before then, in our lifetime? Your husband could return in a month. Or tomorrow.'

She crossed herself.

'Let us not waste our time of happiness,' she had said, and had drawn him down in the bed.

As he rode through a silent wood and then along the edge of a field where peasants were sowing maize, he thought of Blanchette, the wife he had abandoned. He might have tried to force her to love him, but that was not his nature. He did remember her disgust and how her body recoiled from his touch and memories of humiliation surged into his heart. He could never return to that.

But there was such joy in his life now with Marie and their son Bonjoue, with his bilberry eyes and his blue-black hair, crested, like a jay's. Michel, Marie called him; to Astruc, he was Bonjoue and the little boy answered to both names.

The mule's hooves rang out loud on the stony path, while Astruc's thoughts turned sombre again. Of course he had done wrong, by Blanchette and by his brother Thoros. He had sent no news for months. Maybe they never received his first message. Thoros would be desperate to find him, Blanchette would be glad of his absence. And here he was living, more and more, like a Christian. But perhaps that was not important. Yes, of course it was. God had divided all folk into kinds and all lived by the rules of their kind. Merchants and priests, popes and beggars, Jews and Christians. If only he could talk to Thoros . . . he fingered the piece of stuff in his pocket.

In Carpentras market he was lucky, selling his hens and all his eggs in the first hour. And as a pedlar passed with a bag of mended clothes on his back, Astruc saw that he wore the badge. Astruc's heart was beating hard as he called to the man.

'Sir?' asked the pedlar. Astruc felt like embracing him. The pedlar saw a burly young man with a reddish brown thatch of hair under his cowl and a jutting nose, a strong-looking peasant.

'Do you come from Avignon?' asked Astruc, 'from the Street?'

The man nodded warily.

'How is Thoros, the doctor?'

'Who?' asked the pedlar uneasily. 'I have a good cloak here, Master, which will last you seven years. Here, let me show you.'

'I am Thoros's brother Astruc.'

The pedlar's eyes searched for the badge or the hat and he became more uncomfortable by the minute.

'I'm a Jew, Thoros's brother. How is he?'

'What are you doing here, Astruc?' exclaimed the pedlar. 'I know who you are now. Your wife has—' He paused then tried again. 'Don't you know?'

'My brother! How is Thoros?'

'Thoros – I don't know very much, Astruc, but Thoros has not been seen in the Street for months now. He's much missed. They say he went out one night last summer and never returned. But why have you left the Street? Where is your hat, your badge? If they catch you . . . mind you, I took you for one of them.'

'This piece of stuff is for Thoros. See, I've written his name on it in Hebrew, he'll know it's from me. Give it to him.'

'But how can I!'

'And tell Blanchette I will come and see her, very soon. Here's some money for you, and this is for her.'

Astruc handed over all the money he had taken this morning. They'd have to manage without it. One day and one night in Avignon, to explain, and to hear about Thoros; the mule could just about manage the distance in two days with a night's rest in between. Marie would understand.

It was long past midday when Astruc reached the lonely house. He must explain to Marie. She was right,

Bonjoue must be baptised. They had often spoken of Blanchette and what was to be done. He knew how to get a divorce from a woman – it was done simply – and Blanchette would have a hundred suitors.

He rode into the yard and tied the mule to the post, fetched water and fodder for him and put away the empty panniers. All at once he became aware of the silence.

'Marie!' he cried

Nothing stirred. At once his heart, brain, nerves and muscles took up the long prepared positions for a fight. He knew what had happened. Roger, Marie's husband, had returned. They had talked often of how it would be if he returned at night; why, when they had talked about it, had it always happened at night? Well, it had happened by day. Astruc took the cudgel from his belt, thinking that Roger would be waiting inside the door. Marie was his woman now, Bonjoue was their son. Roger had beaten Marie, he had abandoned her. If God was just, he would protect Astruc, Marie and Bonjoue. Thou shalt not kill! cried the voice of the rabbi in his head, but Astruc knew he would not heed it if it were necessary.

He walked to the door; fear, anguish, guilt and anxiety gone, and flung it open.

By the fire sat Marie, cradling Bonjoue in her arms. In the other chair, hunched, sat an old beggar, misshapen in a bundle of old clothes. Both his feet were bare and rested in a crock of water. He was old, with red-rimmed eyes which watered and overflowed. He looked at the door as Astruc came in, squeezing up his eyes against the light.

'Good day, friend,' he said to Astruc in a wheezing voice. 'I cannot see you well and I cannot rise to greet you. I have just returned after two years of wandering to my wife and home. Sit down, master, we're peaceful people.'

Marie turned her face to Astruc, but he could not read her expression. What did she want him to do?

She cooked a meal for the three of them, a fowl and herbs, and Astruc helped her to wash Roger, who had used up the last of his strength, it seemed, to reach his home, and could make little of his surroundings.

'Is there a baby?' he asked Marie, hearing Bonjoue gurgle.

'Yes, Roger,' she said quietly.

'I think our baby died many years ago, didn't it?'

'Yes. Of hunger.'

'So many dying,' murmured Roger. 'But God makes new lives. I'm glad you have a child. It is our child.'

And he began to ramble, about dancing on the bridge, for the streets of Avignon were too narrow. Night and day they danced the *farandole*! But the soldiers of the Pope didn't like us shepherds – then he slept.

At dusk, Astruc began to lock up.

'Too late!' said Marie in a low voice. 'He's here.'

These were the first words Marie had spoken to Astruc since his return. He had told her about the money for the hens and the eggs and how he had sent it to Avignon with the pedlar. She hardly listened. Then he had made up a bed of hay and herbs, by the fire, for Roger.

'I'll sleep in the bed with Bonjoue,' she said. 'And you—'

Astruc saw tears gathering in her eyes.

'I'll sleep in the barn.'

All violence had left him. He felt nothing.

In the morning he knocked softly on the door and Marie came out at once.

'You see how old he has become, Astruc; and he rambles. I see my duty.'

Neither of them had words about what was to become of them, and they stood with their arms around each other, and read in each other's eyes all the pain of what was happening. There was a faint cry from inside the house: Roger.

'Look after Michel, kiss him from me, Marie.'

'Of course. Astruc, take the mule.' Crying, she returned to the house.

Astruc untied the mule and rode towards Avignon to take his ordained place as a Jew in the Street. God had shown him what it was to be happy, and God had closed the door on his happiness. His whole body ached with the loss.

All day he rode, and late in the afternoon he entered the city through the Imbert gate and rode slowly through the narrow streets. Neither the porter at the gate of the Street nor passers-by in the Street itself recognised him. He tied the mule to a ring outside their shop and went in – the shop was empty, and he started climbing the stairs to their room. Nearing the door he thought he heard singing. With every step he had been repeating what he planned to say, but when he opened the door, all he could remember was, 'Blanchette, I've returned.'

Blanchette was startled by the stocky peasant with his face half hidden in the cowl. A Christian, a peasant – How did he get up here, what did he want? In fear, her eyes dilated as she tried to cover the baby at her breast.

'Get away from me, don't touch me!'

She moved backwards to the corner of the room. Astruc had forgotten the lack of space in the room, the darkness, the smell of the house.

'I've not come to harm you, Blanchette. It's Astruc, Blanchette.'

He watched the fear in her face turn to anger, and she began breathing fast. The baby sought her breast, and Astruc watched her trying to breathe normally. At last she spoke. 'If I am angry, he won't drink, the milk will turn sour and harm him.'

'Yes,' he said, smiling at the baby.

The slow wheels in his mind began to turn. Could this be his child? No. It must be a year since he and Blanchette made love. Not his child; so Blanchette was an adulteress, just as he was an adulterer. She was afraid of him, and angry now; but perhaps they might be able to talk, each with an equal burden, and make a kind of life together?

'You sent me money every month, but you abandoned me. How could you?' she asked her voice harsh with resentment.

'I went into hiding, Blanchette, I was attacked and, perhaps, killed the man; I didn't know. But I did not send you money except . . . yesterday, when I gave some to a pedlar from the Street. I . . . I didn't know I was going to be here myself, today. And . . . and I thought you would be selling clothes from the shop. And that Thoros would look after you.'

'So you did not send money,' said Blanchette, winding the clothes tightly around the child until he was a rigid object. 'And if not you – who did?'

'This child—' Astruc began, 'Is it—?'

'You know it cannot be yours. You can divorce me straight after the circumcision.'

A man could put away his wife for infidelity. As for his own, it did not count against him. He had only to ask the rabbi to write the act of divorce, twelve lines to say he was divorcing Blanchette, and these would be handed to her in the presence of three witnesses. Perversely, he felt sad and bereft. And yet he knew that he did not love her any more. But he liked the child, yes, he did.

'What is its name?'

'His name, Astruc, is Joseph.'

Astruc took off his rough cloak and laid it on the bed. Blanchette watched him as though he were a dangerous animal, staring at his strong body, his arms. She said nothing. How long were they going to remain like this? He noticed the blond fluff on Joseph's head. He watched the expressions on her face; anger had given way again to fear. She had become like other women, fearing their husbands.

'I've come to be peaceful,' he said 'Come out of your corner, I'm not angry, can't you see?'

Blanchette came forward with hesitant steps, then resumed feeding the baby while sitting on the chair, while Astruc watched with a smile. She was still beautiful but now he could see this without pain as he no longer wanted her. But Joseph was another matter. If he couldn't have Bonjoue, he would have Joseph and bring him up as his own child, his son. He stretched his hand out to Joseph.

'Don't touch him, Astruc, he's mine!'

Astruc's hand fell back by his side. For a long moment they stared into each other's faces.

'And – Joseph's father?'

'I was alone. I wanted a child. For that I needed a man, and the one who came to me served his purpose – I have not seen him since and I don't expect to see him again.'

'You never wanted my child,' said Astruc, full of the old bitterness.

'In those days,' said Blanchette, turning her head away, 'I loved your brother. I couldn't—'

Astruc's head jerked, as though she had struck him in the face. Watching him, she added in a gentler voice: 'I know how much you love your brother. All we know is that he left here one night last summer, called away to a patient – the Holy Father, it is said, but who knows? We looked for him everywhere – everywhere. We had no word, no sign – and you left me at the same time, without a word or sign either. I became mad with worry. Can't you understand how I felt? Godforsaken.'

'I didn't know, Blanchette. I was in hiding, not daring to return, but I knew Thoros would look after you. I'll tell you what happened—'

'I don't want to know now, Astruc. Our life was not happy and when I was alone I . . . I was . . . I needed something of my own. And then I sinned, it seemed the only way – and you may now put me away and marry another.'

The door flew open and Lea came in carrying a pail of water. She saw Astruc, and knew him at once. She set down the bucket so hard that the water slopped over the rim.

'I open my lips in jubilation, blessed be the Lord! He is back! I knew, I told you he'd be back for the circumcision of his first-born son – but where've you been? Have you eaten? Why have you been so long? Never mind, that'll silence those vicious tongues around here. I told them you would return and here you are. What will you eat? There's nothing in the house. Well, what do you think of your son? He has your nose. Blanchette says not, but see for yourself—'

'He has not, Mother,' Blanchette muttered, but the old woman had heard her and looked at her sharply.

'You, my girl, give thanks to the good Lord that he has returned your man to you, and just in time. We'll give thanks straight away. Here, no need to trouble the rabbi, we'll say the Shema.'

So Astruc, his wife and mother-in-law began to intone the prayer together, and the prayer folded its comforting wings over Astruc's bowed head, wrapped him in the old trusted certainties, and he prayed to his God to keep Marie and Bonjoue safe from harm till, please God, he could return to them.

Chapter 18

Laurent stood awkwardly in the cardinal's great kitchen, where the morning light touched on the copper casseroles, huge unwieldy frying pans requiring a man's two hands to lift, the spit-jack, the cauldrons, the meat-hooks bearing their burden of carcasses and an array of dishes and mortars set out on the long table. Laurent, gaunt in his black gown stood awkwardly, watching Maino, Le Gor's celebrated Italian cook finish making a gallimaufry of mustard, ginger, vinegar, stock and verjuice. Laurent tried not to breathe too deeply; the smell from the rotting wildfowl, hares and pheasants drooping from hooks mingled unpleasantly with that of some crayfish in a bowl which had made their way – too slowly – all the thirty-five hours from Marseilles by cart.

'So my lord thinks you might be a cook?' said Maino, staring at the scarecrow figure in his kitchen.

'My lord is attempting to solve a conundrum: myself. Who am I? All I know is that my hands are asking for work.'

Laurent thought back to the latest of the cardinal's bizarre guesses, when Le Gor had attempted to make gold with Laurent's help – a dismal failure.

'Whatever it was that I did with my hands, I have no notion of alchemy, my lord,' Laurent had said apologetically. 'We have tried many things, in vain. Would you allow me now to return to the hospice, where I was of use?'

'You shall go into the kitchens. It is possible that you were a cook,' said Le Gor. 'If you go back to the hospice, you will become a leper. Why should you deny the will of Jesus who has saved you, by courting death again? I believe it is God's will that you should be restored to your rightful place, and all we have to do is to use the clues you present to us. I have vowed to find out who you are, and I will do just that.'

There are no clues, thought Laurent bitterly. The cardinal is using me as an experiment.

'Watch me!' cried Maino now. 'You're all here to learn! If you become good cooks, you'll never lack employment!'

Laurent and two young cook apprentices were beckoned to the long table and told to watch.

'When making a sauce with spices and bread, pound the spices first and then the bread, since the bread will take up any spices remaining in the mortar and nothing will be lost. Spices cost money. Then we will *boutonner*, meaning to stick meat with cloves. Then we will thread meat with strips of fat—'

Geraud sauntered into the kitchen. Laurent liked the large young page, always friendly and protective of him and watched him sniffing the air in the kitchen, nose in the air like a dog.

'Ah! Geraud, come to report to my lord what he will be eating tonight?' said Maino. 'If you can remember!' Geraud's memory was not for facts, but he loved food. '*Brodo di cappone à la provençale* with fowl giblets, eggs, cinnamon and mace. *Brodo* means soup, Master Geraud. Then a dish of pork, accompanied by hard-boiled eggs, chestnuts and cheese and a few pears if I can find some.

Two brace of those wildfowl on the hooks over there, cooked in garlic because they're a little high. A *comines* of fish to follow for those who like it. What is a *comines*, François?'

'A . . . a jelly. With . . . with apples, Maino?' said the apprentice.

'No. Nicolo?'

'A pudding?'

'A stuffed fish dish which my master likes. With almonds and cumin—'

Maino turned towards Laurent, who was peering at the labelled jars on the spice shelf. 'If you can read, Laurent, I'll give you Taillevent's cookery book.'

Laurent shook his head, and stretching a hand out towards a jar, he began tracing the writing on the label with his finger. Maino walked over to look and read the label out, guiding Laurent's hand: POPPY-SEED OIL.

'Important for health,' said Laurent as to himself.

'Of course,' said Maino. 'Medicine and cooking are sisters.'

The kitchen door was flung open by two servants of Le Gor's, struggling with sacks of sugar and two dead piglets.

'To work,' said Maino. 'Nicolo and François, there are knives to be sharpened – and Nicolo, I have many uses for that honey and those raisins. Their value will be docked from your wages.'

'Come, Laurent,' said Geraud, putting his arm affectionately around Laurent's thin shoulders. 'Maybe this is not where you belong, but fear not, we will find what it is . . . what's the matter?'

Laurent had stopped by the piglets, lying on the scrubbed side table.

'You eat these?' he said. Geraud and Maino looked at each other and Maino touched his forehead.

'Yes,' and, as though speaking to a child, 'you like roast pork, don't you, Laurent?'

'No. Well, I've never eaten any.'

Later, six cardinals, Le Gor's guests, had dined extremely well on Maino's efforts. Candles sent their reflections to the mirrors and were returned as distorted, wavering beams. Dogs were crunching the remains of the roast pork under the table. Silver cups and plates reflected faces shining with grease. Le Gor now called for the *blanc mangier* which Maino brought in himself.

'I shall buy that man from you, Le Gor, if ever I have enough money,' Cardinal Pedro Gomez said, when Maino had left the room.

'No,' said Le Gor. 'He's beyond price.'

They began to talk court business; how much time was devoted to liturgical and how much to judicial duties, and after that the older men began to grumble about the number of times they had to wear the heavier accoutrements. Now that the weather was turning warmer, the weight was cumbersome, particularly when rising from one's knees during Mass. Gaucelme de Jean changed the tone of the conversation.

'On another subject entirely, friends, my auditor came to see me this morning. I employ three legal men – notaries – as well as the auditor; there is the legal messenger and the man who affixes the seals, which makes six on the legal side alone. What with the valets, cooks, bakers, wine stewards, stable lads, lackeys, I'm spending a fortune.'

Then Cardinal de Deaux calculated what his musicians cost, and cardinal de Pres said he was being ruined by his stable full of horses – but he really felt they were a necessary expense.

Le Gor nodded. 'A necessary expense is one which contributes to the standing of a cardinal's household, and reflects the glory of the Holy Father's court! And now, friends, I would like to offer a present to each of you, to show my appreciation of your companionship.'

Silk purses and rings were brought and distributed and there was clapping.

'I remember,' continued Le Gor, 'His late Holiness' *De honestate cardinalium.* You'll remember that he decreed that no cardinal should have more than twenty young knights in his household, and not more than ten chaplains. Of course the Court then was not what it is today – the centre and heart of the Christian world. Well, and now for a surprise!'

All the cardinals, who were regular guests at Le Gor's table knew what the surprise was, and there were some irritable looks cast in Geraud's direction as he stepped forward from behind a curtain, holding his lute.

Geraud looked at the old faces around the table and his heart sank. They did not like his songs much; and he always felt the great gulf between their ages and his, between the power they wielded in Avignon and himself: a penniless young page dependent on the benevolence of Le Gor. He would sing because Le Gor loved his voice. Only – Geraud's large, guileless eyes looked anxiously at his master – each of his recitals ended the same way.

'You know the madrigal by Jacopo of Florence!' Le Gor exclaimed and began to hum in a tuneless voice:

I do not praise a singer who shouts loudly
Loud shouting does not make good singing
But with smooth and sweet melody
Lovely singing pleases, given skill . . .

There was polite clapping.

'Let us hear something by Francesco Landini,' said Le Gor. He turned to the cardinals: 'You have your horses and your musicians, but I believe that in Geraud here, I have the best tenor voice in Avignon. Sing *De! dimmi tu,* Geraud.'

The cardinals exchanged glances.

Geraud plucked a string, softly, and it responded like a woodpigeon cooing. In his scarlet tunic, with his long hair parted in the centre and his tall bearing, the lute in his hands, he seemed to have stepped out of the new picture by Matteo Giavonetti, which the Holy Father had just hung in his study.

De! dimmi tu che se'così fregiato
Tell me, you who are so adorned with golden necklaces
Who do you think you are when you look at yourself?
You believe there is no one to equal you
But what you consider glory, ornaments, fine clothes
Is but a rope to me . . .

Geraud's high tenor soared above the grey heads and its sad message of love denied entered hearts not used to those feelings. When it came to a close the lute continued softly till at last there was silence. It was broken by Cardinal de Pres, old and deaf, who turned to his neighbour and asked in his deep bass voice, 'Tell me what has been said to make our host weep?'

But Le Gor, without bothering to wipe away his tears, called to Geraud, '*Ecco la primavera*! Spring has come to make all hearts joyful. That is what we want to hear now, Geraud!'

Cardinal Le Gor's residence was large. He had bought twelve houses from the citizens of Villeneuve; some of them tall and narrow, others squat and small. They had been joined together to form a bewildering whole, so that there were stairs and corridors which led nowhere, and rooms and alcoves which were never used. At night, many of the cardinal's retinue slept in corners, or four together under the steep roofs of a multitude of garrets, icy or baking according to season; cooks and apprentices close to the kitchen.

Laurent slept in an alcove near the dining room and had lain on his pallet, listening to voices and music from there. Wrapped in two cloaks, he heard the guests depart and then he slept.

In his dream he stretched out his hands to men and women whom he knew, and they embraced him in turn, and the warmth enveloped his body and soul. When he woke again, he found he was holding a cat which had chosen him for warmth and comfort and was purring in the crook of his arm.

Laurent knew that part of him was dead, perhaps for ever, and that his fever had destroyed something which, because it had been destroyed, he was unable to name.

Lying in the dark, stroking the cat, he despaired of ever finding the people who had been close to him again. And he was cold. He had better go down to the kitchens, where the fires were not allowed to die down, and look for a bench on which to lie near the great hearth.

As he opened the door of the kitchen, he heard groans. In the kitchen, two men were bending over another who was stretched on the floor in a gathering pool of blood.

Laurent walked up to the three men. 'Let me see,' he demanded.

Laurent removed his outer cloak and laid it, rolled up, under the head of the injured man.

'He's been beaten, Laurent, we found him in the passage. Look, there's blood oozing from his mouth,' gabbled Nicolo, one of the apprentices.

Laurent looked across at the shelf of jars. 'Fetch me . . .' then his voice wavered and he looked at the floor, 'a priest.'

'Who was he?' asked Laurent, when a priest had been fetched and the man on the floor was, at last, silent.

'Giacomo, my lord's messenger.'

Chapter 19

In the bedchamber at the top of the great tower of Montolieu, Gui told his father that he was now on his way to Avignon. 'De Chauliac is the best doctor in Avignon,' Gui said to the unmoving face and closed eyes. François de Montolieu had tossed in fevered dreams all night. 'I'll return with him tomorrow. Yves, wipe away the pus, then bathe him in rosewater, change his linen.'

'As before, Master Gui,' said the old man who had not moved from François's side since father and son had returned from Apt on the weary horse, François barely clinging to his son.

Gui embraced his father and ran down the stairs two at a time, all three flights; he hoped to be back tomorrow at nightfall.

Yves piled olive and lavender and myrtle branches on the hearth to warm the sick man and make the chamber smell good. Turning to observe his master he thought he noticed a change – it was hard to say. He chased flies away from the livid face running with sweat, and wished he were outside; there was so much work in April! But he, and his father before him, had served the master of Montolieu, his place was here.

I am older than the master, thought Yves, and thought I would surely die before him. If – he crossed himself – the master were to die, he and all the other villeins owed the heriot, the forfeit of their best possession, to the new master; that would be Gui. I've ploughed his fields, sowed his seeds, cut the hay and harvested the crops, thought Yves. When there was a storm, the master's harvest came first, and when there was the plague of rats two years ago, we had to save the master's fields first; when that was done, it was too late for us villeins to save our own. That is how it has always been.

Yves had heard of villeins who rose against the masters. And what about the priests? Who said that we owed a tax to God? Every year I've paid whatever I had: eggs, a hen, a piglet – we can ill spare a mouthful of food, let alone a piglet! Master, master, don't die . . .

Yves looked at him. When had he last stirred? Minutes ago – no, much longer. Then he saw there was indeed a change, God help us all, and by the time the doctor came, it might be all over, and – God forgive this thought at such a time – he would not be able to avoid the heriot. It would mean the horse, he would still have the mule, but without the horse – no, but the master must live. What was that noise? A rasping breath came from the bed. Where was his wife? He needed another soul to help, was that her slow step on the stairs? It was a long climb for her, with her bad leg. The rattling breath came again but with such force that Yves stepped back in fear. Gui could not have gone far, perhaps still saddling the horse . . .

The path from the tower of Montolieu led downhill and circled a deep ravine. On the far side of this ravine six peasants from the village lay sprawled under a huge olive tree, resting from their labours in the vineyard where they had been working since dawn. They were all thin, and due to the little food they ate – and that often rotten – none of them were strong. The April sun had made them sweat. Sitting or lying on cool pillows of herbs, thyme and marjoram and bright green spring grass, they were breaking their fast with dry bread and a few onions. A water-bottle made from a sheep's stomach was passed round.

'He's still sick, then?' enquired Hugues, face furrowed like a ploughed field.

'By his own hand; well, by his own will. Who forced him to go with the flagellants? A bad conscience, maybe,' said Jehan, in charge of the men.

'It is all one to us,' said Gautier, coughing, his chest hollow like a spoon. 'What does he do but eat what we provide with our labour and spend money on his pretty son to clothe him in silks, with golden spurs on his heels; and what have we got?'

'Gautier—' began Hugues. 'Save your breath—'

But Gautier, snatching at air, cried in a rasping voice: 'He hasn't kept his bargain! We work for him, and he in turn must defend us. Not he; not any noble. They live on our blood and sweat! What we earn in a year, the master spends in an hour. And when the brigands came and took our beasts and our carts and killed the pigs, where was the *seigneur* of Montolieu then? But, brothers, we can harm the nobles, they're only men, after all – look what the shepherds did to them.'

'At least we're not starving, not quite.'

'And do you want to wait until the cup of misery over-flows here, too?' gasped Gautier. 'My Catherine cannot feed the child, her breast dry and her stomach swelled up from the mouldy rye bread. Why should we starve? Mouldy bread and a drink of water – do we not sleep and love and cry like the nobles? I say we might be free, and work for ourselves. The shepherds have killed their masters, in France, and burned their houses. I say we are ready.'

None of the men spoke. There was no need. They were ready to parley with the *seigneur*, at the very least, and wait for the outcome. The earth felt warm beneath them as they rested their bones which ached from bending over the vines. Thomas broke the silence. 'If the *seigneur* doesn't live, we'll have pretty Gui, no better than his father. But the heriot! It will be the end of us. All I have left is the pig, and they'll take that. Then we'll be beggars. As for me, I'll join a band, like the master, but it'll be the shepherds for me, not the flagellants.' He picked up the short curved knife with which he had worked on the vines: 'And this will be my companion.'

'Come, to work, or we will not eat at all,' Jehan said.

The men rose, groaning, to go back to the vines, tying up the young shoots. Gautier stopped after a few minutes, shielding his eyes. 'There's someone – it is the young *seigneur*, coming this way – I recognise the horse. Let's stop him, let's tell him all of this.'

Gui had to ride through the vineyard on his way to Avignon, and he saw the villeins from the village among the vines. He decided to stop for a moment to give them news of his father, they would wish to know. He stopped his horse at the edge of the vineyard, and the men slowly came towards him.

Gui looked into their stony faces, and saw anger and contempt. Not one bade him good day. He looked at the dirty rags they wore, tied with hemp around the wrists, waist and ankles, unshaven and unwashed, and he saw a short curved knife in each man's hand.

Gautier seized the bridle of Gui's horse. Gui knew him as a troublemaker, but, thought Gui, I haven't time to listen to his grievance now, I must get the doctor.

'Let go of the bridle, Gautier,' said Gui. 'The *seigneur* is very ill, I am going to fetch a doctor.'

'While we are met like this,' said Gautier, with a look of fiery contempt which entered Gui like a knife, 'and as the master is so ill, if my lord would listen to us a moment—'

'Later, on my return!'

Gautier kept hold of the bridle and his flayed face, skin stretched over bone and muscle, contorted with hate. 'You hold us peasants in contempt. You think of us as cattle, stupid and to be driven where you please. With many pains – of body and soul, Master Gui – we furnish you with our labour and we groan to see it dissipated by you. I look at the clothes you're wearing, your hat, your silver spurs, and I say to myself, who bought you all this ? We did – Jehan, Hugues, Thomas – we dressed you for the city, we paid for your poppy-coloured surcoat, your velvet hat with a curling white feather! You peacock! You . . .'

A spasm shook him, and he trembled in its wake.

Gui, multi-coloured with the golden sheen of beauty and ease, stared at Gautier. Tooth decay had robbed him of his front teeth, dysentery visibly cramped his body while he spoke, interrupting each sentence with his cough. Gautier's words were like so many drops of poison to Gui and, because he was surprised and horri-

fied by what he had heard, he took refuge in his position. The villein was preventing him from riding away,
daring to stop him, Gui de Montolieu, from getting help.
'Let go of the bridle. My father is dying!' shouted Gui,
drawing his sword.

Gautier let go of the bridle, but he held his pruning
knife up. As the sun caught the blade, and before Gui
could spur his horse on, the villeins had surrounded
him.

In the last months Gui had experienced fear, and
love, and sadness. He had asked himself why his father
was suffering in the name of religion, and why God
allowed this and sickness and poverty. As a noble, he had
to protect the weak and helpless – and these villeins; for
was poverty not weakness and helplessness? Would not
Jesus urge him to help these peasants? Gui wished, very
devoutly, to please God. He sheathed his sword; he must
listen.

Gauthier took the gesture as one of fear, moved
forward and with a sudden movement pulled Gui from
the horse. Gui was unprepared and his feet were still
thrust in the stirrups – forced suddenly from his horse
he hung for a moment upside-down till he could free his
feet from the stirrups. Rolling on the stony path, he
curled into a ball but could not avoid the blows and kicks
which the villeins aimed at his stomach and head,
cursing him viciously in revenge for a lifetime of humili-
ations.

Gui, choking on the dust, winded by the blows and
kicks from all sides, repeated hoarsely through a
mouthful of dust that he must get to Avignon, for the
doctor.

The six villeins had stopped kicking, and stood silently, purged of rage for the moment, looking at the young man on the ground whom they had beaten and insulted. Each face expressed guilt at what had been done, and fear; men had paid with their lives for less.

'We've gone too far,' said old Thomas, and walked over to Gui. With his trembling hands he tried to brush the dust off the scarlet tunic. The velvet hat lay where it had been stamped into the ground, its feather broken.

'Master Gui,' said Thomas, 'I beg you to forget what we have done – or at least try to forgive us. Hunger and misery have driven us this far.'

The sound of hooves on the stony path rang out and all of them turned to see Yves, spurring his mule on as fast as it could trot. As he came closer, they saw his face. Old Thomas crossed himself as Yves dismounted awkwardly in front of Gui, whose dirty clothes he did not appear to notice. Yves knelt on the ground and Gui saw that his face was streaked with tears.

'I bring bad news of your father,' said Yves softly. 'You are our *seigneur* now.'

The peasants stared. Yves rose, helped by Thomas, and stood awkwardly with the other men, whispering among themselves.

Gui turned his face away and walked in silence to the olive tree, a few paces away, where his horse stood patiently in the shade. He turned his face away from the silent group of villeins and leant his face against the horse's flank so no one would see his tears.

The villains no longer stared. They stood waiting, their eyes cast down, not wanting to go back into the vineyard, not knowing what words to speak to their new master. Yves watched Gui, saw him stroking the horse's flank and left the silent group of peasants. Slowly and hesitantly he went over to Gui, placing his hand on his sleeve, feeling the sobs shake the young man's body. 'The master is with God in paradise,' said the old man. 'And you will see him again there. It is a hard and weary journey towards the eternal home.' He paused. 'I will be there before you, Master Gui. I saw you when you were six hours old. May God grant you many years yet.'

Gui took his face away from the horse's flank and knelt down beneath the olive tree to pray. Strong scent rose from the bruised thyme and a little breeze turned over the slender silver leaves of the olive tree. Yves and the other peasants knelt down to pray with him, except for Gauthier, who stood coughing and retching.

Gui looked away from them across the vineyard and the meadows, bright with flowers, towards the bluish haze around Mount Ventoux's bald peak. On the ground, close by him, lay Gauthier's pruning knife, dropped and forgotten.

Chapter 20

Cardinal Le Gor knew how Cardinal Annibal de Ceccano must be feeling; fortunately Le Gor was merely a guest today. They were both in their heavy robes and had been standing for the past half hour on the steps of the Ceccano palace in Gentilly – they and twenty chaplains, wearing heavy ornaments, arranged on the steps of de Ceccano's palace in procession order, with the priest holding the heavy cross in front. Le Gor comforted Annibal de Ceccano; 'Any minute now.'

De Ceccano, a very ambitious man, had spared no effort today. He was by now beside himself with anxiety and his face was suffused with blood. He clutched Le Gor's sleeve. 'That controller of the household, Saint-Amant, can't be trusted with time-keeping these days, they say he's possessed. Tell me what you can see, Le Gor – could the Holy Father be indisposed? I wish I had not accepted this honour.'

'They're coming by the garden gate!' cried Geraud, taller than the others.

'No. His Holiness would not shame Monseigneur thus,' said an old priest. 'And I suggest you keep your mouth closed, page, or the devil might fly in.'

'He's arriving by the kitchen gate!' said Geraud, quite loudly. He was as bored and hot as everyone else. There was laughter.

'Hush!' cried Le Gor, 'His Holiness is here!'

They saw the Pope descending from his palfrey and sweeping through the side gate into the garden. Saint-Amant had known that the front steps were to be used, the rehearsal had gone perfectly – he must indeed be mad – and de Ceccano signalled frantically to the procession to reform, hissing at Saint-Amant, whose eyes would not meet his, that he would speak to him later. The procession made its way to the chapel, where hangings of gold and silk masked the walls and carpets hid the stone floors.

Cardinal de Ceccano, so red in the face, had gone very pale, Le Gor noted. In fact his features swam vaguely across his face like those of the man in the moon. Le Gor blinked, and de Ceccano looked as he always did: a sharp-featured man inordinately concerned with the impression he was making.

I can't trust my eyes any longer, thought Le Gor, kneeling in his place in the chapel. What is happening to me? O Lord, let me not be struck by blindness.

Meanwhile, Clement had mounted a throne covered by a gold cloth and prayed for a short while. De Ceccano noted how tired the Holy Father looked, reassured himself that the bedchamber, decked out in wonderful tapestries, was ready for him. Clement blessed all present and left the chapel with halting gait – so his delay was due to indisposition, de Ceccano thought – and heard the Holy Father ask whether he might rest a while. De Ceccano showed him to his room, begging him to rest after the journey.

Clement, left alone, eased himself gratefully onto the huge bed and, before he closed his eyes, became aware of the design on the hangings around the bed, recog-

nising his own armorial bearings woven into the fabric;
he must remember to congratulate de Ceccano . . .
When he awoke, it was time to go to table. He hoped that
he would be able to do justice to the feast, and that he
would be able to show pleased surprise. Never, so far, had
he disappointed a host, whatever his state of health; and
Cardinal de Ceccano would have taken infinite trouble.

Later, with pandemonium in the kitchens behind
them, Le Gor, with Geraud at his side, stood with fifteen
other cardinals, a group of other clerics, and several
highborn guests, about twenty in all, in the cardinal's
great hall. The Pope finally entered, looking rested,
bestowing his brilliant smile on every single guest. He
blessed the table and all took their seats.

Cardinal de Ceccano was well aware of the competition for Clement's favour; it was usual among the cardinals for each to offer the Pope lavish entertainment, and
so he had secretly prepared a *pièce de résistance*. At a
smaller table were seated twelve young boys, all related
to Clement in some degree, and all were in their twelfth
year, and in front of each boy lay a purse containing a
gold florin, the gift of de Ceccano. Clement was truly
astonished and delighted to see the children and
thanked de Ceccano with so much genuine feeling that
the cardinal felt, for a brief moment, that all was well –
but there was time for much to go wrong.

There were to be nine courses, each composed of
three dishes. After the third course, the head cook
brought a baked fortress on a dish which held cooked
gamebirds, as well as a model of a stag.

During the fourth course, the cardinal's servants
paraded around the long table, and his page, when he

reached the Pope, made his announcement. 'Holy Father, there is a beautiful horse below, which Monseigneur my lord wishes to offer you, as well as this topaz ring and this sapphire ring; also this gold cup with a cover.'

Clement expressed his grateful thanks with a short and witty speech and, amid clapping, servants brought presents for everyone in the room.

During the seventh course, ten knights entered the hall. Le Gor saw that one of them was Gui . . . there could be no mistake, he smiled at him in recognition! Le Gor put down his knife and pushed away his plate – joy had taken the place of appetite. One of the knights carried the cardinal's banner and they engaged in mock battle, jousting with wooden horses until the eighth course appeared.

Le Gor took a deep draught of wine, and another and another. He had been tricked by his eyesight and by his need to see Gui again; but Gui was not among the knights. Geraud whispered to him, but Le Gor called loudly and angrily for more wine. Fencers appeared now and, after them, to accompany the ninth course, a choir sang movingly, unseen but heard. Le Gor sobbed quietly into his goblet. Music affects my master thus, Geraud explained but the guests were by now drunk themselves or at least merry enough to have lost their interest in explanations; they were waiting for the dessert and the dessert wines.

By the time the dessert appeared, Le Gor had emptied another whole flagon of wine, and did not see the two trees which were carried into the hall: one, painted silver, bore apples, pears, peaches and grapes;

the other remained its natural green and bore candied fruits. When nearly all had been consumed, the kitchen helpers entered and danced the *farandole* around the table, singing as they went.

The Pope now announced that he was retiring to his room, too exhausted for what de Ceccano had plannëd to follow, while the guests dispersed to the gardens, to sleep the sudden sleep of the drunk under a fruit tree or a rosebush.

Geraud needed all his strength to help Le Gor to a pallet in a secluded chamber.

The April sun gilded the bedchamber when the Pope woke after an hour, refreshed, and drew him to the window, where he found himself looking out over the silvery river Sorgue, bordered by gardens and meadows. His host knocked and entered and joined Clement at the window, from where he gave a signal to a group of horsemen decorated with coloured favours who had gathered in the meadow below. At this sign a troupe of dancers with tambourines and fifes led the horsemen across a little bridge. A large crowd soon followed them, until suddenly there were shouts and screams and laughter. The bridge, erected for show only, had given way under the massed feet, and the shallow water was full of struggling guests. Clement laughed – he realised that this little scene had been staged for him.

Later, he officiated at vespers and, that evening, Clement left his host and rode to his own palace of Pont-sur-Sorgue, leaving de Ceccano very happy and rather poorer. Clement, riding towards his palace with more than a touch of indigestion, thought that his enemies would rightly reproach his way of life, and his thoughts became sombre.

Guillaume de Saint-Amant hardly heard de Ceccano's reproaches; they did not reach the core of his being where there was no room except for the same thoughts, repeated till every muscle in his body had knotted with anguish. As he made his way back to Avignon, after the feast, he checked the preparations in his mind. The child was surely born, he *must* be born by now. Elinor had a cradle next to her bed, all ready. But – supposing it was a girl – was it worth all he had to accomplish for a girl? Yes, he thought it was.

Having arrived at the palace, he began pacing the corridors and stairs: to the Laurent Tower, on to the Wardrobe Tower then to the Gache Tower, to the treasurer's chamber, the notaries' room, finally to the kitchens, checking as was his duty. Let them not pretend that he was neglecting his duties! Out to Pope Urban's orchard, then to see the gardeners planting roses in the new garden.

Finally he could not keep from Elinor's room any longer. It was a small room near the kitchen. As he entered, he saw she was feeding her child. Saint-Amant watched her, tapping his foot.

Elinor had been promised money to send to her family in some village, Saint-Amant had forgotten where. He could see she was frightened of him. She was only about fifteen, he supposed. At first she had asked questions. 'Is it your child, sir? And will the mother not pine for it?'

'Yes,' he had answered, 'and no.'

'But, sir—' The answer puzzled her.

'Elinor, I have chosen you because you already have a child, and milk for two, you say; because you're clean, and because you're not stupid.'

Elinor had accepted, proud that she, at fifteen, earned enough to keep her whole family from starvation. Saint-Amant told her that she would learn more about her task as the child grew up, he would instruct her as time passed. This evening he stared through her, as always, without seeing her. 'What is your village called?'

'Caromb, sir, at the foot of Mont Ventoux.'

'And your child's father lives in that village?'

'No, sir. In Avignon. I explained to you before, sir, that I cannot marry the father of my child. There is a young man in Caromb—'

'Marry the father of your child, here in Avignon.'

'Oh no, sir, that is impossible! I did explain, sir, I know I tried to—'

'Why is it impossible?'

Elinor trembled and the baby stopped sucking. She whispered a name.

Saint-Amant, white with rage, slapped her face. Elinor began to cry and the baby joined her.

'It is not true!' cried Saint-Amant. 'And you never said so before!'

Elinor sobbed.

'I swear by the Virgin, sir.'

Saint-Amant shuddered. It was always said that this happened. Who knew? And there might even be others . . . he tried to calm his breathing. 'And will he not . . . that is to say . . . will he, does he make provision for his child? Surely.'

'I expect he would if he knew,' said Elinor without bitterness. 'But he will not learn from me, sir.'

'The Church must be grateful to you, Elinor,' said Saint-Amant after a pause, deflected from his thoughts for a moment by her generosity, but even as he spoke, he considered how what he had just heard might affect the future of his own son. 'If you married your lover in Caromb, with a good dowry, would he accept two children, this one and mine, if, say, something were to happen to me . . . an accident?'

'I think that Rostain – my lover, he's a swineherd, sir – would accept that, if you made it possible for us to live.'

'You think a purse with golden florins would decide him?'

Elinor nodded. Thanks be to the Virgin, who had once more protected her. 'I'm ready, sir, for whenever you bring him. I have plenty of milk for two.'

The baby woke Marie at dawn. It was nearly summer and the dawns came early. She rose and placed a pitcher of water by her sleeping husband's side. She fed Bonjoue, then tied him with a strip of cloth to her back where he would be contented all day. Then she set the big, torn straw hat on her head, the one Astruc had worn and went out into the beanfield. She talked to Bonjoue all day, calling him by the Jewish name Astruc had called his son. Roger sat on his chair all day, while she had to hoe the rows of vegetables which Astruc had planted, alone. There was too much work.

At midday, tired, she gave the child her breast and made her way back to the house, where she drank a pitcher of water and shared some bread and onions with

Roger. Today, for once, he was not rambling, but contemplated her and Bonjoue for a long time. What had he in mind? Was he plotting some harm to herself and her child? Perhaps today she might get an answer to her questions. Or perhaps he would ask the questions – whose child is this?

'Where have you been all this time, Roger?' she said, as she had done many times before; and for the first time, he replied.

'We went towards Avignon, Marie, but not directly. Give me water, I'm still thirsty. What we did . . . well, for instance, when we got to Malaucene, we went to attack the town hall, to burn the tax records. They fought back, of course, and that was when my leg got broken. A barber set it, but not well. They pulled me on a cart, the comrades. The plan was to go to Avignon, get to the palace and seize as many of the Pope's possessions as we could – his and his cardinals' and his priests – and such money and jewels as we could seize – and give it to the poor people. They feast on course after course of meats – did you know that the Pope and his cardinals eat a banquet every week? And wear rings with precious stones? And drink fine wines, and lie with all the women they want?'

Marie listened. Nothing, yet, about her, about the father of her child.

Roger wiped his face with his sleeve. The fever left him no peace. 'We advanced on Avignon but they heard about us coming, their blood froze, they'd heard the tales about us – give me some wine, Marie, my fever is bad today and my leg is sore. Then, the Pope was crafty, he made an edict that no one was to give us bread on pain of death. Next, he ordered his soldiers to attack us. But we never got as far as the walls of Avignon; the Pope's men went out to search for us and they got us at Vedene – men like us, Marie, but they wore the Pope's colours. We were hungry, very hungry . . . oh, I remember the hunger. People had fed us until then, you see, because we fought the Church and the rich on their behalf but now they didn't dare. People were for us, for the shepherds, until that cursed edict of the Pope's. At Vedene they shut the doors in our faces.'

Roger's face, furrowed and lined with pain, looked pitiful to Marie. Into her mind came the face of the young man she had married, smooth with youth, and ignorant of the terrible future.

'So, when the Pope's men came, we first invited them to join us shepherds. Instead they seized our leaders and hanged them from the trees in the square. We fought them with our cudgels and knives but they had swords and daggers. I think they were hired men, from Italy. They hung thirty of my comrades that day, and our captains and sergeants were killed, so I was told, but, being sick, I crept into a cellar in Vedene and stayed there. I had this fever . . . I remember next that all the soldiers had gone. I slipped in and out of that fever which still plagues me – a woman looked after me, and sometimes I worked a little and I begged, sometimes. The Pope, curse him, got the better of us. So here I am, Marie, the worse for wear.'

Marie nodded, and went back to the hot fields and her hoeing. Briefly she thought about Astruc, but that was over, finished, a glimpse into a life that she would never have now. God gave, God took away, blessed be His name. She had better have the child baptised – in the name of Jean.

That evening she sat opposite Roger, smiling at the baby. She had decided that he was too weak, and too confused, to harm either her or her child.

'Tomorrow I will have the boy baptised, Roger.'

He hadn't heard her. He was back with the shepherds, roaming the roads of the *comtat*. 'They promised us a thousand years of happiness, Marie, and it was for that to happen that we killed those who would stand in our way.'

'Roger—'

'We were a band called together by God. Some of the band really were shepherds, but there were soldiers too and some of our leaders were priests who had been rejected by the Church, for the Church itself is impious, a priest among us said so; and there were even two nobles among us. Our leaders said that the time would come when all were equal, when the rich, proud Pope would give his riches to the poor! Was Jesus rich?'

'I'm going to market tomorrow, and to have Jean baptised.'

'Leave me bread, wife,' said Roger in a whining voice. 'I beg you, Marie, do not leave me without bread. You and I, we worked for bread all our lives, and never sure of not starving.'

'We have enough,' she said gently.

'We have more than enough,' he said with a sly smile, tapping his belt. She had noticed the heavy purse sewn into it when she first washed him. If you touch it, I'll kill you! he had said to her then.

'Nobles' money. They cried out, they screamed for mercy in their great houses, the *seigneurs* and their ladies! Their last hour had come . . . don't cry for them, Marie, they should have led better lives! Money – I have enough.'

But he had not given her any.

At the market, she sold her produce. The money from the eggs alone bought baptism from a priest, to whom she explained that the father, Roger, was ill and that the boy should be christened Jean. On the way home she dismounted in a secluded dell, where the mule could browse in the shade and gave the child her breast and, watching him gurgling and smiling, remarked again his bilberry eyes and resolved, now that her son had been christened Jean, to call him Bonjoue, as Astruc had wished.

Chapter 21

Astruc was holding Bonjoue in his arms, trying to quieten him while Marie was still asleep. He woke to find Blanchette standing by his bed in Thoros's room, hushing her crying baby. Bonjoue, Bonjoue, thought Astruc, desolate. Blanchette stared at him coldly.

'I hardly slept, Astruc, thinking about the circumcision. I know it's early morning, but till we come to a decision I can get no rest. Now, you said last night—'

'And I'll say the same this morning. It is the husband's task to circumcise.'

'The father's task.'

'You tell me he can't,' said Astruc, yawning. 'Isn't it time you told me why not?'

'What about you?' countered Blanchette, stroking the blond fluff on Joseph's head. 'Have I asked you what you did while you were away?'

'If you want to know,' he said, sitting up in Thoros's bed, 'I'll tell you now.'

'Oh,' said Blanchette wearily, 'I don't know why I asked you. I don't want to know. You will divorce me after the circumcision, that is your right, but there's one thing I will not permit; I want my son for myself, you're not to touch him.'

'Blanchette, I would be happy to—'

'No. As for the circumcision, the law says that it must be carried out by a Jew, and one who is used to the operation. You are not used to it, and you are not the child's father. I have chosen Vidal Farrusol who has four sons and has done it four times.'

On the day of the delayed circumcision – it should have been done eight days after the boy's birth – there was a crowd in the *escole*. Word had got out that the baby was different, special in some way.

The chairs near the ark stood ready, covered with velvet cloth. Vidal Ferrusol washed his hands once more, drying them, with their long sharp nails, on a small towel which Lea, the boy's grandmother, handed him, and picked up the knife with its polished copper handle. Joseph, who had just been bathed in a bowl, in view of all spectators, was lifted out and dried by Blanchette. David, the godfather, and Vidal now stood side by side, with Jessue and Astruc near them. Jessue called the ritual words which began the ceremony, 'Bring what we need!'

A group of boys stepped forward. One carried the candlestick bearing twelve small candles representing the twelve tribes of Israel. Another balanced a tray with several brimming goblets of wine, another held a plate of sand, and another a cup of olive oil in which soaked narrow strips of cloth to bandage the wound. The boys arranged themselves around Vidal; they were here to learn from him, and would in turn, one day, receive a fat fee for a circumcision.

Lea had spiced wine ready, so that the mixture of alcohol and herbs would succour the parents of the child, in case they were distressed by the sufferings of their boy. The godfather, David, now took his place on one of the velvet-covered chairs, while Vidal faced him and began to chant the prescribed verses from Exodus, after the crossing of the Red Sea:

I will sing to the Lord, for He has risen up in triumph,
The horse and the rider He has hurled into the sea
The Lord is my refuge and my defence –

And, as he sang for many minutes, Blanchette and her mother handed the child to David. This was the signal for all those in the body of the *escole* to rise. David resumed his seat carefully, holding Joseph, and as he sat down a cry went up from all throats, '*Baruch habba!* Blessed is he who is among us!' This was to welcome the prophet Elijah, who, when a boy is circumcised, sits down in the empty chair next to the godfather to see that the ceremony is carried out properly, which is why, when the two chairs are hung with velvet before the ceremony, the godfather must be present and must say clearly, so as to be heard by Elijah's spirit, 'This is the seat of the prophet Elijah.'

If this is not done at least three days before the ceremony, the prophet may not attend the ceremony, a very bad omen indeed.

Vidal took up the knife and pronounced, 'Glory to God, king of the universe, whose commandments we follow and who has ordered us to circumcise this child.'

And as he spoke he cut a small piece from Joseph's foreskin and threw it onto the plate of sand. Blanchette was trembling. Handing the knife to a bystander, Vidal took a goblet of wine, took a sip and spat it out into the child's face. Joseph, who had begun crying when Vidal used the knife, now set up a great howl. Vidal proceeded to suck the wound which had started bleeding, to stop the flow; and then he spat out the blood into the goblet of wine and onto the plate of sand.

When the bleeding stopped he seized the foreskin with his long nails and pushed it back, which evidently made Joseph suffer, and his piercing cries pulled Blanchette towards him. Several hands held her back and Lea put her arms around her daughter.

'Nearly finished, Lolo. He won't remember it, I swear,' she whispered.

Already Vidal was wrapping the strips of material softened by the oil around the wound, while David, who had held the squirming child during the whole procedure, wrapped him in his clothes. 'Praised be thou, Eternal God, who has ordered us to keep the promise of Abraham,' recited Vidal and the *escole* filled with the sound of the reply from a hundred throats:

'As this child inherits the promise made to Abraham, let him also observe the law of Moses and live honourably and in virtue.'

Joseph's screams abated while David spoke to him softly, and Blanchette, now that it was over, burst into tears. Vidal was washing his mouth and hands, then took another goblet of wine and blessed it. 'God of our fathers, strengthen this child and preserve it in the care of its parents and enable it to take its place among the people of Israel. Let the father find joy in the fruit of his loins—'

Blanchette was seized by a cough, or a sneeze, or a sob. Vidal waited for the paroxysm to pass, then continued. 'And his mother in the fruit of her womb. As it is written. The prophet also said: I see you and you are lying in your blood; you shall live.'

He dipped his finger into that goblet of wine into which he had spat the blood which he had sucked from the baby's wound, and passed the finger three times over Joseph's mouth, just opening for another loud cry.

'The blood will protect him and give him long life,' Lea murmured into Blanchette's ear.

Blanchette took Joseph from David's arms and thanked him. Astruc stood close to his wife, intent on showing that they were a united family.

A feast followed and Astruc was congratulated on the birth of his son. Asked – over and over – where he had been, he told his tale, without mentioning that the family of kind Christians who had hidden him consisted of one person, Marie. The rabbi said a special prayer of thanks for this Christian family.

After the guests had gone, neither Blanchette nor Astruc found words to speak to each other, and fell into an exhausted sleep in their separate rooms.

Astruc, waking next morning in Thoros's room remembered the mornings at Marie's house, the quiet and the light. Here the tall houses opposite thrust their deep shadows into the room. A little rectangle of light fell on Thoros's books and a few clothes. Astruc felt the absence of Thoros, the ache of loss; if he had not sent word, he must be dead.

He heard Joseph cry, and began thinking about him, Blanchette and divorce. Yet, since he had resumed his life in the Street, he might as well stay with Blanchette, and beget more sons. But, Marie . . . he escaped from his thoughts into the morning prayers and ablutions, then went down into the shop, opened the splintery wooden shutters, pushed away clothes on which Blanchette had been working, set cups and platters and what remained from last night's feast on the table. Blanchette, carrying Joseph, came down the stairs looking pale and unwilling to talk. She seemed shy with him this morning. But it was time she spoke frankly to him, and he began by asking her how she had managed without him, without Thoros.

'Very well.'

'How did you sell the clothes you made?'

'Old Jacob took them into Avignon for me and sold them.'

'That's a better idea than peddling them in the countryside like I did! And did you make enough money?'

'Jacob and I shared what there was, but I had enough because I also had a purse left once a month with the porter. At first I thought it was from you, then I . . . I realised it was from Joseph's father.'

Astruc suddenly seized on something.

'If he – the father – left a purse with the porter, it is because he's outside! Not from the Street.'

Blanchette's face closed, she turned pale and shrank back as far as she could from him. 'Yes, he lives outside the street . . . not only is Joseph a bastard, but his father is a Christian. Divorce me, but don't touch the child,' she said, in a low voice.

'You think I would harm him? I couldn't, Blanchette.'

She nodded. 'No one knows, though they may guess.'

'I came back at the right time. No one will know if we live together as man and wife.'

Thrusting towards speech came the thought that he had done the same as Blanchette, he could tell her about Marie and Bonjoue, although her sin was greater in the eyes of the law. But his weakness whispered to him that, if he said nothing, he would at least have a wife who would fear and obey him from now on.

'I understand,' he said. 'I accept Joseph.'

Blanchette looked at him in surprise, then smiled and began to laugh in disbelief and finally cried with relief. He watched her face change from one emotion to the next till at last she got up, handed him the baby in order to put her arms around him and kiss him.

'You are a good man and a forgiving husband,' she said.

He blushed and she observed his blush, but if she began to guess at the cause of his forgiveness, there was no chance to say more, for old Jacob the rag gatherer came into the shop at this moment. Humming a tune, he winked at Astruc. 'Together again! That's nice. They say you killed a Christian, Astruc! They say you attacked him first. How I laughed. You're a joker, Astruc. You wouldn't attack another Jew, let alone a Christian!'

Astruc looked at the old man, and something in his manner warned old Jacob that this strong young man he was mocking was not the Astruc he used to know. And Astruc looked at Jacob and remembered that without him Blanchette would not have sold her clothes, and that Jacob, old as he was, might be jealous of him, Astruc, whose return deprived Jacob of the protection he had been able to give the most beautiful woman in the Street. 'Take me into the city with you, Jacob, and show me what you do. I'd like to learn from you,' said Astruc and saw the old man smile.

Chapter 22

Blanchette watched her husband moving around the room, looking for a sack in which to put the rags. He seemed so much bigger, he filled the small room. Her feelings confused her; she thought she had finished with her marriage, but this was a very different man from the one she had married.

'I almost forgot,' said Astruc suddenly. 'I lost my hat – I can't leave the Street without one.'

'I'll make you a *rouelle*,' said Blanchette, and took a piece of stuff from a heap she was sorting.

'Yellow moiré silk,' said Jacob, fingering the stuff. 'Woven in Lyon, a courtier's *surcot*. Make me one too, Blanchette.'

Blanchette cut a circle into the silk, the breadth of a hand, and cut the centre from it in the shape of an 'O'. She sewed it onto Astruc's grey cloak.

'Make one for me, then I won't have to wear my yellow hat,' whined Jacob. 'I would rather wear a *rouelle*. Ah, I long for the Messiah to come if only to dress as I please. If I don't wear my hat, I'll get fined again and I won't pay and the *baylons* will have to pay for me and that's another telling-off I shall get. Don't annoy the Christians, Jacob, you're bringing us into disrepute with the Christians, Jacob! Who is the only good Christian, Astruc? The Pope, blessed is his name, I can't complain, he lets me get on with my business.'

Jacob got his *rouelle*, and he and Astruc slung their empty sacks across their shoulders and walked through the Street. They stood for a moment in the archway of the gatehouse. The crowd was as dense outside as within.

'Living with Christians, eh?' said Jacob slyly. 'I expect you can tell a few stories, eh? You ate pork, Astruc, didn't you?'

'Come on, Jacob, show me how you deal with Christians, you're with them all day, too.'

'Very true, Astruc. Now listen, young man. There are seven churchyards in Avignon, for there are seven churches. We are going to chose one which is—' he squinted up at the sun, '—in the shade now. Tell me – how many gates are there in the wall around the city?'

'Twelve,' said Astruc. 'Why?'

'There. You pedlars know all the routes out of town. And I know all the churchyards, and for good reason. We'll start with St Didiers's.'

At St Didier's Astruc was amazed at the crowd swarming over graves and tombstones. The Jews' cemetery was a sacred place, unlike the resting-place of the Christian dead which was treated by all with great familiarity. People met, bought and sold, and haggled loudly.

'Why are there so many here?' asked Astruc.

'Where else should they go? There's little space anywhere. The palace sends soldiers now and then to clear the churchyard – an insult to religion, they say – selling cattle, and worse, on holy ground. When I say worse, I've seen fornication, adultery and even murder. But the Pope doesn't mind me.'

'How do you know?'

'He said that the little people who sell and buy do no harm and they may use the churchyard.'

A young man approached Jacob and passed over some clothes, and Astruc saw that they were almost new. The vendor whispered in Jacob's ear insistently, took a good many coins of Jacob's and disappeared.

'Did you notice the state of the clothes,' said Jacob. 'A bit of luck, there. It seems that two smartly dressed messengers from Orleans, having finished their business at the palace yesterday decided to dine well. And they went to sleep in their beds at the Golden Fleece last night; but they woke up in this very churchyard, naked as the day they were born . . . look out!'

A great cry had gone up from the fish stall as a rider wearing papal livery, on a huge black mare, rode through the crowd, scattering people and fish onto the churned ground, recently turned for burial. Jacob was knocked onto a tombstone. Astruc lifted him bodily and carried him to the churchyard wall, where he wheezed and panted and invoked the psalms.

'Shall we return to the Street, Jacob?'

'Are you tired? I'm not!'

They made their way from market to market, from the tripe-sellers at Saint-Pierre, the vegetable-sellers in Saint-Symphorien, money-changers, dealers in precious stones, dealers in new and old stuff and clothes. Sometimes Jacob bought, sometimes sold. Astruc observed, and thought of the silent woods and fields.

'One more,' said Jacob. 'The curia bury their dead here. Ah, there is a funeral taking place. See them digging? They often dig through an old coffin, then they pile the bones over there. No, my dear,' he said to a young woman who had seized Astruc's sleeve. 'We're busy.'

Astruc followed the old man, but saw that the woman had joined two others who were laughing at him, and as he looked he saw her make an obscene gesture. Sitting on a flat tombstone, four men were playing cards, shouting to be heard above a dozen bleating sheep hemmed up against the church wall next to them. The woman who had pulled at Astruc's sleeve had found a client and Astruc saw them disappear into a hut.

'A good place for tools and coffins,' said Jacob, 'and goings on. You know what Christians are.'

'The same as Jews,' said Astruc impatiently.

'Here's Jeanne, now, Astruc. She's in and out of the palace, a palace rat we call her. What have you got for me, Jeanne?'

Jeanne handed over small objects: a cup, some forks, a pitcher, shoes, a waistcoat.

'And where does she find these things? Belonging to drunken messengers, Jacob?' asked Astruc. He felt a disgust with the crowd, with the haggling and the smells. Jeanne pocketed Jacob's coins and melted into the crowd.

'Not she, not Jeanne. She sells herself to the palace guards, but that's not enough to keep her from starving. She goes to the hospices, they give her what the sick leave behind. Come this way, I'm ready for a rest.'

Jacob led the way into a dark alley, so narrow that they could touch both walls as they stumbled over heaps of ordure, but within a minute's walk the tall walls receded into a tiny square and here water welled up into a stone basin with a step on either side. Astruc, who was carrying both sacks, put them down and held his wrists in the water, waiting for the coolness to travel to his heart and head, then Jacob said a prayer and drank in great gulps. They rested as the sounds of the crowd dwindled to a murmur in this secret place.

'I would not ask to live forever,' said Jacob, after a long silence. 'But I do not want to go before I have seen the Messiah.'

'Is he coming to Avignon?'

'Of course he is coming, and we will know in Avignon. When he comes he will work miracles. He will have his wedding, and there will be a great feast to mark it. It must be in Avignon, for this is the most important town in the world, isn't it? Ah, we will all be great lords then! And the Christians will be our servants. But all will be happy and contented, the corn will grow where it has not been sown and the rain will come when we ask for it . . . and we will all . . . all . . .' His voice died away and his head dropped onto his chest as he slept.

When Jacob woke, a hot fetid wind had sprung up. Wearily the old man explained that they must still visit the hospices, for it would be the Sabbath tomorrow and then the Christians' Sunday; two days without work.

They made their way to the leprosy hospital of Saint-Lazare, to the convent of the De La Major brethren, and at last to the hospice by the bridge of St Benezet, and at each stop the porter gave Jacob rags, and sometimes clothes.

'They have been washed,' said Jacob. 'The brothers prepare a tincture which kills the poisons left behind by unclean and diseased bodies.'

The sacks were heavy now.

'Shall we return to the Street?'

'One more,' said the old man, 'and it will be worth it.'

He stopped in a quiet street, in front of a high door, above which Astruc read the inscription HOUSE OF THE REPENTANT SISTERS OF ST MARY MAGDALENE.

A very old man answered their knock.

'Jacob,' said the old Jew. 'Come to ask whether you have anyone new.'

'Discretion forbids a reply.'

He winked and closed the door. Astruc picked up the sacks and prepared to go home.

'Not yet, Astruc.'

Five minutes later, the old porter opened the door and handed Jacob a large basket. 'I want that basket back, and do not tarry too long or you'll find I've gone to paradise.'

'God bless you, I shall not tarry,' said Jacob. 'Here or in paradise, we'll meet soon.'

'If I go first, I'll put in a good word for you. And God bless you too.'

'A friend,' murmured Jacob. 'No, don't look into the basket till we get home.'

And there, in the Street, Blanchette, Lea, Astruc and Jacob sat down that evening to the Friday evening meal. The *shamas* had passed earlier, blowing his ram's-horn and alternating that sad and savage sound with his cry: 'Light up! Light up! The sabbath begins!'

Astruc, tired and dispirited, thought how he had longed for the sabbath meal among his own people, and now that I have what I wanted, he thought, I wish I were with Marie.

'Let's open the basket, now!' cried Blanchette, and they crowded around it while Blanchette exclaimed over every item, some made from silks and velvets, some encrusted with gold thread. Astruc watched, bemused.

'I'll tell you, Astruc,' said Jacob. 'It's like this. Ricau, the old porter, and I were friends many years ago when he was a groom in the stables of the Pope – not this one, the one before. He is seventy-five years of age. That is why he is allowed to hold the post of porter at the House of the Sisters. He guards forty young women in that convent, all young and beautiful. They're courtesans, but ladies, not like Jeanne – the palace rat – and some were very rich. They are there once they have repented of the life they led. When they first come, they are isolated so they may reflect. After eight days, and if the woman is still of the same mind, she may ask to be admitted to the sisterhood. She then hears the Mass of the Holy Ghost and speaks her vows, promising obedience, poverty and chastity.'

'Why?' asked Blanchette.

'Hush,' said her mother.

'And then,' continued Jacob, 'she is protected from the world behind an iron grille.'

Later that night, Astruc lay beside Blanchette in the bed where their marriage had begun. They had made love and now lay on the narrow bed, listening to the sounds from Joseph's cot, and the flies buzzing behind the nailed-up window.

I feel that I have betrayed Marie, thought Astruc, and yet this is my lawful wife. Surely Marie will not be sleeping with Roger . . . surely, he's too ill, too old. At least they will not be making love.

'I wonder if Thoros is alive.' It was her nightly question, her scratching at the wound she would not allow to heal. 'If I knew that he was dead, would I feel less unhappy?' And Blanchette knew that without hope, there would be no life for her.

The wind rattled the shutters, and curses and shouting rose from the well of the house. Neither of them could bring themselves to say what they wanted, but after a while Blanchette said she would feed the child, perhaps he would sleep better in her arms, afterwards . . .

Gratefully, Astruc rose and sought his bed in Thoros's old room.

Chapter 23

The large room faced north and was cool but even so Le Gor felt particularly irritable this afternoon. His eyes itched, and his conscience gave him no rest. A game with Laurent, who had become a constant companion, would keep black thoughts at bay, for a while at least.

He watched Laurent approach. The barber had cut Laurent's hair and beard neatly, and his face had put on some flesh, but his body was still that of a scarecrow. Yet Le Gor noticed that he walked with more assurance these days, and his black deep-set eyes were alert.

Le Gor's initial desire to solve an intriguing puzzle had turned to real concern for this stray creature who tantalised Le Gor by seeming about to declare himself – yet could not do so. With Christ's help, thought Le Gor, I can create a future for him even if he has no past.

Geraud, strong as an ox, carried in a heavy chessboard in the form of a one-legged oak table, ready set with all the pieces carved from ivory and ebony. Laurent bowed to Le Gor and took his place at the table, while Le Gor rubbed his eyes, sore and swollen.

Laurent was looking at him intently. For a moment Le Gor imagined him as a lawyer, or a soldier or even a cardinal; there was definitely a change in him. Yet Laurent was still too sombre, still too sad; the transformation – if it were to happen – was still a long way off and he must continue to show patience.

'I'll take white,' said Le Gor. Geraud hovered, waiting to be dismissed, but the cardinal told him to stay and watch the game, try to learn. Geraud yawned, and watched the moves vacantly.

'Do you think you may have played before?' said Le Gor to Laurent. 'I have a theory—'

'You're going to lose that pawn, my lord,' remarked Laurent, but the cardinal seemed to have lost interest in the game and Laurent won easily, remarking that he thought that his lordship's many cares prevented him from giving his attention to the game.

'The problems of chess pale before the riddle you pose, Laurent,' said Le Gor. 'Now what about you, Geraud? A game? No? '

Geraud eagerly carried the chessboard away and brought a flagon of Baume de Venise. The cardinal took a sip. 'I want to try this theory out, Laurent. Should I speak a name, or mention an object or a person, which calls forth an echo in your mind, even a faint echo, tell me. Yes, you may stay, Geraud, this is certainly part of the education which I promised your father you would receive in this house.'

The three men sat in ornate armchairs, carved with swan's necks and heads and painted in white and gold. Geraud's robust body filled his chair entirely, Le Gor seemed fluid in his crimson robe and Laurent, awkwardly hunched into his grey gown, appeared to hover rather than to sit.

'Baldo degli Ubaldi,' said Le Gor suddenly, 'a great civil lawyer, teaches at the university here in Avignon. Well?'

Laurent shook his head.

'John of Legnano, the great canon lawyer from Bologna?'

Laurent shook his head again.

'You need not shake your head every time!' said Le Gor impatiently.

'No, my lord,' said Laurent, looking down.

'Look at me, I cannot see your face!' said Le Gor sharply. 'It is for you to recollect what manner of man you were, what station in life God had reserved for you! I hope I'm carrying out God's purpose. I am trying to help you!'

'I am very grateful, my lord . . .'

'I can't see you properly, there seems to be a mist before my eyes . . .' In a frenzy of irritation Le Gor plucked at his eyelids.

'Your eyesight is changing,' said Laurent suddenly in a firm voice. 'Glass can be ground and mounted on gold wire, one before each eye, to fasten behind your ears. With one of these—'

'Yes!' cried Geraud. 'The architect Pison has those.'

'Very well,' said Le Gor, smiling, relieved. 'I will send for some. As for my theory, Laurent; I now think you may be a victim of learning.'

Laurent looked up, eagerly it seemed to Le Gor. The cardinal was gratified. 'Why do men throng this city? For gold and for preferment, for learning and scholarship. You are neither merchant nor peasant nor soldier. You are a scholar. Fill up the glasses, Geraud.

'At our university here, study for the doctorate takes ten years. How can a man finance ten years of study? He must receive benefices from a patron, of course. You sought – like all the others – help from the Pope's generosity. But there are too many like you, working through the night, hoping for preferment. What was your field of study? Civil law? Canon law? Or Decretals, perhaps – those, Geraud, are papal judgements which will form new precedents – or Clementines, collections of laws issued by our present Holy Father, or maybe the Extravagantes, so-called . . . Geraud! Where are you going?'

'A call of nature,' said Geraud, hurrying away.

'He will never learn anything,' said Le Gor angrily, 'except new songs. Now Gui, my page who served here before Geraud—,' he fell silent for a moment. 'Where was I? So, night after night you read in the Palace library so as to outdo other scholars and be noticed in the throng. Your very industry is your undoing and at last your brain, burdened beyond endurance, falters and plunges you into sickness. Well? I can't see your expression.'

'I am very interested to hear about the university here,' replied Laurent. 'The concept of a university seems familiar.'

'You were never a clerk? A priest? A notary? Or secretary?'

'No, my lord. All the apparatus of the Church is unknown to me, though study is a familiar field.'

Le Gor remained silent, returning in his mind to his own troubles at the papal court. Clement was aware of the strength and the weaknesses of his cardinals, but for the moment the Pope's mind was occupied with other matters; he was talking of another crusade, he was being urged to return to Rome and resisting. Rome seemed a dangerous place indeed. Not long ago the papal legate di Ceccano had only just escaped death at the hands of two assassins while making a pilgrimage to the great churches of Rome. Clement was right to stay in Avignon. And as long as the Holy Father had plenty to occupy his mind, he would not examine Le Gor's actions too closely. Surely.

Le Gor's gaze, unfocused for the space of these reflections returned to the dark face of Laurent, sitting silently before him. But what was this expression, alert, questioning, which the cardinal had never seen on his face before; it pierced Le Gor, as though Laurent could read his mind. Involuntarily the cardinal put his hand up to shield his face, then covered his mouth as though he had been yawning. An uncontrollable shiver ran through his body. Could Laurent be, might he be an informer who had been placed in the cardinal's residence to gain his confidence and having now done so would report to his master at the palace; such incidents as the attempt at black magic, or the making of gold? This was no poor pathetic victim, a household pet, familiar, harmless, but a man who was waiting, listening, reporting to the palace. An intolerable thought.

Le Gor rose, a formidable figure in his brilliant robe, trembling with hate and fear. 'I do not know who you are, but I can guess who sent you,' he said in a low hissing voice. 'Your spying will cease, from today. Go where you please, viper, whom I took into my household for Christ's sake.'

He took a menacing step towards Laurent, screwing up his face in order to see him more clearly and pointing to the door in a wild gesture, he cried out. 'I saw you staring at me! You thought I would not detect you! When you thought I wasn't watching, your face changed! Out! Leave my house before I have you thrown out!'

Geraud came bounding into the room and stopped short, astonished at what he found. Laurent had risen from his chair and was standing facing Le Gor. The two

men were very close to each other, for Laurent, instead
of fleeing the cardinal's wrath, had walked up to him. Le
Gor's face was suffused with blood and his arm was
raised to strike Laurent.

'My lord,' said Laurent quietly. 'You are distressed.
Please follow me to the window.'

Le Gor, totally surprised, let his arm drop by his side.

'I will leave your residence where I have been so
generously cared for immediately, but with great sorrow,'
said Laurent, putting his arm around Le Gor's shoulders, 'as soon as I have looked at your eyes. We will need
the shutters opened, Geraud.'

Geraud, as in a dream, moved to open the shutters,
and the cardinal allowed Laurent to guide him to the
window. Le Gor seemed not to notice Laurent's guiding
arm around his shoulders, and it was as though Laurent
was the commanding figure; Le Gor, for all his crimson
robe, the sufferer. Geraud thought that he would
remember this scene all his life, however long.

At the window, Laurent looked deep into Le Gor's eyes.

'It is as I thought. The tears cannot flow across your
eyes and wash them, as they should, because you have an
impediment, perhaps an infection, in the tear sacs. In
both, yes, in both your eyes, my lord. A surgeon-physi-
cian can, with the Lord's blessing, make incisions so that
the tears can flow again.' He paused, then added in a
firm and joyous voice, 'I say this because I am both a
physician and a surgeon.'

Le Gor lifted his face up and the two men embraced.

'Glory be to God!' cried Le Gor.

'Glory be to God,' echoed Laurent, and Geraud lifted
up his glorious, sonorous voice and sang a four-fold Amen.

Chapter 24

The ox-cart tipped from side to side, hobbling along the rutted road from rock to hole, then grinding along the sandy stretches. The peasant urging on his ox was on his way home from Avignon, and the cart stank of the pigs which he had sold there. Astruc, sitting on a wooden board above the evil-smelling straw, clung to the side of the cart, keeping his bag of clothes to sell well above the sodden straw below him.

The cart was going west, not east. East were roads to Sorgue, Bedarrides, Entraigues, Monteux, where Astruc knew every path, abandoned shepherds' huts, friendly porters at the gatehouse of abbeys and convents where the fierce dogs were to be avoided. And if he had left the city by one of the usual gates to go east of Avignon, as he used to do, he would have walked without stopping until he reached Marie's house. So he was going west.

He had trudged all morning and, meeting no one on the lonely roads the new yellow hat stayed in his pocket. When an ox-cart overtook him, Astruc had accepted the invitation to ride in it, in exchange for something in Astruc's bag; the peasant liked the look of a leather jerkin.

'If you give me the jerkin, that'll do, as long as it is leather. Fair exchange?'

'Yes.'

In front of Astruc the peasant was cursing the ox. Although there was shade among the trees and shrubs bordering the track, the heat, combined with the stink of pig's detritus was nauseating. Once the sun reached the cart, Astruc thought, he might hand over the jerkin and walk. Weeks cooped up in the Street had given him a longing for the freedom of the woods and fields, away from Blanchette, alone with his thoughts. Such as: Where was Thoros? Had he loved Blanchette? His wife and brother lovers . . . if true, he found the thought was bearable, as nothing compared to the pain of losing Marie, which stabbed him with every breath as the ox-cart travelled through wild country, with the river shimmering through the tangle of trees and bushes, and here and there a proper view of the broad expanse of water.

'That's the island of Barthelasse,' shouted the peasant, pointing at the river, 'there's La Grande Montagne. Another half hour and we'll be out of the shade. After that, it's not far to my village.'

And then I'll have to put my hat on, thought Astruc. His new hat was a disgusting object to Astruc. He had watched Blanchette cut up the yellow linen and sew a large brim onto the crown. The thought of wearing it after the freedom of working in Marie's fields like a Christian, no yellow hat, just a peasant, was hard to contemplate.

While Blanchette sewed his hat she had worn a dress of green silk, with ballooning sleeves of green and white, and twenty-five gold buttons from neck to hem which she had discovered among the clothes from the Penitent Sisters, and now she wore it all the time: she had fed the child in that dress, emptied the slops, made a fire and cooked soup, swept the room in that dress, and resumed her sewing in the dusty, dark work room like a lush green plant in a desolate spot. Yes, she was beautiful. But it was Thoros she wanted.

And if he, Astruc, went back to Marie?

There was sun ahead. The peasant would get a surprise once they had left the mountain shade behind. Astruc shrugged. Nowadays, he feared no one.

At the brow of the hill, the sun struck them with full force, and Astruc put on his yellow hat. The peasant's eyes, small and intelligent like his pigs', fixed on Astruc's head covering with an odd expression, and he suddenly stopped the cart under an oak by the wayside. While the ox browsed on the lush spring grass, the two men sat down in the shade and the peasant offered Astruc a drink of water from his leather bottle. Astruc waited.

'Last year,' said the peasant, 'my wife Dousseline and I went to Avignon for the Pope's Easter procession. Dousseline took ill. When blood issued from her nose and mouth, they told me at the inn to get the doctor who attended the innkeeper – an excellent doctor – and his name was Salamon Mosse from the Street of the Jews. I got to the door in the archway through which you pass into the Street – do you know it?'

'I live there,' said Astruc.

'The porter stopped us because, he said, during Holy Week the Jews are not allowed out for their own protection. But then he said that, for a grave case, for my poor wife, he was permitted to allow a doctor out. But since Salamon Mosse was attending a woman in labour, another doctor came with me to the inn, and he tested Dousseline's urine and then he bled her. I remember the bells ringing and ringing, for it was Holy Week. Dousseline begged us to stop the bells, she was in agony, but what could we do?'

'Did she live?' ventured Astruc after a long pause. Flies hummed around the head and tail of the ox. The peasant turned to stare past Astruc, and shook his head. 'That doctor fought for her life all day and into the night, neither resting nor taking food himself. I shall remember his name always: it was Thoros Bonivassin. You are a Jew, pedlar, and I have no quarrel with Jews. I don't need your leather jerkin – keep it.'

'My brother,' said Astruc. 'That was my brother Thoros. I was away from home when he went out one day, and never returned.'

'Well, pedlar, come and eat and drink in my house where, since my Dousseline died, there is no one but myself and the pigs and they don't care whether you're a Jew or a Christian as long as they have enough to eat and drink and that's how I feel. Your brother is a good man . . . you're a good man.'

He gave Astruc a pat on the shoulder and laughed. Then they climbed back into the cart and rumbled down hill towards Pujaut.

The sun was burning through the cypresses lining the road to Avignon along which Gui, dressed all in black, rode slowly. Now there were no peasants to bar his way. They were busy in the fields; their fields. Gui thought of their astonishment when he made his declaration, immediately after his father's funeral.

His hands rested slackly on the saddle and the horse, receiving no encouragement, stopped by the wayside and grazed. I don't want to go to Avignon either, thought Gui, and turned the horse onto a little track among chestnuts and olive trees. After his great decision, there was emptiness in his mind. He dropped from the horse's back, heavy as lead, in a little glade where bees hummed amid tufts of lavender and lay face down on a cushion of moss. He fell asleep at once.

When he opened his eyes his gaze was arrested by a pair of naked feet close to his head, human feet covered with a horny substance, almost like a horse's hoof. Gui's eyes travelled upwards to the hem of a rough black robe, held by a cord. Above that he saw the two points of a white beard, a long brown face and on the head a skull-cap. A monk? A hermit, far from habitations out here, probably.

'So you're not dead,' teased the hermit, smiling.

'No,' said Gui with a sigh. 'But I have just buried my father.'

'Sleep is the preparation for death,' said the hermit cheerfully. 'Death's kingdom is the whole earth. Life is only a dance which leads to the grave.'

Gui sat up. There might be help here.

'There is something which is troubling me, Father, and which I would like to put to you; from your words it seems you are concerned with death.'

The hermit nodded and settled on a low stone.

'I have had no one to whom I could speak since my father died and my thoughts are heavy to bear on my own. You are a man of God – will you listen to me?'

The hermit smiled and nodded again. 'God has placed me here to listen to you.'

'I was not with my father when he died. The peasant who was with him in the last minutes told me that my father did not speak. Our priest told me that, if my father did not say the prayer he will be condemned to misery for all eternity.'

'Set your mind at rest. If your father was not conscious, God will yet have accepted his thought. And you yourself would do well – in spite of your youth – to repeat those words each day when composing yourself for sleep. Even here, on a pillow of moss, for who knows whether you will wake in this world? Commit your soul to God! Say with me: Into Thy hands, O Lord, I commend my spirit. Thou hast redeemed me, O Lord, Thou God of truth.'

Gui murmured these words which should have been on the dying man's lips; if he had spoken them, he would have passed into eternity in happiness. Gui wanted to believe, but he could not help remembering that his father's death had been caused by his religious beliefs. However, in his present state, any oracle was better than none, and so he turned to the smiling hermit again . . . what had he to smile about? Gui envied his peace of mind. 'I don't know what to do next.'

The hermit smiled even more broadly. 'You look as though you lead the life of a knight, with a house and land and peasants to serve you.'

'I have left my house, and given my land to the peasants.'

'Why?'

'God made me see the injustice of my position,' said Gui, 'But my action has left me in limbo.'

'You have put the need of others before your own. Your reward will be that your soul is redeemed and taken up to Paradise.'

'But now, Father, what should I do now? I have unfinished business in Avignon, something of which I am not proud, something I fear, Father—'

'Then go, face your fear. You will be in my prayers.
Keep me in yours.'

Gui watched the hermit move away, skipping across
the stony soil as lightly as a goat. The hermit's advice was
sound on prayer but shed no light on his coming ordeal.
How could it? Soon he would be in the cardinal's residence, among the mirrors, the pictures and statues, the
rich hangings, the silks and gold. The great house full of
shining memories for him; and the dark stables, where
Giacomo had violated him, humiliated him on the straw,
by the horse's hooves.

He called into his mind Le Gor himself: bold, strong,
clever and powerful, with his agile mind and great influence at the papal court. For many months Gui had shut
his mind against these memories, but now, painfully, he
allowed himself to remember that he had been much
loved, that he owed much to Le Gor, and that he had left
without a word, too humiliated to show himself or speak
of what Giacomo had done to him.

What would his punishment be? He had taken the
cardinal's horse. Some thieves had an ear or a fist cut off.
A robber, caught stealing from the chapel, was sewn into
a sack and drowned in the river. In Avignon a man and a
woman who had sworn an oath on the belly of the Blessed
Virgin had their tongues cut out. But, surely, Le Gor
would not make him submit to a punishment of this kind?

Wouldn't he? Le Gor had been betrayed.

Fear and conscience struggled in Gui's mind, as well
as the need to see the cardinal again and to ask his
forgiveness. As for Giacomo . . .

Gui mounted his horse. He was bringing the horse
back to Le Gor, so he wasn't a thief, was he, and he would

plead for forgiveness and, perhaps, be allowed to explain. But as for Giacomo, he would kill the bullying bastard and if thus he lost all chances of Paradise in the hereafter, he would find means of atoning . . . later.

The sun was setting as Gui slipped off the horse's back in front of the great gate let into the wall. After knocking, he glanced across the river at the thousand roofs of the city of Avignon, at so many heights and angles under the rock on which the massive palace glowered in the dusk, sombre and watchful.

'Gui of Montolieu,' he told the porter, whom he didn't know.

'My lord the Cardinal is indisposed. I am not to admit anyone.'

'I was his page,' Gui tried. 'He will want to see me.'

The porter glanced at Gui's black clothes, judged him to be a knight, set off for the inner apartments and returned in a while, to admit Gui and to call a servant to lead the horse to the stables. The stables . . . but that could wait, thought Gui, suddenly seized with excitement and fear. His heart thudded as he ran up the shallow marble steps of the great staircase, dimly lit by candles set into niches all the way up. A valet stopped him outside the bedchamber and made Gui wait; impatient, apprehensive, on edge with the conflict within him and when the valet returned, nodding, he entered the great bedchamber, at last.

Three steps into the darkened room he stopped, trying to make out what he saw. Two figures, one recumbent with the bedclothes covering the face. His throat constricted, he appealed silently to the Virgin. Had he come too late?

Was that Le Gor? The other figure, bent over the bed, turned at the sound from the door and advanced towards Gui holding out his hand. 'I am Maître Thoros Bonivassin, physician and surgeon. The cardinal is my patient. He is recovering from operations on both eyes. Do not startle him; the slightest movement may loosen the sutures.'

Gui stared at the figure on the bed.

'Is it really Gui? My page, Gui?'

'My lord,' cried Gui with a sob. 'It's Gui, your page, returned to beg your forgiveness!'

'Let him come forward, Laurent.'

Thoros nodded 'You may go forward. Softly—'

Gui moved towards the bed. What he had taken for the sheet were bandages covering the cardinal's eyes, forehead and nose. Only the mouth was uncovered and from the lips came, so faint, Le Gor's voice . . .

'You see me here,' said Le Gor. 'I wish I could see you.'

He coughed and the doctor moved forward with a cup of water: 'You must not cough, my lord! Think of your eyes.'

The cardinal struggled to contain his cough as Gui watched. Was he about to lose another man he loved? Gui's thoughts were, briefly, entirely for himself. Then he remembered his rehearsed speech. 'I will explain, my lord—' he began.

'Yes, sometime,' said Le Gor in his faint voice. 'I have prayed many times for your return.'

Astonished, Gui remained silent. Then he began again. 'When you hear how it came about, my lord—'

'That is of no significance,' said Le Gor. 'When you cannot see, the dark is peopled by demons. I admit that

when I could see, there were demons, there were fears.
But I kept them at bay, Gui. Now, though, in the dark,
they overcome me. Yet sometimes they wrestle with
angels, and, since you are here, I assume that the angels
have obtained a victory. I did not deserve the Lord to be
merciful; yet He was.'

The cardinal fell silent. Tears ran down Gui's face.

Thoros whispered that they should leave, and drew
him out to the vestibule, where he told the valet to watch
over his master.

'What happened to my lord,' asked Gui, 'Maître
Laurent? Or is it Maître Thoros?'

'I am both Laurent and Thoros . . . An incision had to be
made in both tear sacs where an infection had lodged. My
lord has spoken of you many, many times, Master Gui, and
he will recover more quickly now that you have returned.'

'And his sight?'

'In God's hands.'

'Did you perform the operation, *maître*?'

'No. I called on Maître Guy de Chauliac, who attends
the Holy Father.'

'But you are my lord's physician?'

'Now, yes. He took me into his household when I was
sick and had lost my memory; he was the means by which
I recaptured my real self. I was Laurent, now I am Maître
Thoros Bonivassin again.'

It was dark, but then it was always dark, now. His thoughts
surged forward, unstoppable as they were unwelcome,
only briefly interrupted by the visit of Gui – was it really
Gui? Perhaps he had imagined it. I was, thought Le Gor,

one of the inner group around the Pope. Three years ago at the great conference at Avignon attended by delegates from France and England, Clement praised my wisdom. He relies on me for advice in the most delicate situations. Did I delude myself that I exercised real power then – and why, why? By degrees, I have been excluded from the small group of cardinals close to Clement. I am not the only one; Cardinal de Ceccano told me not long ago that Clement had rejected his advice and had thrown him out like a cracked vessel and had reduced him, he felt, to the level of a simple priest.

We cardinals were all simple priests once, thought Le Gor. But the red hat and the ring were powerful magnets. I strove, he told himself for the hundredth time, not only for myself but for the Holy Father and the Church.

A cough gathered in his throat. He must not cough. 'Water,' he croaked.

At once an arm lifted up his head and the cup was set against his lips. He drank two cups, conquered the spasm and lay down again, searching with his hand for the hand of the man who had devotedly sat with him for days and nights, he had lost count. He pressed the hand. 'Thank you, Laurent. For many hours, lying here, I have been considering my life. I trust you, Laurent, with my conclusions, you who have shown me such care. I am sated with favours and cabals and banquets and possessions. I have seen, owned, tasted everything. Power and wealth pall. All knowledge I realise now comes to us through the senses. I have been ruled by them – except for the knowledge and love of God. . . And now one of my chief senses is gone—' He paused and sighed. 'There is one who means everything to me – I know it now.

Earlier tonight I was almost persuaded that he stood by my bed . . . how childish I have become to make my wish become reality.'

The hand he was clasping pressed his, firmly.

'I am holding your hand; I, Gui. I have taken Maître Thoros's place while he sleeps.'

'Many times I heard a demon whisper: "I am Gui". What are you?'

'I am Gui of Montolieu, the son of the master of Montolieu who died five days ago from wounds he inflicted on himself when he followed the flagellants. I am Gui who was your page, but no longer the lord of Montolieu. I am your page who fled on your horse many months ago after having been raped in your stables by Giacomo. I was ashamed—'

'Giacomo is dead,' murmured Le Gor. 'Laurent told me so.'

Gui saw Giacomo consumed, but still burning, in the everlasting flames of Hell.

'I am Gui,' he began again. 'Do you not know my voice?'

'Do I know whether a demon is speaking with your voice? Laurent, pray that I am delivered from a demon who assumes Gui's voice.'

'I am Gui. I am he!'

And he leant over the bandaged head to kiss the only visible part of the face, the mouth.

'You are Gui,' said Le Gor after a while. 'Perhaps God will return me to health now.'

Chapter 25

Beauchamp lies between Avignon and Carpentras, a tiny village. At seven o'clock on a May morning, the sun dazzled an old priest emerging, blinking, from the small stone chapel behind him, and danced across the green meadow, sheltering graves and their tombstones. Half hidden in the long grass smouldered the scarlet of the poppies and the feathery blue of cornflowers. He had said Mass to three old women, and was now contemplating the loan of a scythe to tidy up his little churchyard, when he became aware of a hunchbacked figure, on a mule approaching the chapel. The shape resolved itself into a woman, with a baby strapped to her in front and a heavy sack lashed to the mule behind her. She dismounted with some difficulty. The sack stayed where it was.

'Father,' she pleaded. 'I live alone, two hours' ride away, with my sick husband and my baby. My husband . . . yesterday, he, he . . . will you give burial to my husband's body? That is he, on the back of the mule.'

The priest stared at the sack and crossed himself.

'I can pay, Father.'

Marie drew from under her cloak a purse, the one she had found tied to her husband's body with a thong.

Roger was buried that morning in the green meadow full of flowers, and Marie now had time, since his death yesterday, to remember Roger as he was long ago when he came courting her one spring, in the mountains at Caromb, young and strong. She cried for him and for herself; for what he had become, and for the loneliness awaiting her. Then she paid the priest and the peasant who had dug the grave, tied Bonjoue securely to her, mounted the mule and rode back to her valley.

Lying in her bed that night, she contemplated a visit to the street of the Jews, now that she was free. Surely Astruc would like to see his son? But who would feed the hens, who would lock up the animals? She had never been to Avignon. Could she get there and return in one day? And Astruc's wife . . . no, she thought, I will send him word by a pedlar that I am alone now and he will surely come to me as soon as he hears that . . .

The dog growled.

She had pushed the great chest against the door as they used to do, she and Astruc, when they feared armed men searching for him. Someone stealing the mule or the hens? But the dog went back to sleep.

She touched the purse under her pillow taken from Roger's body. In the end his death had been quiet. He had taken a sip of wine and closed his eyes – and never opened them again. Her fingers felt the purse, full of gold coins. She was rich. She would go to Carpentras and hire a man at the hiring fair, to help. Just once in her life she had been blessed with good fortune and given two things she desired: a loving man and a purse full of money. She had the gold, and her loving man would surely return soon. She fell asleep with Bonjoue in her arm and dreamed of Astruc.

It was evening of the next day when Marie heard knocking on the door. The dog barked and would not stop growling and baring his teeth.

'Is this Roger's house?' cried a man's voice. 'We're old friends, come to see him.'

Marie had not had time to push the chest across the door. She did not reply. The dog growled by the door. Through the hole in the wooden shutter over the window she saw two men, dust-covered, tall. She saw their long legs were thrust into leather boots reaching to their thighs and in their belts they carried daggers, sticks and knives. Huge leather hats hid part of their faces, but they had sharp mouths and eyes set among dirty wrinkles.

They were whispering now. They knew she was in her house.

'Is Roger there?' shouted one. 'We've brought him a gift.'

'I am his wife,' Marie said boldly. 'His widow. Roger died a few days ago.'

She crossed herself.

'Then you shall have the gift we brought,' said one of the men. 'We've come a long way for news of our old comrade. A drink of water or of wine and the taste of bread would help us forget our fatigue.'

Never, never open the door after dark.

'For Jesus' sake,' shouted one of the men. 'We've travelled with Roger, and fought with Roger, and escaped the Pope's men – and now his widow refuses us shelter!'

Her guilt about Roger, whom she had deceived with Astruc, swayed her. She moved the heavy bolts on the door and opened it slowly. The men walked in, silently, looking about them. The dog approached them, growling, and one of them kicked, sending it whining across the room. A cold shiver shook Marie, but she hurried to hang the iron soup kettle above the hearth. They watched in silence, perched on the chair and the stool, as she served them soup and bread. When they had eaten most of what she had, without speaking a word, they stretched their long legs in front of the hearth, observing her.

She looked at their narrow sunburnt faces covered in stubble as they wiped their knives on their greasy boots. They stank of sweat and dirt. Marie thought they might be brothers, and they might be shepherds.

She stood observing them, Bonjoue in her arms, the old dog cowering in the corner. Why should they harm her, widow of their old comrade?

But she feared them. Wouldn't they go now?

'And now,' said one of them – were they brothers? – 'we have come to fetch what is ours.'

'You said you had a gift for Roger,' said Marie, trembling. Jesus, Mary, she prayed, forgive me my adultery.

'Yes,' said one of the men, pulling a stick from his belt. 'We were going to give him a tap with this. And now he has gone. Do you know what Roger did? He ran away when trouble began. Did he tell you?'

'Yes,' whispered Marie. 'But he was ill and frightened.'

'And did he tell you that he took the purse that held all the money we had? Money belonging to us and three others? When we escaped from the Pope's men?'

'Yes' whispered Marie.

'Then give us our purse.'

Without a word Marie fetched the purse from its place under her pillow.

One of the brothers took it from her and put it into his scrip. Then, without haste, the brothers went to the door. Marie took a deep breath. They were leaving. The Virgin had protected her, in spite of her adultery.

They were outside when one of the men turned to the other 'One more thing—'

'Is it necessary, brother?'

'Yes.'

He walked back into the house and seized the child from Marie's arms. Bonjoue screamed as the man threw him onto the bed. The old dog rose painfully and launched himself at the man, who seized him by the throat and threw him against the wall. Blood welled from his mouth, he kicked his legs twice and moved no more. Bonjoue cried.

Marie stood paralysed with fear, unable to move to her child, watching the man pull out a dagger. Could she – but with another movement he sent her staggering against the bed and as she fell, he caught her skirts in one skilful movement and pulled them over her head. Her cries were muffled by her own clothes. She fought for breath, even more important than his violent painful thrust inside her. His weight was crushing her lungs, her mouth was full of fluid, her lungs were bursting. She cried out once more, then he clamped his hands around her throat.

After a while, the other brother came back into the house and observed the still figure of Marie on the bed, with the baby crying beside her. He shook his head.

'And the child?'

'What is one more?' asked the shepherd. He killed Bonjoue with one blow and then the brothers began to break up the little furniture which Marie had possessed, heaping the broken wood on the bed and, taking a brand from the hearth, set fire to the pile.

It had been many months and many deaths ago that the brothers had felt qualms and they felt none now.

They gathered the hens into a sack, mounted the mule and rode into the darkness. The fire burned brightly in Marie's house behind the brothers, and in minutes the darkness had swallowed them up.

Chapter 26

'They're both away from home – the pedlar and the doctor. The pedlar's name is Astruc and the other one, the husband's brother, the doctor, has not been seen since last autumn; so . . . now. Now. Yes, now.'

Muttering, Guillaume de Saint-Amant stood on the bank and stared down at the waters of the Rhône, as they changed from green to blue with the oncoming dusk. Black shadows gaped beneath the arches of St Benezet's bridge. On this fine evening in the first week in June there were plenty of strollers along the banks of the river, walking across the fading, parched grass, sniffing the scent of the many aromatic bushes, watching the boats and barges tying up for the night. Some laughed at the high official, muttering angrily to himself, but took care not to approach.

Prosperity showed in the citizens' dress. Long silk dresses stroked the low-growing lavender and thyme. Young men with brightly clad legs, like storks, strolled past, looking for assignations. Saint-Amant cursed any who came near him.

'I must not wait any longer,' he said aloud as his eye caught the windows of the palace looming behind him, calling him. He knew that at the palace officials and servants were beginning to mock him, for his anguish appeared to them as dementia and they smelt failure on him and disgrace to come.

At the palace, he mounted a dozen stairs to Elinor's tiny room, where she sat sewing and singing cheerfully all day like a caged bird. He held his nose against the smell of soiled linen and stale food, glanced at the baby gurgling and at Elinor who looked up at him with her face full of joy. 'The Holy Father has been to see me! He came with his sister, the lady Guillemette. He came to give me this purse, sir. He kissed the baby, sir.'

Saint-Amant began to form a question. 'Does . . . is he . . . ?'

'The lady carried the purse, she had noticed the Holy Father's interest and she asked me questions like you did, sir. She told me I should go back to the country with the child, for his health's sake.'

'What ails your child?' asked Saint-Amant sharply.

'Nothing, yet, but the lady Guillemette says that in the country there is less illness. And he, the Holy Father, asked me to—'

She blushed.

'Well?' Saint-Amant said. By misfortune, the Holy Father's interest might put his own plan in jeopardy.

'He asked me to pray for him, to forgive him, the Holy Father! He said he had sinned like other men. I said I prayed for him every night. I mean, at the time I didn't know who he was, sir. And the lady asked me about my Rostain and whether he would marry me if I went back to the village with my child, and when I said yes, Rostain won't mind, she gave me this purse, and the Holy Father blessed me and there were tears in his eyes.'

'Really,' murmured Saint-Amant. Would Rostain marry her with two children, though? As for himself, the Church must realise that he was bringing them a soul . . . he supposed his resolve was being tested, obstacles were put in his way to make atonement difficult. That was what he wanted.

'That he should take the trouble, sir.'

'And my proposal, Elinor? Don't you want the purse I promised you?'

Two purses! Calculation and fear chased each other across Elinor's face, so like the Madonna in Simone Martini's picture below in the Audience chamber; so unlike her at this moment.

Elinor was only fifteen, thought Saint-Amant, and too much was expected of her. But his plan! He must frighten her. 'You promised me, and you shall do as you promised. Or I will . . . I will tell the lady Guillemette that you have not been frank with her.'

A silly threat, thought Saint-Amant, with a sinking heart. The lady Guillemette had long ago understood her brother's weakness, surely, but to his surprise and relief he saw Elinor turn pale.

'Is it now that you want me, sir?'

'Very soon, Elinor.'

At sunset, when the gates were locked, the Street ceased to be two rows of houses and became one huge dwelling. Secure, it became a courtyard, a playground, a meeting place. This June night old people had brought their chairs out to catch the breeze and sat gossiping. Young women with babies stood together and in the *escole* the *baylons* were wrangling about widows; should they be exempt from the community tax? Apart from the *baylons* there were few men about this weekday night, for most of them were on the roads of the *comtat* and Provence.

Blanchette, her mother and her friend Rachel sat outside the shop till late, Joseph asleep in Blanchette's arms, while the women ate cherries, delighting in the breeze which stirred Blanchette's curls, cooled their hot faces and ruffled the strange golden fluff on Joseph's head – which seemed slow to darken, as Lea remarked.

David now came out of the *escole*, where the meeting had broken up in disunity, to look at his godson and particularly at his mother. He loved Blanchette, but with the return of Astruc he had to give up hope.

At ten Blanchette kissed her mother and locked the door behind her. Esther went into her house, but left her street door unlocked so that her Christian lover could come to her later. Knowing Esther's habits, the other inhabitants made sure that the doors of their own rooms were securely locked, complaining that Esther's habits endangered all on their staircase.

As usual, the porter had closed and locked the main gate, as well as the barrier which sealed off the other end of the Street. There was a rota among the *baylons* to ensure someone locked the gate from the inside as well. This night, old Sema Rouget had been asked to take the place of an absent *baylon*, but he was busy elsewhere and had not yet appeared to carry out this task.

At eleven, Saint-Amant knocked on the porter's door. The porter grinned at Saint-Amant whom he now knew well. The knight was dressed as usual in a black cloak with a hood.

'This is the last time you and I meet,' said Saint-Amant with the easy manner of one who can count on obedience. 'Here is double what I've paid you for the last twelve months. Tonight I wish you to accompany me to the shop.'

'Yes sir. And I have not seen you, sir.'

'And you have been paid nothing – not tonight, not at any time. But just in case the shop is locked—'

'There will be no problem even in that case. Trust me, sir.'

They stood in front of Blanchette's shop in the deserted, silent Street and tried the door; it was indeed locked. The porter pointed at the door next to it. 'This one is always open. Immediately you're inside, sir, take the door to your right which, you'll find, leads up to—'

'Sh! Make sure your gate is open. Any delay . . .'

The porter saluted and made his way back to his gate, thinking that now the little transaction with the official was over, he might risk placing a word in the ear of another official at the palace, claiming that he felt qualms, an attack of guilt, or a preference for honesty. They might offer him a reward.

On his way back to the gate he almost collided with Sema Rouget, a very old man to whom the porter had taken a liking. Sema was returning from the *escole*, where he looked after the wash places and cabinets of ease; and he was finally on his way to lock the inside gate. But the porter thought he heard someone call him at the gate – Esther's lover, most likely – and he hurried back without exchanging more than a goodnight with Sema. But there was no one and so the porter allowed himself a few minutes' sleep.

He woke to hear cries, shouts and screams; leaped from his pallet and ran out into the Street through his own porter's door, beside the great gate. Standing inside the gate, and rattling and twisting the lock trying to get through – but in vain, for Sema had locked it and taken the key back to the *escole* – was Saint-Amant, holding in his arms a screaming, wriggling bundle; Joseph Boni-vassin, son of Blanchette.

A crowd was gathering. Old men, many women, a few youths and more came pouring out of their houses, some with candles and lanterns. They saw Blanchette running to the gate, in bare feet and in her nightgown, screaming. 'My child! Assassin! Pig! Robber! He's taken my baby, my son!'

The crowd surged forward. 'Assassin! Robber!' they roared.

'Porter! Where are you, Judas! Why did you lock the gate? Open up!' shouted Saint-Amant.

Saint-Amant's hood fell back, and by the light of the porter's lantern the crowd saw the golden curls on his head – and the golden fluff on the child's.

'The boy is mine!' cried Saint-Amant, turning to face the crowd and holding the child aloft. 'Do you see his hair, the colour of mine? Mine. My child by Blanchette Bonivassin.'

The crowd fell silent. So the evil tongues had been right. Joseph was a *momzer*, a bastard, and Blanchette an adulteress who had fornicated with a Christian. The crowd, mostly women, felt for her, felt her shame and anguish and Blanchette felt their support behind her. They stood silently watching Blanchette with her mother and Esther throw themselves at Saint-Amant. They screamed, 'Give him back!'

Tears ran down Blanchette's face as she tried to take Joseph from Saint-Amant and the boy struggled in vain towards her. Saint-Amant pushed Blanchette away.

'I am taking him with me but believe me, no harm shall come to him. I shall make him a Christian – he will be baptised.'

Blanchette cried out and lunged at him again, now aiming at his eyes with her nails, but he held the child high above his head with one arm, warding Blanchette off with the other. 'You, woman – let me go. Porter! Unlock the gate or I will have you flayed! Let me go,' he said again to Blanchette, 'or I will dash his brains out against this wall.'

Blanchette fell at his feet.

The crowd began to beseech him to have mercy. Some, led by the rabbi, began to pray, others set up high wailing as though the child were already dead. David had run back to the *escole* and now brought back the key to unlock the inner bolt. He dared not try to snatch the child; and the crowd watched helplessly as the bolt was withdrawn and Saint-Amant ran out into the city, pursued by David and three youths. Women and children stood inside, by the open gate, afraid to cross the barrier into the black wicked city beyond, praying and waiting.

Blanchette's screams rent the air. They decided to take her to the underground ritual baths whose deep purple waters looked sinister, as no daylight ever reached them. By the light of candles Esther and Lea helped to immerse her, and the water calmed Blanchette till she sobbed quietly. She was still wrapped in towels when the three women heard shouts from above, 'They've brought him back!'

Wrapped in her bath sheet Blanchette hurried up the steps to the vestibule, where David stood with Joseph in his arms. She kissed him over and over as David put an arm around a youth by his side.

'This is Moshe – without him, Joseph would not be with us now. Praise be, he has no bruises or scratches on him. Moshe threw himself at the man's legs and made him fall – he must have stunned himself so that we had no trouble taking Joseph from him.'

Blanchette nodded at Moshe and at David, unable to speak a single word. Lea took the child while Blanchette dried and dressed herself. David accompanied the women home, past a hundred onlookers. There were murmurs of sympathy. Lea helped her daughter to bed and then returned to the landing where David was waiting. Lea said to him, 'The whole Street knows that she's an adulteress now. It will kill her. She is a good mother and a good daughter to me, David. Why did she do it? Is it my fault? She's my daughter . . .'

David could not think of a reply. He had run through Avignon in the middle of the night, wrested a child from a papal official lying groaning in an alleyway, had stumbled over a tethered mule in the dark, and had brought the boy back to his mother. He was very tired.

'She has Joseph back,' he ventured.

'God give that the child will keep her alive,' said Lea. 'She said she would die of shame.'

Chapter 27

Blanchette woke from fearful dreams: a man had entered her room stealthily and snatched Joseph from her arms while she was so deeply asleep that at first she offered no resistance, then felt the empty place in her arms and fully awake, panic-stricken, screamed –

It hadn't been a dream. It had happened last night. But Joseph was back unharmed, lying peacefully asleep in the crook of her arm. Today was Friday. Astruc would soon be home for the Sabbath, tired and dusty, to hear the tale which everyone in the Street already knew.

When Astruc arrived, he had met Lea on the stairs, who whispered that something had happened – David would tell him. Blanchette was deathly pale.

'Tell him, David, from the beginning,' murmured Blanchette.

David told his tale. So we're not safe, not even in the Street, thought Astruc and for a moment his old fears crowded in on him.

'So we ran after the man who was carrying Joseph; the child was screaming, screaming. There were people in the streets still, so we kept shouting, Stop thief! Moshe is a good runner and was gaining on him, I was behind. Nobody could see we were Jews – no hats, you see! Luckily he ran into an alley and into a tethered mule in the dark and that's when Moshe threw himself at his legs and, as he fell, I caught up and seized Joseph. The

robber is disturbed in his mind, that's my view. A soul for
Christ, he kept saying to us. My son, he said, and my sin.
We left him on the ground and hurried back as fast as we
could with Joseph—'

Astruc embraced David. 'I shall make an announcement to all the Street that the child is my own son, that
the Christian is deranged. Tell the *baylons*, David, tell the
whole Street.'

When David had gone, Astruc looked at Blanchette
with compassion. 'Would it comfort you to know that I,
too, have loved a Christian and that we too have a son? I
have lost them both, Blanchette, for her husband has
returned. You – you have Joseph.'

Blanchette smiled briefly, then shook her head. 'Your
pain does not make my pain and my shame better, Astruc.
Don't tell the whole Street that Joseph is yours – they
won't believe you. It would be best if you divorced me
now, Astruc, for they will make it difficult for us to live
together. They'll punish me, and if you stay, they'll call you
a cuckold. I owe Joseph's life to David. I know David loves
me, he will help me. As for you, you could be free—'

Astruc, sad and bewildered, went to the *escole* to pray
for guidance. In his prayer shawl he stood with the other
men, waiting for a sign from the Almighty, but it was as
he feared; God considered him too insignificant to indicate what Astruc should do. After the service, he sought
out the rabbi who talked for a long time about fornication and advised him, given the circumstances, to
divorce. At last, Astruc nodded. The rabbi called three
other Jews who happened to be talking outside the *escole*,
and asked Astruc to make his statement of divorce in
their presence, there and then.

Now he found himself alone in front of the *escole*, a divorced man, and made his way slowly back to Blanchette. It was she who had asked for this divorce, hadn't she? She had never loved him, but would she be sad now, would she regret this step? He remembered her words about Thoros – it was him she wanted, and Thoros had gone. They were both bereft, he and Blanchette.

'We are no longer man and wife,' he said to her gently. They looked at each other with sadness.

Astruc began to prepare for his departure. First, he went into his brother's room and wrapped Thoros's phylacteries around a couple of books and prayer shawl, and put this at the bottom of his pack.

'What will you do?' asked Blanchette, who had been watching. Her face was blank, but again her eyes expressed. He had no idea what punishment the community would find in the statutes and he felt deeply sorry for her.

'Work in the fields,' said Astruc. 'And you?'

'I'll sew. And when the time is right, I shall send for David.'

'I shall come back in the autumn for the holy days,' said Astruc. He kissed Blanchette and Joseph farewell and set off, out of the gate and onto the road to Carpentras.

This was the way to Marie's valley. He wanted to catch a glimpse of her, that was all – and of Bonjoue, of course.

Astruc cut away from the road through the spiky, scented undergrowth downhill to the valley till he saw the little house half hidden by the cherry trees. How still it lay beneath him! In his pack he carried three presents. A small shirt for Bonjoue, a *cotte* from Lyons for Marie and a jerkin for the old husband. He had decided to tell the husband the truth: that the presents were thanks for Marie who had sheltered him when he was being pursued. How ill the husband had looked, maybe – God forgive him for the thought – he was not long for this world? I'll tell Marie that I have divorced Blanchette, and will wait for her till she too is free. Maybe I'll get a chance to tell her I love her.

A little way from the house, he stopped.

The door is open, swinging in the light breeze. And the window, neither open nor shut – the shutter half-shattered and blackened. By fire. Astruc's breath comes fast and his heart beats in his throat.

He sees that the roof clings precariously to the roof beams and that a huge hole has replaced the chimney. There is no sound in the yard. Where's the dog? Where are the fowls? He does hear a sound of – is it bees? No. Flies.

In the deep silence the sound of flies buzzing maddens him. The sound comes from inside the house. There has been a fire and Marie and her husband have gone with Bonjoue, they're sheltering somewhere. Or could she be still there? He knows she isn't but, near the door, shouts, 'Marie! Marie!'

No sound.

He steps inside and immediately retches because of the smell, which is acrid and nauseating. He stares at the hearth, cold and piled with shards, recognising the shattered jug and parts of the chair. The bowl by the hearth has gone and so has the ham above it and the hanging iron kettle.

No sign of Marie, the husband or Bonjoue. The smell forces him to run outside to the well for water but he finds that the bucket has gone and the wooden covers smashed. When he looks into the well he sees the dark water below but there's no hope of reaching it without the bucket. He remembers the spring, a shallow trickle of water not far, by the olive tree, runs to it and throws himself down, allowing the cool water to run over his face for many minutes.

Must he go back? He fears little nowadays but he finds that his legs are trembling. Marie isn't there, they have gone, shouldn't he too leave this place and find her? But he knows that he cannot leave without having looked once more, seen what there is to see; he must force himself . . . but first he says a prayer, asking God for strength.

Now he is in the house, gagging, catching his breath. Oh Lord, he whispers among the buzzing, do not allow me to witness what I cannot bear.

There is the inner room, with the bed, and he goes forward to look but his body reacts before his mind understands; he clings to the door, sobbing and sensing rather than seeing what is on the bed, but he does see it and vomits. He runs out to the stream and returns to the bedroom with water running from his hair and beard, water to cleanse his eyes as he approaches the bed, their bed. The fire has done its work, but not entirely and he recognises the cloth of Marie's shift. Two skulls, one very small, keep guard over charred bones on what remains of the bed.

Like a candle in a storm, Astruc's mind flickers briefly, he remembers a stone hut in the woods where he knew a holy man lives, and he waits there until the friar returns, carrying wood. Astruc persuades the friar to return with him to the house where, together, they collect the remains. The friar takes Astruc to a small clearing near his hut where Astruc digs a grave. The two men pile stones on top of the loose earth, and the friar ties two olive branches together to make a cross.

'This will do for the present,' the friar says to Astruc. 'I will make a beautiful cross shortly, from olive wood, and carve the names of your wife and child on it. You must tell me their names.' He looks at Astruc whose eyes are glittering like pewter and takes him by the arm. 'Come with me and rest in my hut for a while—'

'I have to wait here, for Marie,' Astruc says dully.

'We have buried Marie,' says the friar.

'I have to clean,' says Astruc. 'Marie likes the house to be fresh and clean.'

'My son—' begins the friar.

Astruc looks past him and murmurs some lines from a Hebrew psalm. Until now he has said little to the friar, only what was absolutely necessary. But now he speaks, 'I am a Jew from the Street in Avignon. Marie is a Christian and she and I love each other and we have a child together, his name is Bonjoue. We are to be married as soon as she returns.'

'What you have witnessed has robbed you of your reason, my poor friend. You will remember what happened later. For now I think you should go home to be with other Jews who will comfort you.'

'That's my home,' says Astruc, pointing back at the ruins of Marie's house. 'I had better start clearing up.'

Chapter 28

Astruc, said Thoros to himself, this is the day, the very day on which I'll see my brother again; perhaps only an hour from now.

This morning was to be his last in the cardinal's residence. He was standing in the vestibule to hand his patient over to Guy de Chauliac, doctor to the Holy Father and a dozen cardinals, who was at this moment mounting the steps of Le Gor's residence.

Gui, his hand on Le Gor's brow, awaited the two doctors at the cardinal's bedside.

'I'm pleased with your progress, cardinal,' said de Chauliac. 'As long as your page here takes great care of you when the bandages are removed, there will be no longer any need of my *confrère*, Maître Thoros here. I understand that you have resolved to present yourself and your case to the learned faculty at Montpellier, *maître?* I will be most interested to hear what they make of it!'

'So will I,' said Thoros. Every day had brought him more knowledge of himself, till at last he was together again. It was time to go home. He ached to be back in the Street, among friends, caring for his patients, eating the food he was used to, listening to his own people speaking their special language, half Provençal, half Hebrew; stand with the others in the *escole*, embrace Astruc, Blanchette, Lea . . .

A few minutes later he left Villeneuve, with a purse of gold coins under his robe, a last gift from Le Gor. He crossed the bridge and traversed Avignon in a dream.

It was midday and very hot when he reached the gate of the Street. He walked past the somnolent porter and through the empty Street to the *escole*, entering its cool lobby and climbing up the steps to where the two stone lions of Juda guarded the great portals. He entered and gave thanks to God who had brought him back from the dead.

A man detached himself from the shadows; the women's Rabbi from Poland, Rabbi Liptois. 'Welcome, stranger. Where have you come from?'

'I am Thoros Bonivassin, doctor to the community—'

'Thoros!' The rabbi embraced him, in tears at the miracle, anticipating the joy of the family and of the community. 'The Lord has sent you back! Tonight you will be at the service – they will all see you there!' He looked at Thoros's narrow, dark face. 'Where have you been? We never thought to see you again – have you been home?'

'Not yet, Rabbi. I came here first to give thanks.'

'Come sit down on this chair, by my side, and I will talk to you a little, before you go home, *maître*. I can see that terrible things have happened to you to turn your hair white and take the flesh from your bones. I did not know you at first, *maître*. We were afraid you were dead, yet we could not mourn you properly.'

'Rabbi, I have been very ill in body and in mind. I have been living the life of a Christian . . . in a cardinal's residence—' The rabbi looked up sharply. 'Without knowing who I was. They treated me kindly, but I knew I was different – all the time my hands were searching for their proper work. My hands were seeking, but my head understood nothing; and then, suddenly, it happened: I came to my senses, and before me stood my benefactor, Cardinal Le Gor . . . he rescued me. I will explain—'

But to his dismay, tears prevented him from continuing.

'Now— began the rabbi.

'Now I'm going home.'

'Wait, wait,' urged the rabbi. 'There have been changes at home . . . oh, nothing, but perhaps more than you need at this moment. Come with me, you're exhausted, come to my room and rest until dusk; you'll need all your strength to face the congregation.'

When Thoros awoke, the rabbi stood before him with a prayer shawl.

'Yours,' he said. 'I took it from its box in the synagogue.'

'The service,' said Thoros. 'Will my brother Astruc be there?'

Rabbi Liptois hesitated. 'No, he is still away.'

The rabbi and Thoros stood in the *escole*, still empty, awaiting the first worshippers. Thoros listened for the murmur of voices. The first to enter were the *baylons*: Daniel Naquet, Cabri Montel, Michel Aron, Abraham de Milhaud, Vidal Farrusol and David Rougier. Thoros whispered each name as each man entered.

David Rougier, the last to enter, stopped and stared at Thoros, whose prayer shawl hid his white hair. David hesitated. 'Thoros – is it you?'

The *baylons* fell silent and those in front heard Thoros say, 'I know you too, David Rougier. I know you all.'

Behind the *baylons,* others arriving pushed forward, puzzled by the group standing in a knot around Thoros.

'What is it?' called a voice. 'Has someone fainted?'

Rabbi Liptois stepped forward. 'Friends!' he began, raising his voice. 'Our Lord in his mercy has returned our *medicus* to us—' But the rabbi did not, in his northern way, understand the Jews of Avignon. Vidal Farrusol whose voice reached from one end of the Street to the other cried out: 'It's Maître Thoros!'

Those in front laughed and shouted. At the back they pushed and shoved and fought each other to see. The women in their synagogue directly under the men's heard and, eager to see, hurried up the stairs and pushed forward, crying, in case there was a tragedy, the Lord protect us!

'Back!' the rabbi ordered the women. 'You are defying custom and precept! And you, men, the service! Calm yourselves, friends!'

A wonderful sound stopped the tumult. Muscat, the *shamas,* had struck the candelabrum a ringing blow and now it swung outraged and agitated in great circles above the hubbub, dripping wax from its candles on the heads below.

Silence restored, the service began, the women trooping down to listen from their places below. Among them sat Blanchette, straight as a candle, on a bench by herself as befitted Blanchette the adulteress. She had not rushed upstairs with the others, and, when they returned, not one woman spoke to her about the reason for the commotion. She felt dreadfully alone. Lea was looking after Joseph; Blanchette longed for the warmth of the little boy against her body, to temper the icy silence of her neighbours. Yet hadn't she felt support from the women when Joseph was taken? Since then the *baylons* had isolated her, and the *baylons* embodied the law . . .

Suddenly the rabbi changed from the Hebrew of the prayer to Judeo-Provençal, which all present understood. 'We now offer heartfelt thanks for the safe return of Maître Bonivassin, our friend and master, one of the glories of our community. He has helped so many – not only in the Street, but in the city of Avignon; even in the highest place of that city!'

Blanchette made no movement. With eyes closed, she heard the great shout of 'Amen' which reverberated around the *escole* and which filtered down to the women through the hole pierced in the great chamber's floor. Then her head dropped forward and she slipped to the floor.

The women carried her to the back of the room and wetted her face, while one ran to fetch Lea, who was told the news on her way to the *escole*, and within minutes stood, Joseph in her arms, looking down at the pale face of her daughter, recovering from her faint.

'Trouble,' said Lea. 'More trouble. So, Thoros is back. What about us, his family? Not one word in twelve months. Living with Christians, I hear! Eating we know not what – pork even, who knows.'

'Hush, Lea, the service is not finished.'

'Don't hush me! Now, get up, Blanchette, we had better prepare for your brother-in-law who has not been home for a year. I would like to hear his reasons!'

Blanchette staggered to her feet, her heart thudding and the blood returning to her aching head and, as she left with her mother, she heard the women behind her convulsed with laughter.

Outside, Blanchette stopped. 'Go on home, Mother. I want to see him.'

Thoros came out, at last, with the *baylons* crowding around him, as well as patients and the curious. She saw him briefly – his hair was white! – then he was hidden from view. When the crowd parted, she saw him again, searching for someone: Astruc, of course. Later, she supposed he would come home, tonight he would be sleeping in the room just across the landing from hers. But how soon would he hear what she had done? Fornication with a Christian, bearing his child, deceiving Astruc.

The crowd moved forward, parted.

Thoros was not among them. Blanchette went home.

Rabbi Liptois had taken Thoros by the arm, inviting him to attend the *baylons* in the Azara, the solemn meeting room in the *escole*, and to deferring his homecoming till after he had given a full account of his attendance on the Holy Father.

Chapter 29

Parchment and pens lay on the table in the Azara. On one side the *baylons* casting glances at Thoros's white hair and black beard; on the other Thoros, glancing in turn at the *baylons* and Rabbi Liptois. Minutes ago they had acclaimed his return. Thoros saw them now in their official function.

The *baylons* regulated income and expenditure, controlled the community coffers, the charities, bought candles for the services, held the key to the Jerusalem collection box, decided who should be punished and how, according to a set of laws drawn up every ten years and amended yearly. As Thoros knew, there was a rule for everything, of whatever importance.

The joy of his return began to ebb away. Why hadn't he gone home first? He knew the *baylons* well, and a great lassitude seized him, as the treasurer opened the proceedings. 'Welcome to this assembly of *baylons, maître*. Permit me to get straight to the heart of this business, as I see it. Ten years ago, this community paid for your *studium* at Montpellier. As a qualified doctor, you left your patients, a year ago, without—'

'One moment, treasurer,' said Jacob de Carcassonne quickly. 'We, the elected *baylons*, must give thanks for your safe return. The Lord be praised, Amen!'

'Amen!' rumbled the deep voices of the *baylons*.

'Now, *maître*,' continued Jacob. 'You must be aware that your absence caused a great deal of distress to your brother and your sister-in-law.'

'And cost the community a great deal of money,' interrupted the treasurer. 'We were obliged to offer a purse to the papal official to help him search for you. And during the twelve months of your absence we also offered rewards to those who said they had seen you – false, every sighting!'

'Praise the Lord who has allowed Thoros's safe return,' said Rabbi Liptois.

'I shall reimburse the community,' said Thoros impassively. How quickly the welcome had worn thin . . . but he became aware of a smile and looked up at Vidal Farrusol, whom he had cured of a wheezing chest last year; Vidal who had praised and thanked him over and over and asked him now, 'Could you not get word to us? We were so anxious about you, *maître*! Were you held against your will?'

'Thank you for your concern, Vidal. I owe you all an explanation.' Thoros sighed. 'Until very recently, I could not have given you any account whatever . . . it was a June night, like this one, friends, a year ago, is the year now 1347? Yes? Yes . . . I was fetched from my bed to a patient outside the Street and the sick man – to my amazement, as you can imagine – was the Pope himself.'

The *baylons* started up as though Thoros had trodden in an ant's nest, and began to call out questions. Jessue's was the loudest. 'And what if you had not been able to save the sick man? What then?'

' Then . . . but I don't understand the purport of your question, treasurer,' said Thoros.

'I'll tell you what would have happened! You, *maître*, would have been the Jewish *medicus* who had killed the Pope! Not – I can already hear your objection – the *medicus* who could not save a stricken Pope. And the consequence of that, *maître*, would have brought destruction to this community, to us. We have heard dark stories of horror, from Spain and from Germany; for a nothing, a trumped-up tale, we would have perished, as they perished, burnt in a barn, hacked to pieces.'

'But I cured him – or rather, God enabled me to help him regain his health. He lives, friends,' Thoros said softly, into the silence.

The rabbi, conciliatory as ever, nodded at these words. 'They called a Jewish *medicus* to the Holy Father, knowing that he was the best, why else? Thoros's skill will no doubt have reinforced the Pope's high opinion of Jewish doctors.'

'I was called, I believe, because of Maître Guy de Chauliac's absence that night in Montpellier,' said Thoros. 'He is the renowned *medicus* who attends the Holy Father—'

'Yes, yes. You understand, *maître*,' said the treasurer stiffly, 'that our business is to avert danger from this community and calculate what will appease the palace and the city. We buy peace, we buy safety; we are the guardians of the community's purse. What if, through our mismanagement, there is no money to do that?'

'What was I to do, Jessue – refuse?'

'Well, tell us your tale, *maître*,' said the rabbi. 'We're all anxious to hear.'

'The Holy Father,' said Thoros, 'was suffering from a severe attack of pain caused by a stone which eventually passed from his body. I remained at the palace until midday, feeling very tired. Going home in the heat of the sun, my state of exhaustion was such that I felt death approaching; it was the onset of my disease . . .'

The *baylons* listened attentively as Thoros described all that had happened to him in the past year, and their faces mirrored his bewilderment and misery.

'So you could not send word?' asked the treasurer when Thoros fell silent.

'To whom? I didn't know my own name.'

For once there was no arguing; even Jessue's face showed concern.

'Will one of you tell me now where my brother is?' said Thoros into the silence. 'He never misses a sabbath!'

'On the day you left us, so did Astruc. He returned but – I will explain later – he has left again—' said David.

'And Blanchette—?'

'Was all alone for many months, *maître*. And this is something I urge you to remember when you come to hear her story,' said David, loyal as ever. 'We made provision for her; she also received money from . . . we assumed it was Astruc, but, in fact—'

'Let me explain, David,' said the treasurer impatiently. 'Your brother believed he had killed a stonemason and hid till he thought it was safe to return.'

'Astruc?' cried Thoros. 'He would never even fight, let alone kill someone. You must be mistaken.'

'Your brother came back for his son's circumcision. Then it transpired that little Joseph was not his son at all, but that of a Christian – a high official at the palace.'

'Who tried to steal him!' cried David. 'But we caught up with the man and the boy is safe and sound with his mother now—'

Thoros stared at each speaker in turn. The dream seemed to become a nightmare.

'It seems that the very official who came to fetch you to the Holy Father's bedside was the child's father. He came to pay you, Blanchette took the money, one thing led to another, I suppose,' said Farrusol. 'So then Astruc divorced Blanchette, as was his right. They say he has gone to live with a woman who sheltered him for months—'

'Depriving us,' said the treasurer harshly, 'of his contribution to several funds.'

'Treasurer,' the rabbi began in a beseeching voice, but the treasurer continued, his voice rising. 'While you and your brother have been away, a new cardinal has been promoted and, as you know, we have to pay for the illuminations when that happens. They also asked us to pay for a new set of silver-thread hangings for the Fête-Dieu. Why do I mention these occurrences? Because we need the contributions each of us makes to the community coffers, *maître*. Now; your brother has become what the *escamots* call a *translador*, that is, he has taken up his abode outside the community. According to this *escamot* he has to give three months' warning. As he omitted to do so, he has incurred a fine—'

'I will pay,' said Thoros dully.

'And,' said the treasurer vehemently, 'please do not cast me in the role of villain! I am trying to carry out my duties, as instructed by the community!'

Thoros looked around him at the men he used to know and respect, and bitterness welled up in him. They were stifling among their *escamots* and the narrowness of their one Street was reflected in their thoughts. He heard the women's rabbi clear his throat. 'I speak in the absence – through illness – of the community's rabbi, and I speak to you, *maître*, as the head of your family. Blanchette has incurred a number of punishments. The *baylons* considered the reading of the oath, the *herem*. You will remember: she may not enter the *escole*, no one may buy from her, no one may sell her food. We decided, however—'

'She would have starved!' shouted David.

'That's why we decided on a modified form,' continued the rabbi. 'But what will become of her and the child? As Providence has returned you to us, you could make good the damage, or at least mitigate it by taking her as your wife.'

David leapt to his feet and cried, 'I intend to marry her myself!'

'She is of course a divorced woman; but it would be more correct,' said Jacob de Carcassonne in his old and mild voice, glancing at Thoros who stared dully ahead – was this never going to end? – 'if you, *maître*, were to treat her as your brother's widow; in which case you would of course marry her as is the prescribed form. We would then be able to lift the *herem*.'

Thoros stood up. The old lassitude seized him; he would have liked to lie down on his pallet in the cardinal's residence, but they were waiting for him to speak. '*Baylons* of the community and Rabbi,' he said in a hesitant voice. 'A few days ago I did not know my own name, I did not know that I was a Jew and a physician. My mind is not used to the strain put upon it today. I simply cannot seize the importance of what you are saying.'

'We are failing in understanding,' said Rabbi Liptois at once. 'It is we who are mistaken in speaking to you so soon! Let him go, friends, let him rest.'

Thoros walked out of the grand Azara, leaving the door open behind him, and they heard his dragging steps on the marble stairs.

David Rougier rose and closed the door, returned to the table and remained standing. 'I am far from being the richest man here,' he said with heat. 'But I have been elected like the rest of you even if I do represent only the poorest grade of the community. The Lord has guided our *maître* back to us and what do we do? We speak to him of taxes and dues!' He turned and left, slamming the door behind him.

'Blanchette won't marry him,' said Cabri Montel, the first words he had spoken since the meeting began. 'That is the trouble.'

The *baylons* nodded, shrugged their shoulders and fell to discussing rubbish disposal in this hot weather.

When the *baylons* dispersed at last, Rabbi Liptois remained sitting in the council chamber. He wondered how the senior rabbi Josue Lyon would have handled this meeting. He, the foreigner from faraway Lublin, had been hired to look after the women; his contract with the community still had a year to run, another year in this disordered town where the *mascarades* and balls and doubtful pleasures in Avignon seeped through the gates into this community, where the prevailing taste for intrigue and assignation and, above all, gold flowed daily from dawn to dusk through the gate into the Street, bringing corruption. Disposing of rubbish, he thought angrily; we legislate and apportion tasks and punishments and collect dues but the filth seeps into our lives; though why our community should be proof against temptations when our neighbours, *messieurs* the Christians, succumb?

He wholly pitied Blanchette. She was not the only beautiful woman in his charge, there were so many lovely women in the Street that men in Avignon and far beyond came expressly to catch sight of them and perhaps more . . . an example had to be made of Blanchette, her downfall had become too public to be overlooked.

Rabbi Liptois, a young man, often thought about the women to whom he taught Hebrew once a week, and particularly about one Nanon whose skin was both bronze and rose and whose long lashes hid chestnut eyes, and he remembered hearing that one of the Pope's Monsignori had declared: which of us would not gladly go to hell if we were there to find the daughters of Abraham?

Thoros's progress to his house was slow, because neighbours and patients – unlike the *baylons* – welcomed him with embraces and tears.

He was very tired when he climbed the stairs to his room, inhaling the familiar fetid smell, stopping at every floor where the doors were open and neighbours called his name. At the top of the staircase Blanchette and Lea were waiting to embrace him. But his hold on the present was slipping. Would it all begin again . . . ? Then he was lying on his own bed, with Lea supporting his head and urging him to drink this hot wine with spices . . . The heat of the liquid burnt his mouth, making a fiery path down his gullet and when it reached his stomach he fell asleep. Minutes later he awoke and stared around him, looking for the pallets of the hospice where, among the dead, he had woken – but no, the room was empty. From three floors below the unmistakable voices of the Street rose, and Lea's voice came faintly from the stairwell. He was home.

'And now of course I cannot remonstrate with a sick man,' said Lea to Blanchette, cradling Joseph in her arms in Blanchette's room. 'You can see that he's different . . . strange . . .'

A knock on the door and David Rougier put his head into the room.

'Come in!' cried Lea. 'You're always welcome!'

Blanchette looked away.

'Will his return,' David pointed behind him in the direction of Thoros's closed door, 'change anything, Blanchette?'

'Yes, David, I hope so.'

'Us?'

'No. I'm sorry, David.'

'Blanchette!' They heard a faint cry from Thoros's room, and Blanchette rose and was gone before David could say another word.

'You deserve better,' said Lea to him. 'I've found you a beautiful girl who can cook like an angel. What is more, she likes you. I have already placed a little word in her ear—'

David touched Lea's cheek gently and shook his head.

'The Almighty knows, David, there are so many beautiful women in the Street. One will love you!'

David left.

'Some of my books are missing, Blanchette,' Thoros mumbled across the landing. 'Where can they be?'

'You took some with you, as well as your bag of instruments, the night you left.'

If he were to look at her, instead of staring at the remaining books on their shelf, he must surely see what she felt.

'Look – I covered your shelf with a fine covering against dust and mice.'

'Thank you. Judah ibn Tibbon said to his son: Examine the Hebrew books you have once a month, the Arabic every two months, and the bound volumes once a quarter. At Passover and Tabernacles, call in the books that you have loaned,' said Thoros in a low voice, speaking to himself.

She hardly existed for him; to be close and yet unseen caused her pain and she felt tears prickling. He had forgotten that the books were lost, not lent. She felt an overwhelming need to touch him.

'Rest,' she said.

His gaze roamed around the room, returning to the books, avoiding her. She took his hand, lying on the cover and he withdrew it, gently, turning on his side on the pallet and closing his eyes.

This is how David must feel, thought Blanchette and, like David, I cannot abandon hope. But if Thoros does get better, he will remember that I have dishonoured his brother and will despise me . . .

One evening, weeks later, Thoros was sitting in his room, reading, when Blanchette entered.

'Are you well, Blanchette?' he said, in his old voice

which sent a pulse of joy throughout her body. 'You have been so kind while I have been occupied with myself without a thought for you. I'm very much to blame both as a brother-in-law and a doctor. We have not spoken of your marriage, of Astruc, of the father of your child, of your isolation, your punishment. Let us talk—'

Had he at last seen what her eyes expressed louder than she could shout?

'Astruc and I—' she began. 'It was not a good marriage . . .' and as she spoke, his eyes were upon her and his face was full of concern. He did not comment until she found herself stumbling to express what had driven her during the months of loneliness.

'You have spoken bravely of what is in your heart, and I see that you have borne the consequences with forti-tude. I'm very anxious for your happiness, Blanchette, and want to help, despite my weakness and . . . and I do feel your warmth and your care – you must forgive me.' He took her hand. 'And your trust gives me courage to tell you what disturbs my mind night and day with waking nightmares; I am so afraid that the sickness could strike again and then I would become nobody as before . . . help me . . . please help me . . .'

'You are Maître Thoros, physician and surgeon, who was consulted by the Holy Father himself. Now tell me who you are!' cried Blanchette.

He repeated her words and fell asleep. She took the book from his lap and settled on the wooden stool to watch over his sleep. An hour later, Lea entered with Joseph, looked at Thoros and whispered, 'Feed your child!'

Back in her own room, Blanchette said to her mother, 'I know why he is troubled now. He's afraid he will lose his memory and fall ill again . . . and he thinks of nothing but that—'

Lea nodded. When Joseph had fallen asleep on the cot and Lea had gone, Blanchette took the candle and crossed to Thoros's room, where she settled the stool by the wall, leant back and closed her eyes.

'Blanchette!'

She woke, cold and cramped, on her stool. The candle was out, but dawn showed through the little window giving onto the Street.

'Where is Astruc?' muttered Thoros. 'I cannot remember.'

'He lives in the country with the woman who bore their son.'

'And do you miss him?'

'No. I told you that our marriage was at an end before I had Joseph. I loved . . . I love another.'

'Ah, yes, I remember now what the *baylons* said. It is David Rougier, isn't it, it's he who wants to marry you.'

'But I will not marry him.'

'Then . . . whom do you love?'

'You, Thoros.'

'But you can see and hear,' said Thoros in a voice which he tried to make resonant but which sounded faint in the stealthy filtering light which left Blanchette's face in shadow, 'that I have hardly recovered.' He sobbed, a single sob. 'I am so weak! Will I ever take up my work again? I have no strength to love you.'

She rose and held him, whispering that he would work again – had not God saved him and brought him back to the Street for that? – and that his strength would return. He kissed her gratefully.

She slipped across the landing to find Joseph sleeping peacefully, undressed and returned to Thoros's room in her shift, wrapped in her blanket, to watch over his uneasy, exhausted sleep. She stayed an hour, then returned to her own room and Joseph.

Thoros dreamed that he held a woman in his arms. Gone was the nightmare about the hospice and the still forms of the dead on the pallets all around him, gone the dream about returning to his own people which haunted him at the cardinal's residence. He dreamed that the woman in his arms was young and beautiful, that he knew her well and that she loved him; and that he loved her.

He woke to find himself alone, but, wide awake with the sun reaching into the room, he knew her name: Blanchette.

Chapter 30

The months have passed. It is almost midnight on the last day of the year.

In Villeneuve-les-Avignon, Cardinal Le Gor is asleep, Gui dozing by his side. Le Gor, whose sight has been restored, wakes, and immediately Gui is awake too.

'I dreamed that I entered the gates of Jerusalem,' said Le Gor. 'Now that I can see, we will make the pilgrimage to Jerusalem, together, Gui . . .'

'And your position as cardinal?'

'How good it will be to lay down that burden!' replies Le Gor.

In the Street there is hurried knocking on Thoros's door and he is awake at once. Even now, each knock in the night reminds him of the call to the ailing Pope in the palace. As he struggles out of bed, Blanchette stirs and whispers, 'Joseph— ?' but the little boy has not woken.

Thoros opens the door to an anxious mother, whose child has the croup and cannot breathe and he leaves with her a few minutes later.

Saint-Amant is at midnight Mass. By his side in the hospice chapel his fellow helpers are on their knees. At the back of the chapel a huddle of lepers, those who have been able to walk here, form a dark mass in the light of the candles whose shadows further distort the ravaged faces. Saint-Amant who, soon after the aborted rescue of his child, had decided to face his fears by caring for the lepers' remains on his knees after the Mass ends, giving thanks to God, as he does every night now, who has kept him from disease. So far.

Astruc, alone in Marie's house, neither knows nor cares what day of the year it is. After he has made the round of the animals in his care, after he has locked the door, said the evening prayer and gone to the bed he has made of rough boughs in a corner of the room, he sleeps lightly, knowing that he will hear the quietest knock: Marie's knock.

After midnight Mass, Pope Clement embraces his sister and slowly climbs the stairs to his private apartments, disrobes with help from the monks of the bedchamber, and settles down on his couch. The monks withdraw and leave him to his thoughts, banished for the past two hours by the never-failing comfort of the Mass. Now though, he is exposed to them and shivers, drawing the fur rug up to his chin. The pain has been watching for him and he recognises the insistent nagging of it: another stone. His mind turns to the Jewish physician for whom he has often prayed; who lost and then regained his memory, so Le Gor said.

Clement had noticed the absence of Le Gor at Mass tonight and supposed that the cardinal's eyes still troubled him. Le Gor: a good cardinal, strong in his faith, efficient in the service of the Church, if weak in certain ways, which Clement dismissed – has always dismissed – as of no importance.

Should he call de Chauliac? But while he thinks about this, he drifts into peacefulness adjacent to slumber. His pain leaves him and he sighs in gratitude – just as the first lightening of the dark sky forecasts a January day. His last conscious task is to whisper the words all Christians say before falling asleep in case God takes them before they wake.

And God sends him a dream.

He dreams that he has sailed down the Rhône to Marseilles, watching a ship tying up; he is told it has sailed all the way from Asia. The sleeping Pope watches the sailors spring ashore to tie up the ropes and, as they cross the planks from ship to shore, as they walk with bundles on their backs and in their arms, they are nearly tripped up by a strange cargo escaping from the ship and making its way between the legs of the sailors. Clement sees sharp muzzles and red eyes, bared teeth and long hairless tails, then these are confounded and run into each other to form a writhing word, inky black: the blackness is a stain, seeping everywhere now, all around. Clement groans and beseeches, 'Help us, Jesus!'

He wakes, remembering everything, the dream and the message: danger, blackness. Is this the blackness in men's hearts? If this is a warning, a warning of what – and what should he, the ruler of Christendom, do?

He thinks that the blackness denotes not the innumerable sins committed ceaselessly, but rather a cataclysm; and knows that all – including himself – are helpless when great disasters strike, he knows this and has experienced it, and he finds himself saying the words of the night prayer again, although morning had broken. 'Into Thy hands, O Lord, I commend my spirit. Thou hast redeemed me, O Lord, Thou God of truth.'

Without calling the monks, he manages to leave his couch and presently stands by his window to look down at Avignon beneath him.

It is a clear, cool morning; and the year has changed from the year of Our Lord 1347 to 1348.

Chapter 31

Astruc woke one morning in the barn where he now slept and listened, immediately on guard, aware of change: it was the sound of rain on the roof which was missing. God be praised! He seized the ladder which he always pulled up behind him onto his bed of hay in the rafters and climbed down. When he opened the door of the barn, sun was glistening on the rough stones of the yard.

The rain which had fallen ceaselessly for months on the fields of Provence had filled him, like all other peasants, with despair. The beans, cabbages and roots he had planted grew mouldy and the vines showed spores of disease on the young shoots. Astruc knew that this year's harvest would fail, like last year's and he would surely go hungry when the winter came.

The sun gave him the courage to go into the house, which he had not entered since he had spent the first night after his return to it. So strong was the feeling of evil manifest in its two rooms that he had slept the autumn and winter in the barn. He decided now that he would give the house a good cleaning, and the bright sunshine, the first for months, sent him inside. He left the door wide open to let out the smell of burning, still trapped inside. As he began scrubbing the floor of rat droppings, he discovered a pile of clean bones. Marie's old dog must have died here, thought Astruc when he found its skull, picked clean. He weighed it in his hands, thinking of the thick fur, the waving tail and the golden intelligent eyes.

Memory began to stir, but he fought it down.

When evening came, the friar who had helped Astruc bury Marie appeared in the yard and joined Astruc on the wooden bench where he was sitting, a hairy, filthy figure, turning an animal's skull over in his hands.

'I came to see how you fared, Astruc.'

The friar pulled a loaf of bread from his bag, and added two dried silvery fishes, narrow as poplar leaves, which he placed next to Astruc.

'I have enough. People bring me food in their charity in spite of their own want. I've come from Carpentras. They have locked the corn store; it is half empty, because of last year's failed harvest. They hand out a little to each man and woman once a week. Two bad summers! We have offended God. This sun warming our bones today comes too late, alas, the grain is rotting on the stalks – many people will starve in the coming winter . . .'

Astruc said nothing.

'A traveller from Paris, a friar like me, slept in my hut last night. He told me there had been a star above the west of the city not long ago, very large and clear by daylight, and one night it broke; some fell on the city and some in the fields outside. Famine and shooting stars! A warning from God. It is not too late to pray, my friend.'

'Thank you for your gifts,' said Astruc at last. 'But I beg you to leave me. I find it hard to speak, let alone pray. I have not prayed for . . . for a long time. Excuse me. I must get the house ready for Marie's return.'

Next day the friar returned. The sight of Astruc crouching, filthy and hairy, clutching an animal skull had

not left him all night. He found the house empty with the
door swinging in the wind. Astruc wasn't in the barn or
in the field, and the hens clucking and scratching under
the cherry tree took no notice of the friar.

He returned along the path to his hut, the scent of
thyme and lavender strong in the sun. He reached the
cool shade of the wood, breathing in the scent of pine
needles when he heard, faintly above the sough of pine
branches in the breeze, the sound of sobbing. Reaching
the clearing, he found the place where he had planted a
cross on the grave of Marie and her child.

On the brown, raw earth now spiked with green
growing shoots lay Astruc, his face pressed into the
earth. When the friar knelt by Astruc's side, he heard
Astruc murmur, over and over, 'Marie . . . Bonjoue . . .'

'You will recover now,' whispered the friar.

The sun shone throughout the months of August and
September, and Astruc was able to grow and sell vegetables. The friar, concerned and also remembering the
Church's exhortation to convert the Jews, came by from
time to time. He knew that a Jew's faith was no more
than superstition, but the Holy Father had enjoined
Christians to respect it. When the autumn came, the
friar came to say goodbye, for he was to spend the winter
in the abbey of Senanque.

'Go back to the Street, Astruc,' he urged. 'You know
that Marie will not return, you have wept on her grave.
Or come with me to the abbey, they will take you in and
they have food, I know.'

But Astruc shook his head.

During the autumn months he picked chestnuts, dug
up roots and found honey. He roasted the chestnuts and

ground the flour, mixing it with water and honey,
kneading the dough into flat cakes which he baked. He
used the axe to make a bed and a table and a bench.
When the nights turned colder in December and the
fierce wind whistled through the holes in his clothes, he
remembered how in the Street the people were penned
up like cattle. Despite the cold out here he was free; and
not ready for the narrow Street and a hundred *escamots*
which prescribed behaviour every minute of the day. He
made his own rules now.

He was fishing in a pool in the woods one cold
morning with a net made from the sleeve of a jerkin,
when he became aware of two men watching him, warily,
half-hidden in the bushes. The reflection in the pool
showed him his face, overgrown with whiskers, beard,
hair, all matted together. Astruc's own reflection scared
him, he they must be terrified at the sight of him.

'Greetings,' he tried in a voice rusty with disuse.

'A *cef.* Look out—!' said the smaller of the two men.

Astruc, whose hearing was now sharpened like that of
any other animal living by its wits in the woods, lifted his
head like a deer. A *cef* was the word for a devil in the
language they spoke among themselves in the Street. He
dropped the net and gave a roar of wonder and joy.
Running, lumbering through the undergrowth, he did
resemble a hairy, powerful devil, and the men sprang
back in alarm.

'It's Cresquet!' cried Astruc, 'and Mosset, son of . . .
wait – yes, son of old Bonafos! Don't you know me? Cresquet! Mosset!'

The men stared. 'The *cef* has taken on the form of a
Jew from our Street. Get back!' Cresquet shouted as

Astruc moved towards them. After conferring for a few minutes, Cresquet called out, 'So you're a Jew from the Street, you say. Tell me then, what is the law, *cef*?'

'The law,' Astruc replied without hesitation, just as he had been taught by old Rabbi Lyon de Milhaud, 'as it is handed down to us, was given by the Lord to Moses.'

'And Moses?'

'Moses was the greatest of the prophets,' said Astruc in a sing-song voice.

'And the Messiah?'

'The Lord will send us the Messiah as foretold by the prophets,' chanted Astruc.

'Our soul?'

'Our soul is immortal and when the hour which God has chosen is at hand, he will recall the dead to life.'

The men conferred.

'Isn't that enough? What more do you want? ' Astruc shouted suddenly. 'I know your names! And mine is Astruc! My mother-in-law that was is called Lea, and she makes the best *coudolles* in the Street, and if you're not impressed with my answers – as taught by Maimonides! – maybe I should add that Lea talks too much—'

The two pedlars started laughing, and walked up to him. Despite the fact that he smelt rankly like a wild animal, they embraced him, saying that he must remember that they had to be wary because the enemies of the sons of Jacob took on many forms.

They were brethren and, because they spoke his language, because they were pedlars like him, Astruc became for the first time since Marie's death curious about the world he had left behind. First, he cooked them a pottage with a handful of barley flavoured with thyme and rosemary, strengthened with an egg. They gave him their bread, and Cresquet rubbed Astruc's face with oil and shaved his beard and whiskers. When his hair had been cut, they said the evening prayer together.

'Your brother Thoros has returned to the Street,' said Mosset. 'And . . . well . . . did you know he has married Blanchette?'

'I'm glad! Thoros alive! Yes, I'm glad he has married Blanchette. I know nothing of how the world has fared since I found my Marie . . .' And he managed to put into words, for his neighbours from the Street, what had been inexpressible. The two pedlars looked at him with sadness.

'So no news has reached you of our great fear, Astruc, hidden away here?' said Mosset, as Astruc brought him water to wash his hands after the meal. 'We heard from a learned foreign rabbi who stayed three days in the guest house of our *escole*. In Paris – I heard him say – they explain the calamity thus—'

'What calamity?' asked Astruc.

'You must know yourself since you've become a peasant, Astruc – the failure of the harvest everywhere, in Italy, in Germany, in the Low Countries, in Africa, we've heard and in China! As for the cause, the rabbi told it thus. Two years ago the fires of the sun drew with such force upon the ocean that they sucked up enough water to make an island sea which changed to vapour and remained suspended in the heavens. These vapours – do you understand so far?'

Astruc shook his head.

'I don't understand either, but I have retained the rabbi's words: the vapours enveloped several parts of the world in a thick fog which, soaking into the ground, created marshes full of worms and toads where nothing grows. In other places they suffered with dreadful dryness and clouds of locusts descended, leaving nothing for people to eat. The rabbi warned that where there was hunger and weakness, men would fall easy prey to a contagion.'

Mosset and Cresquet, with their long noses and mushroom-shaped hats roamed all over Provence, with their neckerchiefs to keep out the rain and their tales of tragedies and miracles which they told to peasants hungry for explanations of the dreadful and inexplicable in their lives.

All three stretched out now in front of the fire blazing in the hearth, and while Astruc thought of Marie holding Bonjoue in her arms, Mosset carried on talking. 'God sends three great evils: famine, war and pestilence. You will say there is always war . . . The English burnt and pillaged Normandy, Calais is now English, they say. Last year the Kings of France and England signed a truce, yet there is fighting in Brittany and in Languedoc. There's always war, as long as we can remember. But the calamity of which we spoke earlier—'

Astruc said nothing. They talked too much, he was not used to so much talking.

'Well, you know how mercenaries ply their trade. When the war was over, they roamed the country, looking for where they could use their swords . . . In the Limousin and in Auvergne they killed and looted in the villages. Some of them had returned from fighting in Africa and that is where the disease started and they carried the contagion wherever they went. If a man died of it, his comrades left the corpse where it lay, corrupt with contagion. They did not trouble to bury their own, these Christians.'

Marie was a Christian, thought Astruc.

'It was the wolves,' Cresquet continued. 'It was they who spread the sickness. If, as happened in Cadenet – there weren't enough men to kill them, a pack of wolves would enter a village and scatter, devouring such a corpse if they found one. When the animals perished in their turn in the fields outside a town and lay there, the flux from their unburied bodies, beasts and men both, caused pestilence. Pestilence is borne on the wind; and who can escape the wind?'

But Astruc had rolled himself into a ball and was asleep with his arms wrapped around his chest, breathing evenly. His hair, though shorter, still looked like the pelt of an animal and the light from the hearth glinted on the red curls on his arms and legs, hardly covered by the tatters he wore. Dreaming, Astruc bared his teeth.

Cresquet and Mosset looked at each other. 'How will he live in the Street, after this?' said Mosset. 'Yet a Jew should not live alone.'

In the morning Astruc woke to find his friends washing and intoning the morning prayers and Astruc, too, washed and prayed. Afterwards, Mosset took him to one side. 'It is not good for a man, let alone a Jew, to live alone. How can you worship? And think of the danger in this lonely place. Remember – remember the reasons for living safely in the Street. We, too, like to roam, but we always return to the Street for the Sabbath. Come back with us.'

'Not yet, I'm not ready.'

Words, words. He longed for stillness, quiet.

At last the pedlars left, handing Astruc the remainder of the bread and oil, embracing him and promising to tell Thoros that his brother was alive.

As Astruc watched their packs and mushroom hats disappear into the woods, he felt relieved at their departure, and resolved that he would reward them for their care and brotherly love one day, in the Street.

He never saw them again.

Chapter 32

The *baylons*, unused to so much rain, grumbled as they made their way over the sodden straw one spring evening to the *escole*. At this time of year it should have been light still in the great Azara where they met, but this gloomy evening David counted fifty beeswax candles burning while he waited for the other *baylons*. He looked up at the brass candelabra which carried crowns and nests of candles from which the smoke ascended like an ancient sacrifice to God. What a waste, thought David. He was here this evening to talk about candles . . . The rain-sodden fields, according to all the pedlars' reports, threatened a ruined harvest. It was time to tighten belts.

Old Farrusol opened the meeting and told the *baylons* that David Rougier had a proposal for them. The *baylons* moved restlessly, conscious of sodden footwear. Naquet started coughing. The subject had come before the *baylons* recently, and there was resentment that David should pursue it again.

'Resuming my proposal,' said David. 'I must remind you that all reports foretell a bad harvest, which will affect our stomachs and our purses. My proposal concerns our habitual shortage of money—' He looked around him at bored and irritated faces. 'Friends, my idea is simple. You tell me that according to precedent and tradition, we must burn all these candles. It would help if one of us were to go to Marseilles and buy them, not only for the *escole* but for the whole Street. On such a large sale the savings should be considerable. Until now we have bought piecemeal from the Italian at His Holiness's court at prices we know are too high, and quite unaffordable for the poorest in this community who elected me.' He paused, then said with authority, 'I will go myself. I need two men for protection and I think they should be *goyim*. I shall obtain a *laissez passer* from the palace office. This will cost us something but I calculate—'

Jessue de Carcassonne interrupted. 'You know what happened when we sent a man to buy citrus fruit—'

'Had he no protection? I cannot remember—' asked Abraham de Monteux, president of the *baylons*.

'On the contrary, he had protection; they were bound hand and foot by robbers! We lost all our money and the *estrogs* . . .'

'His protectors joined the robbers!' cried Cabri Montel, 'and so will the Christians you want to hire as protectors. We should send several men, our own, from the Street – I suggest dealers in mules who know the roads. No protectors. Should one of our own men be robbed, God forbid, the others will return with the goods.'

'I've done the calculations,' said David. 'Even with costs for the *laissez passer*, and two mounted guards, I will show savings which will pay for three dowries for orphaned brides. Never mind dealers in mules. I want to go.'

The *baylons* looked puzzled. Why was he so anxious to go?

'And you'll take the risk yourself?' enquired Cabri. 'Of course we would prefer a *baylon* to take the responsibility—'

The candles lit up jutting noses and black, grey and white beards, troubled eyes. 'And will you reimburse us if you are, God forbid, robbed? You will be carrying the money collected from every family in the Street.'

'I am ready to endanger my life for the good of all. You – who are without exception richer than I am – should stand surety for this money!' said David.

On occasions like this, everyone turned to Rabbi Liptois. As a community, they had no learning, unlike the Polish rabbi.

'David is risking his life. At best, it will be an uncomfortable journey, fraught with danger. I believe the *baylons* of this community are generous men; so let us reward him for his generous gesture. We should stand surety for him; David is affianced now, he has responsibilities.'

'We shall see,' said Abraham de Monteux, feeling – again – a bitter flux rising in his gorge. He had eaten tainted food; perhaps it had been the bread. He should have avoided it since a blight had covered the stalks of rye as they stood in the rain-drenched fields . . .

'Abraham?'

'I close this meeting,' said Abraham and, to set an example, he blew out the candles nearest to him. They really cost too much, these candles.

Next morning he met the other two *baylons* of the richest *main*, as they called each of the electoral groups. They decided to underwrite David's journey, and thus they sealed David's fate.

After the meeting in the *escole* David walked along the Street to the staircase on which the family of his affianced bride lived, feeling in his pocket for the orange he had brought for her. Her name was Alysa and she was twelve years old, just a month short of thirteen, when she would be of an age to observe the Law; her father was responsible for any foolishness of hers before that age. Alysa, although tall and well-grown, seemed young for her age to David, watching her bite into the orange and squeezing juice into his mouth as well as her own. He tried to laugh with her, but his heart was heavy. Still, he wanted to be married, and Alysa Duranton was good-natured and pretty.

Isaac Duranton took David's arm and drew him to one side. 'This wedding, David, when is it to be? I have the dowry ready and the money for the festivities and there is no obstacle that I can see—'

'Yes: I have to go to Marseilles on behalf of the *baylons*, but I will be able to tell you the date very soon, Isaac.'

He embraced his future parents-in-law and Alysa, who clung to him, and swiftly ran down the stairs. When he reached the Street he crossed it in two bounds, avoiding a dog fighting another over a fish head and climbed the stairs to where Thoros, Blanchette and Joseph lived.

Thoros was attending an old man with boils, said Blanchette, holding Joseph up to David to be kissed. David kissed the boy, while looking at his mother. Would he never be rid of this pain in his heart?

'Is all well? Are you happy?' he asked her.

'Of course I'm happy, and I hope you are. Have you come from seeing Alysa? I think she is a pretty little thing – what a good choice you've made.'

David absolved her from cruelty. She had greeted the news of a bride for him with relief. Happy herself, she wanted happiness for him. He decided on a last attempt. 'I shall be going to Marseilles soon, to buy candles for the whole Street,' he began.

'You will be making a dangerous journey,' she said at once looking at him with concern which filled him with joy. 'I shall think of you and ask for God's protection—'

He stepped forward swiftly, seized her hands and the blood rushed into his face as he bent to kiss her.

'No,' she said. 'No! Marry, David. Do not torture yourself.'

He left soon after this, embracing the little boy and murmuring farewell. She wished him a safe journey once more, in a low voice.

David returned to Duranton's dwelling straight away, and told him to prepare everything for the wedding. He had decided to go to Marseilles at the end of the month, and if there was danger, so much the better.

Chapter 33

It was an uncommonly cold spring day.

Guy de Chauliac, *medicus* to the Pope, sat shivering in his *cabinet de travail* in the palace, shivering in spite of his squirrel-skin robe, reading once more a letter which was dated last November. It trembled in his hands which were blue with cold.

The letter was signed by three men, friends from his student days in Montpellier, many years ago now – all three serving the Faculty of Medicine in Paris. They wrote because they knew that Pope Clement was in his care; they wrote that they had been required by Philippe de Valois, King of France, to prepare a document on the evil pestilence which had struck the coastal towns of France and Italy and which was advancing northwards murderously fast. We have been asked to explain, they wrote, how we propose to combat this tribulation.

Though the letter had been sent in November, its seal had been broken, and it was evident to de Chauliac that for the past months it must have been seen by many eyes before reaching him. Useless to find the culprit, the damage was done.

De Chauliac rose and walked to the window – of glass, unlike most in the palace which were covered with waxed canvas – and looked down at the roseate tiled rooves of Avignon below, still wet from a squall. There were 20,000 souls below; at great risk, according to the letter. All this would be swept away, amid scenes he could hardly imagine.

His own, puny knowledge could perhaps affect a few. Before him lay his unfinished treatise on surgery, the field in which he was a master and which would be irrelevant for the time being – he might as well put it away. Thinking of the most illustrious patient in his care, he read the letter again. His colleagues had found an explanation, reached together with the royal astrologers, who declared, as they would, that the main causes were astrological. He disentangled the proliferating loops and hooks of the document to read that the nefarious conjunction of . . . fourteenth degree . . . the position of the three planets . . . He was impatient for a diagnosis, but above all he thought of the impotence of doctors in this manifestation of God's wrath. He returned to the letter:

. . . *the position of the three planets on the twentieth of March two years ago, followed by the entry of the evil planet Mars, in conjunction with the sign of the Lion on the sixth of October of this year and its subsequent encounter with the dragon head meant, in sum, that the stars were against man: This was the cause as far as the heavens were concerned.*

The terrestrial cause was the corruption of the air by evil vapours. The southerly wind, given the conjunction of the stars, penetrated to the very hearts of men, whose breathing would be affected; and the overlying dampness would cause the inner organs to rot, causing death.

De Chauliac searched for precedents, and so had his correspondents: he read that doctors and astrologers agreed, and the wise men of antiquity, as well as the Arab masters such as Avicenna, Razes and Averroes, who had come to the same conclusions long ago; and the same causes would, as they did then, produce the same effects. He searched the letter for suggestions regarding treatment, and found none.

De Chauliac was used to writing down his observations, to clear his mind. He now dipped his pen in the inkhorn and wrote:

The great conjunction of the stars foretell marvellous events which act powerfully and may lead to occurrences which we fear; such as the disappearance of a great ruler or the coming of a prophet – but what we fear most is the death of a great number.

As a farm boy long ago, he had set the leg of a young girl who had fallen from her horse, and her grateful father had paid for his studies. A brilliant student, he had been wearing the purple robe of a *medicus* and *physicus* for many years now, the best *mège* in Avignon – well, perhaps Thoros Bonivassin in the Street was equally good . . . He pulled himself up sharply. We *mèges* are puny figures to fight Mars and an evil conjunction of the stars; how can our skills cure a miasma which clings to fields and meadows and is breathed in by all men? 'We doctors will fail the people,' he cried aloud. 'Only God can save us and His Church must intercede for us!'

All men feared Satan, who gathered in his image all other fears of evil and terror; thus it was today. But tomorrow, fear of the pestilence would drive away even the fear of Satan.

He knelt to pray that God would enhance his skills. He had often been humbled before a sick man whose pain he could not alleviate. Like his *confrères*, he hid his impotence from the sick for their comfort.

'Guide Your servant Guy so that he can protect the Holy Father. Give me the knowledge to heal, and make me your instrument in keeping safe the life of the ruler of Christendom—'

It would be presumptuous to pray that he might deliver all men from the pestilence, but surely God would hear his prayer to protect His vicar on earth? And his practised mind slipped into prayer after prayer until his knees hurt and he rose slowly, to read once more the last page of the letter.

Our Italian brothers tried their skills when the pestilence cast its sinister shadows over the seaports of the great Sea in the south. The truth, terrible to contemplate, is that nothing is to be gained by treatment, not even alleviation of symptoms and consequently most of them, even the humble barber-surgeon, abandoned their visits to those sick of the pestilence, for fear of becoming infected themselves, and those who persisted in visiting ceased to prescribe, for, with or without prescriptions, their patients died within two days.

We recommend you, our illustrious colleague and mège at the court of the Holy Father the following: We urge you to separate the healthy from the sick, once the pestilence reaches you; and we know that it is making its way north from Marseilles. Persuade His Holiness to abandon Avignon; and go with him. In one word: flee.

Below these words there were three signatures and the imprint of the great seal of the Faculty of Medicine at the Sorbonne.

The Pope will not abandon Avignon, thought de Chauliac. What can I do to protect him?

The same day, across the Rhône in Villeneuve-les-Avignon, a sharp wind tugged at the sheets tied over heavy carts as the horses laboured up the steep incline to the cardinal's residence, bringing goods and chattels from Périgord, the property of the incoming cardinal. Inside the building, the new cardinal's servants were helping those Le Gor had left behind with the tasks of sweeping and mopping, polishing copper and silver, and hanging the incoming cardinal's pictures and tapestries. The new cardinal, a large man with a gross appetite, had offered a fortune to the cook, who had consented to stay and was preparing Périgordine specialities against the arrival of the new cardinal, expected any minute now, helped by a new kitchen boy from Périgord, who kept questioning the cook on his old master. 'I can tell you that Cardinal Le Gor spent well on himself, as well as on his household,' said the cook, 'And now I'll ask you to get all these feathers off that bird, or someone will hurt themselves on roasted goose, boy!'

'Did your cardinal go to Jerusalem for a penance?' the boy asked.

'Is that your business? A thanksgiving, that's what he's gone for. The Pope's doctor, Maître de Chauliac, operated on both his eyes, and our cardinal recovered his sight. Why are you holding that knife by the blade? Have your senses gone wandering?'

'How could the cardinal leave all this,' said the boy. 'Isn't a pilgrimage for an old man used to such luxury dangerous? And did many servants accompany him?'

'He took just one to serve him, his page, Gui. He went on a pilgrimage, boy, not a procession, remember. Ah,

Cardinal Le Gor . . . I never had a better master. He put away his cardinal's robe and undertook the pilgrimage in a woollen cloak and a pilgrim's hat and stave and scrip – and I hope we will see him safely back from Jerusalem. He left us last September. God speed him home—'

And as he spoke, the new cardinal's horses and coach clattered into the courtyard.

Across the bridge in Avignon, two nuns were leaving the palace by way of the Holy Father's garden, which, despite the winter season, looked inviting. Cypresses and laurels lined the paths where Clement walked every day, scattering crumbs from the *brioches* which the kitchen sent up to him since his teeth had begun troubling him again. Songbirds, as tame as poultry, hopped around the nuns' feet as they passed the huts where the Pope kept the precious foreign beasts – presents from kings in the south – who needed shelter from the cold.

Old Jacob, from the Street, saw the nuns and followed them back to their Benedictine convent close by. Unlike the nuns, who had begged for the money to buy new habits and had received it, Jacob had been unlucky at the palace today. He wanted to give and had so little for Blanchette, who cared for him now that he was getting so old and so tired. As he followed the women, Jacob pulled his hat off and hid it in his pocket. He had called at the convent many times. They knew him as a pedlar and would let him have a little sleep in the kitchen, seeing it was such dreadful weather. When a novice opened the door to the two nuns, she greeted Jacob as well, and though the passing cellarer with her jangling bunch of keys stepped forward with a frown she recognised the old man.

'Our visitor from the Street!' she greeted him, smiling. 'Alas – we gave our old clothes to another last week! I'm truly sorry. But come in and warm yourself.'

In the kitchen, comfortably settled on the bench against the huge stove, he was soon dreaming, not disturbed by the bells which rang for Nones, evensong and compline, and was finally woken by a nun on kitchen duty late that night. When the abbess was consulted, she said that if that was the old Jew from the Street, he did no harm and should pass the night in the convent's dormitory for the homeless, as the Street gates would be locked by now. The nun who woke him told him that he had permission to sleep in the dormitory. 'You will be safe there,' she said. She was to remember those words.

Jacob settled on the bed, a wooden platform which covered nearly all the floor, so that he had to step over several travellers to get to a space. Jacob said his prayers and lay down, head to toe with his neighbours, in the long line of weary bodies. High above their heads a few candles stuck in niches burnt down, and only a narrow slit in one wall allowed a sliver of moonlight to enter the dormitory. Jacob woke several times to cries and babble and moans.

Soon after dawn a nun brought a basket of bread and two large platters of broken meats from the refectory. A pitcher of water went from hand to hand and mouth to mouth. Jacob's stomach churned at the sight of the cold, greasy scraps of meat. The nuns expected all those whom they had sheltered to go to Mass before they left, but Jacob longed to go straight back to the Street. When the travellers and beggars made for the door, to face another cold and windy day, the man who had lain next to Jacob did not rise. His livid face turned towards Jacob and he was about to speak when a spasm of coughing seized him and he contracted his body like a caterpillar. The dreadful coughing brought a nun. A few men still stood by the open door, waiting to brave the wind.

'I need help to carry this man to the infirmary—' began the nun and Jacob, despite his age, stepped forward to do a good deed, as the law commands. He and three others carried the sick man to the infirmary, where Jacob suddenly swayed, fell, and lay on the ground unable to rise. He was placed on a cot next to the sick man.

Within one day all those in the infirmary were coughing and spitting blood.

The pestilence had reached Avignon.

One afternoon at the end of that blustery and cold January, Blanchette was getting ready for David and Alysa's wedding that night. Blanchette, with a reputation for clever needlework to sustain, was trying on garments, watched by Thoros, hunched in his black robe. Suddenly she abandoned the clothes and sat on the bed, holding her head in her hands. 'I can't bear to think that he died among strangers.'

'If Jacob had died here,' said Thoros sharply, 'the consequences for the whole Street, as I told you at the time, Blanchette—'

He was interrupted by a volley of knocks and Blanchette, opening the door to an anxious patient, as she supposed, was confronted by a Christian, who asked if he could speak to the *medicus* who was to go with him, now, on urgent business at His Holiness's palace.

'No one,' said Blanchette, 'has the power to order my husband to the palace.'

The messenger was taken aback. Blanchette staring at him fiercely saw, not him, but Saint-Amant in his pale blue silk clothes with the gold decoration shining like a star on his breast . . . Joseph's father . . . no! Not a second time . . . she shook her head to dispel the memory of what had followed.

'Please go,' she said, 'you bring ill luck.'

The young messenger, very uneasy, spoke to Thoros directly, 'Are you Master Thoros Bonivassin?'

'Yes. Who are you? Who sent you?'

'I am an apprentice apothecary, learning at the feet of my master, Guy de Chauliac, who sends for you to attend an urgent consultation; all doctors are bidden to his cabinet today, sir.'

'I hope the Holy Father . . . is he indisposed? Has he sent for me?'

'No, sir, he is well. I have others to call and I must go. Four o'clock in my master's cabinet.'

Blanchette's calm had deserted her. 'Don't go! What happened the last time you went to the palace? Do not go. If you love me, do not go.'

She picked up Joseph, playing with sand and a spoon, in a violent gesture and the child began to cry.

'You have seen me leave this room a hundred times to attend a sick person since I returned to myself, Blanchette. If de Chauliac has summoned physicians and surgeons – and has not forgotten me – I must attend! We, all Avignon, are threatened. When Jacob died, I warned you.'

'I fear for you,' whispered Blanchette, hushing Joseph. Thoros, looking at her, thanked God for the hundredth time for his luck. He found her as beautiful as always; he admired the force behind her vehemence and loved her black locks which she tossed over her shoulders, her eyes brilliant with tears gathering and the corners of her mouth trembling. She was tall and slim, taller than he was nowadays with his wasted body which had not really recovered its strength after the illness.

'Enjoy the wedding,' he said. 'I will not be able to attend. I am sorry you and I had such a small, quiet wedding – so enjoy this one! Dance, eat and drink!'

'What will you discuss at the Palace?'

'I can't tell you,' he said.

She misunderstood, 'Thoros! Can I not be trusted?'

'I cannot tell you because I do not know what plans will be devised –'

'Thoros!' cried Blanchette, beside herself. 'You don't trust me, and I know the reason! Because I bore a bastard while I was your brother's wife, that's why!'

And she wept so vehemently that he was shaken.

'Bastard or not, I love the boy like my own son, Blanchette, be reasonable! There is a meeting of doctors which I cannot but attend, seeing the grave danger which threatens all of us! But Blanchette – you know I cannot live without you.'

'I didn't know that,' said Blanchette quietly. She kissed him and let him go.

Thoros walked with dragging steps through the alley-ways to the palace. Blanchette was stronger than he was in health, spirits and determination. How he, weak and sickly, shrunk in body and half impotent, could keep the love of this woman, remained a mysterious gift from God.

As he splashed through the puddles, his mind turned to the catastrophe to come.

Chapter 34

Alysa had lived her thirteen years like any female child in the Street, loved but of little account. There were two occasions when her life would rise from obscurity: her engagement and her wedding. On the day of her engagement she knew that she counted as always in the eyes of God, who knew the fall of a sparrow, but also in the eyes of the Street.

Her family and friends were assembled in one of the warren of rooms in the *escole*, and all the boys and young men had been given a clay pot. A *baylon* who seemed ancient to her, Jessue de Carcassonne, had read the marriage contract out aloud to all the party, while David held her hand and had announced the day of their wedding: 24 April 1347. Then there was a crashing of clay pots as they broke on the ground, thrown with a will. Alysa knew that this was a symbol of abundance to come; although she knew there was little of that at the moment. A hum rose from a corner of the room and the six singers burst into loud song. Dancing began, *gaillardes* and *branles*. Alysa loved the *branle* when all held hands and the chain of people wound skipping around the room, and as the dancers became heated Alysa's father handed out wine and honey cakes, sugar plums and pine kernel-studded biscuits. Alysa was happy. David was soon drunk.

The night before the wedding, Alysa, stiff with fear, was taken to the ritual bath – built deep underneath the *escole* – by her mother and an aunt, who carried little handbells which they rang now and then as the small group walked to the *escole*. There they descended the dark stairs and passed along a corridor to another stone staircase, narrower and slippery with moisture, lit only by the candles they held in their hands. Alysa saw that the steps led right down into the black water of a basin, the size of a small room. Her mother's hands on her back urged her forwards. Trembling, she walked into the icy water, dark and oily in the shimmering light of the candles, till she was submerged up to her neck. Soon she lost the feeling in her limbs and her teeth began to chatter, when suddenly her mother traitorously pushed Alysa's head under water. It was only seconds before she rose to the surface, screaming. Her mother and her aunt, laughing, helped her out and rubbed her dry with towels.

The next day was her wedding day.

Alysa stood in her best clothes and a veil over her face, fingering her gilt-fringed belt, a present from David. He would be wearing her present, a belt with silver droplets attached to it. Her mother and sister hummed the old wedding songs as they waited, till there was a shout from the window: the bridegroom is here!

David and his friends and Alysa's father set off for the *escole*, Alysa and the women a few steps behind, and as they walked, neighbours called out blessings.

In the wedding room, Alysa and the other women started the ceremony by walking three times round David who stood in the middle, staring at nothing, swaying slightly and very pale. Next, the women stood back as David took his bride's hand and guided her in a circle around him, while everyone showered the couple with pellets of yeast, so that they might prosper and multiply. Then Alysa was told to stand to the right of David and he turned her head so that she should look towards the south – just as the conjugal bed must be placed if the bride was to bear a boy.

Rabbi Liptois now stepped forward. Since old Rabbi Lyon had taken to his bed, Rabbi Liptois – well rehearsed by now in the ways of the Street – celebrated weddings. He took a corner of the prayer shawl around David's shoulders and covered Alysa's head with it, then blessed a glass of wine and offered it to the young couple. Alysa's mother stepped forward and wiped a few drops from her daughter's lips, as was the custom. Then the rabbi took a ring, showed it to all present before putting it onto Alysa's finger. Next, he read the marriage contract aloud. Again he gave wine to the couple; David drank most of it, then threw the glass on the stone floor where it broke. This was always done in memory of the destruction of the temple.

Throughout these ceremonies Alysa smiled and looked about her. As for David, he looked ever paler and the sweat poured down his face. After the ceremony, friends crowded into the bride's new home, David's large room above his shop. A meal was brought; the first course consisted of two steaming cooked fowls which were set before the bride; and beside the dish lay an egg. Alysa was told to tear the birds with her hands until they were in fragments which she did amid much laughter and clapping. She knew she was to bear childbirth with joy, as the fowl lays an egg with cackling song. Other dishes were brought and eaten, there was singing and David and Alysa led another *branle*.

Instead of celebrating eight days, as was usual, David had decided that, as times were bad and moreover he was to go to Marseilles, they would celebrate for four days only. On 28 April, therefore, he left for the coast. At dawn, Alysa waited for him by the gate, shivering while David fetched the horse from its stable at the other end of the Street. He led it by the bridle to the gate, just opened, where they could see the two protectors waiting and yawning on the town side. As soon as the men saw her, they called out jokes and blew Alysa kisses, which made her shy as she timidly embraced her husband of four days. David whispered into her ear, 'A month, and I'll be home.'

Alysa returned to her parents. For the last four days she had shared a room with just one person, David, and had marvelled at the space, but now that he had gone, she was happy to be once more with her sisters, the baby and her parents. For twelve years she had slept in one bed with her sisters and grandmother. Last year one sister had married and her grandparents had died, leaving more space. Her father slept behind a curtain in an alcove in the same room, and her sister, brother-in-law and the baby in a large open cupboard, also curtained off. Often, after dark or when it rained, someone would open their door from the next door house, on the same floor – the fourth – and walk past their beds till they reached their own rooms, maybe four houses along; but David's room was unusual in that it did not communicate horizontally, like almost all others, so that he and Alysa were alone during their honeymoon.

The first night after David's departure, Alysa curled up like a kitten against her mother's warm body, comforting herself against the memory of the hurt he had done her.

All day she had carried water up from the Street, peeled roots and pounded millet, scrubbed the floor, ran down to buy fish, up and down again for herbs from the country as the peasants cried their wares. Tired out, she did fall asleep at once. But after a brief sleep between her mother and her little sister, she woke up and tried to stifle the sobs which rose to her throat and which would soon wake them all. Her shaking body awoke her mother.

'Why are you crying?'

Alysa could not speak, but clung to her mother.

'Did he hurt you?' whispered her mother.

Alysa clung tighter and murmured something.

'I can't hear you, my lamb. I thought he was so gentle, your David, but you never can tell. Now, stop crying – this is nothing. Wait till the children come, then you can cry! Did he frighten you? He'll be gone a month, and you'll soon be longing for him, you'll see. That's how it'll be, my lamb, so hush your crying and may the angel of the night send you sweet dreams.'

Her mother, tired as always, fell asleep again within a minute, while Alysa lay quietly now, thinking. She felt pain, but not in her body, it was in her heart and quite unlike what she felt when she was a child, four days ago, before the wedding. She was a woman now, but hadn't been one long enough to know how to deal with this pain. She wouldn't tell her mother, she would find a way herself. A memory shot through her, piercing her heart. But he was hers now, her husband.

The best thing to do was to arrange a meeting, see and hear for herself, face to face.

Chapter 35

The tall friar was hurrying up a staircase in the palace when he felt a tug at his sleeve. Turning, he saw a stout woman in a blue mantle and hood which had slipped and uncovered long matted hair and black eyes which stared at him without modesty. She sank to her knees, and clutched the hem of his robe. He tugged gently but she held fast.

'I want a little of your time,' she implored. He looked at her; her gaze, her strangeness. A friar should make himself available, he thought, but there was a problem. 'Could you come to – let us say – the Pope's garden, in half an hour?'

People were pushing past the two of them, but the woman remained kneeling and he thought he heard her saying in a low voice something about his study. His heart missed a beat.

'Your study!' she said in a louder voice.

'Move on!' barked an official. 'You're blocking the way!' and he unceremoniously pushed them both to the wall. The friar helped the woman to rise, and she thanked him and kissed his hand which he tried to withdraw.

'Do you know who—'

'Many of us know, Holy Father. And I have come a long way to give you an urgent message. In private, Holy Father.'

Clement decided that he had better see her, he was not sure why, and told her to follow in half an hour. He thought, with regret, that his days as a friar were numbered.

She entered the study punctually and knelt before him, as before. He asked her name and her business with him.

'The Egyptian, that is what they call me.'

She looked about her, staring at the painted walls, the flowers, vines, birds and fishes in their living colours and likenesses glowing in all the splendour of imagination and new paint. She pointed, 'You capture their likenesses so that you can use your magic to win power over them too – the animals, the birds – as you have power over humans?'

'No, no. These paintings represent the beauty of the world, created to show the glory of its maker. Now, what is it you want to tell me?'

'Others don't know what I know. Some have time; you do not.'

'I do not? Time for what purpose?'

'Listen, Pope Clement, to what I am saying. It is already late.'

He looked at her sharply, at the layers of multi-coloured gauze floating around her short body, at the bulbous-headed pins studded with crystals in her wild hair, at her eyes which looked through him now to the window beyond. She was delaying her message, he thought, to heighten the anticipation before the impact.

'If it is already late, why don't you tell me quickly?' he tried, but she wasn't ready yet.

'Your animals in the menagerie remind me of home . . . the camels, the beautiful fish-catching birds . . .'

'Why are you here?' he made an impatient movement.

'It is hard to say what I must, Clement. I see the future. Often I do not reply to those who ask me what their fate will be – but you shall hear. I have made the journey expressly for that reason.'

Clement smiled at her. This heathen woman had come to warn him, and he must be attentive and grateful. He saw that she had decided to speak.

'Death will come to Avignon, Clement. It will claim twenty thousand lives in your city. It has come from the east to Africa and has leapt over the sea and is now travelling north from Marseilles, up the Rhône. It moves as fast as a trotting horse – not yet cantering, not galloping yet, but it will be here in days. It may be here already, as we speak. I see you have turned pale.

'They will die quickly from sickness in the lungs – so many that soon you will not be able to find graves; you must consecrate new burial grounds now. As for your power, the power of your Church, you will pray and repent and you will devise strategies, but all to no avail. I can hear the cries of the stricken, of those in fear and those in agony, and of the bereaved. More burial grounds, that is all you can do, Clement.'

He crossed himself. Was she right? How did she know? He remembered the dream he had: Black Death. But how had she known him, in his friar's robe? Could a messenger from God take on the shape of an Egyptian fortune-teller, and why?

'Please—' he began, but she held up her hand.

'I have brought a terrible message, Pope Clement, but I have also brought you something to make amends – a

little. You see this ring on my finger? It is as important as
the ring they kiss on yours. I shall give it to you, but on
condition you wear it.'

He wrenched his thoughts away from nightmare
pictures and looked at her with the genuine warmth
which made him so loved. 'I do thank you from the
heart, my daughter, but I cannot accept.'

'I am not your daughter and you must take my ring.
Turn it on your finger as you look where the wind blows
from and it will offer protection from the contagion
from that quarter.'

'I cannot accept—'

'Will you really refuse its power because you do not
believe in it? Will you – because you say you abhor super-
stition – lose the chance of saving lives? Yet they say you
are wise!'

Clement could not reply at once and she continued.
'I am a soothsayer in my country where a crouching
beast with a woman's face, the size of one of your
churches, guards the pyramids and the desert, and I can
tell you that my religion is as powerless against this
disaster as yours will be. I have been granted some
insight, I have come to offer you help and it resides in
this ring.'

She pulled it from her finger and held it out to him.
He took it and put it on his finger. Evidently made of
glass, it looked puny next to the great ring of St Peter,
heavy with its burden of huge precious stones.

'I am deeply indebted to you,' said Clement. 'What
can I offer in return?'

'Nothing I cannot obtain for myself. But I would like
to add to my gift, for I know you are a good man. You

would surely like to know whether you yourself will
survive?'

'Yes, I think I would like to know, in order to make
those dispositions—'

'No need to explain yourself,' she said, 'is it not
natural? Yes, Clement, you will live, and do much for
your people.'

'And will you live? You too surely do much good.'

Her face closed and became indistinct, as though one
of her gauzy garments had blown across it. She kissed his
hand one last time, touched her ring on his finger and
was gone without another word. He did not pursue her,
nor ask a servant to call her back, and then went to kneel
in his private chapel. He tried to pray, but thoughts
slipped between the well-known words. To believe in the
ring's power was to bow to superstition. Twenty thousand
deaths in Avignon, the Egyptian had said. He must speak
to the doctors – but first, he must see his sister,
Guillemette, always calm and always wise.

'Yes, brother, I have known for some days,' she told him
quietly. 'I learned from the prior at the leprosy hospital
where Saint-Amant now works, caring for the lepers – he
told me that all the occupants of the Benedictine Infirmary died within two days of falling sick, of a contagion,
a pestilence . . . what have we done, what sins had they
committed? Has God condemned our world?'

There were tears in her eyes. Brother and sister
embraced, and Guillemette left him. O Lord, said
Clement to his God, if many are to die, how shall I recon-
cile the people with your will? And those who point the
finger at the so-called opulence of my court will crow,

saying my bad example has called forth the just wrath of God . . . I must bring sinners back to the Church through repentance. If I survive this pestilence – and the Egyptian has told me I would – if I live . . . O Lord, relieve me of this pain in my back, in my knees, I have to be physically strong enough . . .

He remained on his knees for a while, praying and arguing with his God. As Pope, he set before his Maker his hopes and his fears. As ruler of Christendom, he must find help and consult. As for the ring, he would give it to the next beggar who approached him. Now he must call Guy de Chauliac, and see what the doctors proposed.

Ten minutes' walk from the palace, Blanchette tried to imagine Thoros speaking with the Pope's doctors. Since the arrival of the first messenger, Thoros had been called to the palace three times in as many days to confer with the doctors of Avignon. At night he wrapped his thin body around hers, and fell asleep at once. The third day he returned in the evening, after many hours in the palace, ate the soup she had prepared without speaking, and asked her to fetch her mother.

'But it's late, Thoros, she will be asleep—'

'Please, wife, go—'

'Lolo!' cried her mother, still awake. 'I am glad that you can spare a few moments to talk to your old mother! How is my grandson? Nothing amiss?'

'You saw him only an hour ago, mother. Thoros wants you to hear some news from the palace, so will you come with me now, he begs you.'

The old woman was happy to wrap herself in a big shawl and hear what Thoros had to say – who else had news directly from the palace? Not those sluts in the street who had pointed the finger at Blanchette! The two women passed quietly through room after room, picking their way by the light of small braziers, set over sand because of the danger of fire. As it was late, mother and daughter passed through silent rooms where the families of the Street lay dreaming, as mother and daughter crept on tiptoe, startling a child here and there who sat up, gaping at them, believing they were creatures in his dreams.

'You are my family,' said Thoros softly when Blanchette and Lea had settled back in his room.

'And have you fetched me from my bed to tell me that?' interrupted Lea at once.

'And, somewhere, there is Astruc, though he has given no sign of life,' continued Thoros. 'Before I speak to the *baylons*, I must tell you first.'

'And Jacob – surely he had become part of our family, and he would be with us if he were not . . .' Lea dabbed at her eyes and blew her nose.

'If he were not dead,' said Thoros, 'and it is Jacob's death, and what will follow that concerns us. I have something very difficult to tell you.'

'I'm glad you include me, Thoros. I often think you do not listen to what I have to say—'

'Hush, Mother.'

'Lea, Blanchette, Jacob's death concerns us – in this room, in this Street, in Avignon.' He paused, then said vehemently, 'I can set broken bones, pull teeth, cut open a tumour. I know the four humours: sanguine, phlegmatic, choleric, melancholic and their importance in treatment. I understand the spasms of the brain, epilepsy and apoplexy, I know how to detect illness in urine – in short, I know how to detect symptoms, but only God can effect a cure. For many hours I have searched with Guy de Chauliac and the other Christian doctors – in their belts of silver threads and their embroidered gloves – for remedies. We have tried everything . . . rosewater mixed with vinegar, pills of powdered stag's horn, a paste of myrrh and saffron, a compound of spices and powdered emeralds—'

Lea sniffed. 'Where shall we get that? We're too poor!'

'It doesn't cure the patient, Lea. No more than praying to the Virgin, like the Christians, nor to the relics of their saints. We cannot relieve symptoms of this disease, we cannot cure it, we cannot prevent death. As a physician, I must not destroy hope, but I have to tell you there is little hope. I have determined that you must hear the worst, or you will not accept my solution.'

Mother and daughter stared at Thoros's narrow head and sunken eyes. He continued. 'Let me go back to Jacob, who slept one night in a convent dormitory. One of the sleepers, we think, had made his way from Marseilles. Neither the other sleepers nor the nuns can tell us now, because they have all succumbed, everyone of them—'

'But can't any of the learned doctors devise—' began Blanchette.

'What? How? We have searched feverishly. This is a sickness against which we have . . . well, nothing. Nothing.'

'With your great knowledge—'

'No!' shouted Thoros, waking Joseph. 'No! If my own wife will not understand, how shall I convince the whole Street?'

'How dare you shout at Blanchette,' said Lea angrily. 'Let me remind you, doctor though you may be, that I've seen sickness come – and go. We must all die, it is God's will and I am resigned to go if I must, but I cannot abide a faint heart! When you were still at your studies in Montpellier, there was much sickness in the Street, and they came to me for my herbal remedies. I tell you—'

Thoros put his hand up to stop her talking. 'Blanchette, forgive me. I am desperate. Herb remedies, mouthwashes, praying, repenting, abjuring evil, or supping with the Devil for all I know, will not make one jot of difference, for this is the pestilence, do you understand? No, you cannot, how could you . . . we have read of the symptoms. What happens, is this: the pestilence kills within two or three days.'

Blanchette had picked up Joseph, now wide awake, and she and Lea stared at Thoros horror-stricken. Lea's mouth worked, her lips forming words which she could not utter.

'How does it begin?' asked Blanchette, quietly.

'With a fever. Then comes the spitting of blood. Within two days it is over, but the patient has passed it on to his wife, mother, child.'   They flinched.

'So quickly,' muttered Lea.

'And . . . is it always thus? ' asked Blanchette.

'We have not seen one soul recovered. De Chauliac, the Pope's doctor, has received reports, letters from doctors which report the same thing – I fear great mortality among doctors. Our duty is with the sick. This means . . .' he stopped and put his face into his cupped hands. Blanchette rose and embraced him, and Lea clung to them both, and they felt his body shake with sobs.

He told them that five days after the death of Jacob, there had been notification to the papal authorities of a hundred deaths. Many more, he thought, had been unrecorded. Reports from villages near Avignon told that an evil wind carrying dust and ashes emanating from the conjunction of certain planets had infected the birds who were dropping to the ground. Herds of cattle had made their way back to their stables from the fields without their herdsmen who were left dead in the fields. Fish were dying, unable to escape some evil in the water. In Avignon, Thoros told them that he had passed by the churchyard of the Dominicans and had seen the bodies of the newly dead lying in long lines, awaiting burial.

'As yet, we are safe in the Street, inside our gates. Do not go out. What I fear are those Christians who enter to buy clothes.'

'But if no one buys my clothes, how shall we live?' asked Blanchette.

'If they do come into the Street, none of us will survive. I want everyone in the Street to be given the warning; beginning with the *baylons*, at first light. No – we will wake them now, tonight.'

'You will get no thanks from them if you wake them now!' said Lea. 'A gaggle of goats they are, prouder than peacocks with the same ugly voices and no more sense than a newborn child between them, grey beards and all. Remember when I asked—'

'Mother—' Blanchette began, wearily.

'You are right, Lea,' said Thoros. 'If they haven't drawn up an *escamot* to cover this particular case, weeks may go by while they argue; and we have only days. But we had better wait till morning, or there will be panic. We must tell them, and each of them must tell five people, and those must tell five – and within the hour everyone will know to remain in the Street.'

Blanchette lay down next to Thoros, but neither slept. Thoros knew that even if no one ventured outside the Street, death would stalk them; there was only one way they might escape. He must persuade the *baylons* to accept his solution.

Blanchette knew that Thoros would continue to care for the sick. Sooner or later, therefore, the corruption would leap from a dying patient to him. She resolved to be as much with him as he allowed, and to die with him when the time came.

Chapter 36

Thoros knew that the *baylons* would need to be made thoroughly afraid to accept his plan – a plan he must urge on them, dangerous and uncertain of success though it might be. Before first light he decided that he, Blanchette and Lea would go out to wake the *baylons* and, without explanation, beg them to assemble for an urgent meeting in the *escole*. He counted on their curiosity and the endemic fear that the Street was somehow threatened. The women wrapped themselves in black cloaks and Joseph was enveloped against the chilly dawn in a red one. Each had the task of rousing three *baylons* and urging them to meet in the *escole*, before the door of the chamber known as Little Azara, in an hour's time.

Day followed night without apparent change in the light cast into the dismal abyss of the street, as Thoros and the women knocked on doors – all on the first and second floors of the houses, as befitted *baylons*. Eight *baylons* accepted, and those whom Blanchette, with Joseph on her arm, woke, even smiled.

An hour later, lamps had been lit in the Little Azara, and Jessue de Carcassonne turned the pages of the last set of *escamots*, drawn up six years ago and endorsed by the *viguier*, the papal official in charge – signed, authorised, stamped and paid for; and, as far as Jessue was concerned, learned by heart. One by one the other *baylons* arrived and took their seats round the table, yawning, and last came Thoros with Lea, Blanchette and Joseph. They were kept standing.

'I have called you because I have grave news for you,' said Thoros in his deep voice, 'which calls for urgent action. I thought it best to bring my family. May we sit down with you?'

'No,' said Jessue without hesitation. 'We do not permit women and children to attend our meetings, as I am sure you know. They may wait for you outside.'

'They are part of the case I wish to present to the *baylons*, Jessue.'

'I insist on the ancient tradition of the Street. Once you break with tradition you have weakened the backbone of the community, Thoros, as we have seen demonstrated many—'

'They will stay, Jessue! Or I will not reveal to you my plan which concerns the life of every inhabitant of the Street! You too have mothers, wives and children. Look at my little family and think of your own.'

There were murmurs of concern around the table. Jessue caught their drift.

'Sit down, *mège*,' said Jessue. 'We owe you respect. Your family may sit on those chairs by the window.' He gathered authority into his voice: ' I hope you have not called us out of bed at this early hour of the morning to waste our time.'

Thoros remained standing. His bent figure looked insubstantial in the mild lamplight. He steadied himself by placing his trembling hand on the table and looked at each *baylon* in turn before he spoke.

'Last week, old Jacob – who was known to many of you – was taken ill in the infirmary of a convent in Avignon, and died there. His body lies with others outside the church of the Dominicans, awaiting burial.'

Jessue leapt from his chair. 'Why were we not told? Why has the society for the burial of the dead not been informed? You of all people know the rules, Doctor!'

'There was one thing which prevented our normal procedure, Jessue: he died of the pestilence.'

'So he died of the pestilence. Do we deny any body the comfort of being buried according to the rights of his forefathers? You take too much on yourself. I shall give orders—'

'That would be ill-advised,' said Thoros. ' Do not quarrel with me, Jessue, you have need of me, and if you will all listen you shall hear why.'

There were pale faces and eyes mirroring the turmoil beginning in minds and hearts.

'Friends and *baylons*, I see that, sheltered as we are here from knowing what the pestilence is, you are in ignorance of the very great danger threatening all of us. I will tell you, with a very heavy heart. So far it has killed just one of us, may his soul rest in peace.'

They murmured Amen.

'But outside our gates, in Avignon, the pestilence has so far killed two hundred Christians that we, the doctors of Avignon, know of and almost certainly many more. Some are buried, others await their turn. We have news from the coast, where *confrères* speak of the extent of this contagion and warn that the exhalation of the dying and the corruption of the dead, and their effect upon the living, is horrifying – as is the speed at which the pestilence travels . . . My master, Guy de Chauliac, who is physician and surgeon to the Pope, and many others have searched the books for precedents. We have tried the treatment our forbears recommended. So far, friends, without success.'

He paused. Could he persuade them? There was complete silence as pale faces were turned towards him.

'May the Lord soon wake me from this evil dream,' said a voice.

'Tell us what to do, *mège*,' cried another *baylon*.

'The pestilence kills within three days. But . . . it does not only kill the body. A traveller from Marseilles, where the pestilence arrived on ships from Africa and beyond—'

'David—' interrupted Jessue, 'David is there, buying candles—'

'May the Lord protect him! – The traveller also observed how the disease kills even the natural ties of love between members of the same family, who fear the corrupted breath of father, mother, wife and husband, yes, even of their child. In this very city, de Chauliac was called by the family of a high official at the Palace, who was taken sick and abandoned in an outhouse with water and food beside him; and none ventured to help him when he cried out in his agony. There he died, alone, like a beast in the fields . . . his family would not bury him but paid a servant to do so. Next day, the other members of the dead man's family fell ill and they died in their turn.

'This happened just outside the gates of Avignon! And, *baylons*, this may well happen to us, here in our Street, for the pestilence is blown on the wind which does not recognise gates.'

The *baylons* took out handkerchiefs and wiped the cold sweat from their brows, felt for the fringes of their shawls, murmured prayers under their breaths.

'What has been decided in Avignon,' said Thoros softly, 'is to forbid the selling of old clothes, in the town and in our Street, for already some beggars have been stripping the corpses of their clothes. There is mortal danger in these rags and in all finery taken from unburied bodies; they carry corruption and will kill the beggars. We must issue a decree, on pain of *herem*, stating that all commerce is forbidden – on pain of excommunication. We must forbid all commerce with outside: None may enter; it would be inviting death into our houses.'

'You are right, Thoros,' said Jessue, pale as a ghost. 'What you say – and we must believe . . . exceeds . . . I cannot find words. Yes, we have stores of barley and maize in the granary, though depleted; will the Christians support us if we close the gates?'

'Yes, that is their intention. They will put guards on the town side of the gates,' said Thoros.

'And the drinking water – our women must go outside the gates to fetch it.'

'They may, but no one must come in.'

'Many of the poor,' Abraham de Monteux began, 'only earn enough each day for their needs. They must go out; what is to become of them?'

'They cannot go out, Abraham,' said Thoros sharply. 'Since they will be fed from our stores, they will not suffer.'

'The sellers of fruit and herbs from the country—'

'Brothers, *baylons* of our Street,' said Thoros in a voice yet deeper than before. 'Death is within the gates of Avignon. One minute you fear it and your blood runs cold, the next you wish for fresh herbs and fruit from the country. The Lord above has not announced when the pestilence will abate! Measures to combat the pestilence, I've told you, are uncertain. No – I must say it – they are useless. We can forbid contact with the sufferers in the town, but there is only one effective remedy, and it is one which you – and I, friends – find hard to contemplate, but we must. The most certain remedy is flight. De Chauliac is recommending it to the Holy Father; and I recommend it to you. We must leave the Street. We have not done so in our lifetime, and our forefathers did not do so in theirs. Yet we must go, or die.

'I say that we – all of us, men, women and children – should gather our belongings and food stores in our carts, harness horses and mules and leave the Street.'

'When?' whispered Abraham de Monteux.

'Tomorrow,' said Thoros.

He sat down; a sick man still, as the *baylons* could see. They began to whisper among themselves; heads drew together.

At the foot of the table sat old Farrusol who was very deaf. He had heard very little of what had been said, but had been observing faces. He now beckoned Thoros to him and Thoros knelt close to the old man, whose bright eyes showed him in full possession of his wits.

'Old Jacob has died, you said, Thoros?'

Thoros, kneeling, spoke directly into Farrusol's ear, 'Yes, alas, of the pestilence.'

'You say pestilence? As we had in . . . in . . . when I was a boy?'

'Yes.'

'He was related to you, was he? You want money to bury him, and you're asking for money from the burial fund, is that right?'

'No. There is contagion in the bodies of those whom the pestilence has killed. We must abandon the body; he died in the town and we must not bring him back here.'

'But our cemetery is outside the Street,' said Farrusol after reflection.

'It is. But if we were to bury him, someone would have to go into Avignon to fetch the body, and the contagion would enter the Street that way.'

'I remember 1307,' said Farrusol abruptly. 'The year of great sickness. Yes. But why are these women and that child here?'

'To remind you all that you too have mothers and wives and children and that, if we do not leave the Street . . . LEAVE THE STREET! . . . YOU ARE RISKING THEIR LIVES!' Thoros shouted into the old man's ear. Then he turned to the other *baylons*. 'We must leave, before we start dying like the Christians in the town.'

'Ah!' said old Farrusol loudly into the silence. 'They shut the gates at Aix, in 1307, I remember now. The community put guards on the gates, but of course guards have pockets, and the gates could be made to open. That's how the community lost a few pedlars, for they never came back. Of course, they could have run away from their wives or their creditors, ha ha!'

'Thank you, Thoros,' said Jessue. 'I know without looking up the old *escamots* that this calamity has not been legislated for. *Baylons* . . .' he turned to them, 'we must decide now.'

Old Farrusol cackled and blew a kiss to Blanchette as they left.

Blanchette and Thoros walked back to their dwelling in silence, listening to Lea with Joseph behind them scold the boy, toddling from one iridescent puddle to another. 'You'll stink of horse's piss!'

In their dwelling, Thoros offered the back room, where Blanchette and Astruc had spent their married lives, to Lea, for the few days – maybe only one – till they left. When the old woman had returned to her room down the street to gather her few belongings, Blanchette turned to her husband. They sat close on the bed, and Blanchette began to speak with the vehemence which she often found hard to control. 'I understand the danger, but the *baylons* will not wish to. It is too terrible to imagine.'

He held her close, and nodded.

'You have told us what to do, but what of you? I know you have sworn an oath to succour the sick. Will you still care for them, those that are . . . I cannot bring myself to name it. I am not a fool. The sickness may be amongst us already—'

'No one yet,' he said, 'and God forbid—'

'God forbid!' she cried. 'God has allowed, He has allowed the death of innocent people! What had Jacob done, how had he sinned? What I am thinking is that you go out into Avignon and back to us daily. If you continue, you might as well – yes, I shall say it – you might as well bring Jacob's corpse back with you. What use is barring the gates when you yourself—' she fought for breath and burst into tears. He held her, trying to soothe her while she cried: 'Don't go! You must not go!'

'You're right, my love, flight is the only remedy. I shall not go back.'

She embraced and kissed him, but felt his body stiffen, resistant in her arms.

'You are right,' he said again. 'But consider this. The Pope has – and it is against the ruling of the Church – given permission for the examination, the dissection and study of those who have perished by the pestilence. If they should, on opening the corpse of a victim, find the cause of the pestilence, if they should happen on it, am I to be deprived of this knowledge, because I am absent? For such knowledge will give me the weapons I need to cure, perhaps.'

Blanchette wiped her eyes and turned to him with an expression he could not fathom: anger, despair, love? He could not always read her face, but he knew she was strong, and that she loved him.

'So you will continue to go into the town?'

'No. No. That is, perhaps, were I to hear that the dissection has revealed something of use, yes, I would have to go. And I know what you're thinking; I would be at risk, but I might bring back a cure, you see, to save thousands—'

Blanchette looked at him in silent anguish and he read the sadness and despair in her eyes.

'Blanchette, I will now say how happy I have been with you. Alas, I have not given you a child. I am not much use now, but at least I have given the *baylons* the alarm; they know and you know what the community must do. If . . . if I go back into Avignon, and should I feel that the pestilence has seized me, I shall know, and I shall die outside this Street. If two days go by and I have not returned—'

'Thoros! You said that you would stay with me!'

'We will leave here very soon, my love, we will be in the country, though of course at the mercy of the wind which will blow, whatever we plan.'

He rubbed his eyes. His feelings were at war with his mind.

'So we are not safe outside, either,' said Blanchette quietly.

'Safer, much safer than here. Remember my words. Remember that if I do return to Avignon not to search for me should I not return.'

'I will remember that we have been very happy,' she said.

Chapter 37

All around brother Raimond Durand the city was turbulent, awash with speculation and fear of the pestilence, but within his cell he was considering the Holy Father's thinking, not even pursuing his nightly reading of Saint Augustine's *Confessions*, open in front of him. Raimond wondered as he often did, with regret, why the Holy Father – a renowned scholar, after all – would not extend the *studium generale*, which Raimond taught to students who desired the *licentia ubique docendi*. Thirty-five years ago at the council of Vienna, Avignon had been promised chairs of Arabic, Hebrew and Chaldean, which the universities of Paris, Oxford, Bologna and Salamanca offered, all of them, where as here in Avignon the emphasis was on Theology, and the other chairs remained promises . . . He shivered. When the summer came with its unbearable heat, he would be glad of the moist massive stones which constituted the thick walls of the theological faculty. If he survived to see another summer; he was well aware that the corpses in the churchyards were increasing in numbers daily, nightly.

The cat on his lap tore rhythmically at the rough robe with its claws, but suddenly stopped purring and crouched ready for flight. He too now heard footsteps on his stair, and then a familiar scratching on his door. Raimond remembered who scratched instead of knocking. 'Come in! Welcome, Guillaume!'

Saint-Amant entered the cell, the two men embraced and Saint-Amant shed the large black cloak which enveloped him from head to foot. Raimond looked at his friend with amazement. Saint-Amant stood before him dressed in blue and red, white ermine showing at the sleeves of his *soubreveste*, gold buttons marching down the scintillating red and gold cloth covering his chest, held by a broad belt with a golden buckle around the waist. He wore one red and one white stocking, and his golden curls – so like Joseph's – sprung up as soon as he freed them from the hood on his cloak.

Brother Raimond looked at him with affection and said: 'You rival the bird of paradise in the Holy Father's garden of animals! Have you brought a message from him?' As Saint-Amant shook his head, Raimond added, sighing; 'I might as well ask if you're bringing a message for my cat. I sometimes wonder why the Pope is not more interested in the work of the university . . . You haven't been to see me for months. Is His Holiness appreciative of your work?'

Saint-Amant sat down and stroked the cat. 'This is the first time in many months that I have put on this finery. Months ago . . . do you remember that I then came to you with . . . questions?'

'Yes,' said the theologian. 'I had to elucidate the rules on the forbidden relationships between Christians and Jews, I remember.'

Saint-Amant in his peacock garb looked around the austere room, at the pallet, the books, the water pitcher, the bare floor. 'I have a cell like this now, Raimond, and day and night I wear a grey robe with a rope around the waist. These fine clothes which were mine when I was His

Holiness's Master of the Household have lain folded in a coffer for many months. I left the Pope's employment last summer.'

'Not unconnected with our discussion on the Jews?'

'Not unconnected, no.'

'You did not incur the prescribed punishment, or you would not be sitting here. I suppose you were dealt with leniently in order not to draw attention to the matter, and dismissed the Palace Household in order to carry out a penance? You should have come to me.'

'It is true that the Holy Father had heard gossip, but it was I who begged him to relieve me of my task so that I could do penance. I chose the Friar's Penitent Hospital, and there I have been, caring for the lepers since last summer.'

'The lepers,' said Raimond, nodding. 'Those whose unclean lives have been punished by the disease; the choice presumably meets the committed sin?'

'Yes. My duties are to wash the sick, feed those whose hands have withered away, place food in mouths beneath what had once been a nose, help those to the latrines who no longer have feet . . .'

Raimond, silent, stroked his cat, dark and brindled, and only its purring showed its place on the dark robe of the monk. Saint-Amant continued, 'I am there to bear the revulsion I feel, Raimond; also to pray with them and for them. To repent.'

'God will accept your sacrifice and repentance, Guillaume, and will instil humility in your heart. Then you will experience the joy of His forgiveness and the satisfaction of succouring the sick.'

'That is what I thought would happen.'

'Well?'

'We who care for the lepers do not go forth during the day, but at night we may walk through the streets. For the first time in many months I dressed in my palace clothes and stole away from that place of sighs and lamentations and made my way to the Rocher des Doms, next to the palace for I longed to see; just to catch sight of the Holy Father, who often walks up there. I long for everything I have lost, my high and responsible office, my work.'

'I don't know how seriously you broke the law, but you have earned merit in heaven for your self-imposed penance and sacrifice, my dear friend, and surely you must feel some peace and some happiness even, in caring for the lepers?'

Saint-Amant stood up and walked around the room like a caged wolf.

'No!' he said in a stifled voice. 'I hate the sick! I hate their hideous deformities, their smell disgusts me, nausea rises in me as I feed their terrible faces and wipe the pus from their eyes. Do you know that they lose all sensation from their diseased members, do you know that a finger or a toe may drop off like a rotten fruit from a bough, without the sick man's noticing? Do you know, Raimond, that I am often near to killing them, or myself? I can no longer bear to be with them, I hunger for my former life! I thought I would catch the disease and die, not knowing how slowly death comes to the leprous.'

'So you are prepared to die?'

'I cannot bear to live like this.'

'Well, you may soon obtain your desire. This city and all of us who inhabit it are after all facing death, as you know.'

Saint-Amant looked at his friend with a frown. 'Are we attacked? Who is the enemy? Shut away in the hospice, I hear nothing of the outside world.'

'The enemy is the pestilence. The contagion is said to attack the very air we breathe and the breath of one stricken soul is said to fly like a dart into the throat and lungs of another, with whom he may be speaking and, within two or three days, it will have slain him. Have you not seen the victims lying unburied in the churchyards?'

'No. This is . . . terrible,' said Saint-Amant in a low voice.

'So you do not want to die just yet,' said Raimond, softly.

'Not of this contagion! Ah, Raimond, you must think me craven, cowardly, and after the words I had just spoken—'

'I am afraid myself, but I shall stay here and teach my students, or do such work as the Holy Father requires. He will need me, he will need all those who survive. It seems to me, and I hope this is of comfort to you, that your penance is at an end. You have atoned for your sin and now you should flee the city.'

'I might flee . . . or stay with the lepers. I must reflect . . . I had better return to the hospice, now, Raimond, so let me say farewell and thank you, my true friend, my only friend in Avignon. Will we meet again?'

They embraced with the warmth and anguish of friends saying a final farewell.

'May God protect you, Guillaume,' said the monk. ' I hope to meet you – here, or in Paradise.'

Alysa stood with the other women from the Street by the fountain, just outside the gate, waiting her turn, listening.

There were Christian women waiting too, and, as usual, all the women talked only of the great contagion. After she had drawn water, Alysa hoisted the two slopping buckets onto the wooden yoke across her shoulders and was stopped at the gate to the Street by the two guards, who asked if she was bringing anything except the water. The guards were paid two *sous patas* by the Jews and two by the Christians. The guards joked with Alysa but her thoughts were not on the jokes, not even on the disease, her thoughts were on David. On what she had to do.

One of the guards asked her, as he did every day, whether she would open her door to him tonight. For the first two nights on duty he had been fierce, had not allowed anyone in or out of the Street; no man, woman or merchandise. They had pleaded and protested. Neither buying nor selling, how could they live? But the *baylons* had made the rules, and their authority was never flouted. It was simply circumvented. There was the promised distribution of flour outside the *escole*, but people wanted meat and herbs and somehow these were smuggled into the Street. . .

Alysa knew she was spoilt and had often got her way because she was pretty, but her prettiness would not help her now against one who had ensnared not only two husbands, but a Christian lover as well. With careful steps she entered her doorway and slowly carried her heavy burden up.

'You know Blanchette,' she had said to her mother last night.

'Of course, she was married to Astruc, now married to his brother, has a little boy, Joseph, with yellow curls, like a . . . never mind.'

'The boy's father – is it Astruc, or is it Thoros?'

'Well, you're a married woman now,' said her mother, 'besides, everyone knows.'

'I do not, Mother!'

'Remember when a Christian came into the Street and snatched the little boy? Said he was the father. Of course she is a very beautiful woman. No wonder the men—' she stopped, remembering some half-heard gossip about David, her new son-in-law.

Alysa understood. Now, today, she said to herself. Meanwhile she had to spend the day searching for food, bartering a string of onions for a scrap of meat, carrying more water for a very old woman who rewarded her with two candied plums from Carpentras. At last she slipped down the stairs at dusk and crept up the four flights of stairs in the dwelling where Blanchette lived, and took minutes to pluck up the courage to knock. Blanchette was alone, Thoros with a sick woman, Lea with Joseph in her room.

'I am Alysa—' she began, as Blanchette opened the door to her.

'Alysa! Of course! I danced at your wedding.'

'I did not see you,' Alysa said.

'Of course not, you were far too busy. Come in, Alysa, you must be missing David. Isn't he in Marseilles?'

Alysa stood stiffly, trying to ignore the warmth in Blanchette's voice as she began her rehearsed speech. 'Blanchette,' she said 'you must promise never to see David again.'

Having spoken, her anger overcame her embarrassment and she met Blanchette's astonished look with a cold stare.

'Very well. I will not do so,' said Blanchette after a silence.

'I know what you did,' continued Alysa, holding back her tears,' for in the wedding night, when we were so happy . . . when he . . . just then, at that very moment . . . at that moment he cried out – your name! And again, the next night, and the next. So you must never . . . he is my husband now. You must promise!'

Through her tears she heard Blanchette speak softly. 'David is a friend! We never did anything friends might not do, we never lay together, I swear. By the *herem*, if you wish.'

They would, both of them, suffer much grief before uttering the *herem* which once pronounced laid a heavy burden on the speaker; but even the mention of it stopped Alysa's tears.

'David is your husband, yours of course! and I hope you will see him soon.' May God protect him, thought Blanchette, if he is still living. 'I have a husband whom I love—' she continued, looking up with joy as a thin, stooping man entered the room. Alysa stared at the sunken eyes in the haggard face and recognised the doctor who cared for her mother when her younger sister was born.

'Who is this shedding tears? Are you ill? It is Alysa, wife of David, isn't it? Do you feel, God forbid, feverish? No? Good. Rest on the bed a moment,' said Thoros, touching Alysa's cheek with a light, caressing gesture.

Alysa, helpless and defeated in the face of so much kindness, turned towards the door, but Blanchette begged her to stay, see Joseph, drink a cup of water, eat a piece of *coudolle*. She stayed, and noticed Blanchette kissing her husband, resting her head on his shoulder, forgetting her presence as they talked. The storm in her heart abated while she listened.

'I've just seen the guards let a couple of children into the street, they were playing catch-as-catch-can with the guards. I went to find Abraham de Monteux. You *baylons* refused me when I urged flight, I said to him. People are entering our gates all the time, I told him, and the next visitor will be the angel of death.'

Blanchette seized his hands. 'Make them listen!'

'I warned him that I would carry out my plan without benefit of the *baylons'* support, if necessary. I will make a public announcement.'

'We will need horses and mules. And carts, of course.'

'We will have them. Cardinal Le Gor gave me a purse of gold before he set off for Jerusalem. We could obtain some outside the Street.'

Alysa's mouth was open, her eyes still red-rimmed and smarting, and she remained speechless. It was as it had always been, she thought, the grown people made decisions and she, half understanding, half mutinous, would be bidden to do something she only half understood. But the doctor was asking her something:

'I will take Alysa here for a representative of our people. She shall tell us which course of action she considers the right one. You have heard of the pestilence?'

Alysa nodded.

'If I told you that the only way to escape the contagion is to flee the Street, flee the city?'

'Leave the street? Where would we go? I have never been further than the fountain.'

'And why have you not been out?'

'Because we are safe in the Street, protected from the Christians.'

'And if I were to tell you that there is no safety for Jews or Christians in our city, neither in the Street nor elsewhere, that we would be safer in the country, and that the Christians will pay no attention to us because they are consumed by the same fear of contagion, would you stay or go?'

'Oh, go,' said Alysa. 'Yes, and would we all go?'

'We should,' said Thoros. 'But some prefer to believe that nothing will happen here, in the Street, because it is known, familiar.'

'And where would we go?'

'We would cross the river,' said Thoros slowly, 'and go along the bank until we come to a place where I have seen empty shepherd huts. We would shelter there. We would carry our stores with us – we would wait for the contagion to pass, as I pray and hope, and we would all be together in God's keeping.'

'I want to go,' said Alysa. 'But how would David find us? He is still in Marseilles, you know.'

'We will leave word for him on the gate of the Street. You have answered well, Alysa,' said Thoros and took her hand.

Chapter 38

Lyon de Milhaud had been rabbi in the Street for the past twenty years, for the community had renewed his contract four times. Normally five years were enough to disgust the community with their rabbi, but Rabbi Lyon was a truly wise teacher. He had been bedridden for many months now, and relied on young Rabbi Liptois, the Pole, to do the work.

A quiet knock and Rabbi Liptois entered with his springy step as befitted his twenty-five years, taking his usual place on the stool by the old rabbi's bed.

'Good news?' asked the old rabbi.

'Bad news,' said Rabbi Liptois, smoothing his patched, mud-encrusted robe, looking directly at the old man, whom he loved.

'Let me guess,' said the old rabbi. 'I suppose someone has bribed the guards on the gate?'

'Yes,' said Moshe Liptois. 'Mordechai Delpuget, last Tuesday. He bought contaminated clothes, it is thought, and slipped them past the guards while they were chatting with the women, as usual.'

'How is he?'

'Dead. Of the pestilence. The *baylons* gave orders to bury him at once, near Faret, along the river.'

'Faret? Why not in our cemetery?'

'His Holiness has designated a field near Faret to be the burial ground for Jews who have died of the pestilence. He himself has given us this ground.'

'We must say a special prayer for the Pope, added to the usual one, this sabbath. This is truly a good Pope, perhaps the best advocate this Street has. Clement he is, in word and deed! So the pestilence is among us, because one of us has acted as greedily as the Christians.'

'Their priests tell them that the pestilence is their fault for neglecting God's ways . . . but others, Lyon, are looking for scapegoats. They say that we are at the bottom of this, that we have caused the sickness by poisoning the wells and the fountains, that we have acted in revenge for being forced to wear the hat and the badge.'

'Of course,' said the old rabbi. 'And what do the *baylons* say?'

'They talk, as usual. But they have repudiated Thoros's plan to flee the Street.'

'They will have to give in, Moshe. We should go. The rolls of the Law must go with us in their crowns of silver and the candlesticks, well-wrapped. Remember the ark which Moses and Aaron carried through the wilderness? We too will carry it – and you must go with them, Moshe, I'm too old. I hope it will not be forty years—!'

'There is to be a meeting this evening. The *baylons* have given Thoros permission to speak in the *escole,* they want to hear what the community think of his plan.'

Rabbi Lyon pulled himself upright in his bed by means of a rope which was attached to the ceiling above his bed. His mouth was hardly visible amid the curls of his white beard, though Moshe Liptois knew that the lips mostly curved upwards in an encouraging, amused smile. His large nose rose majestically from the broad expanse of his face, over-shadowed by bushy white hair which supported a little skull-cap, barely anchored on the unruly growth. Rabbi Lyon's fiery nature had been succeeded, in old age, by benevolent calm, and Moshe Liptois was relieved to see him smile.

'They are more afraid of change than of death! Find two men to carry me, Moshe; I must be at the *escole* tonight.'

'Yes. Rabbi, what do you think? They will ask us; what should we advise?'

Rabbi Lyon told him.

That same morning Thoros made his way to see Cresques Bondavid, barber-surgeon, who lived in one of the three houses in the Street which were higher than the others. From the top floor the Bondavid family had to climb a ladder into a cockleshell of wood, precariously perched on the fourth floor of the house. The wooden structure was roofed with reeds and thatch; dangerous in the winter gales. The surgeon-barber lived here with his wife Tourlourette, midwife and layer-out of the dead, and their three young children.

Thoros climbed four flights of stairs and found himself at the foot of the ladder, trying to catch his breath. He knew he ought to speak to his brother in medicine before the evening meeting in the *escole*, but had put off the meeting. When he reached the top of the ladder and set foot in the one room, he was unsurprised to be greeted without warmth.

Thoros stood gasping by the little window, marvelling at the view of hills and meadows. When he turned round, the children hid their scabby faces in their mother's skirts. In the silence which greeted his arrival,

Thoros searched for a chair. Cresques watched him, without a word or gesture of greeting.

'*Ahly*!' began Thoros, speaking the language of the Street. By calling Cresques 'brother', he hoped to persuade the surgeon-barber to abandon his usual hostility.

'*Bardayan*,' replied Cresques, and Thoros knew that meant 'the Lord protect us'. It also meant 'unpleasant nuisance'. Thoros felt suddenly that his legs would never carry him again, and a huge wave of tiredness swept over him. Unexpectedly Tourlourette, a large sad-faced woman with the eyes of one who nurses the dying, thought Thoros, offered him some water.

'Thank you, Tourlourette,' said Thoros, a little revived. 'Persuade your husband to listen to me. We need him.'

Cresques, red of hair and beard, with watery eyes, stared at Thoros with undisguised hatred. Devoted to the sick, a loving father and husband, he had, he believed, one enemy in the Street: Thoros. Now he uttered his first words. 'Listen to the famous *mège*, the physician, the *magister* in *medicina*! You have come to see whether I am ready to receive the *licencia practicandi*, I suppose.'

Cresques had not studied at a university but had learned his trade helping two doctors, and had learned the books by heart. To obtain his licence he had to be examined by two doctors, one of whom had passed him as competent; the other was Thoros. Until Cresques possessed the licence, he could charge only small sums; but during the months of Thoros's absence, Cresques had, on his own, cared for the sick of the Street; on Thoros's return, people had turned to the *mège* with the higher qualification, and Cresques's earnings fell.

He continued. 'And about time too! When will you deign to examine me? I have three hungry children as you know—'

'I have come about an urgent matter: about the contagion,' interrupted Thoros.

'Of course!' cried Cresques. 'You fear my competition, so the examination is put off once again! You are always unwell, or too busy. I should have guessed.'

He is not aware of the horror in the town, thought Thoros, as he is only allowed to practise in the Street. I have failed him, yet surely he must know something? He felt the accusing glances of Tourlourette and Cresques's hatred.

'Cresques, you will obtain your licence, without question. You are competent in theory and practice, as I have found again and again. I cannot find fault – there is much to praise; any delay is due to my weakness. When I return to my room I will write my favourable appraisal.'

Cresques smiled, for this was the only matter of importance for him this January morning.

'We have had trouble paying for the children's food.'

'I have come about a matter of life and death – death, really, Cresques. At our meeting of doctors, yesterday at the palace—' Cresques's face clouded over again immediately. As a humble surgeon-barber he had not been invited.

'It was reported that the following have been tried against the plague. Pills for purging, of aloes. Purifying the air with fires. Giving the sick plants to smell. Ordering the populace not to approach ditches, marshes and lakes. Ensuring that all windows to the south are closed, wind from the south being nefarious. Burning plants and woods, such as honeysuckle, cypress, rosemary, vines, oak. Burning also the following: resin, incense, marjoram and the stalks of cabbages. Folk are not to wrestle, run, throw balls. And no hot baths.'

Thoros laughed dryly and coughed.

'That is what we have at present, Cresques, against the pulmonary plague, which kills in two to three days.'

Cresques and Tourlourette stared at him with open mouths. Cresques rose and stood aghast. Of course, he said, he had heard. The sickness had come, it would surely go. Perhaps, he thought, perhaps it would make his fortune? He needed money, they were in debt to the neighbours. For the moment though, fear gripped him by the throat and he croaked, 'Have these measures, um, been effective?'

'What do you think, surgeon-barber, about to receive your licence?'

'I would think . . . not . . .' said Cresques slowly.

'You are right. Pope Clement, may the Lord reward him, has shown courage and energy, he has bought land for cemeteries, and huts and dwellings outside the city and has had the sick installed there. He sends carts full of food from the palace kitchens.'

'Is there room for all?'

'Yes, alas. Those newly sick take the place of those who die. And the Pope has installed a hut for doctors, where we are to open up bodies to see whether the cause of the plague can be established.'

'And can it?'

Thoros looked away, across the roofs of the city.

'Some of those who died had been coughing up blood, from infected lungs. But two new forms have been discovered: one causes boils to erupt under the armpits, and another causes boils in the groin. All three kinds kill within days. That is what has been established.'

'But, Thoros, our religion forbids the cutting open of the dead. Are the Christians permitted . . . ?'

'No. But the Pope has made special provision, nevertheless. Now, Cresques, you must help me persuade our people. I believe that we will be safer – not safe, but safer – in the country. I have called a meeting in the *escole* this evening. Help me to persuade our people, Cresques! The Pope will send food to the shepherd huts, where we should go. There is room for us and we will be fed. You will come, I can count on you, can't I? Your example will reassure the fearful. Cresques, you understand the danger! And whatever I have done to offend you, forgive me. You and I are the doctors, it is to us they turn and we must not fail them.'

'Yes. Yes,' said Cresques. Thoros saw his pale, frightened face and thought he could count on him, said farewell and began his descent, backwards down the ladder. What were those encrusted sores on the children's faces, though, and how was Cresques treating them? He must have a word with the doctor aspirant, sometime soon, if ever there was time . . .

As soon as Thoros had gone, Cresques, suddenly full of energy, turned to his wife and rubbed his hands. 'He can go, and we will stay. Don't you see . . . some will go, but most will prefer the known to the wilderness outside. And once again there will only be myself to care for them; just as before when the great *mège*, who cured the Pope of a stone, had lost his mind. A stone! I could have done as much as he did.'

Tourlourette slapped the hand of her eldest, scratching at a scab. 'Mordecai! Stop it! But, Cresques, this disease . . .'

'Wife – what do we know except what Master Thoros chooses to tell us? We barber-surgeons are practical men, not given to theorising like Thoros. I have a recipe given to me by old Dieulosal, may he rest in peace, so let us see what can be done instead of crying "Flee!" and giving up. The Jews in this street will not suddenly leave the safety of their homes. I know them.'

Tourlourette dipped a cloth in a bowl of vinegar and applied it to Mordecai's face, who was wailing and scratching, and the two smaller ones joined in while Cresques began again. 'I take half an ounce of bitter aloes, oil of iris root, some camphor . . .' He mumbled the rest of the prescription to himself and suddenly cried, 'Yes! There are some in the Street whose fortunes will allow them to buy my prescription without trouble! In truth, everyone will do anything to find the money, but they will – or they may pay us in food. I will cure this contagion, wife, I will.'

'I am afraid,' said Tourlourette.

'Come, wife, disease is my companion, my friend, this is how I earn my living. Where would I be without it? You will see that I can turn it to our advantage.'

'Oh, Cresques, I do wish the children were better, I fear for them. Look at Mordecai. Now he is scratching his chest.'

Cresques took his son on his lap, and examined the angry rash on Mordecai's chest. What had Thoros . . . ?

He searched under the boy's arm, then in his groin – nothing. Forgetting all else, he hurried to fetch his mortar and pestle and began to mix ointment from the little store he had left, and, as the boy grew feverish, he forgot his plans to combat the plague, as well as Thoros's request.

Chapter 39

That evening, the *escole* was full. The women had been allowed to sit with the men. Small children crawled on the floor and between the feet of those standing against the walls. The noise swelled, and the candles cast their light on puzzled and anxious faces, as Thoros stepped onto the dais and attempted to speak. No one heard him. The crowd seemed in a fever of apprehension, for a rumour had spread that the Christians were ready to attack the Street, that the gates would be locked and that they would all burn. Thoros saw that Moshe Liptois, the Polish rabbi, was shouldering his way through the crowd to stand beside him.

'Let us pray!' shouted Moshe.

But the crowd continued to groan and high-pitched shouts echoed among the candelabra. Rabbi Liptois waved his arms in the air, motioning for silence, but the crowd just waved back until suddenly there were women screaming and someone had fallen. The wailing of babes in arms rose shrilly. When Thoros looked at the rabbi for help, he saw to his dismay that Moshe Liptois had disappeared. But moments later he stood again by Thoros's side and in his hands he held the *shofar*, the ram's-horn, which he raised to his lips and blew with all his might. The piercingly sad sound set forth across the hall and rebounded with echoes from the stone walls. Astonished mouths stopped in mid-cry, for this animal sound was only heard at New Year and on the Day of Atonement. When Moshe lowered the *shofar* there was complete silence in the *escole* during which old Farussol could be heard asking loudly whether the rabbi had taken leave of his senses. Moshe Liptois whispered to Thoros that he should speak now, before the noise resumed.

'Friends,' said Thoros into the silence. 'Most of you know me, I think. Sons and daughters of Jacob, you are aware that there is a contagion beyond our gates which kills men women and children within three days. And if there are any among you who either have not heard, or, having heard, do not believe the reports, I will tell you now that in the city, beyond our gates, the contagion has killed many hundreds. As I speak to you, the carts are trundling carrying the victims of this *grande mortalité*. In the alleyways and squares of Avignon, in the houses of the Christians, they are waiting for death. In the palaces of the rich some fall ill still wearing the wreaths of flowers which crowned their heads during a feast a few hours before; and they have but a few hours to live. The victims are people like ourselves and what is killing them, will kill us.

'Despite our precautions, Delpuget brought into our Street what had been expressly forbidden: old clothes. They were contaminated. Delpuget is dead and his body has been carried to the new cemetery at Faret—'

He stopped for a scuffle had broken out in the hall. Gourdin, the dead man's brother-in-law, was recognised, seized and forcibly ejected from the *escole* in spite of his protests, for they understood that he was unclean, perhaps already stricken.

Thoros waited again for silence. Small muscles in his face, around his mouth and eyes, jumped and he had to wipe sweat from his brow. Then he continued.

'You ask – what is to be done? There is only one thing I recommend. Now that we have had one case of the plague in the Street, we must leave it. Come with me and my family, cross the bridge over the river and take up our abode among the fields and meadows where the contagion has not appeared yet, so I believe. Will we be perfectly safe there? I think we will be safer and I have found a place for us on the island of Barthelasse in huts abandoned by fishermen, shepherds and charcoal burners. We must leave the Street. We must leave tomorrow; yesterday would have been better.'

A voice called from the hall, 'What of the old and sick? And what of our possessions?'

'I can pay for handcarts – it is Giacatiro, isn't it? – I have prepared this exodus; but I am not Moses, Giacatiro.'

'How long will we be away from the Street, *mège*?'

'The Lord knows, Bondevin, I do not. Weeks, months? I speak from great concern, great fear. As the prayer says: O guardian of Israel, guard the remnant of Israel and suffer not Israel to perish!'

The congregation of the Street murmured Amen.

As Thoros sat down he saw that Cabri Montel was making his way forward to the dais. Cabri was rich. He owned horses and mules, he and his family lived on two floors of a house in the Street and besides he owned a vineyard and three fields, tilled by Christians. Envied and admired, tall and thin like a poplar, with sparse hair turning white, he was known to be a master at all calculations.

'For those among you who do not know me, I am Cabri Montel, an elected *baylon* of the *première main*.'

The crowd listened in silence; many of the poor did not even know him by sight, for Cabri represented the richest in the Street and was often on the roads of Provence.

'You have heard our respected *mège*. He is a devoted doctor and a learned man, and we, your *baylons*, value his judgement. We have considered his proposal, which he had made known to us before this meeting. We *baylons* know what happens beyond these gates; I myself know the world of the Christians, for I have had business with them for many years. I shall not gainsay what Maître Thoros has just told you, the disease is indeed in Avignon, and it is mortal. But – forgive me, *maître* – he has not told you what the Christians are saying, taken up with the most devoted care of the sick as he is. What are they saying? Having accused the winds, the conjunction of the stars, and the wickedness of each other's lives, they are beginning to say that the disease is perhaps caused by poison in the wells. And who are the poisoners? Who poisons the drinking water, and the food, and the very air? The Jews, of course.

'Far away in Germany, so we have heard, Jews have been herded into barns and burned like straw. Why? For the reason that they caused this contagion, this great mortality. Our Christian neighbours, here in Avignon, are beginning to suspect that we have spread poison. Here in Avignon we live under the sheltering protection of the Pope, and here, in our Street, close to our protector's palace we are safe. Not in the countryside, salubrious though it may be and, you heard Maître Thoros say, safer; not safe, only safer.'

Thoros, hunched on his chair, knew that the battle was lost. Watching Cabri, upright in his dark brown cloak beside him, he thought, not a poplar; more a dark cypress in the fading light. Cabri's arrogant, confident voice continued.

'Jacob Delpuget is dead. His family – except his brother-in-law, who has just been ejected from our *escole* – have left the Street. We have learnt our lesson. Our Street will become a fortress, with the gate permanently locked. Your *baylons* have ascertained that the stores contain enough food for three months and the treasurer and two other officials will see that all needs are met. A few weeks of restrictions and the danger will have passed. As for the loss of earnings, the food from the store shall not cost you one *sou*. We of the *première main* will pay. I say to you: Stay in the Street. We are safer here.'

As Thoros rose to reply, a voice called out, 'What shall we eat, if we leave the Street? How will we find employment? I am a tailor and not used to the ways of sheep and goats!'

'The Pope has set up places where all may obtain food and medicines,' said Thoros. 'He has named the Friars Penitent, the Hospitallers, the Knights of St John, the Franciscans, the Austin Friars, the Carmelites and the Benedictine Nuns as depots, and we may send carts to these places twice daily to collect our portion, which we will take back to our huts on the island of Barthelasse.'

Abraham de Monteux made his way to the dais: He hid the fear in his heart well, and his calm voice rang out clearly: 'Friends, you have heard Thoros and Cabri and you must today decide where you will be safe – and from what! From the disease? From the malevolence of Christians, looking for poisoners? What do you fear most?'

A new hubbub arose, but Thoros stood up once more, and the hall quietened.

'I must persuade you to leave.' They saw his mouth working and at last he forced out, 'I swear on the *herem*, there is no time to lose.'

A dull murmur went through the crowd. Even to mention the oath could bring God's vengeance on one who spoke the name of the oath in vain. Thoros made a visible effort to speak more loudly, but his voice was failing. 'Delpugets's body has gone and the family's dwelling, I have heard, has been walled up. But the wind blows and respects neither gate nor high walls. This contagion has no face, no sword. It will not batter down our locked gates, it will sail over them, soaring like a bird of prey. As for the attack of the Christians, I do not believe it will happen, for the good reason that they are sick, and concerned with their own mortality. Therefore, I implore you to risk your lives . . . in order to save them. Tomorrow morning, all those who wish to choose life over death, all those who wish to go with me, are to assemble outside the *escole* after morning service with those goods you are to take with you. I shall place a parchment in the vestibule of the *escole* so that each family can inscribe their name and the number of members, so that we have enough handcarts and mules, for which I can pay; and, friends, the *baylons* have offered those who will go enough food for seven days, from our stores.'

'What does our rabbi say? Rabbi Lyon!' cried a voice from the crowd.

There was a commotion, as helping hands enabled Rabbi Lyon to rise in his seat.

'I am here,' he said, clinging to Moshe Liptois. 'Angels of mercy, usher in our petition before the Lord of mercy—'

'Yes,' called the same voice, 'but should we go or should we stay?'

'I am a teacher,' said old Lyon, 'and not, alas, a prophet. We two rabbis have decided to stay with both sides, with all the community, that is: Rabbi Liptois will go, and I will stay with those remaining in the Street, should there be any, and the scrolls of the law will remain here in the *escole*.'

Rabbi Moshe Liptois helped the old man to lower himself into his seat, then made his way through the throng to the dais, and Thoros, watching his progress, thought that the young foreigner had survived much adversity on his long journey from Poland, and thrived on it. He held himself upright and spoke with energy and assurance. 'We will now pray from our hearts for our protector Pope Clement! And for those who stay, and for us, who are leaving the Street tomorrow.'

And all of them in the great hall of the *escole* lost themselves in prayer and in the strength and joy of their religion.

Chapter 40

'Like Moses, come to lead us to the promised land,' said Lea. 'A leader of men, my son-in-law.'

They were choosing what they needed for their stay on the island of Barthelasse. Lea prattled on. Seventy-three years old, she had spent all of them in the Street and knew nothing of the town by sight, though she had a treasury of stories about the town and especially about the Pope, whose clothes, habits, taste in food and sayings she knew well; for the pedlars earned many a meal at her table by telling her gossip gathered in the papal kitchens.

Thoros set off to read the list of names and see to the carts while Lea began to prepare the evening meal and Blanchette picked up the old misshapen leather buckets for water. She reached the gate to find that the porter and guards had stopped a group of women; no one was allowed out. Blanchette stepped forward and was recognised.

'Porter,' she called to him. 'Will you ask the Christian women outside to go away after they have drawn water? Tell them that we'll come out when they have gone. Thus they will not catch the contagion from us; nor we from them.'

And she handed him two *sous*. He obeyed; people usually did when Blanchette asked.

Blanchette returned to their rooms, having carried the buckets up four flights without pausing and set them down with a sigh.

'And tomorrow?' asked Lea.

'The Lord will provide,' said Blanchette. Mother and daughter looked at each other and saw the bleakness of the future mirrored in each other's eyes. They were sitting on the bale of cloth which held their belongings when Thoros returned, exhausted.

'Twenty names, twenty families so far, out of a hundred or so families, I don't know exactly. I met Rabbi Liptois; he told me that when the Israelites set off for Egypt there were six thousand men on foot, as well as their dependants and of course cattle, flocks and herds; and dough from which they baked unleavened bread because they had no time to get food ready.'

'I have bread already baked,' said Blanchette. 'Thoros, we are not to go into Avignon yet we must in order to get to the island! Explain.'

'Yes, we must risk an hour or two in the streets.'

'I am thinking of another risk. When you spoke in the *escole*, no one asked you, but they must be asking themselves now, and they're bound to enquire soon; if we are forbidden to go into Avignon, how will we obtain food from the Pope's stores?'

'Well, we may not need to. I should have said that they will send us carts and we will not leave the island—'

'Oh?'

'Dearest Blanchette, my thoughts were on how to persuade people to leave and I said what might well be questioned. But I really do not think we will starve. We are, after all, taking stores—'

'And is it truly safer in the country?'

'I would not strain every muscle in my body and cudgel the few wits left to me to lead you and all of us to a place as dangerous as the Street will become. I am trying to make sure that we have the best chance of our prayers being heard by heaven, and that the judgement on all of us will be suspended; may the Lord be merciful.'

'I love you, Thoros,' said Blanchette.

At dawn, twenty-five carts stood ready, for the twenty-five families had worked through the night. Rabbi Lyon had again been carried to the *escole*, where the departing families, and many of those who were remaining in the Street, had gathered.

'Children of Jacob,' said Lyon. 'Today a hundred sons and daughters of the Street are leaving its shelter. The women and children do not know the world outside, though you men knew something of it before this great disaster struck. What dangers await you outside we do not know, and disaster may well strike us, left behind. But, as the psalmist says: indeed man is but a puff of wind. Yes; and the psalmist says: hear my prayer, O Lord, listen to my cry, hold not Thy peace at my tears for I find shelter with Thee. I am Thy guest, as all my fathers were. Frown on me no more and let me smile again, before I go away and cease to be.'

Thoros, with tears coursing down his hollow cheeks, embraced Rabbi Lyon and many others did the same.

Outside the carts stood ready, in a long line, loaded high. Thoros looked in vain for Cresques. At least the Street would have his services if he remained behind – not that they would avail against the plague. But ready by their carts stood Alysa, with her family, old Farrusol with his older sister, Giacatiro, and Bondevin. There was also . . . he peered at the loaded cart, beside which stood two women and three little boys – surely that was the family of Cabri Montel? Who had spoken so eloquently for remaining in the Street?

The first light of dawn picked out Cabri, emerging from the *escole*, who approached Thoros and seized his hand in both of his.

'*Maitre*,' said Cabri. 'I have thought much about your arguments and I believe you are right.' He lowered his voice. 'I have some – that is – part of my fortune with me, at your disposal. I hear you paid for most of the carts out of your own pocket. Yesterday—'

Blanchette stepped forward and interrupted Cabri angrily. 'So you have decided to come with us? And what of all those whom you persuaded yesterday to stay here, to die of the contagion?'

'They heard your husband's words just as I did! Yesterday I spoke in good faith, but *maître* Thoros's eloquence persuaded me. And I hope that when others see me leave, they may follow my example. Is it too late?'

'Yes,' said Thoros. 'We cannot wait. Why, are there any more *baylons* who have followed your example?'

They walked down the long line of carts, but saw no more *baylons* and their families. They did see the Milhauds, the Lisbonnes, the Dignes and the Jouves, dogs on ropes of hemp, others with poultry in cages, some chairs, buckets, cooking pots.

Thoros and Blanchette walked back to the first cart in line, where Lea waited with Joseph.

'I have lived in the Street all my life. Just now I packed my belongings in half an hour. It does not seem long, Lolo, to pack up a life,' said Lea, sadly.

'Mother,' said Blanchette, her voice breaking. 'Say good-bye to the neighbours. Thoros says we must be gone.'

There were more tears as neighbours clung together, while mules and horses twitched their ears and stamped their feet till at last Blanchette, leading the first cart, gave a loud cry: Forward! and the carts slipped and lurched over the stinking straw towards the gate. The porter, standing by the closed gate, cried out aghast. 'Where will you go? And what am I to say when the Palace official asks where you are? I see you men are all wearing your yellow hats – I never thought to see such a sight . . . how many carts? Why are you going? The Holy Virgin protect us, the Jews are leaving . . . where is the permission from the Papal office?'

Cabri held out a parchment and the obligatory purse.

'Here is the authorisation from His Holiness's administrator. You may keep it, porter, and here is a purse for your trouble. Other families are remaining behind, so there is work for you. Lock the gate behind us and keep it locked!'

The porter, troubled and mumbling to himself, pocketed parchment and purse, and unlocked the gate. After the carts had trundled through, he locked it again, crossing himself.

'I had forgotten the porter,' said Thoros to Cabri. 'How did you, in the short time—?'

'I gave him a tax demand from the chancellery, it still has the official seal on it. I know he cannot read.'

'But the taxes?' asked Thoros.

'With death about everywhere, the chancellery will not collect much longer – if you are right, the Christians have other matters on their minds.'

The carts trundled forward slowly, swaying with their heavy load of bundles, children and old women. Thoros walked in front with Cabri, behind Blanchette leading her cart with Lea and Joseph riding on it, behind her Dousseline, Cabri's wife, held the reins of a horse easily pulling a large cart on which three little Montel boys whooped and shouted at the marvellous strangeness of this morning, and soon the children on all the carts behind joined in. Cabri held up his hand, and all the carts stopped at the agreed signal; then he ran back, placing his finger on his lips for silence, and all nodded, well knowing the danger while crossing the city of Avignon, aware that they were as helpless as a snail without its shell.

The carts followed the narrow lane which twisted away until it met the rue de la Saunerie, where they were to turn northwards to the Grande Fusterie, making their away along to the gate of the bridge, passing through it and onto the bridge. Crossing the Isle de Piot they would head northwards along a spit of land to the Isle de la Barthelasse and the empty huts.

The carts set off again, their rumblings over the cobbles like thunder in the ears of the long line of Jews, the men wearing their yellow hats according to the decree and therefore in order; but also easily recognised, thought Thoros. If the times had not been out of joint, they would be open to attack, probably – certainly halted and turned back. But for the first few minutes they encountered no one. Why not? Where were they?

Rabbi Liptois brought up the rear. His few belongings had been accepted by the cart in front. He felt, young as he was, that he, the rabbi, was ultimately responsible for all these people. As he turned round to look once more at the towering buildings of the Street, he missed old Lyon, already, and begged God to protect those left behind.

'My boy Daniel,' Cabri said suddenly to Thoros, as they trudged along, 'looks like a Christian boy; no one will notice a boy like him running through the streets. I would like to send him ahead to warn us of danger. He is clever and courageous and he'll be proud to be chosen for such a task.'

Thoros looked uncertain but Cabri called the boy, and Daniel Montel, ten years old, listened to his father and leaped at once from the cart, with his heart beating fast and pride filling his whole being.

Meanwhile the carts rolled forwards, filling almost the entire space between the houses, whose walls of clay showed tufts of straw sticking out between gaps. Above, large stones held the wooden roofs safe against the ever-lasting wind. The few windows were closed with shutters. After ten minutes during which, perversely, the empti-ness of the streets seemed more menacing, they saw two women, mouths gaping at the strange procession, pressing themselves against the wall of their house to let the carts go by; otherwise the streets were empty.

'This absence of people . . . I wonder, is today some Christian festival?' Thoros asked Cabri, who shook his head. Behind them, pale faces on the carts turned this way and that, fearing a sudden noise, an ambush.

It was not until they reached the rue de la Saunerie, where they had to turn left towards the river, that those in front heard an unusual sound. Thoros held up his hand and the carts behind him stopped and when the last distant rumblings had ceased, most of them heard. Cabri climbed on his cart so that he could be seen, cupped his hands over his ears and pointed to the street ahead, crossing the rue de la Saunerie.

'Where is Daniel?' murmured Blanchette. 'There is something humming ahead; Cabri was wrong to send Daniel.'

Cabri was hearing reproaches from his wife and their whispered altercation continued as the carts moved forward again at Thoros's signal, the Montels peering ahead for a sight of Daniel. The rue Palapharnerie crossed their street twenty paces ahead when Thoros signed for the carts to stop once more, and the Jews silently watched the sight none had ever seen.

Twenty paces away priests, nuns and monks, looking neither right towards the line of carts nor left, came into sight with crosses – they counted three – held aloft. There was a murmur of prayers, then chanting. They crossed in front of the carts, and if one or other were to look in their direction, Thoros realised, they would only see the front cart in the narrow street, waiting for the procession to pass. Those carrying the crosses were engrossed by their task – the crosses were large and heavy; and behind pressed a great throng of people. Some were bare-footed, some wore sackcloth and had blackened their faces and hair with ashes, some were weeping and others tearing their hair as they walked, calling on God and the Virgin. For twenty long minutes they passed – was the whole town walking in procession? Nuns passed now, carrying a relic, and they were followed by penitents in black, beating themselves with whips. Thoros shuddered, Lea gave a low cry.

'Daniel! Where's my Daniel?' Cabri whispered and Thoros and Blanchette had to hold him back. A new group passed through the narrow field of their vision; white-robed priests bearing banners and singing a funeral dirge. As the Jews remained immobile by their carts, staring, they saw a friar stumble and fall. He lay writhing on the ground among the moving feet, with no one giving him succour till at last two others friars lifted him out of the way and propped him against a wall. Thoros observing the man's livid face, recognised the *grande mortalité*. Yet more and more passed, some dragging chains, some singing dirges, some praying, till at last the procession became more sparse, leaving two more bodies on the ground. Prayers and lamentations died away.

Now the children in the carts began to whisper, horses and mules stamped their feet. Cabri stood, deathly pale, with his arms around his wife. Thoros waited another five minutes, then held up his arms and the carts moved forwards again.

There was no sign of Daniel.

'He knows the city,' said Cabri several times to his ashen-faced wife. 'He has been with me here again and again!'

Thoros told Blanchette that the Pope had surely himself ordered this procession. 'They will be making for the usual place; crowds often gather under his window, for his blessing. We will not be noticed. The Lord has protected us so far . . .'

Moshe Liptois, walking behind the last cart, remembered that the Lord had sent an angel ahead of the Israelites on their exodus from Egypt. Moshe was ruminating on the fallacy in Thoros's promise that they would seek food from the depositories in the city; but who among them would go to fetch it and risk his life?

Daniel Cabri was no angel leading the Israelites to safety, but he was a fearless boy. He had crept ahead of the carts; aglow with his task he had got so close to the crowd marching in the penitent procession that an arm pulled him suddenly – 'This way, boy!' among the marching feet of a group carrying, ten of them together, a huge cross bearing the wooden Christ. For a long moment he was swept forward among the heavy robes bunched close together. Hemmed in, afraid of treading on the bleeding, naked feet Daniel was borne along between them, unseen, for their eyes were cast heaven-wards or on the black-robed figure in front, and when Daniel was able to break free he found himself on the far side of where he had started. Dazzled, he watched the candle bearers, the gilded relic in its ornate case and wished he were a Christian boy and could march with the procession.

At last the street was empty. Daniel knew he should return to report to his father that the street was safe. But the tide of penitents had swept him forward, nearer the palace. Alone and now afraid, he heard the rumble of carts, and ran that way, and found himself minutes later in his mother's arms.

'They've gone,' he said, gasping, 'towards the Palace! And there's no one about, just a few men lying on the ground.'

The carts moved forwards again through the empty streets, every man and woman fearful, some praying aloud, till they reached the river gate; and as they approached, Daniel saw them first. He ran back to his father and walked by Cabri's side, his hand in his father's.

The air had become fetid.

'We must advance,' said Thoros, looking. 'There is no help for it.'

The carts rolled slowly towards the gate, all voices dying away as each family saw the row of those dead of the contagion, heaped close to the gate. Mothers covered their children's faces with their skirts, men and women pulled their hats well down and covered their mouths with kerchiefs, as the carts approached the river gate in complete silence. Cabri said:

'I have a purse ready, as well as a pass asking that His Holiness's Jews be afforded safe passage. I signed it myself. It is a rare guard who can read.'

Chapter 41

The river gate was massive. Iron bands bearing round buckles barred the two wings. Strangely, the gates were half open and a shaft of light entered from the sunny world outside.

'They haven't locked it after the last traveller,' murmured Cabri. 'They maybe outside—'

The large lock, an iron box with a key protruding like the haft of a sword, needed two guards to turn it.

'Or they're in their shelter,' said Cabri. 'That's where they play cards.'

The city wall towered above them, casting its shadow of deepest black over the entrance to the guard shelter.

'I will see to this,' added Cabri, confidently. Behind him the carts were silent, and Cabri, feeling both their apprehension and their support, knew that they trusted him. He walked forward slowly, holding in his hand the *laissez-passer*, every word of which he had written himself early that morning. Having obtained his wealth by means which pleased neither God nor man, such as sharp dealing and counterfeiting, he hoped that this action would redeem him. His clothes were damp with sweat. Everyone in the carts behind depended on him, *baylon* Cabri. He took another two steps forward and cried.

'The Lord be with you! I am the bearer of a *laissez-passer* from His Holiness's office.'

There was silence, no sound from the guards, none from the carts. Thoros stepped up to him. 'They're in their shelter, asleep perhaps. Waking will not improve their tempers, but we must . . .' He cried, 'Hey! Ho!'

Cabri pushed him gently aside and went into the guards' hut, stepping out again backwards, ashen-faced and retching. Thoros held his head as he vomited and his wife came running.

'Daniel,' said Blanchette to the boy. 'Run along and tell each cart that there are no guards. They have . . . they have joined the procession. Tell them to move forward and, as they go through the gate, to keep their mouths well covered. Well covered, do you hear?'

Daniel ran while Cabri, recovering, put his shoulders to the gate to move both wings wide open, and found Blanchette among the men who were helping. Cabri found time to marvel at Blanchette. She had directed Daniel down the line of carts; she seemed as strong as a man. Now she was comforting Thoros who stood hunched, coughing.

And the carts rolled through the open gates. Once outside, Cabri sent Daniel back once more to tell Rabbi Liptois to leave the gates open.

As the carts rolled forward over the bridge straddling the Rhône, people began to talk at first in low voices, then loudly. The sun sparkled on the river below and suddenly relief broke into laughter, a snatch of song, a baby's cries. The Duranton dog bit through his rope of hemp, escaped and ran ahead, barking at the space and the sound of the carts on the bridge. The bridge, which Thoros remembered as thronged with people, was empty except for a couple of cantering horsemen passing who stared curiously at the procession of carts and Jews with their yellow hats, but did not stop.

When they reached the chapel on the bridge a man who had been hidden in its shadow stepped out and then ran forward crying.

'Hey! *Chelleduf!* Maître Thoros! Do you not know me? *Baylon* Montel! Where are you *jusieux* going? It's me, Abranet!'

Thoros knew him at once; Abranet worked jewellery for those who wished to shine at the papal court, and Thoros had once treated a hoarseness of his throat. While Abranet heard what had happened and where they were bound, he looked doubtful. The carts had halted again and men and women gathered round Abranet now.

'The Isle de la Barthelasse? There's no room! The citizens of Avignon have taken all the huts for themselves with their kith and kin and all their belongings. The Pope has been sending his carts of mercy there, food and medicaments—'

'But further upstream, the huts of the parchment washers, what about those, Abranet?' called a voice.

'I would not advise you to try those; each one of those is now a tomb.'

Abranet, small and wizened, hoarse, with his sack on his shoulder, was not accustomed to have a crowd listen to him in silence.

'Well, there are other huts,' he said, scratching his beard. 'But—' his voice died away, while they waited. All laughter had ceased, the mood of the Jews had become sombre.

'I have seen things to shake your faith, may God pardon me,' Abranet began again. 'And there is no safety – at least, in Avignon or close. Friends, I'll come with you, for I know of somewhere; I saw the place on my way to Nîmes, the other side of Les Issarts, so we must go downstream. Unless some others . . . but let us go now, at once. It is a long way.'

Thoros looked at the faces around him, strained, calculating, worrying. They had heard.

'What choice have we?' said Blanchette. 'Let us be on our way. Return to your carts and tell your women. The children will be tired and hungry. Tell everyone that we have chosen a new place and that we have a guide.'

Cabri thought he had never met a woman like Blanchette; the men accepted her authority without further discussion, returned to their carts and the mules and horses strained once again to pull their burdens.

Thoros walked on, exhausted, next to Abranet who pointed to distant hills and named them. Leaving the bridge, the carts turned southwards and were now swaying along a sandy path close to the river.

For three more hours the carts crunched along the sandy path, past the Château des Issarts. The family were generous to the poor, Abranet said, and added that another two hours would see them near the place he knew of.

'Is there nowhere nearer?' demanded Blanchette. 'People are too wearied by all that has happened today. Listen to the children crying. And those walking have had enough, too.'

'Grange Neuve, perhaps,' said Abranet.

They reached Grange Neuve with the last of their strength, Thoros lying on the cart with Joseph, while Lea, with the same strength as Blanchette, walked by the side of the cart. They found that Grange Neuve was a huge barn, cruciform in conception; *neuve* might be its name, but its large stone foundation had crumbled in places, and its wooden door was rotten. The roof was sound, though. There were no windows. Cabri calculated that a hundred people could find shelter for the night here. Abranet easily prised away the lock and pushed the doors open with the help of twenty pairs of hands. They peered inside.

'Hay!' cried Abranet. 'Just what is needed.'

There were cries of relief that this was the end of today's journey at last, and the twenty-five carts were ranged in a circle outside the barn. The hay took up barely one quarter of the huge space inside. They unharnessed the animals and led them towards the hay. Each family chose a place of their own, and carried hay to it for sleeping; the children were sent to the riverbank, under the supervision of Lea, and returned with buckets of water; the first bucketfuls were given to the mules and the horses. In his corner, Moshe Liptois pulled his prayer shawl over his head and, turning his face south towards Jerusalem intoned,

Not to us, not to us, O Lord
But to Thy name ascribe Thy glory
For Thy true love and Thy constancy
O praise the Lord—

Other voices joined him.

The women had unpacked, fires were lit outside the barn on the sandy patch, food had been cooked and eaten. The children were beside themselves with new experiences – the space, the sights and sounds of the river, the absence of houses. They had been forbidden to stray from the barn, and were now playing inside. Their piercing screams and laughter came from a dark corner where they were sliding down the pile of hay. Their voices, silenced during the flight from Avignon, rang out, rejoicing at the escape from their small enclosed world. But suddenly there was silence, followed by whispering. Blanchette, Lea and other women hurried over to the group of children, Blanchette taking the lead as always, but afraid of what she might see.

What she saw was a gift from heaven. The children had uncovered a store of food. There were grains, roots and bottles of oil, a sack containing dried fish, as well as many flagons of wine. Whose stores were these, and would they return to claim them?

'Don't touch!' commanded Blanchette, as the women and children fell silent, disappointment and dismay on all faces.

Abranet stepped forward.

'Lady,' he said to Blanchette in his hoarse voice, grinning. 'I know the owner of this barn; he used to give me shelter. When I was walking to the bridge, I saw him, down by the river, and he was dead. So, we must not let the children fetch water from the river alone; one of us must always go with them, in case they find another person dead. We must beware, look out. But note that the man lay dead by the bridge of Avignon, and we have walked for three hours away from there. The owner of these stores – may he enjoy Paradise even as I speak – will not need them now. They're ours.'

Then, although they had eaten, the women set to preparing another meal, a porridge of crushed grains, honey and water, enough for two days. They put the dried fish to soak, and broke open the flagons. For once these Jews, so abstemious in the Street, celebrated their escape in wine and forgot their fears until they were very drunk and fell asleep in the hay, dreaming of Jerusalem and Paradise.

Chapter 42

The Pope took a step back from the window, where he had just blessed the crowd below, framed by the intricate tracery round the shutters. He heard their murmuring, in protest at his announcement, dirty and tired as they were from the long march through the streets of Avignon, from church to convent to shrine, singing and praying.

At first, Clement encouraged these processions, but now there were fewer processions and more in the cemeteries. He could no longer bear to look at the figures presented to him every day. The rage of the disease had not abated – on the contrary; and one day de Chauliac said to him: 'Holy Father, since this disease leaps from one body to another, and as the penitents are very close to each other during the processions, I suggest that there should be no more.'

Clement agreed and had just told the crowd. Now they stared at him with consternation, still hungry for his blessing and his reassurance that God would show mercy. When, Lord, thought Clement, will that be? At present, he knew that the populace believed that they were unwilling witnesses of God's visitation on a sinful world; how long, he wondered, before they believed that God was also punishing a sinful Church; or even a sinful Pope . . . ?

His valet entered and helped him change into a linen tunic, a soutane of white wool. He gave him the warm purple cap without rim, trimmed with ermine, and his soft red shoes with the embroidered gold crosses. Dressed, he sent for his sloping table, the quills in the lapis lazuli vase and his ivory knife with which he began to sharpen a goose quill. It was time to devise his sermon.

Greatly learned, well beyond the understanding of most who heard him, Clement had found a way to make the most uninstructed listen; he played with words. Sometimes he tried a torrent of words all beginning with the same letter, at other times he chose a word with several meanings and juxtaposed different thoughts – like turning the facets of a diamond ring. His words were a tool to open closed and sometimes obstinate minds, and he took enormous trouble with each sermon.

What should he say this time? Five thousand houses in this city stood empty, their owners and tenants lying in shallow graves in the new cemeteries. There were noticeably fewer at each Mass and at each procession. He reflected on whether the Church had indeed failed the people; had he himself failed in his task? If so . . . if so, he thought, with the remainder of his old arrogance, I will only be judged by God. It was right, though, to castigate the Church.

Then his body issued the warning he had come to heed, indicating something more than tiredness; the almost certain onset of disease. Before my own dissolution, thought Clement, as so often, I have still so much to do. What is this plague but the rider on the pale horse of which Revelations speaks? Are these days perhaps the precursor of the end of the world? He seized his pen. The end of the world, he thought, and we must meet it with dignity, charity and courage. Firstly he must persuade his priests to care for those stricken, to act with true love and charity and not allow themselves to become paralysed by their own terror, letting their flocks perish without the comfort of the Holy Sacraments. He wrote: *'Priests must hear confessions even of those stricken by the plague, converse with the sick and accompany the dead to their graves.'*

A knock: Eble Dupuis, his *chambrier* prelate, entered. He looked like a small bear in his heavy fur robe, such as danced on its hind-legs at Arles fair. Dupuis took no notice of the quill in Clement's hand. He had his task to carry out.

'For tonight, Holy Father, I have laid out the red robe, an underrobe of wool and your leggings. The cold in the dining room is death to old bones—' he stopped in confusion and Clement laughed.

'Your new purple—'

'Stop, Eble. I have no heart for tonight's dinner with the cardinals.'

'The purple cap, to keep out the cold,' Eble went on, inexorably. 'You are welcoming a new cardinal, the one who has taken cardinal Le Gor's position.'

Clement hesitated.

'The cardinals say – I have heard talk, Holy Father – that you have promised to direct the way they, in turn, should direct the clergy during these terrible times; they need your advice, Holy Father.'

At eight he sat down with his cardinals, and, as he looked around and smiled at them, he acknowledged each man's greeting – Gaucelme de Jean, Annibal de

Ceccano, Jean de Comminges, Pedro Gomez, Guillaume de Peire de Godin, the new cardinal, the three cardinals of Italian origin. They had been appointed because they were good administrators, or judges, or reliable when it came to chasing heretics or travelling on behalf of the Church, chosen for their skill in making decisions. Petrarch's words came to him, too: '*The cardinals – arrogant, swollen with cupidity and voluptuousness, satraps covered in gold and purple.*' Petrarch at his most vehemently critical of his Court. They did not look as though they needed his advice; but they should have it.

'Where is Cardinal Le Gor now, uncle?' asked Pierre Roger de Beaufort, his sister's son, sitting on Clement's right; his favourite nephew.

'In Jerusalem by now, I hope, giving thanks for his restored eyesight,' said Clement, briefly remembering Le Gor's minor sins and his major contribution. As for Pierre Roger, not yet a cardinal, he resolved to make him one very soon, before the plague could carry him off.

Apart from his nephew, there was another guest at this dinner of cardinals: Etienne Asselin, who had treated his foot successfully with sea water, back in 1343. *Mège* Asselin caught his eye, and he sent a page down to where the doctor sat to bid him come to his study after the meal.

I must address them, thought Clement, as the servants removed the silver dishes in which fruit and salads had been served and brought in others – pounded almonds whipped with cream, a pâté of duck and another of crab. Pedro Gomez, on Clement's left, now remarked whether they might be permitted to hear the subject of tomorrow's sermon? Very well, thought

Clement, why not now before their minds are fuddled with wine, and he swallowed his spoonful of almond and cream. As his gaze swept around the table, conversation ceased.

'The subject of my sermon,' he said, 'will be the responsibility of the Church, and the abdication of their duties by many priests. Cardinals, whatever your private fears, you must put them to one side and lead our Church through these black days.'

Pierre de Pres had been talking to Annibal de Ceccano about their journey in the winter of 1343, when they had made their way from the camp of Edward III to that of the Duke of Normandy, sent by Clement to resolve their quarrel, in which, after much pleading, they succeeded. Both cardinals were of the opinion that the Holy Father was failing. There had been signs. They caught each other's eyes, and now waited for instruction, perfectly aware that a great disaster had struck.

But the Pope sat silent; subject, they saw, to that pessimism of which the ancients spoke. Eble, aware of the hiatus, at once gave a signal, and six kitchen maids brought in three tureens of soup: one of millet, herbs, fennel and mustard, one of pears, the other of quinces. Then, as Clement sat without speaking further, sunk in thought, Bertrand de Deaux thought he might as well report a strange happening, which would surely jolt the Holy Father out of his accidie. He begged leave to speak – a full report would be presented at the next *concilium*, but meanwhile . . .

Clement listened in silence. A young Breton fisherman had apparently heard the sound of heavenly voices, and saw what was indubitably a figure walking on the sea near Concarneau. Investigation was proceeding. Clement listened, his thoughts elsewhere, till he saw that Bertrand had stopped, with an injured expression. The cardinals looked significantly at each other. Gaucelme de Jean began to relate how he had been called to a false Franciscan, now in prison in Avignon, who had turned eloquent on the fate which awaited them all, Pope, cardinals, everyone.

Clement gave these reports a fraction of his attention, looking around his dining room; at the floor, strewn with flowers of camomile and pine needles, so that every step released scents, and at the yellow balls of mimosas in the huge silver vases which cast their heady scent like a benediction into the room. I cannot talk of sickness, death and the role of the Church here, now while they are feeding, snouts in troughs, he thought suddenly and nodded at Eble, anxious to hasten the end of the banquet.

The roasts were brought: veal, duck, pheasants, accompanied by their sauces – parsley, garlic, vanilla, broom flowers. Corsican wine flavoured with cinnamon and honey was poured, and, as the talk increased in volume and circled his aching head, he shook his head at the servants offering dried meats from Italy. Eble, after one look at his master, waved them away and called for the sweets; light confections of nuts, honey and limes.

Clement looked angrily at the faces around the table, gulping and feasting; his cardinals. It is I, though, who had brought them here to feast, so how can I grudge them their feast, for tomorrow they might be dead?

Sitting or slumping at ease in their violet copes, their red hats attached by ribbons to the upright of each man's chair, the cardinals' conversation had turned to the *code canonique*, a favourite topic once the cardinals were in their cups. The code forbade certain dress for clerics.

'They persist in wearing green and red!' cried Pierre de la Forêt, striking the table with his fist. 'And they must have striped jerkins! Spurs on their boots or – I have seen them at Mass – in cutaway shoes with points so long they trip when they rise from prayer!'

'They have huge feathers on their hats!'

'Long hair, curled and perfumed.'

'I saw this day a priest in a parti-coloured *justaucorps*.'

'Who will respect them?'

Clement could bear no more. This was not the time to speak his message. He rose, inclined his head and cut off all conversation with that gesture. Into the silence he spoke the usual prayer, and then, with Eble's help, made his slow way around the table, leaving faces gleaming with grease and napkins balled on the table among peel and dirty spoons. He left the feast, asking himself again whether he had not encouraged such levity and such luxury, in times which had suddenly turned so grave; had he not led his own astray?

Chapter 43

'Doctor Asselin,' announced Clement's valet.

Clement, exhausted and dispirited, had already disrobed, having forgotten that he had told Asselin to attend him after the feast. Asselin entered, bowed low.

'I saw that you were indisposed during the banquet?'

'Illness is commonplace at my age,' said Clement impatiently. 'You have something to tell me that cannot wait?'

Asselin, fifty-seven years old – as was the Pope – but quite untroubled by ill health, sighed. 'As dissection proceeded today, we, Doctors de Chauliac and Jean de Parme and myself, confirmed new symptoms. You asked that anything new be brought to your attention immediately. There is further change in the disease. Large carbuncles now appear in the victims' armpits and groin, and whereas the lung infection kills within three days, these abscesses – carbuncles – kill within five. When these carbuncles grow, limbs blacken, the body is shaken by convulsions – I will spare you the rest. We have ordered masks for ourselves and for the nurses and the grave diggers. We continue to burn clothes and to pile lime on the bodies.'

Asselin took a deep breath. A large man, his fur robe made him seem huge, menacing in the flickering candle light.

'I have waited until after tonight's banquet, Holy Father, to tell you that your auditor, Simon de Brossano, lies sick in his room in your palace. I did not attend him, as I was to be a guest at your banquet, but a friar who did sent word that de Brossano complains of black and livid patches on arms and thighs. It seems that these black patches—'

'—are the messengers of death. I already knew, *mège*. Months ago, I saw it in a dream. Is he dead?'

'He will die. I have come to inform you . . . to urge you . . .' Asselin seemed to make an effort to speak. 'Seeing that, unfortunately, the disease has entered your palace, Holy Father, you yourself must go. The plague . . .' he whispered, mopping his brow. 'So we, your doctors, have made plans for your safety.'

Clement remained in silent prayer, his face contorted as though in pain. Asselin waited.

'Come back tomorrow, early,' said Clement. 'Thank you, but it is late. Too late.'

A few minutes later, his door opened softly again – not Asselin, but Guillemette. He embraced his sister warmly, feeling the comfort of another body and he caught himself longing for his mother's embrace; he, at the head of Christendom, and at the end of his life.

'They said you left the banquet early. I came to see how you were.'

'Guillemette, I had the physician Asselin with me just now. The plague has taken a new turn; I must tell you of a dream I had the last night of the old year, of rats, their bodies black, like dried blood. Asselin reports black patches on the skin. It is the black plague, and it is here, in the palace; there is a man dying of it now, in one of our rooms, of the very disease of which the ancients suffered – and, O God, there is no remedy!'

There was a long silence while brother and sister contemplated, each alone, the future. At last Guillemette said, 'Have we sinned so deeply?'

'Yes. Each one has sinned. There is no denying that the Church has played its part, as well as myself the shepherd. We have called down the wrath of God on us.'

A bell rang twice and other bells from the many churches of Avignon echoed the sound, but it was quiet in the bedchamber, solid masonry stifling the sounds in the huge building where people went about the Pope's business, night and day; guards, monks, servants, member of the Pope's *familia*, moving through corridors, into chapels, stairways, stores, preparing for the new day four hours before daylight. The candles in the bedchamber were casting a doubtful flickering light on the wall paintings and the silk hangings stirred over the door in a sudden draught, waking the thrush in its cage which began to sing.

'I will send for more candles,' said Guillemette at last, like one waking from a deep sleep. 'And we will discuss the measures to be taken.'

'Taking measures . . . what would you propose? Against the wrath of God?'

'You are the Pope,' said Guillemette rising and placing a hand on her brother's brow. 'You are feverish, as I thought. All Christendom looks to you, to your indomitable spirit! We have sinned, but Christ forgives sinners. Let us show repentance, let us devise ways of showing repentance, not by small acts, but by a major act which will draw in all sinners. An act which . . . which will show God that his people repent of their sins.'

Clement looked at Guillemette with surprise and then with hope; and with gratitude. They moved to his study, candles were brought and a valet fetched Clement's great cloak with the hood and Guillemette's cloak of ermine.

They sat down together at the work table inlaid with ivory whorls and scrolls, and Clement showed Guillemette an unfinished letter addressed to Petrarch, asking whether the poet would like a position as librarian at the palace.

'But why? Since he has attacked you many times!' protested Guillemette.

'I love him and admire his work,' replied Clement. He showed her a book on astronomy written by Levi ben Gerson, a Jewish scholar; and a letter from Jean de Murs, whom Clement had asked to calculate the Golden Number.

'Jean de Murs,' said Clement. 'He is busy unravelling the mysteries of God's world—'

'To our task!' said Guillemette, reverting to the commanding tone she, his elder sister, had often used to Clement when they were children. ' I have thought what to do.'

And Clement thought, not for the first time, that she had a mind as good as his, perhaps better; but, being a woman, she had lacked opportunity. Her eyes flashed as she continued. 'Listen to me, brother: I propose that you, the Holy Father, declare this year of 1348 to be a Holy Year, and exhort all the world to make their way to Rome, to fast and pray together there, and hope thus to calm the divine anger.'

'A remarkable idea! But I must point out that the next Holy Year is due in . . . in fifty-two years, which takes us to the year 1400. It was in 1300 that my prede-

cessor Boniface granted full indulgences to all repentant and confessed sinners who in the course of that
year went on a pilgrimage to Rome. Pope Boniface
then decreed that there should be a holy year every
hundred years. But five years ago I reduced the
interval, for various reasons, to fifty years. As it is
written in Leviticus: Ye shall hallow the fiftieth year and
proclaim liberty through all the land and unto all the
inhabitants thereof.'

'Well, brother, call it what you will! '

Clement smiled. Her idea was good, and after a
moment he said, 'It shall be called . . . the name is important . . . let me see . . . Jubilee Year. People are to make a
pilgrimage to Rome, to the tombs of the apostles Peter
and Paul, and it is to take place in 1350; surely by then
the plague will have left us and the survivors can obtain
absolution as well as give thanks. What do you say?'

'No. Too late. Now is the winter of our sickness, the
spring of death. I say that tomorrow you announce at
Mass that this is to be the year of Jubilee, this is the year
they are to go to Rome. Let the pilgrims assemble in
Rome – they have all year. No, let them go for Easter;
what better time?'

He tested the idea in his mind.

'It would enable all those who have stout legs and a
mind to repent truly to make their peace with God. I
shall declare the Jubilee tomorrow, and silence those
who attack me about the sale of indulgences. This is a
gift, within my power, no money is involved. Not all will
go, not all can go but, for the moment, it is an important
gesture.'

They embraced and each sought their bed.

Guillemette, an hour later, during which time neither she nor he had slept, watched Clement, robed for Mass, pass through the great sculpted entrance into his own chapel, nicknamed the Clementine. As he passed through the double doors, he nodded to the carved angels – ten on a ledge above the door, twelve more above them, then glanced to the right to acknowledge the damned, carved either enveloped by flames or in the mouth of Leviathan; angels and hellfire clearly telling the unlettered that entered by this door the choice each Christian could make. The sun flamed through the coloured glass; Clement still owed de Cantinave, glass maker, 450 florins, a fortune – but what glory, what joy! A hymn to God in glass.

The congregation were watching a small door in front, near the altar, through which Clement usually entered, but a chorister, turning round, heard his soft step and all heads turned to watch him as he walked up the aisle.

He celebrated Mass. Then he stood up in the *cathedra*, and the gold cloth above his head turned dusky pink and deep green as the sun sent shafts of colour through the stained glass. He told them in simple words what they knew to their cost and sorrow; that the plague was among them.

'I urge you therefore,' he said, 'to repent and to make a pilgrimage to Rome, in the course of this year which shall be called Jubilee year. When you reach Rome, you may obtain full remission, without payment, of your purgatorial pain.

'And to those who attack the granting, hitherto against payment, of indulgences, I repeat: one drop of Christ's blood would suffice for the redemption of the whole human race. Out of the abundant superfluity of His sacrifice there has come treasure which is not to be hidden in a napkin or buried in a field; but it is to be used. This treasure has been committed by God to his vicars on earth, the Popes, to be used for the full or partial remission.'

So far, the congregation had heard the arguments regarding indulgences many times. They were anxious to hear more about the pilgrimage to Rome, new and unexpected, but Clement stopped speaking at the sound of a man falling, then another and another, a commonplace occurrence in the streets and houses, though, so far, never in this chapel. People tried to move away from the bodies, but the chapel was full. There was an uneasy silence . . . why did the Holy Father not continue? Was he ill? Had he too . . . but that could not be. God would not take the Pope from them, their intercessor; but Clement had fallen silent, in the full flow of his peroration.

Clement was wrestling with his own spirit. As he spoke, urging them to make the pilgrimage to Rome, the plague had entered the chapel, had seized three men in this his special domain. Did this signify that God was displeased with the pilgrimage? Was this, then, not a true way to show repentance? Yes, it was, he felt in his heart and mind that it was; he must urge them to go.

'And thus I urge you—' he began again, to the relief of the congregation, 'to flee this contagion and make your way to Rome, within the year, which is to be called Jubilee Year! *Adieu*, my people; *à Dieu.*'

They cannot all flee, he said to himself when he had regained his own apartments, and he cupped his face in his hands, and sat thus until Doctor Asselin was announced, with his plans for the safety of the Pope.

Chapter 44

The vessel lay becalmed on the glittering, oily water, for the fifteenth day in a row, while its captain stared across the sea towards a strip of land, clearly visible. In spite of the turban wound across head and face, and the loose chemise and baggy trousers, Captain Achmed felt consumed by the heat. He craved a drink of water, but held back; they all craved water, but he must set an example. Rations were low. A man approached him now, wrapped against the burning April sun like himself; only his eyes were visible. The eyes were blue. Before the man could speak, Captain Achmed said, 'The answer is still no. Here; what's this?'

He pointed at a place on the map he was holding, speaking in French as usual, as the other man had little Arabic. They had taken a liking to each other since the passenger had joined the vessel a month ago, in Algiers.

'An inland lake.'

'I think this is an inland sea – here, by the wind-rose, do you see? The étang de Vaccares,' said the captain. The passenger nodded and pointed at a point on the map. His voice shook.

'There! "St.M.d.l.M"! Remember our bargain, remember your promise? Put me down on the shore, here. I know what those letters stand for.'

'No. Remember what they said in Sardinia? The warning? I will not land on the shores of Provence.'

'I do not ask you to land, Captain Achmed, I am asking you to approach close enough for me to land. I know where we are; those letters stand for Saintes-Maries-de-la-Mer. I need a small boat, that's all.'

'What you have paid covered your food and lodgings on my vessel, sir, it does not pay for a boat.'

'You said it would!'

'We've been becalmed for fifteen days. I cannot land to sell my goods. I dare not land here, I will be out of pocket. You know yourself that rations are already short; but I dare not land.'

Captain Achmed had taken a risk allowing a Christian on board; what ideas might he not put into the heads of the sailors? The passenger refused to kneel on the deck with the others, heads turned towards Mecca.

'You could make a raft of the planks over there,' he said after a tense silence. 'But truly, I urge you to stay with us . . . I have grown to like you. There is disease and death on the coast, and inland, they say. What draws you to this shore? I have never asked you. Money? Family?'

'I was born not far from Avignon, a great city on the river Rhône. The centre of all Christendom, Captain.'

The captain spat on the planks.

'And I have a message for the Pope, who resides there, in a magnificent palace, Achmed. Although there is no hurry, I want to deliver the message, and then go home.'

'So there is no hurry, but you are to deliver it to your sheik, your sultan—'

'Pope Clement, Captain. The message is from one of his servants, which he cannot now deliver himself, and I have promised before God to deliver it.'

'I cannot give you the boat,' said Achmed. 'But I shall keep my promise so that you can keep your vow to God, as I would myself.'

And he ordered the seamen to tie some loose timbers together, and gave the traveller his own knife. 'How long you will survive on that hostile shore Allah only knows.'

The seamen heaved the improvised raft overboard, and the young Christian was carefully lowered after it, landing on it without capsizing. A little wind blew shorewards. The raft swayed and turned, but carried him, obeying, very sluggishly, his efforts to steer with a loose plank the sailors had given him. In his baggy trousers with the turban wrapped around his head, he was moderately well protected from the heat and for the next hours drifted shorewards, gently and slowly, with the sailors' gifts – a leather bottle of water and a pouch of food – to sustain him.

Late afternoon, with lips beginning to crack, he sipped a few drops and used the knife to carve some dried meat from the chunk the sailors had given him. He contrasted their generosity with the savagery of the pirates who had captured him on the way to the Holy Land, last autumn, as the two of them journeyed to Acre from Marseilles. Tears of rage, even after all these months, filled his eyes at the bitter memories.

Still the little breeze steered his raft towards the shore. His attempts at rowing left the raft at, he saw with a sinking heart, always the same distance from the shore. And supposing the wind changed and blew him out to sea again? But that evening God sent a stronger breeze which pushed the raft close to the beckoning land, till he had drifted near enough to wade ashore. He stripped off his turban, cloak and baggy trousers and went back into the cool water, washing off the sweat and soaking the garments. After he had sat, naked, drying himself and his clothes in the last of the day's heat, he knelt to give thanks for his freedom and his return to Provence. The salt had irritated many wounds on his body; prickling around the ankles, where the shackles had caused a suppurating ring of pain for months, the wounds hardly healed. All over his body the flesh was puckered where the shackles had rubbed. Salt matted his long yellow hair and, as he pulled it under the turban, winding it around the head – one musulman fashion which served him well – he heard a sound. It was a dog, whining but too afraid to come close. Did animals succumb to the plague? The dog kept its distance. Weariness overcame him suddenly and as he slept on the silvery shore he was half aware of the dog creeping closer; and in the morning it seized a ship's biscuit, but kept its distance.

He set off towards Saintes-Maries-de-la-Mer, walking through a group of huts and dwellings, sheltering under the fortified walls, looking about him. All men were enemies, each a bearer of contagion, he knew that much; for on board the pirate ship, as well as on the vessel he had just left, the talk was of the plague. In the past seven months, he had been used badly, he had encountered pain of body and heart, torture and death; he was the stronger for it and determined to live.

Among the huts he looked in vain for inhabitants; there were only hens scratching in the dirt road between silent houses. He seized a fowl, looked up and down the silent road and swiftly killed it. He could hardly eat it raw; he would enter one of the cottages and make a fire.

The cottages were abandoned; no one from whom to catch the plague; and he was hungry. Holding his knife unsheathed, he walked to the open door of the next ramshackle dwelling, and peered inside.

One look, and he vomited on the doorstep.

He recovered by and by, and put the knife away. What he had seen and smelt was the plague. He dropped the hen he had killed – the dog seized it and ran away at full tilt. I will never again eat flesh, for flesh putrefied, he thought. In the stinking black hold of the pirate ship, he had thought of nothing but survival. On Captain Achmed's vessel, he had thought only of return to his country. The plague had not been his strongest concern. Now it was.

He stood in the road, watching the dog devour the hen.

He stared at the ramparts, the towers; better not to enter the town. His way lay north, slightly north-east, that way lay Avignon. He took a well-used path between salty marshes, crossing a huge expanse, flat with bright green patches. Spring had come to this huge salty marsh and, among the stunted grasses, his heart leapt to see marguerites, narcissus, asphodel, tamarisks; and among the flowers huge butterflies the size of his hand, dancing and dipping. It was good to breathe clean air now, with only the dog and huge birds about; some he saw wading in shallow pools, some flying out to sea. He felt as though he were the last man alive, and had inherited the earth.

The dog near him suddenly barked and ran away. The young man felt the earth tremble and flung himself behind a spiky bush; hardly shelter, but against what? He was not alone on earth, then.

Yet he could see nothing though the ground reverberated with sound. Then finally he saw an advancing
black cloud, heard the thunderous sound of hooves
striking the ground and a mass of gleaming bodies, bulls,
running tightly packed and faster than horses, within a
stone's throw of him, making for the sea.

Walking north, he made his way until another village
appeared in the distance, shimmering in the noon haze.
When he reached it, the same silence greeted him as
before but, as he passed the church, the door opened
and a priest emerged, dazzled by his passage from the
dark into the hot, blinding midday heat, shielding his
eyes.

The young knight drew his knife, whose blade flashed
in the sun. 'Keep your distance!'

'I will,' said the priest. 'I see you are a musulman, far
from home. This is the village of Albaron, sir, a popula-
tion of ninety-three souls. I have buried all my parish-
ioners except a dozen or so who fled . . . but I do not
suppose you can speak my language.'

'Perfectly, Father. I am a Christian, born in the region
of Avignon. I was held on a pirate vessel, and made my
way back to Provence on another musulman ship . . . for
the moment, I would beg some food and drink from
you.' He still held the knife out before him.

'There is no need to threaten me,' said the priest.
'What could I do to you?'

'Give me the plague. I must live, Father. I have a
message for the Pope.' He put the knife away as the
priest smiled.

'There is bread, uneaten, in the bakers . . . but perhaps
you should not touch it. Walk a few minutes beyond the

last cottage and look for the mayor's store house; untouched since before the plague reached us here.'

'And you, Father?'

'I have stores, my son, but I may not need them much longer. Farewell and may God preserve you.'

'Amen,' said the young man with feeling. 'And may God keep you too.'

He found the storehouse, broke the lock with two blows of a stone and ate a strange meal of olives, raw onion and dried raisins, washed down with the local wine, which felled him. When he woke it was with a fierce pain in his gut and a raging thirst. He filled his scrip with onions, olives and raisins and went forward again, hoping to find a spring among the salt marshes, and at last found a fresh water spring where tall birds, pink as a sunset, were drinking.

After two days of trudging, nights spent in the open, weary, with swollen ankles and blistered feet, he saw a city on the horizon. They had both come this way last autumn, riding southwards on their mules, full of talk about Jerusalem. This city should be Arles, by his reckoning. Meanwhile there were other travellers on the road, on foot, on horseback, in carts. At first he brandished his knife, shouting: Keep away! But soon he realised that no one would come close, each lonely in his own fear. He noticed ownerless animals grazing, and decided to choose two horses, leaping on the back of one which still bore its bridle and attaching the other which bore a rope around its neck to the first. He could no longer walk, the wounds on his ankles in fiery revolt. He rode into the city, where there were a handful of people in the streets. He called to one of them, the knife well in evidence, to say what name the city bore.

'Arles,' said the man, shrinking back from the mounted Arab brandishing a knife. 'Spare us, master, we have enough deaths in this city.'

The young man allowed the horses to guide him through the empty city, and, their hooves ringing loudly on the cobbles, the horses led him down to the bridge over the Rhône, where he let them drink great draughts from the river. In an adjacent river meadow he saw nuns, monks and friars burying the dead in ditches. He crossed himself, whispered a prayer, and led the horses to the water to drink, while he drew strength and hope from the great river. Along the quay boats had been tied; from here they would have been towed towards Lyons, passing Avignon; the Rhône flowed strongly the other way towards the sea. He remembered the barges being pulled towards Lyons, when he used to stand on the bridge at Avignon, horses and mules straining on the ropes against the flow. He only had two horses; could they pull a barge, with no load except himself?

Suddenly a child, a small girl, came running out of the hold of one of the barges across the gangplank. Running like a startled hare, she saw him, hesitated, and hid behind a barrel on the quayside. When she peered out from behind it, after a minute while he stood still, debating what to do, he saw tears on her face. Not more than six years old at the most, he thought, and then she made up her mind and ran towards him.

'Stop!' he cried, showing her the knife. She stopped in the middle of a sob. The precepts of religion, the vows of knighthood, common humanity, the protection of the weak against the strong – where were they now, he thought? I am threatening a small child who needs me. But I must live, he said aloud, and reach Avignon. Not only because I want to reach Avignon with my message for the Holy Father. I want to live. I am young, I have survived much and I will not let myself be infected. The precepts of religion are nothing to me now. I may go to Hell, if I believe in Hell; but Hell is here, now.

'Help me,' said the child, softly.

He did not answer. If she were to come nearer, he would have to run away; a grown man running away from a little girl! There was no question of using the knife. He stared at her face, forbidding her to come closer . . . 'Keep away!' he called, and she obeyed. Her eyes were larger than they should be, weren't they? They were looking at him with longing, with hope, but he could see a strange expression on her pinched, small face; she seemed to look inwards. At what sights? What sounds? She was being called and her plea for help was answered from another quarter, for she twisted and fell, such a little way to fall, he thought, and as he watched he saw that she was now beyond his help, as she lay still on the blistering cobbles of the quay-side. If she was still alive he could not tell, for he moved away, not looking at her body, to untie his horses. His steps did not falter as he made a large circle around the place where she lay. He mounted one of the horses and rode along the quayside, towards Avignon, and as he rode the face of the little girl swam before his eyes, half-closed against the dazzling light: What could I have done for her? he said to himself, twice, as tears forced their way under his lids and ran down his dark, sun-scorched cheeks.

Chapter 45

Three days of riding north, along the paths beside the Rhône, the only folk he saw were those burying the dead. No horses dragged barges northwards, no barges made their way south. When he reached Tarascon, he rested for two days beneath trees by the river, till one morning he heard whispers. Help me, help me . . . but it was only the wind rustling the leaves above him. Though he was weary and in pain from his wounds, he spent only a further two days in the saddle before he found himself within sight of Avignon.

He rode slowly, himself and both horses exhausted, till he came to the bridge near Villeneuve-les-Avignon, and suddenly his heart lifted, for every stone and every tree seemed to welcome him. Only the cardinal's palace on the crest of the road looked blankly down on him with closed shutters. He tied the horses to a sweet chestnut in the shade beneath which he had rested himself many times and walked back down to the river that had accompanied his long ride from the coast, but his gorge rose as he saw the bodies floating in it, and his heart lurched within him. Of course, death had reached Avignon too; they said that it moved a league north, every day. But was there no one here to bury the dead?

Staring at the floating shapes in the fast-flowing river, he wondered what had become of those he knew? Was the Holy Father still alive? He became aware of a small group of people camped near the river, watching him, but no one approached him, of course. So there were survivors. But he did not allow himself to rejoice, not yet, although he had reached his goal: Avignon! Avignon: the focus of all his thoughts. The city lay across the river; all he had to do was to cross the bridge and enter it.

He untied his horses, mounted and rode across the bridge, through the gate into the city of his dreams. It was mid-morning.

Avignon was, he saw at once, like the other towns through which he had passed, but the contrast with what had been was heartbreaking. He was riding through a dead city. Those who had neither died nor fled were huddled in their houses, speaking to no one, afraid and hungry, and he met no more than half a dozen muffled cloaked figures as he rode through the turns and twists of the narrow streets he knew so well. A sweet nauseating smell clung to the houses and made him gag. He wrapped the ends of his turban across his mouth and nose and wished for a moment for the clean salt-laden breezes of the sea. A last twist of the narrow lane brought him into the huge square in front of the palace, the papal fortress hiding the opulence within.

He looked for the sentries by the gate; there were none, but he had not really expected to see any. Unhindered, he entered the great courtyard, walking towards the Tour de la Garderobe. He was unsettled by the silence. Where would the Pope be now, mid-morning? Would he be holding an audience or should he try the Clementine chapel? Then close to him, from a window, a voice cried, 'What do you want?'

He saw a head at one of the vestry windows, behind bars.

'I have a message for His Holiness. Please tell him so.'

'From the Grand Vizier, I suppose? Clear off. This is no place for a heathen.'

The young man unrolled his turban and shook his long blond hair free. The watcher at the window called:

'You're like a mermaid, half-fish, half-flesh, only with you it's half heathen, half—'

'Please take a message to the Holy Father, and say it is from Cardinal Le Gor!'

'There is no Cardinal Le Gor,' said the mocking voice at the window. 'I know the names of all the cardinals. Mind you, we have lost quite a few – six of them, so far: Cardinal Gomez, Cardinal Colonna—'

The young man uttered an oath, walked through the nearest open door and found himself in one of the many corridors which he remembered as leading into the great audience chamber, where he thought that the tribunal of the Rota used to hold its meetings. He found it empty. All rooms were empty but for the rich hangings, glowing where the sunlight struck gilded threads; the graceful frescoes and the paintings of youths and maidens, his own likeness among them, which Le Gor had offered the Holy Father; representations of animals and humans in marble and bronze. But no human soul about anywhere, where all had been buzz of clerics and courtiers and beseeching claimants.

He found his way along empty corridors and deserted stairways to the Tour Saint-Laurent – was it not here that the Holy Father had his private apartments? Maybe he was mistaken. Desperate now to find him; the goal of his life for so long must be near. Had they perhaps persuaded the Holy Father to retreat to a place of safety, somewhere else, not in Avignon? There was no one about. Were they keeping away from him? Of course, they must be . . . he ran through anterooms and halls, quickening his pace, and finally leaped up the steps in a tower, he no longer knew which. At the top of the flight of stairs there was a wide antechamber – could this be the entrance to the private apartments? Yes, and it seemed unguarded for the moment. Yet here he met with an obstacle; not as he had expected, drawn swords protecting the Pope, but a bank of burning braziers.

Beyond the braziers, kneeling in prayer before a small prie-dieu, he saw the man for whom the message was intended. The Pope himself knelt there, his back towards the braziers and the visitor. A monk, in the shadows of the room, rose and with agitated gestures waved the young man away, but how could he hold himself back now, after so long a journey and so much hope deferred? And he shouted across the burning braziers.

'Holy Father!'

The Pope gave no sign of having heard.

'Forgive me for disturbing you. I have come a long way with a message for you from Cardinal Le Gor!'

The Pope turned and looked across the braziers at his visitor, rose slowly and awkwardly from his knees and peered at the young man.

'From Cardinal Le Gor?' he said in a tremulous voice. 'Is he well? Is he coming back to us? We need him very much. You were his page, Gui . . . Gui—'

'Gui de Montolieu, Holy Father.'

'I must not go beyond this ring of braziers,' the Pope said slowly, peering through the gloom of the antechamber. 'I hope the cardinal is safe and in good health? We need him, we have lost cardinals. Of course, you are the cardinal's page who cared for him devotedly when he was blind; it will not be forgotten, Gui.'

'Cardinal Le Gor cannot come back to Avignon, Holy Father, alas. The cardinal . . . my master died last autumn at the beginning of his pilgrimage to Jerusalem, from wounds received at the hands of pirates. I was with him when he died. He spoke of you before the end, Holy Father, and he made me promise to return to Avignon to tell you that he . . . that he had some sins on his conscience but that he had always been your faithful servant, Holy Father, and that he hoped to see you in a better world than this.'

'I shall miss him,' said Clement, and both men remained silent for many minutes, while Gui, having at last delivered his message, waited for the Holy Father to say more about Le Gor.

'And you, Gui – what did they do to you?' asked the Pope.

'I was taken with the cardinal. We were outnumbered and both wounded, and they held us in shackles, expecting ransom. After the cardinal's death I escaped, with the help of a musulman, Holy Father. As for my wounds, they are nearly healed.'

The Pope looked directly into Gui's eyes with a show of his old spirit:

'I would so much like to speak with you further, reward you for your loyalty, you who nursed the cardinal with love and devotion . . . but I must not see people, my doctors have forbidden visits, the braziers are to be a barrier. I can do nothing for you at present, I cannot help others, the times are as you see and my health vacillates. We must live out the punishment God has sent us as best we may. I have been persuaded to go to Valence, on Guy de Chauliac's advice; it is said to be safer there. When this tragedy is played out, we will meet and meanwhile you will be in my prayers. Farewell.'

Gui, beyond the braziers, fell on his knees, and the Pope blessed him. Empty of thoughts and feelings, exhausted, Gui made his way out of the empty palace into the streets, then out of the rampart gate towards the Château of Montolieu.

As he rode, he marvelled at the beauty everywhere in this region away from the river, beckoned forward by the shadowy blue mountains many hours of riding ahead, along the familiar winding roads towards the tower of Montolieu. On his right and left the dark cypresses guarded him against the sun. There were no human beings on the roads but he was aware of constant sounds made by the beasts of the forests who, unchecked by men, had multiplied. Huge Aleppo pines pointed to heaven and between them stood isolated oaks, offering shade beneath their fresh green leaves, for which the horses showed a strong desire. He looked out for and passed two mulberry trees, after which the road meandered through a vineyard, then an olive grove and he knew he was coming to a village. A row of cherry trees guarded the first houses and then he saw that he could go no further, for rocks had been placed so that there was no entry. At the sound of his horse's hooves dogs leaped onto the stone barrier and barked with abandon.

Gui understood; a village so far unharmed. He guided the horses through the lush grass around the village, so high that riding, his feet brushed the grass and at once the scent of crushed rosemary, thyme and lavender rose into his nostrils, and he longed intensely for his home.

Back on the road beyond the village, he noticed a field of barley which would soon ripen; no one had weeded or watched over the crop, he saw. The tendrils of young vines curled merrily into the air, for no one had tied the young shoots. The cherries were turning red. Would there be anyone to gather them? In the fields, among the crops, there were cattle everywhere. The herdsmen were dead, thought Gui, wondering whether the animals from long habit would return to their byres for the night or remain in the fields, where the wolves would surely pick them off . . .

The road became a rutted track, and soon his clothes were covered in dust. Gui thought about his meeting with the Holy Father, so long desired, so quickly past. Avignon had been his goal for so long. What now?

His thoughts tangled with what had happened in the palace. The huge reverberating empty halls had disconcerted him; already the search for the Holy Father seemed like a dream. There had been the sound of steps, he suddenly realised, retreating from his own footfalls in that huge silent grove of stone.

Then when he had at last found the Holy Father . . . then, as in a nightmare, he had been baulked of the person he sought. He was looking for the great prince who held the keys of St Peter, but found an old man full of sorrow and despair.

Gui dropped the reins of the horse he was riding and sat quietly, while the two horses tore at the rich juicy grasses by the side of the track. Insects hummed around his head as thoughts formed: I could not speak to the Holy Father about the death of Le Gor; yet I wanted him to ask me . . . though how could he know, and why should he care . . . that I lost the one person I loved?

His heart constricted and he wept, and these tears were the first he had shed over the death of his master, his friend, and now he became aware how much he had counted on the Holy Father to question him, to ask what had happened, how it happened. I wanted him to feel the death of his servant, his cardinal, to talk about him, to shed tears with me. He should have done, I could have spoken, such talk would have shifted, for a little while at least, the burden of loss. But the Holy Father is, of course, surrounded by many deaths and one more cannot have much meaning for him, whereas for me, the cardinal's death was final. Final, in that it means the death of my own heart.

He dried his eyes. He would shed no more tears, he must become hard and he would stay thus; having delivered his message, he had no more obligations.

The world was harsh, and mankind was being punished by a revengeful God. *Sauve qui peut*, he thought: I will please neither man nor God; only myself.

And he rode on towards Montolieu.

Chapter 46

Guy de Chauliac, the Pope's favourite; and now only medical adviser waited, pen in hand in his silent study, deep in the heart of the papal palace. He was listening for footsteps and, as there were few people left in the palace who would guide a visitor, it might well be hours before he found de Chauliac's study. Pope Clement had told him that yesterday a young man had brought news of Cardinal Le Gor's death at the hand of pirates and had actually found his way to the private apartments. This must not happen again; where had the guard been? There were too few of them now; they fell sick. He sighed and started again on his notes, provisionally entitled *Notes of a Doctor at the Court of Pope Clement VI.*

Maître de Chauliac thought of himself as a practical doctor and hoped that one day these notes would be useful to those in his profession who would come after him, and scan his notes eagerly. If they were looking for a successful treatment the search had yet to bear fruit. Better to write, though, than to give himself up to idle melancholia like one or two of his *confrères*. He wrote:

April 12, 1348. My illustrious patient is very low. The placing of braziers inside the palace, in his antechamber, has been mostly successful; at least nobody has been able to approach him closely; though yesterday he received a visit from a young man, formerly

Cardinal Le Gor's page, possibly his catamite? The Holy Father was very disturbed after the visit.

My beautiful young patient Laura des Noves died six days ago today. I have persuaded Louis Sanctus de Beeringen, who knows them both, to write to the poet and scholar Petrarch, who will be devastated – if he is still alive. Who knows?

The Pope frets in his apartments. He has left them a very few times only for I have ordered him not to go out and he has obeyed. He hardly eats, and drinks only water. I bled him yesterday, but he fainted as the leeches began to suck. He asked me if he might go out to bless the waters of the Rhône which have become a sepulchre for so many, as he did a few weeks ago, but I do not feel it is prudent.

I see that this chronicle has deviated from the medical notes with which I began, four months ago. My colleagues in Paris, to whom I applied to know their present thinking, wrote recently that we must obtain for our patients fresh air, rest, drink, food and sleep. I am much advanced! I am now trying fumigation; once at midnight, in the morning and again in the evening, burning the wood of aloes, also of musk and amber when available; am now trying perfumed balm, resin, incense and cabbage stalks.

From my correspondence with Olivier de la Haye I gather the following: patients should avoid meats like beef, pork, goat, hare, deer, and birds which live on the water, as well as fishes. Offer soups composed of peas, lentils, borage, spinach, parsley, beet, mint. He recommends abstention from the pleasures of making love, but urges the patient to live joyously. I ask myself if de la Haye is mocking me—

Regarding the problems of burial. The Holy Father has approved an idea of mine. It is that certain peasants from upper Provence be sent for; they are known as the Gavots and I

remember them as robust and healthy fellows when I travelled in
the region two years ago. We will offer them such payment that
they will not refuse to come and bury our dead.

Recently the Holy Father has instituted a special Mass
against the plague which, the astrologers tell us, is to last for
ten years! Our city is already three-quarters empty; if this is
true, not only Christendom but all the peoples of the earth will
cease to exist. But I will not join in useless speculation. I am a
doctor and they look to me to cure the plague, alas. So far our
efforts are pitiful. I believe the frustration has addled the brain
of my medical colleague Chalin de Vinario whom hitherto I
admired; he maintains that the reason for the advent of this
sickness is the bad behaviour of the people! I asked him whether
he was a priest or a doctor? He left me, showing great anger.

I do, however, have further ideas –

A timid knock on his door was followed by the
appearance of a gaunt figure, wrapped in a cloak, with
dull yellow hair and haunted, bloodshot eyes.

'If you are seeking advice—' began de Chauliac.

'I am Saint-Amant, *mège*, I sent word if I might see you
today and you agreed. Don't you remember me?'

'No. The Chevalier de Saint-Amant sent word that he
wished to see me—'

'I am he, *maître*. I have been nursing lepers since I left
the court. You advised me to do so, when I left the
Household because of . . . you do not remember.'

'No. Why are you here?'

'You do not remember, and I thought that every
man's finger was pointing at me. I had a bastard son with
a Jewess, and tried to snatch him so as to bring him up
as a Christian, in order to atone—'

'*Chevalier*, at present we are fully occupied in fighting the plague. Your scruples are of no interest to me. Thank God that you are alive and leave me to cudgel my mind for ways to combat this most terrible—'

'But what I am here to tell you is relevant. I care for the lepers. But recently my lepers, my charges were attacked by a mob, by a mob of Christians! They broke into our hospice with sticks; they beat the sick and kicked them till my poor charges lay on the ground, like broken vessels, some never to rise again. And why? Because they are being held responsible for the plague! There is no one left at the hospice now. Those who were not struck down have run away, I am alone. I have come here because they say you decide who sees the Holy Father; I beg you to let me see him, to beseech him to utter a denunciation! Lepers do not cause the plague! Allow me to have an audience; he will see me. I was after all the controller of his Household, *mège* . . . a brief meeting will suffice—'

'No one sees the Holy Father, if I can help it. What would you have him do? Not even he can bring your lepers back to life or find those who have run away. My task is to keep the Holy Father alive, *chevalier*; I am sure you approve.'

'*Maître*, I want to draw your attention to the Jews. The mob are looking for scapegoats. That is why they seized on my poor lepers. They have already attacked some Jews; there have been massacres of Jews in Marseilles where the plague began, and then, a few weeks ago, a mob killed forty Jews in Toulon, accused of having poisoned the wells, which caused the plague.'

'But you hate the Jews, *chevalier*,' said de Chauliac slowly, observing Saint-Amant's glittering eyes. 'I believe that you are still obsessed by that fornication of yours with the Jewish woman from the Street, with the son they would not give up to you! You are obsessed, *chevalier*. What is this attack on the Jews to you?'

'What, *maître*! Do you need a good reason to protect the weak from the mob? I have just witnessed what happens when a mob searches for the causes of the plague. I am no longer the coward who came to you months ago with fears about leprosy. I am not better than others; it is true that I begot a child with a Jewess and that I do not want that child killed. Do you believe the mob who say that the Jews poisoned wells and cause the plague?'

'Of course not,' said de Chauliac contemptuously. 'So you want your child protected, is that it?'

'Yes!' said Saint-Amant angrily, red spots on his cheek-bones. 'And not only my child, nor his mother only. If the Holy Father does not protect the Jews – and he has a reputation for protecting the Jews, hasn't he – they will be attacked like the lepers. And since the Holy Father is God's vicar on earth, I ask that he be informed of the horrors perpetrated by Christians, and that he forbids violence on the innocents suspected of causing the plague!'

'The Holy Father is aware of the fate of certain Jews. We have had intelligence from Narbonne and from Carcassonne where the plague has raged all winter. And it is known that there they have killed their Jews. In Savoy, the surgeon Balavigny was tortured and avowed that he had poisoned the fountains of several towns with the venom of snakes and toads, and with desecrated hosts, and with the hearts of Christians whom, as a Jew and a doctor, he had treated. I am as disgusted and horrified as you are.'

Saint-Amant looked at him with feverish eyes.

'So?' he asked. 'What is to be done?'

'His Holiness, when he heard, pronounced excommunication against all those who kill Jews. He has decreed Avignon and the *comtat* Venaissin a refuge for all fugitive Jews. No mob would touch them here.'

Saint-Amant gathered his cloak around his meagre form, only half the man whom the doctor remembered.

'You have set my mind at rest. I suppose the Holy Father can do no more. I shall go to the Street of the Jews now.'

'To search for your child?' asked de Chauliac. 'To take him with you? Is that wise? You did not succeed before . . .'

'Not to take him with me. To see him. To reassure the Jews that they have the Pope's protection.'

'Well, go; but I believe there are not many in the Street now and you may not find him.'

After Saint-Amant had left, de Chauliac felt weary, his mind showing him pictures of cudgels, lepers, Saint-Amant's bloodshot eyes, snakes. I am wearied to death by anxiety and failure, he told himself; the best antidote for the moment is to record what happens – perhaps a pattern will emerge. He picked up his pen and opened his notebook. Strangely, the movement caused pain in his armpits. His mind seemed clouded; words swam about but he could not catch them, write them down. At last he began:

A man came to tell me yesterday that if a man or woman were found with powders or an ointment, fearing that these might injure someone or cause the plague, the owners were forced to swallow the powder or ointment. Some reject stored food less than a year old, in case it is contaminated. On the whole, I am ashamed of my colleagues. Some, a few, show sublime devotion to the sick; most a horrible cowardice. But I believe I am on the cusp of a discovery, and if I am right, the cowards among my colleagues can face their patients and with God's help, cure them and –

He had to put down his pen. There was definitely a pain under his armpits. At once his mind cleared. He would test his new idea on the next patient – and it looked as though that was to be himself – and survive; or the world would have to wait further for effective treatment. My next action, he said aloud, must be to send the Holy Father to a secret house in the country, for it seemed as though he, Maître Guy de Chauliac, might no longer be able to care for him. He felt no fear, but a strong curiosity.

Chapter 47

Why am I in such haste? Gui asked himself when he knew he was a half hour's ride from the Château of Montolieu. Nothing awaits me there; the old servants will have gone.

But in his mind's eye he saw the château which consisted of only one tall tower, its feet buried in grasses and bushes as high as a man, the lavender in flower with its attendant bees, the well in the courtyard shaded by the huge chestnut. Even if the old servants had gone, his past life would enfold him like a father, and tonight he would sleep in the little chamber on the top floor, with the moon peering in through the crowns of trees. Tomorrow at first light he would swim in the pool where his father had taught him, then ride down to the village to see the serfs, to see what they had made of the fields he had given them. And then . . . ?

His father had taught him that a knight should face death without fear or emotion, and Gui thought he would be able to do that when the time came; but how to face life now? Apprehension and melancholia are themselves a plague, he thought, and he who fears loses all appetite for life and draws unto himself the very disease he fears. Therefore I must cast out fear if I wish to live. The cardinal had once told him that Paracelsus taught that a gloomy mood and fear predisposed the body to sickness.

It came to him, as he allowed the horse to slacken its stride and shortly stop altogether, that his own spirits were low enough to attract the plague. Would it matter greatly if he were to die? Yet the sun and shadow alternating on his skin, even the smell of the herbs at this moment, were reasons for living and when he stopped at a little stream to drink he was glad to still be alive.

When at last he rode into the courtyard of Montolieu, and had dismounted, he was not surprised by the weeds grown tall and thick, nor by the rusty chain by which the bucket hung above the well. The sun was setting, and a cloud of biting insects swarmed around his head, plaguing the horses. Of course, the servants were long gone; he was alone. But on the ground, in a corner of the yard attracting flies, he saw eggshells, peel from roots, cherry stones and fish heads; so the servants were still here, after all!

Dusk was approaching and the light was uncertain, but did he see a lit window above him, or was it the reflection of the setting sun on paper which had been made translucent with oil? Was that the flickering of a candle behind the shutters on the floor above? He tried the huge door: locked, as he had expected.

Then he heard a whinnying, and his own horses confirmed the sound by whinnying too. In the old stable he found five horses, standing peacefully in the stalls, feeding on hay, freshly cut, and there were buckets of water for each. His own horses appreciated the hay and the water.

Whose were these horses? Were their owners here? His heart leapt at this evidence of human life. The owners of the horses must be inside the tower, and it was they who had locked the door. Gui had known another way into the tower since he had been a boy. He found the footholds on the massive rough stones and climbed the wall till he reached a small window, always open to air the storeroom behind it. The stores were there, enough of them to keep him from starving for a year. Softly he opened the door onto the little staircase which led to the hall below, from where he could hear muffled sounds.

Carefully he made his way down the stairs by feel, for it was totally dark. He would startle the owner of the horses; although he was more curious than angry at their unbidden presence. Nevertheless he held his knife ready as he quietly descended the last steps.

The hall was dark. All around him were sounds, human sounds which he recognised with astonishment.

Carefully he picked his way in the dark among several pairs of bodies enlaced on the floor. He was walking on carpets; not carpets, his father had never laid down a carpet in the hall. He thought that his guests must have removed the great tapestries from the walls where his father had hung them many years ago, on his return from Flanders. They do not know I am here, amongst them, Gui thought, when suddenly he stumbled, but righted himself, over a couple intent on making love. Too late, he thought of contagion . . . But the sounds of lovemaking roused him, in spite of himself. Fornication, he thought, why not? I am damned, I am already sinning in thought – and this time a man's outstretched leg brought him down upon the floor. The man was asleep, but the woman, seemingly unaware in the dark that Gui was a stranger to her, pulled him to her while he was still considering sins and indulgences. Later, after a brief sleep, he found himself in the arms of another woman, or it might have been the same one; darkness covered all. Around him, men and women coupled with abandon, and he did the same . . .

Much later, he rolled into a corner and fell into deep sleep on his father's Flanders tapestry which depicted amorous shepherds and shepherdesses.

When he woke, it was late morning, as he could tell from the sun on his face. The cloth of his cloak felt rough on his skin and he realised that he was naked beneath it. He sat up, confused at first, then aware that he was in the hall of the tower of Montolieu. There was complete silence around him, yet something in the silence told him that he was not alone in the great hall, it was as though someone, perhaps several people, were breathing cautiously, as though waiting to spring on him. Where was his knife?

A tiny sound, the shuffle of a shoe, gave him the direction in which to look. Nine people – he counted – stood well away from him, near the door. They were fully clothed in resplendent garb, such as he had worn himself when he was Le Gor's page. He saw fur-lined cloaks, gold chains, soft dyed shoes and lace, and all the colours of the rainbow on the four women and five men standing in a group, with their faces turned towards him. Pale faces, marked with fear; with terror. Fear of him? He looked about for his knife but could not see it.

'What are you afraid of?' Gui said at last, breaking the silence. 'I am the master of this château, I am Gui of Montolieu. You are trespassing. But you can see that I am unarmed and naked.'

'Each one of us thought—' began a red-haired woman hesitantly. Gui found her beautiful, her red hair in long tresses hanging down over a white, gold embroidered bodice.

'—that you were one of us,' continued a tall, well-built man, dressed in a green suit with a braided cloak about his shoulders. He pulled at the braid, and avoided Gui's stare.

'So that,' continued an older man with grey-flecked beard and long curled hair, 'we did think we were safe. For each of us knows the others, knows that none of us has the plague. But now . . . since you took part in . . . our lovemaking, our celebration of life, we are afraid that you will have put an end to us all. We thought that if life is to go on, we must love and procreate while there is life in us.'

'Set your minds at rest,' said Gui. 'So far, I have been fortunate.'

There were sighs of relief.

'How . . . how . . .' began the older man again. 'Since we had locked the door, in case of others breaking in?'

'As I noticed,' said Gui. 'I have the means of entering in spite of locks. More to the point, sir, how dare you break into my house! Why are you here, fornicating in my hall, on a tapestry torn from the wall?'

There was silence again. Gui noticed that a little colour had returned to the faces of his guests. He remembered the couplings of last night; had he lain with the red haired woman or with that one, with the jet-black hair? Perhaps. It did not matter. There was no Hell and no Heaven, no sin in fornication, no need to purchase indulgences, no life after this. No truth, no goodness. Life was short, the pestilence was king. Why was he so angry with the intruders? It did not matter.

'It seems you are my guests,' he said into the silence. 'Welcome.'

There were some tentative smiles, and some allowed themselves small movements of the feet or hands but no one spoke. Are they ashamed? thought Gui. It does not matter.

'You found this château empty,' he continued, 'for I was on a pilgrimage to Jerusalem with my master, Cardinal Le Gor, from whom I bore a message to the Holy Father at Avignon; and after seeing him – he is alive, ringed with braziers of fire – I rode back here, to Montolieu, my home . . .' he paused and bowed to the women. 'Where to my astonishment the ladies made me very welcome—'

There was tentative laughter, but the group of nobles found difficulty in meeting Gui's eyes. After a pause the older man with the grey-flecked beard stepped forward.

'We were fleeing from the plague, Knight. We took shelter with one another then, and when food became scarce we moved to another great house where we had friends or family, till there were nine of us always moving northwards out of the path of the plague. All of us had lived in châteaux south of here, some in the mountains behind the sea, others here and there in Provence. My home, *chevalier*, is in the château of Barben, near Salon.'

'And mine and my sister's was at Lambesc; empty now,' said another voice.

'We have the château of Lacoste. There is no one alive in the village.'

'I lived in Beaucet. Only ghosts live there now,' whispered the woman with the jet-black hair.

'We fled from the plague,' said the grey beard. 'On . . . onwards, and not long ago we found this tower empty; and the store room full. Forgive us, *chevalier*. We know that we may not have long to live, so while God spares our lives, we eat, drink and are merry. And we comfort each other.'

He came forward and stretched his hand out to Gui, who took it.

'There are those,' said the grey-bearded man, 'who rob and pillage the dead. There are many cruel and perverse actions committed by those in fear. There are those demanding ransoms, money, who then let the stricken die alone, without at least the comfort of a human soul, if there is no priest. Alone! Who can bear to die alone? As for us, what harm are we doing? And should God be merciful and allow one of our women to conceive, and the child lives, well, we shall have placed new life on this stricken earth. These are the tenets by which we now live.'

A young man with sharp features and a nose like a bird of prey, dressed in a green, silver-braided and slashed doublet now stepped forward and bowed to Gui.

'Chevalier de Montolieu, we owe you an apology. But the tower was empty, there was no one to ask. After this, sir, if I live, you will be an honoured guest for as long as you wish, in my castle on the Luberon, and you will be treated like a king; on my oath!'

'And in mine, Knight! And in mine!' the others cried.

Gui nodded. Why not? Meanwhile he would share Montolieu with this band of nobles, for as long as the plague raged; making music, perhaps, singing and dancing, drinking and feasting. And spending the nights in each other's arms until the plague had either retreated or harvested them.

Chapter 48

The month of June had been the hottest that Blanchette could remember. Waking, she felt the scratch of hay through the blanket. Thoros, asleep in her arms, rolled away from her with a sigh. It was still cool in the barn, the sun had not risen yet and the birds were silent.

For months now, Blanchette had marvelled at the silence all around. At first, after the departure of the others, she had been frightened by it, but now it was precious; something good had come from leaving the Street, not that her mother would ever agree . . . She turned her head to the left where Joseph lay in his nest of hay, like a hare. There was a faint rustle, nearer the wall of the barn and, drifting into half-sleep as the dawn brought the first birdsong, she knew that her mother Lea was rising early. A little later she became aware that Lea was kneeling by her bed, and heard her murmur something.

'What is it, Mother?'

'A prayer for us all. To pray for your health and happiness. To ask protection from the wrath of God. I will be gone in a moment, Lolo.'

And she kissed Joseph, who stirred but did not wake.

'Where are you going?' said Blanchette, sitting up, which woke Thoros.

'What has happened?' he said, alert at once. 'Lea? Are you ill?'

'I am going to look for food,' said Lea with a note of defiance in her voice and face. 'You know we have not much left; enough for this week, no more. Well, maybe a month's provisions. We gave too much to the families when they went north, I said so at the time.'

'Do not—' began Blanchette hesitantly. It was she who looked after everyone, she who made decisions, but with her mother she was gentle and, this morning, beseeching.

'—go close to anyone,' said Lea mimicking Blanchette's voice, 'look where there are bodies and do not approach them whether in fields or meadows or near the river. Do not speak to strangers, do not, above all, take food from them. As if there were any strangers, Lolo. It is empty out there, no people, nothing, God has forgotten us, we are alone in the world. How long before our turn? Why did we leave the Street? What are we doing here in the wilderness? I am tired of fields and meadows, even if the good Lord made them before houses. I wish we were back in the Street, and when I have to die, I'll do so in my own bed. I have a good mind to go back to the Street this morning.'

'Mother, stay with us, I beg you, Mother! We've spoken of this before; there is truly more chance of staying alive here! And you chose not to go with the other families, northwards, to Lyons, so that when the time comes, you will be home quickly.'

'Lyons! Still further away from the Street; not I! Well, I am going to look for food now; someone must.'

'Lea—' began Thoros, gently.

'Oh yes, the pact, Thoros, I remember it, do not fear.'

'Will you repeat it once more?' said Thoros softly. 'We care for you, Lea. Please.'

Lea drew herself up. There was anger in her face and her lips quivered. The little door let into the huge barn door suddenly admitted a blaze of light for a moment, sunshine and birdsong, and they saw little Abranet making his way towards them.

'You make me say it every day, Thoros. How can I forget it?' Lea said sullenly and she recited in a singsong voice:

'If any of us, going about outside the *grange* is taken ill and notices the signs of the contagion in or on their body, they will not return in order that others may live and so protect this family, that some, at least, may survive the wrath of God. If stricken, they will await the decision of the Lord and, if He wills it, die alone.'

'Kiss me, Mother,' said Blanchette, embracing her, and watched the old woman setting off into the glorious bright morning, into the empty fields and meadows, looking for berries and herbs to gather, and to harvest grain in fields where others had sown but had not lived to gather.

Blanchette went out to wash herself and Joseph and then prepared a meal which she offered to Alysa who lay on her side, breathing heavily and still asleep. Abranet ate and went out again, Alysa rose and took Joseph into the grass where he played, and Thoros and Blanchette were alone in their corner of the huge barn.

'What are your thoughts?' Blanchette asked Thoros, stroking his cheek. 'Do you love me?'

'Yes. Yes, of course! As for my thoughts . . . according to Abranet we have evidence now which is important and which of course while I'm here I cannot verify—'

Blanchette sighed.

'I cannot approach the bodies. But it appears that the disease has changed since we left Avignon. Black buboes; Abranet heard talk.'

Blanchette knew what was coming. Her husband's frustration was growing daily.

'Bernard of Montpellier – this I heard just before we left the Street – puts a cloth over the sick man's head so that the breath does not contaminate. Now, can that be right? Surely not!'

'I don't know, Thoros. Even in your absence, I am sure that the doctors are doing all they can.'

'I doubt that! Most of them are afraid of dying. Or, like myself, not so much of dying but of risking the death of my family.'

Blanchette bit her lip to stop herself replying.

'Guy de Chauliac said bleeding was indicated, but of course I am speaking of months ago. Bleeding weakens the patient, though with the blood, morbid humours are expelled. What do I know. I am far away here and have no concept how the sickness may have altered. I have never felt more impotent – as a *medicus*, and I still have not given you a child, either. My skills are useless. Oh, I understand your mother's frustration well; if she knew the extent of mine, she would be surprised! People are dying by the thousand and I am here, idle.'

'You promised to stay with us,' cried Blanchette. 'As for a child, I have you, I have Joseph, I do not need another child.'

'But I would be so happy with a child of ours. Besides, we must create new life, we who are left; which Alysa's David did in the four nights they were together . . . Poor Alysa. Poor David.'

At midday they, and Abranet, Alysa and Joseph sat on the big flat stones outside the barn, in the shade, watching the fast-flowing glittering Rhône not far away, hiding its burden of bodies, while Abranet spoke of ways he had devised to catch birds, to eat.

'We have plenty of stores,' said Blanchette. 'Although my mother frets that we haven't enough.'

'Where is Lea?' asked Alysa listlessly. She had refused food.

'In the fields,' said Blanchette. 'Gathering whatever she can find.'

Alysa stared ahead of her, remembering David's face, searching the empty banks of the river for approaching figures, as she did most of each day.

'I wonder where they are now,' said Alysa. 'Mother and father and the sisters . . .' Her voice died away, and no one spoke.

For three weeks after their arrival at La Grange Neuve, all had gone tolerably well for the twenty-five families. The habits of the Street had taught them to show forbearance and to keep to the rules by which the Street was governed.

They each had their allotted sleeping place and there was plenty of room for all. They cooked food from the store and said their prayers as always. Not far from the barn was a spring; it was, thought Thoros, as good a place as could be found, and as soon as the sickness had abated, they could reach the Street within a day. But a constant stream of weary travellers passed them on their way north to escape the plague and the twenty-five families soon learned to defend their barn. As they understood the extent of the devastation and horror which came advancing up the Rhône, they too began to consider further flight – to Valence, maybe to Lyons.

One morning Cabri came to sit beside Thoros, on the large stones near the entrance to the *grange*.

'We are leaving, Thoros,' he said quietly. 'And I would be happy if you and your family were to come with us. I know that something keeps you near Avignon – I have not asked you why – but come with us now. Will you?'

'Why?'

'Why? The stores will not last for ever. Also, and you know this as well as I, as we have indeed all discovered: we are no longer safe here. Seeing that the disease comes from the south and makes its way northwards, we must travel ahead of it. To Valence; or Lyons, I have a sister married there. Thoros, I think all the families wish to go; will you not come?'

But Thoros shook his head. 'You will find the same dangers there; if not already, you soon will. The plague moves as fast as you can.'

But the prospect of movement inspired hope in the Jews who were leaving and one morning at the break of dawn Rabbi Liptois, who felt it was his duty to remain with the greater number, held a short service in the shade of the barn.

'God, our Lord, who helped us overcome our enemies, who wrought miracles and retribution upon Pharaoh and brought forth the people of Israel from among the dangers to freedom, we beseech Thee to set us free from this plague and protect us who go and those who stay.'

Alysa was one of those who stayed behind; if she were to leave, she said, how would David ever find her when he returned?

Abranet was the other, apart from Thoros and his family. He did not want to be part of a large group of travellers, he felt safer alone, he said, and till he felt the restlessness in his legs again, he would help Thoros look after the women. And so they lived in their corner in the great barn, two men, three women and a child. Not enough men for a *minyan*; but they said their prayers morning and night, though Alysa could seldom be persuaded to join them.

She lived for the child within her and spoke little except that once each day, when she would ask Thoros or Blanchette whether she could go back to the Street today, in case David had returned from the coast and would not know where to seek her. Blanchette and Thoros told her each day that no, she could not go – yet. Next day Alysa would ask again. In spite of her approaching motherhood, Alysa's mind had returned to her life as a child, when she was powerless in the hands of the grown people around her who made decisions.

This morning as always, Alysa approached Thoros, her small pale face frowning, her great stomach of six months pushed forward. Thoros was reading for the seventh or eighth time one of his few books, the *Treaty on Urines* by Theophilus. He saw her and smiled, in spite of the mutinous angry expression on her face, and lowered his book, searching for something new to say. He found it. 'You should know, Alysa, that you are the most important person amongst us! Without you and the child you are carrying, there might never again be Jews in the Street. I hope you are well this morning?'

She appeared not to have heard.

He picked up his book again. Blanchette came to join them, and took her place next to Thoros.

'*Maitre*,' said Alysa as though she had not heard him before. 'Please allow me to go back to the Street. I ask you every day. I beg you to think of David – what will he do when he can't find me?'

Thoros remained silent. Each time she had asked him, he had replied to this question evasively, afraid of speaking the truth which he thought might well harm her and endanger the unborn child. Alysa turned to Blanchette. 'Help me to go back to the Street, Blanchette.'

'You know as well as I do that there is plague in the Street. I don't know, but Thoros thinks that there may be no one alive there anymore. There may be bodies. It's not safe. We have told you a dozen times,' said Blanchette harshly; why would Alysa not grow up?

'You both speak as though we were safe here,' cried Alysa. 'And if I had wanted safety, I could have gone with Cabri and the rabbi and my family! I could have gone with my parents! I want to be at home when David returns. That's what I want!'

She is reasonable, thought Blanchette, except on one point. I must risk the truth. Without a smile and speaking slowly, she said, 'You are carrying David's child. It is yours and David's, but also it carries all our hopes. David may be dead. They say that the sickness came to Marseilles first. I know you loved him for the four days of your marriage. Yes, Alysa, and I grieve for you, both of us do. Don't you want his child to live, though? You would endanger it in the Street; more surely than here. I have had to say these harsh truths to you; and I think that in your heart you know.'

Alysa turned away with a cry, rose with difficulty and ran with lumbering gait back into the barn.

'I could not say it—' began Thoros.

'Then it's as well she heard it from me,' said Blanchette. 'She is a little mad, maybe it is her condition. But she had to hear.'

And she rose to fetch water from the spring. Thoros read. They thought no more about Alysa who, after all, asked the same question every day.

The sun stood overhead when the little group from the Street sat down on the stones in the shade to eat their midday meal; but neither Lea nor Alysa had answered Blanchette's call. If Lea's search had been fruitless, the old woman would not return till later, searching all afternoon; she would come when she was tired. But Alysa—? She was always hungry by midday as it was her only meal of the day. The millet porridge, sweetened with honey and raisins, was steaming before them in its bowl and Abranet had begun to eat when he stopped and listened

'*Nom de bore!* I can hear the cart! There she goes! That *bardayan* of an Alysa has taken it . . . and the mule! She is driving it – Look!'

'To her death,' said Blanchette shading her eyes against the glare. 'What is serious is the loss of our mule and cart—'

'You are heartless,' said Thoros angrily. Blanchette paled; he had never spoken to her in that voice. 'I am going after her—' He abandoned his plate, springing to his feet.

'No!' cried Blanchette. 'I am sorry! Thoros, I meant—'

But Thoros, stronger every day now, was walking away with long strides and, reaching the path along the river, broke into a run. Blanchette, with Joseph, alarmed by the shouting, whimpering in her arms, sat with a face of stone. Presently, she began to feed Joseph.

To Abranet, who was watching her anxiously, she said after Joseph had been fed, into the silence, 'So he has done what he wanted. My words – my stupid words – helped him to get away.'

'Alysa has done what she wanted,' Abranet offered.

'No. My husband has done what he wanted. He has gone after Alysa, yes. It is not Alysa – I know what he wants. Alysa—'

'Well,' said the little pedlar. 'Of course Thoros could have no interest in that young girl – except to fetch her back. With such a wife as you, he would not look elsewhere!'

'He may have set off after Alysa, but he cannot hope to catch her on foot, and of course he knows that. Do you know, Abranet, why we are still here, why we did not go north with the others? We are still here because . . . he . . . he promised me he would not, but now he has—'

Abranet waited, not daring to speak, observing the tears coursing down Blanchette's cheeks, and he envied Thoros such a wife; so beautiful and so full of passion, though often daunting, but in need of comfort at the moment. Maybe there would be chance for him, later of course, if Thoros did not return . . .

'My husband,' said Blanchette drying her eyes on her *cotte*, 'was and is the best *medicus* in Avignon, except one: Guy de Chauliac. I made Thoros promise that he would not practise his art, his skills, so as not to endanger us: my mother, my boy, me, you. Himself.'

'Ah!' said the pedlar. 'He is always spoken of as a *gulbor.'*

'A hero? Is he a hero who carries the plague back to his family? He will not bring Alysa back, Alysa was his excuse. No, he will have gone elsewhere, and I think I know where.'

And she sobbed for a long while, withdrawing angrily from Abranet's comforting touch.

Chapter 49

By late afternoon Thoros had reached the bridge which crosses the river from Villeneuve to Avignon. At the sight of the spires and the towering bulk of the Pope's palace, planted on its rock, he paused. After the first few minutes of running along the riverbank in pursuit of Alysa he knew very well that he had no hope of catching up with her, but he had continued to walk towards Avignon. By now she had reached the Street, and, for her, the die was cast.

But it was not cast for him; he could still turn back, and be safe; he could keep his promise and act like the responsible, trained and experienced *medicus* he was. Trained to save the lives of the sick under oath; but in order to save, he needed knowledge.

He walked forward, across the bridge, towards the Porte du Pont which he had last seen when he led the exodus from the Street. There was the sentry box, its gate stood open. There were no sentries, nor other people about; so much the better. He had never meant to go to the Street. He had needed circumstances like the ones provided by Alysa . . . Guy de Chauliac, the Pope's doctor, in the Palace, would tell him the history of the disease, its mutations, the measures de Chauliac had taken. If he was still alive.

'Forgive me, Blanchette,' he murmured, once through the gate, and inside the wall. He stood still, and, with turmoil in his mind, forced himself once more to see the consequences of his actions. Were he to discover a symptom of the disease on himself – there were new symptoms, it was said – he would carry out the pact, repeated with scorn this morning by old Lea. Out of the corner of his eye he saw a corpse, half-naked, slumped against the wall of a house, twenty paces away. Even at that distance he could distinguish discolouration on the flesh – black patches. So that was the mutation. He did not approach.

If he could speak with de Chauliac, discuss the new symptoms, hear what measures had been tried . . . he hungered for news and for speech with his like. What life was he living at the barn? A half life, not a useful life. God had preserved his life to carry out his calling, not to hide . . .

He began to walk resolutely towards the Palace.

Never had he seen the town like this. The streets were devoid of life, both human and animal, and it was not until he had walked for many minutes, and found himself close to the Palace, that he heard footfalls and the sound of wheels on the cobbles. He had to press himself into a doorway to let a funeral pass in the twisted narrow street. A funeral: two sturdy men were pushing a large barrow. Both were dressed alike in black, wearing high conical hats with kerchiefs attached so that they covered head, neck and face as well, with slits in the black stuff for the eyes. In the barrow were bodies piled high, lying pell-mell upon each other. Thoros saw rags on the corpses, but also lace, a bracelet – were they burying folk with their jewellery now? – some purple velvet, coarse sackcloth, silk dresses, tassels, belts, bicoloured hose. The bodies of rich and poor were trundling towards a burial ground, with no witnesses but himself.

Thoros, despite all he had seen of misery in his life was too affected to walk on. Wiping tears from his eyes, he whispered: God, take pity on us all.

As he stood, covering his nose and mouth with his cloak, he wondered if all the cities had become like this. And what of the land? He thought of the forests reclaiming the tilled fields, the vegetation regaining inhabited places and deer and hares, wild pigs and wolves take men's places on earth as human life succumbed. How long till wild beasts roamed unhindered through Avignon? Would tall grasses grow in the centres of learning, the universities of Montpellier and Paris, the palaces and churches?

His steps had taken him to the huge *place* in front of the Palace and neither doorkeeper nor guards challenged him. He thought the Palace deserted till a voice from an upper window called to him and told him that, yes, Maître Guy de Chauliac was in his chambers and had been alive last night, according to the friar who took him his victuals.

When Thoros reached de Chauliac's door, after twenty minutes' walk through the empty, echoing corridors, he found a hunched form propped against it: a sleeping friar, sleeping, not dead. Ranged against the wall were platters, some full, some empty. Flies buzzed. The friar opened bleary eyes.

'You are advised not to enter. By order of the Maître.'

'I am a doctor.'

The friar scowled.

'Other doctors have not found it necessary to visit Maître de Chauliac. Are you a saint? Welcome.'

He rose and opened the door. '*Mège*, here is one who says he is a doctor.'

Thoros heard a faint call and entered de Chauliac's bedchamber, where he had never been before. Stretched on a pallet he saw the emaciated form of his colleague, uncovered because of the heat, but directly under the small window. The wind which had just sprung up came whistling about the sick man's form; the mistral, thought Thoros, another supplication.

One glance at de Chauliac showed Thoros the discolourations on the sick man's body; the same as those he had noticed from afar on the corpse. He is condemned, thought Thoros at once, yet managed to smile with sweat running down his face, half hearing the moan of the gathering wind; and so am I, for I am here, close to him. We must both die, and I shall not have advanced the cause of medicine by one jot. He clung to the lintel, gasping, thinking that he had risked his life for nothing, made Blanchette a widow; for nothing.

The sick man's eyes marked huge hollow places in his emaciated face, his lips had all but disappeared, leaving a gash below the nose in deep shadow but he was able to speak, in gasps.

'Come in, Thoros . . . friend from the Street . . . the only doctor with the courage to come and see me . . . but who can blame them? They are human first, physicians a long way behind . . . come in, come in. And . . . an astonishing, an amazing thing . . . I want to tell you, you need not fear . . . !'

Thoros stared. Had he heard . . . ? The sick man was still able to speak, might be able to reveal something, perhaps. The Pope's doctor was now his patient; he had a patient again, his last. He nodded and advanced into the room, forcing a smile, knowing that the moment of choice had passed, he was here and must behave according to a doctor's duty and precepts. He must help his patient and *confrère* to die with dignity. Farewell life; de Chauliac's and his own.

He looked carefully at de Chauliac's emaciated body on which several great buboes, black like monstrous plums, glowed. But why was the sick man smiling? De Chauliac began to speak again, hoarsely, rubbing his chest with his sheet, sweating, appearing to welcome the draught from the open window, appearing to welcome the shrill whistle of the wind.

'I am glad the wind has got up – I suffer from the heat. Do you know, Maître Thoros, how long a man with bubonic plague has to live?'

So that is the mutation, thought Thoros. At first pulmonary then these – Thoros looked carefully – these boils. As described among the plagues of Egypt.

'I will tell you,' whispered de Chauliac. 'No longer than five days, mostly not as long. And how long have I been sick? Five weeks, almost to the day. I am going to live, note! . . . I will be cured, do you hear?'

Thoros stood before this man, this victim of the plague and he felt himself shaking, he could not control the trembling of his limbs.

'Sit on this chair,' said de Chauliac. 'I have always admired your skills and now I know that you are a brave man, Thoros. I will tell you, friend and *confrère*, what treatment I devised for myself. I have—' and his voice dropped to a whisper with the effort he made to speak 'had myself bled and purged. Onto these boils, do you observe them, I put a mixture, obtained thus: ripe figs and boiled onion must be chopped and mixed with yeast and butter to make a paste, and the friar you saw applied this paste . . . a good man, a saintly man . . . give me to drink . . . the flagon over there. Thank you. Now. Do you see these livid marks here, and here? Those were buboes which burst and voided their poison, which the mixture drew from them. You see this one, nearly healed? It was the size of a hen's egg. Now it is flat skin, almost, just a shadow, here, to indicate its former place. The flagon again . . . thank you. And the sheet . . .'

He shivered and pulled the sheet up to his face, trembling with the effort of speaking, but he persisted:

'The leeches . . . at first I had them to suck the poison from the buboes, and the wounds they left after they had gorged themselves I scarified and cauterised, myself. I tell you—' he drank. 'This is cumin and water. I tell you that, having cheated the plague, the Black Death, for five weeks, I am going to live! And you, friend, may go now, and I thank you more than I can express.'

But Thoros stayed, changing the mixture which covered the remaining buboes, watching de Chauliac as he snatched minutes of sleep, discussed the news brought by the friar that no new cases of the plague had been notified and that the number of dead to be buried had fallen; even without the treatment which de Chauliac had devised for himself. De Chauliac offered the mixture to Thoros to take back to La Grange Neuve, in case it were to be needed.

Thoros learned that de Chauliac had, just before the onset of his sickness, sent the Holy Father to a secret house a day's ride away, in the mountains where he would stay until the plague had abated. Before Thoros left his exhausted yet triumphant patient whom sleep now claimed, he heard de Chauliac murmur, 'It is coming to an end, the Virgin be praised.'

Thoros slept that night in one of the Palace corridors and at the very moment he left Avignon, at dawn, through the Bridge Gate, his brother Astruc entered the town by the Gate of Saint Lazare. Astruc had been two months on the road to Avignon. One day, at Marie's house, he closed the door. Without a backward glance, he set off for Avignon. In a dream, he had heard his brother's voice, telling him to return to the Street. So he set off in the direction of Avignon, and soon understood that the times were out of joint, that the world had changed in terrible ways while he lived alone and far from its ways, that he would do well to take the utmost care, and that his strength would not help him but that cunning might.

He saw, as he took the forest paths, that there were many sick and dead animals, and then he saw his first dead body. Some nights he perched in a tree, some he slept in a ditch. At first he lived on the food he had taken with him, then on berries. A nun who had buried all her sisters cared for him for ten days in the huge, empty convent, feeding him on goat's milk, parched as he was for he feared the wells, till his strength returned. By slow degrees he approached the city of Avignon, and it was late June when he made his way at last through the same gate through which he had walked out many months ago to a new life with Marie.

Inside the gates he noted the absence of people and the presence of the smell; of rotting flesh, putrid vegetables and of fires burning. He had seen the bodies in the countryside, and anticipated with fear the manner in which it had struck the town.

He reached the tiny *place* with its well, saw that the gate of the Street stood open, and looked straight along it.

How could he or any man or woman ever have lived here? How could he have longed for this man-made ravine with its stained walls, where filth thrown from the upper storeys still clung to the walls; this slimy pavement covered in sodden urine-stained straw, where flies hovered over excrement? The exclusion of the sun because of the height of the houses offered no shade; only a crepuscular air, though it was early morning, and these rancid odours of decay which made him gag. It was for this he had longed amid the sweet-smelling woods, the lavender and gorse.

Though the woods and fields, now, harboured sights and smells which he would rather forget.

Slowly he walked towards the *escole*, avoiding the carcass of a dog and another, a mule. He met no one, there was no sign of his neighbours, his friends. The dead dog, the mule's carcass, told him what had happened here, and his heart constricted.

Stepping into the *escole* past the two stone lions still opening their mouths for a soundless roar, he breathed deeply in the cool entrance hall of the vast building, the heart and brain of the Street, where he had been circumcised and married Blanchette. He stepped forward, comforted by the familiar, through the Little and Big Azaras, into the Temple where behind a curtain the scrolls of the Law were kept. As soon as he entered, he heard the voices of men at prayer. So there were some alive, some who had been spared!

He stood where he was, wishing he had his prayer shawl, observing the men with their backs towards him, praying. The scrolls were held aloft by one of them, swaying; a dozen men or more. Astruc wondered who they were, while the familiar prayers swept into his soul and he began to pray with the others. He could not see the rabbi; would Rabbi Lyons still be alive? He supposed not. Soon the service would end and the men at prayer would turn round and there would be surprise and joy at seeing him – perhaps, thought Astruc, or perhaps he had not been forgiven for leaving the Street, taxes unpaid . . .

The service finished at last. Astruc still waited by the door, feeling more and more unsure of his welcome now. Maybe they would not even recognise him, the savage who had left the Street to live with a Christian woman, spurning the company of other Jews.

One by one the men turned round, and Astruc saw their faces, as they saw his. He did not know a single one of them and they did not know him either, that was clear.

'Greetings, *shalom*,' said Astruc, his voice shaking, to each man as he passed, and to a group of four added a few words about the sickness in the Street, speaking in Judeo-Provençal, as the Street spoke among themselves. And they answered him.

He did not understand one word.

What nightmare is this, thought Astruc, have I lost my senses? And as the last man passed him, he went after him, followed him into one of the houses and up to a door with a sign on it which Astruc could not read. Before the man could enter, Astruc held him by the sleeve.

'Please listen. My name is Astruc, I was born in this Street . . . where are the people, the people of the Street? I have been away; are they all dead? Tell me!'

The man scratched his head and pulled at his beard; the door opened and a young woman with a baby at her breast stared at Astruc.

'This room, this room belonged to—' began Astruc. But he could not remember the name. 'Where are Blanchette and Lea?' he shouted as though he could be heard and understood better, 'Abraham de Monteux? Rabbi Liptois?'

The stranger smiled, but Astruc saw the fear behind the smile and he took his hand from the stranger's sleeve. He tried again. 'I can see you are a Jew – but what are you doing here?'

The man swallowed twice before he could use his voice and Astruc realised that, large and burly as he had become with two months' growth of beard, he must appear a threatening figure. When the man spoke at last, it was in Hebrew; but spoken with an accent which made Astruc, whose own Hebrew had not been used for so long, beg him to speak slowly and to repeat many times what he was saying.

At last Astruc understood that a small group of Jews, survivors, had come from Worms in Germany to the *comtat* Venaissin, to Avignon which was the Pope's domain, for here the Holy Father protected Jews, everyone knew that. Here they could find sanctuary from persecution, so they had come, and on the road had met others, fleeing, from Strasbourg and elsewhere. Thousands of other Jews had perished as instigators of the plague, accused of poisoning wells and other crimes, burnt, hanged. He and his wife and young child, said the man, and eleven other men with wives and children were the remnants . . . of hundreds . . . of a thousand murdered. He hid his face and wept.

Astruc turned away, confused and overwhelmed, his mind full of the evil buzz of words he had just heard. So Avignon was a safe place because of the Pope, the Street a refuge for foreign Jews . . . but still he did not know the fate of his family, his neighbours . . . thousands killed because they had caused – but how could they? – the plague. He turned from the man and walked down the stairs of the house and towards his own, walking slowly, understanding that sickness and evil had taken over the world; where could he flee?

Slowly he walked up his own staircase, to go to his own room. To be alone and to hide. Where else could he go?

He knew there would be no one there; only a dozen men had been in the *escole*, all the houses would be standing empty.

He opened the door to the dark room, his home, where he and Blanchette had lived out their miserable marriage.

At once he was blinded by sunlight streaming in from the townside where the window had been nailed up, by decree, since he could remember. Someone had taken down the shutters, thought Astruc. There were not enough Christians left alive to enforce the decree. And elsewhere they were killing Jews. At least the plague struck all, Christians as well. All at once he became aware of someone lying fast asleep on his bed, a man who held in his hands a string of beads, a rosary. On the wall there was a small painting, hanging from a nail; it depicted a woman and a child – her whom the Christians called the Virgin.

Rage swelled Astruc's chest, he could feel it bursting, swamping his mind; had he survived to find an enemy on his bed? Kill him! roared in Astruc's ears but the man had woken and leapt from the bed holding his hands out before him. Astruc choked back violence, he felt the muscles in his arms relax, his clenched fists uncurled. God would judge, not he. He spoke to the intruder in a quiet voice. 'Go. This is my room.'

The intruder, like a subservient cur, fell on his back onto the pallet, opened his arms to show he had no weapon and bared his teeth in an anxious smile.

'There is a reason for my presence in this room, please hear me out. The woman who bore my son used to live here, this was her room, her name was Blanchette, a dressmaker.'

'Ah,' said Astruc calmly. 'You are speaking of Blanchette who was my wife. You are the one who cuck-olded me.'

The man shrank from him as far as he could in the small room and whispered, 'I was . . . I am . . . the Cheva-lier de Saint-Amant. I realised I wanted to see Blanchette, to atone. She has gone with the child, they have all gone; here in her room I was near to her, to our child . . . I know I have wronged you.'

Astruc leaned against the wall, not aware of the picture behind him, which he displaced; it fell on the ground. Neither man moved.

'Do you know,' said Astruc quietly, 'it is all one to me? The plague is devouring us all, Jews and Christians. Let us try to keep alive. I have no stomach for a fight. Stay where you are, *chevalier*, you may rest on my bed. I shall go across the landing to the room where my brother used to sleep. Who knows what or whom I might find there—' and he began to laugh suddenly, and just as suddenly stopped.

But all he found in Thoros's room were the bare planks of Thoros's bed, on which he lay down, having commended his soul to God, and slept.

Chapter 50

At La Grange Neuve, Joseph was playing with snail shells, while Blanchette walked up and down without cease, whispering a few words now and then and uttering a dry sob at times. Since Thoros had left yesterday, little Abranet attempted words of comfort but Blanchette had not heard. Although it was now late afternoon, the sun still burned so fiercely that she took Joseph into the deeper shade to one side of the great barn, where the umbrella pines had shed some needles to make a cushioned floor. She laid her red cloak down and drew Joseph onto her lap and tried to calm herself by breathing in the scented air. Soon she became aware that a hot wind had got up – the mistral, she realised. When it blew, it brought aching temples, exasperation and violence.

Thoros has been away for a day and a night and Blanchette had been aware of every passing empty hour. Thoros, forgive my hasty tongue and return, she said, turning her head towards Avignon.

She thought back to her life in the Street, the restrictions and punishments she had endured as an adulteress; and of the confined space, the darkness, the smell of rottenness, her incessant unsatisfied longing for sun and air. I will never go back! she said aloud.

Joseph tried to seize a lizard clinging to a stone in a patch of sunlight, his body bent into two curves, but was left holding the tail as the animal darted away. Damaged, thought Blanchette, but it has escaped and will grow another and live well enough; and so will I. But only if I have Thoros; and he has gone.

Thoros, come back. Without you . . . but no; I must begin to learn to live without you. I wish now that I had told you. Now you may never know. It was you who devised our pact, and you will keep to it. That devilish pact . . . are you already stricken by the disease? They say it kills quickly, but how quickly? And are you already suffering . . . what? What are the first symptoms? I shall not know, I will not be there, I will never see you again . . . And tears, which she had not shed since Thoros left, began to flow, and she hugged Joseph, who struggled, to her.

And she was aware that her mother too had been gone for a day and a night; Lea, who hated the fields and meadows. Blanchette had to face, now, at this moment, the loss of both her mother and Thoros. The strength and the hardness which had carried her through a loveless marriage, fornication with a Christian, her punishments, the abduction of Joseph, were confronted now by one terrible truth: Thoros gone. Perhaps already sick.

Joseph tore himself free to look for another lizard. He and I, thought Blanchette, with a surge of her usual courage, will live in the great world, after the passing of the plague. Outside the Street, we will be accepted everywhere thanks to Joseph's golden head. Everything will be different after the plague. People would not be herded into a Street and separated into sheep and goats, Jews and Christians. How would she live, though, a woman alone among strangers? A shameful thought came to her; she would seek out the boy's father and beg him to help . . . but no, of course not. One reason was that he might be dead. She understood how few were still alive. For another, she had always made her own way with her needle; however few people there would be in this new world, they would surely need clothes. And thirdly, she loved Thoros and no one else.

How could she live without him? She would die – so easy at this present time, the touch of a corpse would soon see to that. But then, what would become of her child?

By night-time Blanchette's composure finally left her. Neither her mother nor Thoros had returned. It was little Abranet who cooked and then fed the boy for Blanchette could only walk to and fro, moaning, listening for footsteps which never came. Once, at midnight, she sank to the ground and slept for a few minutes. Never would Lea have spent the night out of doors. Mother! she sobbed. The accursed pact; she wanted to care for her mother, they would die together.

So was she was ready to condemn her little son to death, Joseph, who had his whole life before him? Whatever punishment God was meting out for their sins, Joseph deserved none of it and without her, who would care for him? And that other little one, who had not lived yet?

She must live, however hard that would prove to be.

She cried heart-rending tears, and little Abranet held her in his arms, beside herself as she was, for many hours.

At dawn, Blanchette left the barn, left Abranet rolled up like a hedgehog, snoring in the hay, and Joseph sucking his thumb, moving restlessly in a dream.

A cool mist hid the river. The sun had not yet touched the colours of the river-bank, and the wind was light.

Bushes and trees loomed, grey shapes. She thought she saw movement along the river-bank – an animal? A traveller? Please God, she prayed, let it be my mother, safe and sound, or Thoros. The outline, grey in the greyness, was that of a human being.

'Mother?' she called, and after a pause, 'Thoros?'

Her dress was caught by a gorse bush, all scent and prickles.

'Blanchette!' whispered a voice. It was Thoros.

She saw him now, God be praised, twenty paces away from her, and hurried towards him, whispering his name at first then calling his name loudly, tearing her dress as she ran through the gorse bushes between them. As she hurried forwards, she saw him retreat and understood at once.

'Thoros! Where—?' she called, but how could they speak at this distance?

'I went to the Palace. I did not see Alysa, she was too far ahead.'

Blanchette nodded. Of course.

'I saw de Chauliac, the Pope's doctor and he . . . he is sick with the plague. But . . . but recovering . . . do you hear me? Now that is very significant—'

'Significant! Fool!' thought Blanchette bitterly; my husband, so brilliant, doesn't he realise what I thought? What I felt? I love him, but how could he be so foolish? He is back! But now what will we do?

She saw Thoros advance to ten paces from where she stood and saw he was limping.

'We must not be nearer to each other than this until . . . I will explain, Blanchette. You see, I found de Chauliac recovering from the plague; until now a person did not, could not recover from the plague. The sickness is receding! Blanchette?'

'I hear you,' she said. She loved him; but he had risked himself, her, Joseph, Abranet.

'It means that, if I have been infected, I can be cured! For seven months there has been no cure, we have been fighting the pulmonary plague, and then the bubonic plague, with rosewater, vomit of toad, magic, abracadabra! De Chauliac has shown me what he did and I have what I need with me. But I am confident that I have not been infected: I think the Lord will protect me; I think that the disease has exhausted itself, and is in retreat. God has lifted the burden from us, He is merciful, the plague is abating!'

'God has forgiven us,' she murmured.

Now she heard the birds singing at full throat, the sky was full of birdsong, the colours of the river dazzled her in the morning light. She rejoiced in the green of the riverbank, the scent of the gorse and of the pines, the silvery leaves of the lavender. She pulled a twig and rubbed it between her fingers, smelling the strong scent as though she never had before.

'I shall not come nearer than this,' she heard Thoros say 'for a – yes, a week. Then, if I am well which I expect to be . . . oh, Blanchette, I have thought about you all the weary way back from Avignon, I knew what you must have been thinking and feeling, forgive me. And then on the way back I turned my ankle, and it slowed my progress, that is why I spent another night on the way—'

'I missed you,' said Blanchette.' I missed you. I thought . . .'

In a day or two – no, when the week is over, she added in her mind, when I know that he is well I will tell him that I am carrying his child. A child to replenish the Street, I shall say, for our new life in the Street – or better, here, in the sunny great world.

On a golden September evening in that same year of the plague, two groups of people, a smaller and a larger, sat on benches in the Street of the Jews, separated by only a few steps. A great effort had been made by the small number of men and women to clear the detritus under foot so that they could all take the evening air. Most of the dwellings stood deserted, and the survivors knew that whole generations of Jews had been lost to the burial grounds which the Pope had designated for the plague victims. None of the inhabitants left behind when the twenty-five families departed eight months ago had survived; their few sticks of furniture gathered together by the foreign Jews made a few dwellings habitable.

The strangeness of the open gate struck Thoros, Astruc, Blanchette and Alysa anew every time they glanced that way. Tonight the air of late September, if not as pure as in La Grange Neuve, was carried through the Street by a little refreshing breeze.

Thoros and Astruc, Blanchette and Alysa watched the antics of Joseph, who was making his way down the Street to where the foreign Jews sat and where Joseph had seen two little children he wanted to greet. But before he had gone far he fell and Thoros hurried to scoop him up in his arms and return him to Blanchette.

Alysa was nursing her child, one month old, born nine months after David had left the Street, never to return. This child, a girl, had been named Lea, after Blanchette's mother. Blanchette knew that her mother was dead. She and Thoros had searched for many days, but Lea was never found. She died alone, thought Blanchette often with anguish, so as to protect us, our family. Since returning to the Street, she still looked up in hope whenever she heard a step on the stairs . . . but in her heart Blanchette knew that she would not see her mother again and one night she abandoned even vain hope and lay crying on her mother's bed, alone, till dawn.

Alysa had been fortunate when she left La Grange Neuve in the stolen cart. She had never driven a cart before, but fortunately the mule was as anxious as she was to regain his stable in the Street, and he took her there safely. Once in the Street she had been startled and relieved to find the dozen foreign Jews, their wives and children. Seeing her condition they had cared for her as a matter of course.

When Alysa's time came, Thoros and Blanchette were living in the Street once more and it was Blanchette and Thoros who helped little Lea into the world.

The brothers Bonivassin were deeply thankful to have found each other again; when Thoros, returning full of fears as to what he might find, discovered Astruc in his room, there were tears of joy. The brothers decided that Alysa would make a good wife for Astruc.

'If you do not marry her, you are unlikely to find another woman, nor she a husband,' said Thoros. 'For you and I must found large families. Life has ebbed from this Street like a terrible blood-letting. We have lost so many, generations have been wiped out. It will be fifty years before this Street will be full of Jews, as it was.'

Astruc was willing enough, and saw the wisdom of Thoros's words – though who could replace Marie?

Alysa, though mourning David, accepted Astruc as a father for little Lea. It appeared that the foreign Jews had no rabbi among their number to marry Astruc and Alysa, but Blanchette remarked that God would understand, that these were strange times and that they should consider themselves married.

Blanchette had been persuaded back into the Street by Thoros. He understood her need to live in the world, instead of the Street, but he assured her that life in the Street would never be as closed and shut off as before; the Black Death had seen to that, destroying, along with lives, the old ways, and sweeping away the old rules. He was going back, his work lay there; and where Thoros was, Blanchette would be. And it was true that life in the Street was different now, untrammelled, free. Meanwhile they awaited the birth of their child with great happiness.

On this late September evening, dusk had come and the air was cooling down. Both little groups were about to return to their rooms, when noise from the gate alerted them to something unusual. The men from the group of foreign Jews, Thoros and Astruc stood ready to repel marauders. The gate was loose on its hinges, the key lost; they were vulnerable.

Thoros moved forward, ready to parlay with whoever was coming their way. He saw three dilapidated carts which had halted in the little square with the well. The carts held dusty, weary people, a few household belongings and some hens, as well as a goat bleating loudly. At the sight of Thoros there were shouts and Thoros stared at Cabri, almost unrecognisable, older, bowed, and his sons, including Daniel. There was old Farrusol waving both his arms in

greeting and his sister Jolie, in tears of joy; Jessue de
Carcassonne, hardly recognisable beneath his mask of
dust, his wife sobbing loudly with relief and his children, laughing and screaming with excitement; and
Rabbi Liptois, quite unchanged, who was the first to
leap down and embrace Thoros. The carts rolled into
the Street among shouts, laughter and tears, bleating
and barking. The foreign Jews came to stare and later
to join in prayers of thanksgiving in the *escole*.

What brought them back, thought Blanchette, to the
dark forbidding houses? Why did they shed tears of joy
and sing God's praises? Because they had not been
seized and devoured by the Black Death, of course; but
why return here, as did animals released from their
cages, bewildered by the outside world, return volun-
tarily to captivity?

She questioned those who had returned, who had
settled contentedly into their old rooms. Because – she
understood having heard their tales – the world outside
was harsher even than life in this, their home.

Pope Clement returned to Avignon that September,
quite without pomp or show of any kind. There were few
people in the huge palace, but the city, overrun by rats,
thieves and brigands, was slowly coming to life again.

One morning, after having celebrated Mass, Clement
was walking back to his private apartments when he
caught sight of a familiar face in one of the corridors.
Clement hesitated.

'Saint-Amant?'

'Yes! Welcome back, your Holiness! We have all
prayed for your survival and I am overjoyed to see you! I

am here . . . I have come to ask you . . . I would like to serve you again, in any capacity.'

'I am delighted to see you, Knight. I recollect that you tended to lepers, after you left me. No doubt your life was spared for that reason! But I understand that the leper hospices were dispersed. What has happened to you – where have you been?'

I've been to Hell, thought Saint-Amant. Losing my son. Caring for lepers. Returning, for a few days only, to the Street, hoping for Blanchette's return, but soon realising that there was no place for me among Jews and that I have lost my son for ever. Forgiven by Astruc and counselled by him to return to the Pope's employment, as controller of his household, or any other position.

'I have been away,' he said quietly.

Clement considered for a moment.

'My household has shrunk,' he said. 'But perhaps you should take up your old duties again, *chevalier*, though they may be different now. Avignon is reduced to a spectre of itself. There are, it is reported, seven thousand empty houses in the town. And around us, in the countryside, bears and wolves roam through deserted villages. We must give hope to the survivors; at least there will be fewer to share what is left of the harvest. We must devise the best means of giving help.'

Saint-Amant knelt and kissed the Pope's hand.

'Walk with me to my apartments,' murmured Clement. 'I too welcome you back, Saint-Amant. I am sure you have suffered. We must live with our memories, terrible though they may be. Ah, here is Eble, who has also survived and who has been caring for me in the country.'

The two men embraced.

'Your first task shall be to gather a household around me. A few have returned from the country. My household should be small.' He smiled. 'Faith and belief are our only weapons now, the only remedy for the anguish we have suffered. Prayer, and deeds; the poor and the bereaved need us.'

As the October sun was setting, three peasants in the Montolieu vinyard straightened their backs and slipped their knives into their belts. It was as though nature had been generous to those who had survived the plague; there would be enough grapes to make more wine than the survivors could drink. The three men – all that remained of the inhabitants in the village of Montolieu – had been toiling in the vinyard all day and sweat soaked the rags which were wound around their bodies. The tallest of them unbound his leather bottle from the thong around his waist and passed it to his companions:

'Let us drink to a good harvest, to peace among us, to good health!'

'May the Lord hear you, Master Gui!' replied the two peasants, smiling and wiping their lips.

In the following spring, 1349, the poet-scholar Francesco Petrarca sat in his small house at Fontaine-la-Vaucluse, set in a strip of garden in the narrow valley bounded by steep rocks on both sides, close against the bank of a rushing green torrent which surged from a cavern a hundred paces beyond the cottage. Before him on the rough table lay a painting of Laura, whom he had loved for many years, shown wearing a green velvet dress, her wavy golden hair bound with a pearl-studded velvet band, her delicate face turned slightly away from him – as she did in life, thought Petrarch with sadness; Laura whom he had loved and lost to the plague, last year. A breeze stirred some poems dedicated to her, and about her, which lay on the table.

His ears – as always when he stayed at Fontaine-la-Vaucluse – were filled with the unceasing sound of the green foaming stream within a few paces, and he saw the silvery arc of a fish leaping, as he took up his pen and wrote:

I will never think of the year 1348 without shedding tears; this year robbed us of what we held most dear, death with his scythe cut short the lives of those we loved most. Those who come after us will find it hard to believe that there was a time when, not by lightning, nor by fire, nor by war, the entire world was depopulated over its entire surface. Who has ever seen the like? Where have you read of deserted houses, empty cities, fields growing wild, meadows piled with corpses and fearful emptiness all around us? If you consult historians, they will remain silent; ask the physicians, who are frozen with fear – speak to the philosophers and they will make a negative sign.

Will those who come after us believe in so much misery, when we who have witnessed it can hardly believe it, we who are tempted to believe we have dreamed what we have seen with our own eyes . . .

Happy our great-grandsons who have not witnessed these calamities and who, perhaps, will believe that our stories of this time are nothing but fables.